BEGGAR OF LOVE

Acclaim for *Beggar of Love*

"Lee Lynch has not only created some of the most memorable and treasured characters in all of lesbian literature, she's given us the added pleasure of having them turn up in each other's stories. You'll recognize many of them in this novel with its roots in the roiling seventies and featuring the complex, deeply real Jefferson. *Beggar of Love* ranks with Lee Lynch's richest and most candid portrayals of lesbian life."—Katherine V. Forrest, Lambda Literary Award–winning author of *Curious Wine* and the Kate Delafield series

"Lee Lynch reads as an old friend, and in a way she is. Our lesbian years overlap and much in *Beggar of Love* rings true to me. Lynch provides a good read, sexy, touching, involving—Jefferson, the butch heart of the novel, loves being a lover; Lynch depicts almost fifty years of her complex and erotic lesbian life here, ranging from the bars of New York to the rural communities of New Hampshire. Lynch has always written lesbian history with a velvet touch, and this story of touch and taste, of loss and redemption, is true to her life's work—telling lesbian stories of erotic adventuring that lead to deeper places."—Joan Nestle, Lambda Literary Award–winning author and co-founder of the Lesbian Herstory Archives

"I've been a fan of Lee Lynch since I read her novel *Rafferty Street* many years ago. Her books—especially her deeply human characters—never disappoint. *Beggar Of Love*, the newest in her gifted oeuvre, is the tale of Amelia "Jef" Jefferson, a tale of love lost and love found. Toward the end of the book, Lynch gives us a description of Jef: 'Her hands could shape mountains.' When I read that, I knew I'd found the perfect metaphor for Lee and her writing. *Beggar of Love* is a story not to be missed!"—Ellen Hart, Lambda Literary Award –winning author of the Jane Lawless Mystery series

Praise for Lee Lynch

"*Sweet Creek* is Lynch's first book in eight years, and one that shows the maturing of her craft. In a time when much of lesbian writing is more about formula than finding the truths of our lives, she has written a breakthrough book that is evidence of her unique gifts as a storyteller and her undeniable talent in creating characters that move us and remain with us long after the final page is turned."
—*Sacred Ground: News and Views on Lesbian Writing*

Sweet Creek "…is a textured read, almost epic in scope but still wonderfully intimate. Lynch, with a dozen novels to her credit dating back to the early days of Naiad Press, has earned her stripes as a writerly elder—she was contributing stories…four decades ago. But this latest is sublimely in tune with the times."—Richard LaBonte, *Q Syndicate*

"…the sweeping scope of Lynch's abilities…The sheer quality of this work is proof-positive…that writing honestly from a place of authenticity and real experience is what separates literature from 'books.'"—*Lambda Book Report*

"Novelist Lee Lynch—author of a dozen books including *Old Dyke Tales* and *Morton River Valley*—has been creating richly woven lesbian stories since she was a contributor to *The Ladder* in the '60s. She's done it again with the beautifully rendered tale *Sweet Creek*. The sharply focused snapshot of the women of Waterfall Falls, a tourist stop along Oregon's Interstate 5, *Sweet Creek* takes us inside the lives of aging gay hippies, trannies, lesbian cops, womyn's landers and rural couples by tackling broad themes that affect us all: love, death, gender and aging. Lynch possesses an authentic rural voice—so rare in lesbian literature—and offers up stories that are simple and moving, infused with a kaleidoscope of emotions, that remind us of the fiercely loving way lesbians find wholeness. A must read for dykes of all ages."—*Curve* magazine

"[Lynch's stories] go right to my heart, then stay and teach me...I think these are some of the most important stories in the dykedom."—*Feminist Bookstore News*

"Lee Lynch fills her stories with adventure, vision and great courage, but the abiding and overriding concept is love. Her characters love each other and we love them for caring."—*This Week in Texas*

"Lee Lynch explores the elements of survival, the complexities of defining community and the power of claiming our place."—*Gay & Lesbian Times*

"Lee Lynch's books and stories [are] rich with characterization and loving, detailed descriptions."—*Gay Community News*

"[Lee Lynch's work] is a salute to the literary and bonding traditions of our lesbian past, as well as the acceptance we continue to demand and achieve within a larger society."—*The Lavender Network*

"Lee Lynch is a mature novelist who retains the freshness of outlook of a young writer. Her independent, self reliant women... are ever ready to face the challenges that all lesbians meet."—Sarah Aldridge

"[Lee Lynch's] writing is a delight, full of heart, wisdom and humor."—Ann Bannon

Visit us at www.boldstrokesbooks.com

By the Author

From BOLD STROKES BOOKS

Sweet Creek

Beggar of Love

From NAIAD PRESS

Toothpick House

Old Dyke Tales

The Swashbuckler

Home In Your Hands

Dusty's Queen of Hearts Diner

The Amazon Trail

Sue Slate, Private Eye

That Old Studebaker

Morton River Valley

Cactus Love

From NEW VICTORIA PUBLISHERS

Rafferty Street

Off the Rag, Edited with Akia Woods

From TRP COOKBOOKS

Butch Cook Book, Edited with Sue Hardesty and Nel Ward

BEGGAR OF LOVE

by

Lee Lynch

2009

BEGGAR OF LOVE

ISBN 10: 1-60282-122-4
ISBN 13: 978-1-60282-122-4

THIS TRADE PAPERBACK ORIGINAL IS PUBLISHED BY
BOLD STROKES BOOKS, INC.
P.O. BOX 249
VALLEY FALLS, NY 12185

FIRST EDITION: OCTOBER 2009

CREDITS
EDITORS: JENNIFER KNIGHT AND SHELLEY THRASHER
PRODUCTION DESIGN: STACIA SEAMAN
COVER DESIGN BY SHERI (GRAPHICARTIST2020@HOTMAIL.COM)

Acknowledgments

Thank you:

Len Barot for caring about my work.

Shelley Thrasher for your careful editing, suggestions, and cheers.

Stacia Seaman for her caring work.

Connie Ward for your personal and professional support.

Lee Coats for sharing your stories.

Jennifer Fulton for telling me I'm a literary writer.

Jackie Brown for your friendship and enthusiasm.

Jean Sirius for your encouragement in writing down the hard parts and for Ginger's flip-flops.

Marilyn Silver for your help with 21st-century New York City.

Joy Parks for your support.

Dedication

This book is dedicated to

Nel Ward and Sue Hardesty.
Thank you for your friendship, love, and shelter.

And to

Elaine Mulligan
for giving me back my stories.

CHAPTER ONE

G inger wasn't coming back this time, Jefferson felt it. She didn't blame Ginger, but for the final break to come over a mistake, a misunderstanding—the pain of it pummeled her. She'd only gone to Shirley's room to finish apologizing and to get to know her without sex hanging them up. Then they walked around the corner to the coffee shop as Jefferson had originally planned, as she told Ginger she would. She was bursting with herself when she got home.

"I'm home, Ginge! I really had a good time seeing Shirley," she'd planned to tell Ginger. "Talked and laughed with her without once feeling like I had to seduce her." It was so good to be free of the compulsion to get physical with a woman. She'd finally unloaded some of her guilt. For so long she carried it around in an imaginary old cloth sack she dragged by its drawstring closure everywhere she went.

She'd bounded up the stairs instead of waiting for the slow elevator, unlocked the door to the apartment, and went in, panting, smiling, ready to shout, "I'm free!" First she'd stopped drinking; now she knew she was serious about being faithful. They'd celebrate with a bottle of sparkling cranberry juice.

"Ginger?" she'd called into the hollow-sounding apartment, startled when the refrigerator made the clunking sound that signaled a defrost cycle.

She could hear Ginger's heavy Bronx accent as she read the note Ginger had left. "I ran into Elisa from Hunter," it said, "at the recital. She saw you at the Hotel August in the elevator with another woman. You promised I wouldn't have to endure this again. I should have known better. This time I'm really done."

Since then she'd heard nothing. Ginger's Aunt Tilly had barred her from Ginger's dance school. None of their friends had heard from Ginger. Jefferson couldn't sleep; the line between consciousness and unconsciousness became more and more thin. So here she was, on a personal stakeout, spending winter break watching Ginger's dance school for signs of her. In years past, waiting to meet Ginger, she'd gotten friendly with the waitresses in the restaurant where she now sat hunkered in her worn brown leather bomber jacket by the window, and they kept the coffee coming as she watched across the snow for a chance to explain that, this time, she hadn't strayed. If she'd lost Ginger again, what had been the sense of getting sober and staying away from other women? She ran both hands through her hair, combing it back. Oh, sure, at the program they'd tell her she'd done it for herself, but who *was* she without Ginger?

She'd always loved the city in the snow. It tamped down the noise, the traffic, the hustle. The snow was deep enough that each infrequent vehicle drove in the tracks of the last one. Everything wore a clean icy tarp about two inches thick. Buses were sparse and no passengers waited at the stop down the block. New York was as much at peace as she'd experienced it since the last blackout.

The next blow came like a roaring avalanche. A car pulled up outside the Dance Loft and Ginger, bundled in the pouffy coat with the fake fur collar Jefferson had given her last year, hurried to it, wheeling her huge green suitcase. Their gay friend Mitchell Para got out and opened the trunk. She'd never thought to call him.

He hugged Ginger, long and tight, then loaded the suitcase while Ginger went back to the doorway for—oh, no, she thought. All her luggage? What was going on? Mitchell was following Ginger now, shadowing her, not six inches away, his arms outlining her, as if to protect her or to shepherd her to the building. Ginger's face looked like it belonged on an injured athlete, the pain was so obvious. Was she sick? No, you didn't haul four suitcases to a hospital. Had one of her brothers fallen at a building site? No, that didn't make sense either. Four suitcases? Had she packed every one of her prized collection of flip-flops?

Mitchell opened the door for Ginger and then got in the driver's seat. Jefferson should have been lunging out of the restaurant to catch Ginger, but she sat there and watched Mitchell lay his arm across Ginger's shoulders, draw her to him and kiss her. Jefferson stood, but within seconds, all she could see of them was the roof of the car, darting into a side street.

Breathless with shock, she stepped outside and looked for a taxi. But Ginger could be going anywhere: Mitchell's place, out of the city, out of the state, out of the country. She imagined herself foolishly shouting, "Follow that car!" and lowered her arm. She slumped against the bare little tree beside her, a ginkgo she'd watched city workers plant two years ago. She clearly wasn't wanted on Ginger's voyage. Ginger had every right not to wait around for an explanation after so many of Jefferson's lies.

She charged across the street and through the gate of Ginger's Washington Heights Dance Loft. It was the only building in the area with chain-link fencing around it; with its red stone walls, it resembled a little armory. Despite the weight she'd been putting on for the last ten years, again she sprang up the flight of wooden steps two at a time to the second floor. Ginger's two instructors were holding classes. Aunt Tilly was at the reception desk. Jefferson placed her hands flat on the desk and waited in silence until the old woman looked up. Still formidable, she had to be in her eighties by now. She'd retired as a school secretary and come to work part-time when Ginger's enrollment ballooned.

"You need to leave," she told Jefferson. "Ginger doesn't want to see you."

Jefferson was streaming sweat and unzipped her leather jacket. "Where did she go?"

"I'm not at liberty to say." Aunt Tilly averted her eyes.

Aisha was a student who had started taking lessons at the Neighborhood House, where Ginger first taught. A hefty, clumsy, but determined adolescent back in modern dance classes, Aisha now emerged from the classroom where she taught modern dance herself. Jefferson always thought of Aisha as an elongated butterfly who had emerged from her cocoon of baby fat. Several preschoolers in ballet slippers trailed her. Jefferson hugged her, then followed her into the girls' changing room.

"Do *you* know where Ginger went?" she asked.

Aisha had an apologetic expression as she shook her head. "Ginger called me and Ronna"—the other full-time teacher—"into the office and introduced us to Milly Falls."

"Ginger's old teacher from college?"

"That's her. Milly's on sabbatical. She's taking over Ginger's classes for a while."

"While Ginger—"

"I don't know, Jef. She didn't tell you neither?"

"I wouldn't be asking if she had," regretting immediately that she sounded irritated at sensitive Aisha.

"Don't get all odd about it. All's I know is I saw your bud Mitchell hanging around night and day, like some old manly husband to her. I always thought he was as gay as us. I got to tell you, Jef, I have never seen Miss G. so stone-cold all-business. It's been like her heart seized up on her and her face froze this last week. Especially those eyes. I have seen warmer eyes on a damn statue."

It should have come to her the minute she saw Ginger with Mitchell and the suitcases, but it didn't hit her until Aisha, with her puzzled words, spoke the eulogy for their decades of love. The giant oak of herself fell to the ground, uprooted by the ice storm that had hovered over every lover since the beginning of time.

Was this what Ginger felt every night Jefferson didn't come home or returned reeking of the scent of calumny? Ginger was beautiful, but what she'd taken for quietness in Ginger had become a savage coldness in recent years. Had Ginger felt this way while staring through their apartment windows at the iron balcony railing, fenced into a relationship full of spikes and bars? Was there a way to survive this devastation?

The city under its dirty crust of snow looked shredded and ravaged. Jefferson, spent in every cell of her body, walked the nearly sixty blocks home, every street bringing back a pulverizing memory of Ginger, every side street the one into which Ginger had disappeared. She felt as if she was crawling all the way.

CHAPTER TWO

At four, she was too big for the church. Emmy, her mother, had dressed her in a navy blue Easter coat with a white lace collar, white gloves, lace-topped white anklets, shiny black shoes with straps, and a flowered dress that stopped, like the coat, short of her skinned knees. She felt like she had been shrunk in the wash and stuffed into doll clothes. She hated doll clothes. She hated dolls. She hated church and the drone of the organ that filled the stuffy air with its sad wheezing.

If only she could stretch tall. Instead, she did a silent inside stretch, but it only made her smile to pretend she would pop the buttons on her dress and inflate right to the ceiling of this big building. Her tight fists would smash through the stained-glass windows, and on the way up her shoulders, wide as Popeye's, would nudge the scary cross off the wall so she wouldn't have to look at that poor man and his bleeding hands.

She, Amelia Jefferson, would be like Alice in Wonderland—so tall she'd fill the rabbit hole and crash through the peaked roof and never have to be a little Episcopalian princess again.

"Amelia, stand still," hissed Emmy, who had complained of a splitting headache on the way to church. Amelia knew she would have a headache today because she'd heard Emmy throwing up in the master bath on the other side of the wall during the night. She was never going to drink; first the grown-ups got silly and then they got sick. It was the only time they hugged her and cuddled her, though.

"Sing," Emmy said.

She sang loud. She sang like she was yelling the hymn at the boys up the street when they played cowboys and Indians. She yelled out all her squirmishness. She yelled so she wouldn't stretch so big she'd destroy the church. She sounded like those great big opera singers Emmy and Jarvy listened to on records.

"Quietly," commanded her father, Jarvy, on the other side of her. His hand shook as it held hers, and his breath had that awful smell of peppermint toothpaste and whiskey.

"Sweetly," said Emmy.

Amelia didn't know how. She wanted to explain why she couldn't sing quietly, but she wasn't allowed to talk. If she did tell them why, they'd look at her the way they did when she was being wrong, and she was always being wrong. The light in the church, already dim, grew dimmer. So she marched then, which sometimes helped keep the dark away, whispered the words she guessed she was supposed to sing, and lifted her knees up, down, up and down, to keep time. Everything kept getting darker. She rested the rifle on her shoulder, its butt in the palm of her hand. Jack and Glen up the street were the Indians and she was going to shoot them. The boys were good at grunting, spinning, and gasping out a last breath.

Once they were dead she'd lead the little girls across the street out of danger, hitch a horse to the covered wagon, and make her tongue go "Cluck-cluck, cluck-cluck" as she and the other girls traveled out West to build a cabin where the sun was.

"Amelia!" came Emmy's whisper. She'd been clucking aloud and not paying attention. It was time to sit. She was sleepy, but she wasn't allowed to nap in church. She would think about something. She would think about the girls across the street, Cynthia and Fern. Was it okay to smile? She guessed not. Last week Cynthia was home from first grade. Fern was with their grandma because she had a cold and couldn't go to kindergarten. Cynthia was a big girl and mostly didn't like to play with Amelia. But that day, with her sister away, she did.

Why did they get in trouble? Cynthia was playing on her bed. She had Tinkertoys. Amelia got on the bed to play too. They made a train and then got under the covers to make a tunnel. The sheets were snow. Their legs were mountains. It was nice under there and she felt awful good, tingly shivery all over. She wanted to snuggle with Cynthia and take a nap. Maybe Cynthia would kiss her on the top of her head like Emmy did before she went to a party. Both mothers came into the girls' bedroom and yelled at them. Why weren't they allowed to be under the covers together?

She sat so still she would never be able to move again. Why did she have to do things she didn't like doing? Why couldn't she do what she liked to do? That darkness came around her, like night. She tried not to cry, but she felt awful. She wished she had a magic potion like the one in the story her grandmother read to her. It would make her think good thoughts.

Maybe Jack and Glen would be home after Easter dinner. In back of their house was a hill down to the brook. This time, if none of the bigger boys were playing, she'd win at King of the Hill. Last time she got rolled down the hill and she'd ended up with a nose full of dirt. She didn't go crying to Emmy like the little kids. She blew her nose on some big leaves and scrubbed the dirt off with water from the brook. She still got in trouble for the grass stains, but the big kids got in more trouble for tearing up the grass.

Thinking about playing King of the Hill made her feel strong. Late afternoons, sometimes the sun looked like pancake syrup dripping through the trees. She would twirl Jack around and around and then let go at the top of the hill so he'd fall and roll to the bottom. Glen was six; she might have to wrestle him down and then give him a push. She was stronger than those two. She was stronger than the other girls. She'd dance on the hilltop, the big winner, then climb the fence and run into the woods before they ganged up on her. That fence! This was the first year she could climb it. It was all up-and-down wood boards, but she knew how to shimmy up the posts now, grab hold of the acorn-looking things on top, and pull herself over.

They could never catch her when she ran, not even the big boys. She was faster and she was smarter. When they'd be about to grab her she'd jump behind a tree and run back the way she came. It was like when Emmy and Jarvy took her to the football game after the tailgate party and one of the big boys on the field ran in and out of the other boys who were trying to knock him down. She could be a football player when she grew up.

When she grew up and got married—she supposed she'd marry Jack or Glen—their children would call them Mommy and Daddy like Jack and Glen did with their parents. Emmy said Amelia couldn't call her and Jarvy "Mommy and Daddy" because it made her feel too old. Emmy called Jarvy Jarvis when she was mad at him. Sometimes Emmy called him Daddy, she heard her. Whose Daddy was Jarvy, Emmy's or hers?

That man up front was talking about the baby Jesus. Did ladies ever get to talk up front? Did the baby Jesus have to go to church with his mother and father like her? Did he feel like he didn't belong too? If she was God she'd want these people outside in the woods or a park, not in some fancy building a bunch of sweaty guys had hammered together. Instead of sitting and being bored, they could plant trees, or play handball or something fun, right out there in daylight where God could see them. She bet baby Jesus would like that better than this.

Emmy told her to wake up and follow Jarvy out to the street. She could see their dark, shiny new Oldsmobile parked a little way up the street. "A '63!" Jarvy told everybody, even if you weren't supposed to brag. Maybe they'd go to the city today. She loved staying at Grandma and Grandpa Thorpe's apartment in the city. That's where they lived when she was just born, before they bought the house here on the hillside over the Hudson River in Dutchess. Sometimes they went back down to the city for days at a time. There was so much to see out the city window, especially after they put her to bed and the babysitter left her alone in the bedroom. In Dutchess, she couldn't see anything but the patio and the hedges.

The minister was saying something to her. He could get her in trouble with God, so she said "Yes," and looked down at her feet. They were always wanting her to say yes. They loved to say she was bashful when she didn't have anything to say to the grown-ups.

"She is such a self-possessed little girl," the minister told Emmy. Jarvy was lighting a cigarette with his gold lighter. "Like a little adult going about her business with utter self-confidence, unconcerned with the opinions of you or me."

"Thank you," her mother said and added, "I think."

Jarvy, above her, said, "She's a strange little one all right."

Emmy nodded to her and Amelia took off running—smack into the car! Then she hopped on one leg to the sidewalk and pretended a hopscotch game was chalked there. She could go fast. She bet she could hop to the corner and back to the car without stopping before they finished talking to the minister, plus twirl around on one leg at the corner. She'd see if her cousins Ruth and Raymond could beat her at this.

Aunt Jillian lived in another old house, but hers was right on Main Street and had a gold thing on the front that Emmy said made the house part of history. Aunt Jillian had a lot of big framed pictures on the walls and this huge mirror that showed the big old houses across Main Street, like Aunt Jillian wanted the houses to be able to see how pretty they were. When she was little, Amelia would lie on the floor and rotate her body, looking at the picture-window homes, the mirrored trees, a hunting picture, the family portrait, the other scenery pictures, and the one of her grandfather. Since it was Easter, Grandmother and Grandfather were at Aunt Jillian's too, even though they had moved part-time to the apartment in the city where they were close to his office and the things her grandmother liked to do, like the ballet and Bonwit Tellers.

You could see the house from the sidewalk, old-fashioned, like a little castle. Sometimes people going by would stop and snap pictures. When Amelia could get away, she would go out on the deep covered front porch and watch them watching the house, or she would lie on the cedar porch swing, out of sight of the viewers, so the creaking swing would look like it had a ghost moving it.

Mostly, she had to stay in the parlor with the family at Aunt Jillian's. Now that she was four she had to dress like a young lady and sit on the couch, not talk to her cousins Raymond and Ruth. Everyone would be dressed up. Cousin Ruth, who was sixteen, wore nail polish and lipstick and drank long-stemmed glasses of wine. Why would she do all that before she was grown up and had to? Her father and Uncle Stephen drank highballs and talked about what they'd read in the papers, and Aunt Jillian and Emmy talked about the food they bought and clothing styles.

Eighteen-year-old Cousin Raymond was, her mother said, portly, and he tried to join in the conversation with the older men, smoking and with a drink in his hand too. His father said he would learn to drink responsibly by doing it at home. Amelia was never going to drink and get loud. Cousin Ruth would ask what grade Amelia was in and tell her what she could look forward to as a big girl at Dutchess Academy. Then it was usually time to eat roast beef, scalloped potatoes, and green beans in sauce, which was a lot better than listening to Cousin Ruth's dumb stories about trying to get a boyfriend.

She'd wonder if someday she was really going to have a little Amelia or a Ruth and Raymond of her own, with some man like Uncle Stephen. She gagged on her green beans. The sauce tasted like sour milk. She wasn't going to spend her life sitting in parlors with boring people. But what else was there? Did kids one day give in and turn into parents? She wouldn't, that was for sure. And she wouldn't cook scalloped potatoes or shop at Bonwit Tellers or go to the philharmonic. She would run. She would play games. Suddenly she knew what she wanted to be:

a New York Yankee! When it wasn't summer she'd teach the little kids to play games like she did now, teach them to play baseball like Mickey Mantle.

After dinner she couldn't climb the trees in the yard because she was still in the Sunday dress Emmy bought last week. She couldn't race anybody because her cousins were too fancy-pants. While the grown-up laughter and the record player inside got louder and louder, she lay on the porch swing playing ghost and thought about what she would do, who she would be like, if she would live in the city or upstate in Dutchess. She had no idea.

She bounced her pink Spaldeen down the wood porch steps and back up, down and back up again and again. She challenged herself to do it perfectly: one bounce per step, no skipped steps, hit the middle of each step. When she got all that right she had to bounce higher and use the same rules. Then harder, higher—the ball went into a prickly bush. It didn't have any leaves, so she could see it.

The front door opened. She was trying to get out of the bush. Her dress was still caught on so many stickers. Emmy's face looked like she was watching horror movies on TV. She didn't say anything to Amelia. She only turned around and slammed back into the house.

Amelia felt like the nightmare she always had of free-falling through a hole to China, screaming "Emmy! Jarvy!" and they had no arms to catch her. But she wasn't falling. She was stuck.

CHAPTER THREE

By the time she was fifteen, everyone but her family called her Jefferson. At Dutchess Academy she was on the volleyball, field hockey, and softball teams. It was an exciting year: Billie Jean King founded the Women's Tennis Association. She planned to be captain of them all by her junior or senior year. Her parents had been to see the counselors about ten times to try and get her out of sports and onto the junior-miss committee or some other dumb thing, but her coaches couldn't afford to lose her. A talented athlete, they called her. She knew that already, but she had a secret weapon besides her body: she shone at team playing.

She remembered the exact game that woke her up to team spirit—a field-hockey game against Newby Prep when she was fourteen. It was on the hottest day that fall and she hadn't been playing well. Besides wilting from the heat, she had the first day of the curse. The darkness that sometimes weighed down on her like a storm cloud she couldn't get rid of was out in full force that day. She wanted to go back to bed, but her coach knew she could play better so she left Jefferson out on the field for the hour remaining of the game.

What she didn't know then, what she was seeing now as she watched her teammates, was that when fine athletes are doing poorly, they improve during the course of a game. Despite everything, they somehow come out on top. When the coach left her in the game she was saying, "I believe in you, Jeff." So she scored twice and they won. She would never mention having the curse, but the other players knew she'd been feeling punk and piled up around her, hugging her and smacking her on the back to give her an extra-special hero's boost. She felt heroic that day because she'd triumphed over the weather and her body and the tent of darkness—the team had needed her. There were the individual players and there was the coach and there was her, but this whole other being, separate from any of them, called the team, was what got her through a tough day over and over.

Now when they wanted her to run miles on her own and try out for the Olympics, she had no interest. She preferred strategy and bringing a team member from nowhere to score. She could understand wanting to be best in the world at something and maybe she could do it, but it couldn't beat the rising-sun-daybreak high at the end of a winning game when the team hugged and yelled and sang all the way home on the bus.

It didn't hurt that Angela Tabor—a townie who attended every game—was one of the women cheering her on.

Jefferson at fifteen, in the year the Twin Towers were born, was sandy-haired and smiled in a crooked way that deepened the dimple to the left of her mouth. She was tall and solid, loose-limbed, and loved to dance. Dumb dances like the Pogo and the Freak were popular, but she could do the Hustle like a pro, as long as she led. Later, she would love disco, that freeform movement that allowed her to toss Angela around like dandelion fluff. She also did the Bump and Grind, which Angela taught her one night when Dutchess Academy had a town-and-gown mixer. By the time the music stopped she knew the way her heart beat at the sight of Angela was something she should only experience for a boy, but it was such a thrill she didn't care. It was like winning a game, like her team being in sync, like she had found exactly where she belonged and who she was.

After their kiss it would not be the Bear Mountain Spring Beer Fest that Jefferson remembered, it would not be the end of a winter of longing; it would not be the kids tossing balls, the couples holding hands, or the daffodils laughing in the breeze. It would not be her first beer, poured into a huge paper cup by an overworked server in a vest that looked more like a corset with straps and a blouse with big puffy short sleeves. It would be none of those things. It would be the beer-bitter kiss Angela gave her right there on Main Street, in Dutchess, New York, the kiss that, like spring, changed everything.

Lesbian lives may not always be pretty lives, but they abound in pretty moments. To Jefferson that dizzying first kiss felt like the two of them were the center of a whirlpool. Their neighbors, classmates, the shopkeepers they'd known since they were toddlers, their teachers, families were swirling around them, and all of their small Hudson River community was swirling around Flower Park; and all of New York State, the whole Atlantic Seaboard swirled around Dutchess, the whole of the country, all the world swirling in elation around and around the village of Dutchess while Jefferson kissed Angela with the passion of the moment and the passion of a hundred moments when they'd held back.

Her dark days were over. Her wondering, puzzled days of bursting with feelings that had no name and no outlet were history. It was the end of all torment. There could be no more holding back. This was her first woman's kiss, and her first kiss. The thought of kissing a boy made her burp.

Angela was a different story. Young men seemed to like her angular eyebrows and long, narrow eyes—light toast brown was how Jefferson thought of Angela's eyes. The boys did not seem to mind that her nose curved like the near beak on her grandmother's face in an old photograph Angela had shown her, or that her lips looked as if someone had etched them, so precise and deep were their lines. They did not mind the dusky brown hair that should have been black like her mother's or red like her father's, and that had natural waves so tight it looked ruffled. Boys had kissed Angela, and Jefferson was to have kissing lessons all spring and summer long from the girl who had practiced on them.

Much later she wondered if her half of the cup of beer had enhanced that magnificent kiss. From that moment she became greedy for both women and whatever liquor a sixteen-year-old girl could easily come by. Had her life since been one long yearning to recreate that moment?

It had been noon. Someone at the pristine white Congregational church set its bells ringing. Then the Episcopalians, never to be outdone, swung theirs in the old stone bell tower while the Catholics played their taped bells across town. The air-raid siren switched on for its weekly test, its mournful wail transformed in Jefferson's ears to a nasal bellow of glee. The boats on the river bleated and tooted, loosed from their winter moorings this first warm day of the year. The ferry across the Hudson was loudest of all, as if the captain knew there was a first kiss to celebrate. The owners of Mercurys and Buicks, British sports cars and ugly French Citroens beeped greetings at one another and rolled down their windows.

The grown-ups called to one another and lifted toddlers from strollers. Older children, excited by the festival, shrieked and shrilled and squealed with excitement until the old cannon in the little park at the end of Cannon Street boomed once to celebrate the day. The town caretaker had been keeping it ready for their kiss, whispered Angela, even as Jefferson wondered why no one had noticed or objected to two girls kissing.

It could not have been a more momentous kiss. When she opened her eyes she saw bright streamers lifting in the breeze and colorful beer pennants waving, or perhaps that was before she opened her eyes. For sure, when she opened her eyes, there was Angela, holding both of her hands, her best friend since Angela had moved to town six months earlier. Angela's parents had taken over Hiram's Soda Fountain in Dutchess.

Poor Angela had obviously been bored after living in the city where adventure awaited her on every corner, jingling the change in its pockets. Angela was a lush girl at fifteen, five months younger than Jefferson, a gorgeous eligible girl whose family was making sure their daughter would have every frill imaginable at a glorious wedding.

Angela Tabor didn't seem interested in her eligibility. She told Jefferson that boys were boring pigs. Jefferson had seen her slap one who'd grabbed for her at school. Perhaps for the daughter of immigrants in a town that seemed well content to be separated from the melting pot of New York City by a forty-five-minute northbound train ride, it was her sense of herself as a stranger that inclined her to Jefferson, who also felt she fit nowhere. Pledging allegiance to the American flag, she'd confided to Jefferson, turned her insides to grateful, inspired mush, and she said she had learned, on assembly days, to brazenly bear her teachers' sympathetic looks when they noticed her stealthily wipe tears from her eyes after singing "America, the Beautiful." Jefferson found her slight accent electrifying.

Was this why Angela first spoke to Jefferson—could she tell that Jefferson was different too? Had Angela noticed that Jefferson never giggled about boys, never thrust out a newly swelled chest to provoke them? Jefferson herself slouched, as if to emphasize that whatever treasures lay beneath her blouse were not being cultivated for male adolescent riffraff. Then again, it may have been Jefferson's name itself, so very American.

Angela had already erased most traces of her first languages, Greek and a smattering of her father's native Czech. She wanted to be really American, so no one could tell she'd been conceived in no country but on a freighter—conceived by a father fed up with a homeland that didn't like Jews and a mother whose family had always survived by smuggling off the coast of Greece. Why not smuggle people? The family had never before lost a daughter to one of their refugees.

Maybe a Jefferson, her eyes seemed to plead, maybe a Jefferson from the big house that looked down on the river, whose aunt owned that classic beauty right in town, set back from Main Street, with an iron gate out front and a sign that said it was built in 1889, maybe a Jefferson could give her what she had not inherited in her blood: the American arrogance and matter-of-factness about having—having freedom, having possessions, having education.

After the kiss, Jefferson withdrew her hands from Angela's, but continued to hold her. She wanted Angela, half a foot shorter than her, to feel cherished. With the festival at high pitch around them and her heart pressed to Angela, she believed with her whole pleased and uproariously beating heart that the world—her team—was celebrating the first spring of forever with her Angela.

CHAPTER FOUR

Once, when Jefferson's father was shaving in his bathroom, he let her stand on the toilet seat next to the sink and lather shaving cream on her little-girl cheeks. He kept the razor to himself so she lost interest and watched him until he used a washcloth to clean the foamy stuff off her face. He used his index finger inside the washcloth lightly, as if it was his shaver slicing through the cream. It tickled. She laughed so much he couldn't finish and gave her the cloth to get the last bits. It was fun, but after that he always kept the bathroom door shut when he shaved, and she couldn't reach his shaving cream up in the medicine cabinet. Now and then, though, for the rest of her life, she would rub her jaw as if feeling for whiskers, like her father did.

Sometimes, both in Dutchess and in the city, she sat on the floor next to Emmy's vanity while Emmy, on an upholstered stool, put on makeup. There was a small rug in the Dutchess house, with a raised flower pattern, green on green, with little yellow and light blue specks. She would settle on it and sometimes trace the outlines of the flowers, sometimes run her hand up and down the smooth round pieces of the vanity's legs while she watched her mother.

The best part was the little things Emmy used. The eyebrow pencil was red and had a sharpener, and Emmy left red and tan peels on the low-down part where everything was laid out. The vanity had little wooden beads along the front and four deep drawers Jefferson wasn't allowed to open. Emmy used a shiny thing to curl her eyelashes up and then a tiny brush that made them dark. She scraped the brush on a pad in a red holder as little as a matchbook. There was powder too, in a round marshmallow-colored box. The pink powder puff sent up smoke signals as Emmy patted it into the white stuff.

When Emmy was finished, Amelia collected the pencil shavings and sniffed them. They smelled better than the powder and perfume. The perfume was named Prince Matchabelly, Emmy said. Emmy got up and stood in her black silky slip. She was very pretty. Her cheeks were all pink then and her eyes were dark. She smiled at Jefferson like a mother in a Golden Book. Her hair was up in the back. She looked like a movie star. Amelia felt heat fill the bedroom. They were going to a party at her father's work. "I hope there's dancing," said Emmy, stepping into high heels, her hand, with red fingernails, on Amelia's father's shoulder to keep from falling over.

The wood shavings curled around Amelia's fingers and fell to the floor. She bent over and picked them up again. Emmy turned her back to Amelia's father and he zipped up her slinky dress. Amelia went back to the vanity and climbed on Emmy's vanity stool. She picked up the eyebrow pencil and drew a mustache over her lips. Her father's mustache was neater. Emmy slipped the pencil from between her small fingers and placed it in a drawer, then put away the Maybelline and moved the powder and perfume out of reach. Jarvy picked up the lipstick and dabbed a little on Amelia's lips, then, with great care, applied it to Emmy's lips.

Amelia looked in the mirror. She had a mustache and lipstick! She laughed and showed her face to Emmy, who didn't look, then to her father, who was putting on his black shiny shoes. She ran her tongue along her lower lip. The lipstick tasted like a candle. Emmy folded a tissue and popped her lips up and down on it—Amelia could hear the little popping sound like Emmy was kissing the tissue—until there was a red mark on the tissue.

She used the side of her hand to wipe the slimy stuff off herself. When she looked up, her father was in his good blue suit. She liked his black-and-red striped tie. She liked all his ties. It was magic, the way it was a long flat thing and then he put it around his neck and it made him handsome. Her hand was red from the lipstick. She hid it in her bathrobe pocket so Emmy wouldn't notice.

Cousin Ruth arrived to babysit her. As soon as her mother and father left, Ruth put her to bed and went out in the living room to smoke cigarettes and listen to the record player all night. Amelia's mustache kept away the dark-cloud feeling she usually had on Friday and Saturday nights when Emmy and Jarvy were gone.

All these years later, smoke from Angela's cigarette stung her nose and she stood to avoid it, as she always tried to avoid her family's smoke, losing her reverie. Angela lay on the new spring grass in Cannon Park. Bright new dandelions and tiny white daisies with yolk-yellow centers were clustered everywhere, like glowing fallen stars. Bits of streamers had been left behind from someone's wedding.

"Look at this magnificent carpet, Jefferson! Summer's here in full swing now that you're sixteen."

"Summer never looked so good before, Angie," she said, bending to finger one of the little white flowers.

"You mean, before you?" They'd come from walking along the river, arms wrapped around each other. Angela tickled Jefferson's bare toes with tiny pebbles that she emptied from her shoes.

"No, Angie, before us."

"Before us you were making eyes at your Girl Scouts."

"Hey! You know I wasn't." She leapt to catch a tree branch and pulled it down to tease Angela's nose with a soft blossom. "I didn't know a girl could love a girl before you."

"What about Isadora Dellwood?" Angela teased.

Jefferson dove onto her stomach and hid her face. "I should never have told you about Isadora Dellwood. We were best friends when we were kids, that's all."

"And you shared a tent with her on Bear Mountain every summer."

"We were little girls."

"If only we could share a tent somewhere."

Jefferson dared a look up. "You? In a tent? I thought you didn't like bugs and owls and"—Jefferson half-rose and pretended to pounce—"ferocious night-stalking raccoons."

"In between visits from the menagerie it might be nice. You could show me what you wanted to do with Isadora Dellwood."

"Angie! I never knew there was something *to* do with Iz."

"Aha. You think I corrupted you."

"And how." Jefferson flopped on her back and hugged herself, trying to erase the humiliating memory of what she and Isadora did do.

When it happened, they were only eleven. Iz lay on the couch in her mother's apartment above the hat store and the Chinese laundry. The apartment always smelled like steam from the pressers, and Jefferson could sometimes hear the owners arguing in Chinese, their words quick, incomprehensible bursts that, for all she knew, might not have been hostile, could have been loving, or mundane, maybe about the weather.

That day it was raining. Iz had called for her to come over and play. They'd been friends all through grammar school; play, to Jefferson, meant paper dolls or kickball. She'd loved the few paper-doll books that had boy characters. Iz would dress the girl doll and she would dress the boy to go out on a date, wishing she could wear clothes like theirs, not like the girl's. Sometimes they talked about growing up and having children. Jefferson always wanted to have little boys so she could dress them in tiny gray flannel slacks, white shirts, red vests, and bow ties.

She sighed, remembering how Iz had lain on the green, textured couch in that rainy-day apartment and beckoned her, crooking one finger like movie stars did. She went over and Iz looked at her with an unfamiliar faraway gaze that scared her.

"I got a brassiere this week," Iz told her.

Jefferson remembered the exact feeling of confusion, embarrassment, and interest that made her face get hot as an oven.

Iz reached around Jefferson and felt along her back. "You don't have one yet."

"I don't want one." Her words were fast and firm.

"They're sexy," Iz boasted. "Want to see mine?"

The seconds she waited for Iz to unbutton her yellow blouse felt like a lifetime. The brassiere was plain chalky cotton. Iz sat up, filling the tiny cups with her brand-new, tiny—Jefferson knew the word, but couldn't say it, even to herself.

She looked, then looked away.

"You can touch it," Iz said in a voice that didn't sound like hers.

She shook her head and started to quickly hide her hands behind her back, but Iz caught one of them and placed it on her left breast. The fabric was soft and warm. Iz held her hand there. A bump slowly rose under her index finger. "What's that?" she asked, startled.

Iz laughed at her. "Don't you know anything? That's my nipple."

She'd known it was wrong, that this whole encounter was terribly wrong, but she dared to rub her finger over the bump.

"That felt nice," said Iz. "Do it again."

Jefferson shook her head and tried not to, but at the same time, the sensation was good. It excited her the way it first had when she was nine and touched herself between the legs. Every time she'd done it since, the quickening inside her was as scary as it was now.

"Do you want to touch me somewhere else?" Iz asked.

Had Iz found that place too? She backed away, tried sitting on an armchair and talking to Iz about something, anything, but Iz lay there, smiling in that dreamy way, like she knew everything and Jefferson was being silly, but would come around to Iz's way of thinking.

"My mother said I have to come right home," she mumbled and grabbed her green plaid raincoat and her red umbrella and her black rubber boots and fled down the long steep wooden stairs, through the glass-windowed door to the cool rain outside. She didn't go home, but ran at full speed into the woods, outran that blindness that came on her when things went wrong, ran along a path worn by animals and kids, ran to the field where the foundation of an old house lay, nothing left but it and part of the chimney. The rain had stopped. She sat on the edge of the foundation and relived the touches and the way she'd felt, both terrified and jubilant.

She looked up at Angela now. Was she nuts about Angela because she was something like Iz, a girl from the other side of the tracks? How far would Iz have let her go? Would they have been as happy as she was now, with Angela? Of course not. That had been play; this was love. She looked around. No one was close to them. She ran a hand along Angela's thigh, her hip, the small of her back. How amazing that Angela liked the feel of her fingers and her arms. After a lifetime of touching no one except teammates, she couldn't keep her hands to herself.

Her first year with Angela, school had hardly been an interruption. They simply moved their idyll with them wherever they went. Jefferson felt as if she lived in one of the Impressionist paintings the art teacher had shown them. She answered her French teacher with lyrical Romance words that fell so easily from her mouth she might have been born knowing them. She read "The Lotus Eaters" in her English class with such spirit she might have been singing the rhymes to Angela. The sciences filled her with wonder.

"Life used to seem so full of traps, Angie," Jefferson said, still watching the clouds drift overhead. "Ever since you, I know what to do."

"Except when I get you in trouble."

"Trouble? Like forgetting the time last night? We were only walking."

"And two nights before that. God, I love the way you walk. I swear you never touch the ground, Jefferson. You glide, all in one fluid line, like you're never in a hurry and you've got everything handled."

This was their age of innocence. Young as she was, Jefferson knew that even the bad might be the best it would ever be. That they would recognize real trouble only too well when it came. She didn't yet know that idylls softened real trouble and that two young women in love might not recognize it.

"We're going to wear a path through Dutchess, Angie."

"Then my father won't have to worry where I am at nine o'clock at night. He can follow our trail."

"I don't know about that."

"We'd hear him before he saw anything."

She glanced the palm of her hand over the head of a dandelion. "When you're kissing me, Angie, I don't know where I am."

The heat Angela so easily raised in her came. Angela moved closer and said, "Show me, Jefferson."

"Angie, not here. This place is wide open. My parents could come by, or, worse, my grandparents. You want to get us run out of town?"

"We could go on your bicycle." Angela settled back on her haunches, making a tent of her skirt for modesty. "Can't you see it? We'd honk that wheezy old horn you have and wave and—I know! We'd ride out of town without a stitch on, the two Lady Godivas, with, with"—she spotted the rows of not-quite-blooming rose bushes—"with roses in our hair! And we wouldn't stop until we climbed to the top of Bear Mountain. We'd live on acorns and whatever else Girl Scouts eat and be too busy making whoopee to notice bugs and wild animals."

Jefferson sat up. "You know you're nuttier than a fruitcake."

"You say the nicest things, Miss Jefferson."

Angela was always sneaking Chesterfields out of her father's pack, and she fished another one from the pocket of her dress. She held up a book of matches she'd swiped from her family's store. "Want a smoke?"

Jefferson eyed the crumpled paper and the shreds of tobacco that hung from its end. "How do you stomach those?"

"You don't eat them, Jefferson. Stomachs have nothing to do with it." Angela lit the cigarette and squinted as the smoke drifted upward. She picked tobacco from her bottom lip, then lay back. "I made a smoke ring yesterday."

"Do tell."

"Watch, now that I know how…" She shaped her lips into an "O" and blew a shapeless stream of smoke toward the sky. "Damn."

Jefferson smoothed her own hair back with her hands. She hated when Angela smoked, and when she cursed. Both felt like links to the rest of the world, outside their circle of safety. Why did Angela want those bonds?

Angela had told her that smoking made her feel older and more worldly. Made her feel like Lauren Bacall in *To Have and Have Not*, although she would have been happier if her hair fell, she'd said, loose and silky on her shoulders. They both loved old movies. It had occurred to Jefferson more than once that she watched old movies to find out who she was and where she fit in the world. It was kind of hard with no gay movies out there. Angela sucked the smoke in, let it drift lazily over her bottom lip, and looked at Jefferson through slitted eyes.

"You are something else, Angie Tabor."

She felt that flush again as Angela's chest gently heaved, her eyes radiating desire. Angela watched her: her lips, her chest, her eyes. This was an exquisite new power Jefferson had found, this magical ability to excite another girl. It heightened her excitement in turn. Sometimes she felt exultant, like this was what she had been born to do. Other times she felt a little mean, like she was abusing the gift of love. She could never stop herself, though. The feeling was too delicious, the changes in Angela too pleasant, for both of them. Had that been what Iz had been feeling?

"Jefferson," Angela said, her voice lower than usual, as if every bit of her was focused on the sensual volcano that she and Jefferson became together. "One kiss."

Jefferson crawled to her then, propped on her elbows, and ground a kiss on Angela's mouth. It was short, but the voltage left them panting while Jefferson, going to her knees, slowly surveyed the park.

"That was dangerous," Jefferson said. It was not the only thing they fought about, but it was their most frequent conflict.

"More dangerous than taking me out in your grandfather's skiff in that storm?"

"Cripes, Angie, it was a little storm. I know what I'm doing in a boat and I wanted you to feel it. The excitement. How big Mother Nature is and how little we are."

"I feel that every time I look at you. Mother Nature wrote the book on getting hot, Jefferson. Everything from how I get here," she indicated her breasts, "to how I get here." Her hand swept across her nether parts.

"Angie," Jefferson said, her voice half-swallowed.

"I love how you want me," answered Angela.

She worried that sixteen was far too young to be speaking this language, but their sticky passions enthralled her. Why was she thinking of that movie, *The Snake Pit*, that they watched in reruns on TV? Its scene of lesbian madness and doom couldn't be farther from loving this girl than…than Iz's haughty seductiveness had been.

She sprang to her feet and pulled Angela up, up, up—away from her doubts. She was who she was. They were fine together. Being the way they were was every bit as good as it felt. From now on she wouldn't think what everyone else thought, and she wouldn't let herself get slammed by that monster dark cloud that sometimes swallowed her whole. She'd push what she knew was wrong way back in her brain and never let it surface again.

CHAPTER FIVE

Jefferson was always breathless by the time she reached Angela's candy store on Cannon Street. She wanted to make the most of their time together so she flew on her three-speed bike, though her parents disapproved, tore through the old streets of Dutchess down the hill, let herself out the gate, and raced across town through the park, rushed under the majestic trees and onto Cannon Street toward the center of town. Main Street had the banks, Town Hall, the library, but Cannon boasted the army-navy store, a laundry, two hairdressers, pharmacy, deli, dentists, the A&P, and Angela's candy store.

Angela's candy store. It felt like an amusement park, or the circus. She got those same tingly feelings deep down, although she knew perfectly well she was too old for the cap guns and tiny military figures the Tabors sold, and she'd stopped considering ice-cream sodas to be the summit of her desires. Still, the candy store had always been a treat in childhood and now Angela was there, and Angela was better than a million cap guns. Sexy Angela was her fantasy figure; laughing Angela was her ice-cream soda. She gripped the brass door handle, warm from the sunny spring Saturday afternoon, and peered through the glass, nerves jingling. No sign of Angela.

"Amelia," cried Mr. Tabor at the sight of her. He knew she hated being called Amelia, but he always accompanied his gaffe with a loving bear hug. "Mister Taborrrr," she'd croon in return, smacking his back like guys did. He probably thought he was another father to her, this stocky little redheaded guy with his bibbed apron and hairy arms. His welcome embarrassed her, since she couldn't remember her own father hugging her and never quite knew what to do with her body.

Mrs. Tabor was suspicious of her, she thought, although she bowed to Mrs. Tabor, jollied her along when she made jokes, hugged her hello and good-bye and laughed anytime Mrs. Tabor said something funny. Mrs. Tabor was always inspecting her up and down like Jefferson might have forgotten to put on a blouse or wet her pants or something. It was probably the floppy dungarees Jefferson wore and the plaid Western-style blouses Emmy allowed because she thought they were cute. She tore off her dresses and skirts every chance she got. She felt stupid, unprotected in a big round skirt, unable to run, to sit comfortably, to fend off boys. The dungarees were getting a little worse for the wear, with the bike grease behind the left leg and the grass stains she couldn't scrub out of the knee. But Grandpa Jefferson had made the mistake of giving her the pair she asked for on her birthday, and he hadn't heard the last of that from Grandmother and Emmy. He wouldn't likely give her another pair. He was the one who bought her the bike and took the flak for that too.

"Got a boyfriend yet, Jefferson?" Mrs. Tabor asked.

The way Angela's Mom ritually asked that gave Jefferson the creeps. "What would I do with one of those?" she would joke, giving her the big old smile that always won over her friends' moms.

"Ooh-la-la," Mrs. Tabor cried, fanning herself, as if her ribald hints would make the prospect tempting for Jefferson.

"Your usual?" Mr. Tabor asked while his wife went back to sweeping.

"If you would. Please." Jefferson settled in with her black coffee and cherry Danish until Angela heard her voice or name or sensed her presence and came to ask her into the back.

"You could serve off that floor, Mrs. T," Jefferson always said, to butter up Angela's neatnik mother.

Mrs. Tabor looked around the almost-empty shop and whispered, "Some of them I think would feel like they were home with the cigarette butts in the coffee cups and the chewing gum under the seats. Don't ask me to dinner at their houses."

"You'd come to my place?"

"The grand Jeffersons' house?"

"No, mine, when I get out of school."

"I thought you were going to college too, like my foolish Angela."

"After that school."

"Sure. But you'll have your hands full without visitors," Mrs. Tabor warned in a teasing singsong voice so like and unlike Angela's. "Feeding your husband, maybe a little angel on the way."

She laughed. "You have such wonderful dreams for me, Mrs. T," she lied. "Maybe I'll be an old maid. Or maybe I'll enlist in the WAVES. See the world."

"Stop that talk," Asta Tabor hissed, her expression annoyed. "You're a pretty girl. You'll marry." Angela had told her that Mrs. Tabor hoped Jefferson would introduce Angela to marriageable boys from Dutchess Academy.

To herself Jefferson said, I'll marry your daughter. It was hard to like Mrs. Tabor, and she enjoyed a small perverse satisfaction in defying her, but Angela's father was a different story. She always felt a trickle of hope that Angela's father knew she loved Angela, knew it and was glad somewhere inside. Looking at Damek Tabor, though, with his compact energy, his quick wit, his constant sunniness, she could see the innocence in his eyes. He didn't know. She felt empty at the thought. At all the trust this man placed in the world, in her, when behind his back she was touching his daughter in ways that would horrify him. She would die before getting careless and revealing what they did.

If Angela didn't hear Jefferson arrive, Mr. Tabor would call, "Angel!" into the back of the store when he saw Jefferson come through the door.

She pictured Angela putting down her algebra homework, a hair's breadth from solving a problem, and blowing air from her pursed lips in exasperation. She wouldn't know if he was calling her for help or because someone was there to see her. Jefferson had rushed through the problems, not caring if they were right or wrong. Her class wouldn't graduate tomorrow. Who could be serious about algebra homework now? Her parents would be disappointed in her grades, but she didn't want good grades. Angela wouldn't be able to afford a fancy college. Jefferson planned to do well enough to get in where Angie did. They would room together.

Kids swarmed the candy store. Mr. Tabor moved swiftly back and forth behind the counter in his short-legged, bouncing way. He had originally bought the store so his parents would have an income. With his father, Hiram, sick and needing full-time care from his mother, he had sold his own thriving rivet factory in the Bronx to be near them. He told Jefferson that he thought Angela's prospects would be better up here, away from the city. He wore his apron over brown baggy trousers and a plaid shirt that was frayed and gray at the cuffs. She checked the clock. The Saturday-afternoon matinee at the Cliffs Theater had gotten out. No wonder kids were everywhere.

"Angel, serve for me, will you? Your mother's by your Aunt Rose."

Angela tied on an apron and went behind the counter, rolling her eyes at Jefferson. "That wedding dress is taking longer than the New York Central in a snow storm," she said.

Mr. Tabor explained to Jefferson, "She's Asta's only relative in America, four years old when we came over. It's a big deal."

"Mister Tay-bore," called a little kid with an accent.

Like Angela, Dutchess was a mix of nationalities, a community that called to people who, if rich, built summer or year-round homes, and if not rich, had enough ambition to get out of the city and establish a tenuous toehold in a better place to bring up the kids. The Tabors had always lived behind their businesses and gone without so Mr. Tabor could buy the little bits of land he wanted, and now his investments were paying off.

Angela's mother had returned from Aunt Rose's and now came out of the back room, tying a floral-patterned apron around a pink, blue, and white plaid housedress. She worked in slippers to accommodate the swelling of her feet after a few hours of standing.

"Okay, okay," Asta Tabor cried. "Ragamuffins, scram." She grabbed a circular tray and marched along the counter, inspecting glasses. "Empty? You want more? No? Then go on home. These people want their peace and quiet," she told the kids, indicating Mr. O'Mear's booth and the other adults who had made their way more slowly than the children to the soda fountain.

"So beautiful, your Aunt Rose," she told Angela. "But not as beautiful as you'll be on your wedding day."

Jefferson could feel Angela cringe as she watched the children dawdle in front of the store. It was suddenly too quiet inside and she dreaded the words she knew tormented Angela.

"It will be different for you. When I married Damek, over there, it was midnight. My mother cried like I was dying. My father looked like he would burn your father to cinders with his eyes. The priest was shaking like a leaf, afraid he'd be caught with this refugee, afraid God would strike him down for marrying me to an apostate, although Damek Tabor had been studying with him, hidden in the goat shed, since our first kiss." Her mother stroked Angela's short hair. "On your wedding day the bells will ring, the sun will shine, the whole town will be invited."

"Meanwhile my teachers would like me to get back to my homework," she said. "I can hear them in the back room."

"Asta Tabor and her big dream," said Angela, drawing closed the curtains that separated the living area from the store. "If she'd only had one or two more daughters to marry off, to show off, to count on, but she couldn't."

Angela was her mother's present and future.

Jefferson pulled Angela to her and kissed her, hot but fast, eyeing the curtain. Angela pressed against her, took the stolen kiss, then moved away, fast.

"I want to run into the store and spill my happiness all over them. I'd shout, 'Jefferson and I are in love! We're going to move in together after graduation.' I'd fling my arms around these two people who made me the woman who loves you. Why shouldn't they be excited too?" She stirred the stew.

Jefferson could only agree. They'd made Angela bright and attractive, taught her to laugh. Why should she hide the rest of who she was? Why shouldn't they share her happiness?

Angela gave her a look that made her heart race. "It's all I can do not to run back out there and tell them right now."

"They'd keep me away," she predicted, part of her hoping that wasn't true, although she knew it was. "I'd never get to see you again."

"They couldn't," Angela countered. "What would they do, tie you up?"

Jefferson scowled. "They'd send me away," she told Angela, holding her hand under the jacket on her lap. "Bury me in some prep school where chapel is a requirement and the girls talk about boys from morning till night."

"I'd come to you. Live in the nearest town. I could get work as a waitress. We'd do it on the chapel floor at midnight. I'd steal you away on weekends, and we could be naked together in my little room at the top of some old lady's big house."

"We'd get away with it for about two weeks. We'd get caught. You'd be sent home. I'd be locked in my room except for classes. The other girls would hound me for being...strange. You're such a kid about these things, Angie. If we don't do everything the way the adults want, they have more ways to punish us than God could even imagine. Your parents would be the same."

"So we're going to sneak around forever?"

"Yes."

Angela got angry then and lashed out at Jefferson. "I think you *like* all this hiding and conspiracy, Amelia Jefferson. I think you get a charge out of being scared all the time, that's what I think. It dresses up your little-rich-girl country life, like playing cowboys and Indians when you were a kid. In the Bronx, we played Nazis and Jews on our front stoops, while you were rolling down your green hills."

Jefferson stood up to go. "I'm not a rich kid," she protested, although, compared to Angela, she must seem so. "Maybe you're right. Maybe I do make a game of it in a way. Maybe I've always felt safer than you because my family's been in this county since the dinosaurs. Maybe we're too different to be together."

Outside, she was Gary Cooper in *High Noon*. She could feel the holstered pistols on her hips and scowled at passersby. That did nothing to chase off the black-cloud monster in pursuit. She swung a leg over her bike and rushed toward the hill.

CHAPTER SIX

In certain sunlight the quarried stone blocks in the magnificent Tudor-style railroad station in Dutchess looked Mediterranean pink, in others, a rough gray. The pointed arches gave the many doorways a beckoning depth as the elaborately decorated passageways, brief tunnels most of them, suggested destinations more exotic than Kingston or Albany. One night Angela and Jefferson arrived at the station before the sun set and watched from a bench outside as the stone glowed a rosy gold and the shadowed portals were curtained with a velvety darkness filled with promises.

"Looks like a castle," Jefferson said. She wore a yellow V-neck sweater vest with a wide-collared white blouse and her jeans rolled up into a cuff. Emmy was giving her money to buy her own clothes now. She and Jarvy's crowd had become big drinkers. Jarvy went off to work every day, but Emmy stayed in bed with a hangover. Jefferson told the housekeeper what needed doing and delivered buttered toast or ice to Emmy after school, then left the house until they were gone in the evening to go touch Angela every moment she could. On weekend nights Angela could come over for a while if she wasn't working, but she had to lie; the Tabors thought she was spending too much time alone with Jefferson.

Angela told her parents she was studying with other kids at the library, and they met wherever they could be close to, but out of sight of, the candy store. No one was around outside the railroad station.

Jefferson captured Angela's hand. A year after their first kiss, that neat, warm hand stirred her still. She clasped the narrow fingers and walked her thumb along the pads below them, straying frequently onto that sensitive flesh toward the palm. Jefferson gave Angela her bold, one-dimple smile. Aloud, she said one word: "Angel."

The 6:10 clacked into the Dutchess station. Balding businessmen in sports coats and unbelted slacks, carrying black molded briefcases, strode to their cars or walked toward houses off the main streets. Jefferson scuttled behind the last one, imitating his weary, hunched walk, then swirled around and sped back to Angela.

There wouldn't be another train until Jarvy's at seven. Jefferson pulled Angela up and they wandered toward the building, skirting it to avoid the main room and ticket windows, then strolling down a familiar set of stone steps. Jefferson tucked Angela's arm under her own. She felt as wild and cool as James Dean in *Rebel Without a Cause*.

The platform was deserted, but passengers came and left at all hours, so the station was never locked. The bathrooms were downstairs, as well as wooden benches hidden from the street. The slightest echoing footfall on the wooden platform would break the sentry silence that filled the arches and high-ceilinged room of the empty station. They ducked into a short arched passageway that led to a locked wooden door. It was dark and out of the way.

Jefferson rested against the uneven stones, almost at the door, arms extended. Angela, eyes on Jefferson's lips, moved to her so quickly she put her hands out as brakes. Jefferson's lips touched hers again and again.

"Touch me, Jef. Touch me, touch me, touch me."

"I love you, Ange. I love you," she whispered.

"Jefferson, we have to find a way to be together. All night. All alone." She already had Jefferson's blouse out of her dungarees and was fingering her breasts through their bra. "If only you were going to college here. Why do they have to send you away?"

"Angie, Angie, come on, baby, it's only Hunter in the city, a train ride away." She wasn't entirely sure how it had happened, but Hunter College, her family's second choice, had accepted her, mediocre grades and all. It sounded better to her parents than a state school, and it did have a great reputation for physical-education training. She could do anything, according to her school aptitude tests, but she trusted her body most, so Hunter sounded great to her.

And then there were the bars. Eventually she could go to the gay bars. With or without Angela. She still loved Angela, but she was headed for a whole city of girls. They could be together again after college.

Nothing could stop them then, could it? "You'll transfer there on scholarship," she said to comfort Angela.

"Sure, and I'll be your first lady when you're president of the United States."

"Stranger things have happened," Jefferson said, finally touching Angela's breasts under her bra.

Angela was moving against her like she was desperate. She never got enough of Angela's excitement and wanted to be closer. She reached under Angela's skirt. As always the act excited her past reason. She stopped talking, one hand on a nipple, the other inside Angela's panties. Angela had jumped when she pulled up the skirt. Jefferson laughed quietly, then let herself get swept away. Angela spread her legs as much as she could while standing. She pushed against the heel of Jefferson's hand. There was no effort involved, such slight friction before Angela sighed into her shoulder to the familiar sound of Jefferson's exhaled, "Ange."

"I want to marry you," Angela whispered, hand reaching for Jefferson's zipper. "A big wedding with 'The Wedding March' and flowers and you kissing me in front of all of them." Angela's kiss was wet, full-lipped, lazy with satisfaction, and Jefferson's fingers meandered on Angela's wet parts. Angela stopped trying to get Jefferson's zipper down and opened herself wider, knees bent. "I want to do this again and again on our honeymoon. Who needs to travel? All I want is a bed and a locked door."

"Angie, Angie, we'll have it all," Jefferson promised, open-mouthed kisses muffling her words.

"What are you two doing?"

Jefferson's heart felt like a massive bell struck by a clapper. She stepped minutely back from Angela so that the bottom of the hiked-up skirt would fall. Angela pulled her hands away from Jefferson. She felt cold as a glacier when she met Angela's shocked, unblinking eyes.

The deep, accented voice seemed to boom from the alcove to the now-wide-open wooden door. The man was heavy enough to fill the doorway. He was almost bald, with gray tufts of hair everywhere: on his head, sprouting from his nose, ears, from the back of the hand that held a push broom. Angela tried to hide her face with her jacket. Jefferson stared him down. In a second the frozen feeling was gone. She straightened and summoned an angry defiance, born of defending her teammates, that now prepared her to kid and cajole their way out of this.

"No," Angela whispered. "Don't let him see your face."

"He already did, Ange." She knew seconds, perhaps thirty, had passed, but that they would only have the advantage for a few more.

"Run," Jefferson whispered. "Keep your head down. I'll meet you behind the band shell in the park."

Angela only hesitated for the length of time it took Jefferson to speak. Then they were moving, Angela swift as the shadow of a bird as Jefferson was still pivoting to run—Angela was away—and the hairy arm, like a fat rolling pin, grabbed Angela's arm. Jefferson stopped. Angela pulled away from the hand, twisted, ducked, slipped free, but the hand, the size of four of Jefferson's, caught her skirt. She heard the rip, pushed him, heard the skirt rip more, should have pulled Angela, should have accused him of attacking them, but she still held a hope that no one would find out. He had Angela by the arm again.

"Is that the candy-store kid? What's going on here, girlie?"

She thought of crazy explanations: we were rehearsing for a play; my friend is sick and I was helping her; wish I could stay and talk, but I have to catch a train. She couldn't be flip with him clamped on Angela's arm. She felt a new fire break out in her guts.

Angela cried, "Take your hand off me!"

"I don't think so. Your father should hear about this."

"Hey," Jefferson cried, clawing to get his hands away from Angela, but she could not pry them loose.

"Let me go! He knows," lied Angela.

"Knows his kid's a dirty little queer?"

Angela pulled back her free arm and slapped him, openhanded.

The man shook her. "Damn slut." He looked at Jefferson then. "I know who you are. I guess it wouldn't do any good to let him know about the chip off his own block."

The man watched her reaction. "Or didn't you know? He's not the only good family man in this town who finds the boys at the railroad station more interesting than his wife."

What was he saying? She had a flash of a scene from the musical *Guys and Dolls* of the guys playing craps in an alleyway. She pictured Jarvy crouching against a wall, tipping back a bottle. Her straitlaced father? Did this have something to do with why Jarvy and Emmy drank more and more?

"And I don't mean he's out playing poker with them either. Like father, like daughter—or are you really a son? Maybe he does it to you too."

Jefferson had been feeling helplessly small compared to the janitor's bulk, but at that moment she understood what the man was saying and her whole world opened up in a way that was bewildering and painful and freeing all at once.

No! she thought. The monster cloud was coming, dropping over her like a hooded cape. She'd never be able to think her way out of this situation if she gave in to it. Her trusty body reacted on its own; she kicked his shin viciously. His grip loosened and they ran.

Normally it was exhilarating to run, but she was crying, embarrassed to be such a weakling. She should be the strong one, but how could she stand up to that man? He might as well be the supreme court, the state police, the weight of the whole disapproving world.

They reached the shelter of the band shell and hid behind the wooden enclosure to catch their breath.

"Why did he have to *know* us?"

"Jefferson," Angela said with gentle sympathy. "Jefferson, who in Dutchess doesn't know me?"

"And I guess my family may be a little bit infamous."

"You mean what he said about your father?"

She nodded.

"Could the janitor be lying?'

She couldn't look at Angela. "You know he wasn't."

"No, I don't think he made that up."

"I don't know whether to be happy or upset."

"It's a shock, Jefferson. You need to get over the shock first."

"Okay. But that's beside the point. Do you think he'll tell your father?" She wanted this ugliness over with so they could graduate and play all of their last summer before college.

"Not before I do."

"Oh, God, Angie, he'll hate me!"

"Face it, Jefferson. What else can we do? I want to go straight to Daddy, tell him like I've always wanted to. He says he wants me to be happy and married. He likes you. Why shouldn't you be the one? We'll get an apartment after we graduate, get jobs. You can go to school with me instead of going away."

"Angie." Her nose was stuffed, but she was no longer crying. "Are you nuts? Parents don't say, 'Sure, fine, my kid's a queer, and that's okey-dokey.' They think we're dirty."

"Dirty? We're not the dirty ones. Dirty is how that man looked at me. Dirty was what all those boys tried to do to me before I found you. I haven't for a second felt dirty with you. Only delirious with love."

They were hidden from the street on one side by the band shell, on the other by a clump of bushes. Jefferson wanted to hold her, but was scared to now. She felt like a broken little tree after a storm. Angela moved against her, but Jefferson stepped back.

"What are you so afraid of?"

She was still shaking and didn't want Angela to know it. "They could throw you out."

"I'm their daughter, they would never do that."

"They'll try to change you." She cupped a hand around Angela's breast.

Angela brushed her hand away as she said, "I can't change. I'm yours. I want to spend my life with you!" Angela smiled into her eyes as if to will an infusion of courage into her.

Something in Jefferson shifted. She'd stopped shaking. It wasn't exposure she feared, was it? She loved this girl, but, no, staying in Dutchess was all wrong. She would go away to school. This incident didn't matter much at all as long as they kept it from getting out. Really, she'd known all along that the forever Angela talked about was a kid dream. There would be girls she'd like in college. She'd seen some playing field hockey.

She straightened and put her arms around Angela, then kissed her. She loved her, but good gravy, she was seventeen. "Do you want me with you when you tell him?"

Angela, such a small, sweet cuddly girl, laid her head on Jefferson's shoulder. "No. Stay by the phone."

"If my parents answer, don't say anything to them, okay?"

"You're not going to tell them?" Angela said, pulling back.

"Look, they aren't very interested in me as it is. I don't have as much faith that they'd go along with this as you do."

"What do you have to lose?"

"You. Cripes, they might stop us from seeing each other."

Angela looked at her. "You would let them stop you?"

"Like I'd have a choice?"

When Angela's call came, Jefferson was watching *Gunsmoke* with her parents. Earlier, she had gone to the basketball game at the high school and continued a friendly argument about the restrictions of girls' rules with the coach. She loved watching the game and was looking forward to playing in college, since she'd already made her name in field hockey. She'd completely forgotten that Angela was talking to her father tonight until the call came.

"Jefferson, help me," Angela said on the phone. "He's going to send me to my aunt's in the city until you leave for school."

Gunsmoke was her favorite show. When she went back into the den to watch, she thought about Angela's scheme to run away from home. Angry, of course she'd said no. She'd ride the train down to the city to see her every weekend this summer. Her parents wouldn't think it was strange that Angela was spending the summer with an aunt or that Jefferson wanted to visit her best friend. But no, it turned out that Angela had decided she wasn't going along with her father's scheme and didn't want to leave Dutchess and Jefferson. She begged Jefferson to get an apartment with her.

"No," she'd said, with such firm fury, Angela cried more. Where was this anger coming from? She felt trapped. She needed a way out, but was Angela what she wanted to escape? Was getting stuck in Dutchess forever what she was angry about? She couldn't think. "I'm going to live in the dorm at college and concentrate on school, not take any old job and some slummy apartment. That gets us nothing but poor and unhappy."

She watched Marshal Dillon swagger through Dodge, hips heavy with six-shooters. She loved Angela, but she wasn't giving up her entire future to be with her. The marshal ordered a bad guy out of town. Her decision was final. Damn it.

Chapter Seven

Margo Kurtz was not as striking to look at as Angela, but having spent her childhood in the cities of Europe, she had a worldly manner Jefferson had never before encountered. She also had an aura of glamour that came from teaching German at Hunter College and reading poetry at the Village coffeehouses.

"Rilke," Margo exclaimed over coffee in the cafeteria. "There simply is no greater twentieth-century poet." Margo read some lines about flowers and seasons and how "immemorial sap mounts in our arms when we love." Jefferson wasn't much on poetry, but this guy Rilke got it about making love.

The verse—or Margo—instilled in Jefferson's chest a heat she thought had cooled forever the day last summer Mr. Tabor met with her father to explain why she and Angela must be separated. She'd been right all along to fear every shadow, every odd look, every innuendo about her tomboy ways: the aftermath of their exposure had been sheer hell. They asked her why she was like this and she said she didn't know. That was true. She just loved loving Angela as much as she loved Angela herself.

In the hot summer weeks before her eighteenth birthday she'd felt incurably cold, an exile in her town and from society itself. She'd been too humiliated to show her face on the streets of Dutchess to look for a job and had spent her days idle, on the maple four-poster bed at Grandma and Grandpa Thorpe's roomy old house, up the hill from her parents' home where she felt constant disappointment sweep through the house like a searchlight.

There was no place to hide. An enormous cherry tree shaded her window. It was filled with trilling birds whose enterprising, energetic, and comical comings and goings kept some deep and silent force within her alive with the hope that life might have some intrinsic value for a kid like her. Every time she began to measure methods of suicide, some little gray bird would crane its neck as if to peer in her window, or would burst into a song worthy of an opera hall, or would disappear deep into the branches, absorbed by its own busy life.

She was too ashamed to face meals downstairs and lost eighteen pounds from her spare frame, eating only when she slunk to the kitchen late at night to consume leftovers. The thought of Mr. Tabor's cherry Danishes turned her stomach sour with guilt. Yet on the August day that she reached eighteen and went immediately to the bank to empty her savings account, she didn't gnash her teeth and beat her breast in torment. That final decision she'd made about moving into a dorm at Hunter—well, she wanted her girl. She'd go into the city and sign up for a couple of classes at night to get started. She was defying her parents. She felt like a bird with a beak full of nesting material doing what came naturally as she rented a rinky-dink apartment on the first floor of a big pink house, then waited in an alleyway down the street from the candy store until she saw Angela.

"I wish it could be an engagement ring," she'd whispered, waylaying Angela and taking her into the alley, "but I hope this will do." She presented the lease and watched as Angela scanned it. They hadn't seen or spoken with each other since graduation day when, leaving the grounds of the Academy for the last time, she had seen Angela across the street, smiling and applauding her in gown and mortarboard. She'd had to avert her eyes or cry in front of her parents.

Today Angela's face slowly flushed. She looked up at Jefferson, eyes narrow.

"The birds gave me the idea," Jefferson explained. The heat was smoldering inside her. "First they make a nest. Everything follows from there."

"Do you have a job?"

"No, Angie." She feasted her eyes on Angie, felt one flame, then another lap at her insides. "Nest first, then job and furniture and family fireworks and gas hookup—and love."

Mischievous delight replaced the apprehension in Angela's eyes as she cocked her head like a little bird peering in. "Not necessarily in that order?"

They could not touch, but their eyes locked. Oh, the inferno in her chest. She was sweating. "Definitely not in that order," Jefferson responded. For the first time in weeks she rode her bicycle around town like a triumphant racer, swooping around corners, pedaling uphill without slowing, exploding through empty intersections as if fleeing demons, racing as if rushing into her future.

They moved in the next day.

The family fireworks came next. Appalled, Jefferson's family refused to pay for night classes. She should have made a clean break right then, insisted on leaving Dutchess, but Angela wanted to stay and work things out with her parents.

"It's true I'm not the daughter they planned," Angela had explained, as much to herself, it sounded like, as to Jefferson. "How can I deprive them of the only kid they've got?"

They stayed in town and found whatever work they could: babysitting, waitressing, selling magazines. They made love daily, before rising, after work, in the middle of their nights, all sleepy and passionate. She was determined to put herself through Hunter if she had to commute for ten years so she could stay with Angela. They began to feel the strength of their wings and determination when Angela got a job she liked, almost full-time, assisting a photographer. Jefferson was hired as a layout and paste-up person in the little print shop. She learned to operate the press, bill customers, and drum up business so well that they offered to train her as a backup manager. Arranging hair, applying makeup, and warming up customers for the photographer convinced Angela that she could succeed as a beautician if she could save up the money for school.

All through the fall when Jefferson was supposed to have gone away to college, Emmy and Jarvy, smelling of alcohol fumes, hammered at her to live a normal life and demanded her presence, without Angela, at holiday dinners. Giving up Angela was not an option, but their efforts— we'll send you to school, we'll get your grandparents to revoke your trust fund, how about a year in France—kept her in constant turmoil. She couldn't help but compare the difficulties of her life now with the relative ease of surrender.

Without consciously doing so, she schemed constantly and silently for ways to spirit Angela along if she capitulated and moved to the city to enroll full-time as a PE major at Hunter in the spring. How, she wondered, could she get her hands on the trust money before she was twenty-one? Every other solution involved leaving Dutchess. Angela would not go. The Jeffersons' disdain of Angela and of all things gay was like the Hudson River air, whose damp grew a constant stinking crop of mold in the backs of closets in their apartment. She still loved Angela, but she had also started to feel trapped again.

Angela gave in first. Her father, resigned to her choice of mate, offered not only to put her through beauty school, but to help finance a shop of her own when she was ready. Angela would have to stay in Dutchess and help out at the store when she wasn't in school. And Jefferson, well, she could feel—as Margo, the German professor she would soon meet, recited—her dampened heat rekindle, but it had nothing to do with Angela, who was waiting at home for her. Jefferson's father had finally agreed to give her the money he'd be paying for a dorm so she could keep the apartment and continue to commute to Hunter for the winter semester instead. When Jefferson began commuting, only a short train ride separated her from Angela, but in the stark, dead winter, Angela seemed farther and farther away.

As if Margo had dropped a gauntlet in the middle of the cafeteria table, Jefferson touched her hand—she had become quite a toucher since Angela—and said, "I really like this piece we're reading in lit class." She found it in her text and read about the salley gardens and the poet's love with little snow-white feet. The woman told him he ought to take love easy, but Yeats said he was young and foolish, just like she knew herself to be. He called the poem "An Old Song Resung" so she figured she was in good company.

"Yeats. I would never have taken you for a Yeats lover."

She felt herself flush with this dishonesty; she wasn't a poetry lover at all.

Margo's laugh, despite her frail-looking form, seemed to carry her whole life force up the column of her long pale throat and past her pouty-looking lips. Jefferson would have sat in the cafeteria for hours talking about books and poets, but she had the train home to Dutchess to catch. There was an irony in having persuaded her father to pay her tuition at Hunter College. She hadn't left Angela, or cloistered herself in Dutchess, but sending her to the city every day was a brilliant move on her parents' part. It had taken her back into the larger world, exposed her to promises of urban adventure she found harder and harder to leave as train time neared.

"Immemorial sap." Later, on the train, while passing through the sleety February darkness of Dutchess County, she tasted the words like a delicacy. "Mounts in our arms when we love." Had it been Margo's rendering that made those the sexiest words Jefferson had ever heard? Margo Kurtz was a lesbian, she could feel it in her bones. No, that wasn't where she felt it at all. Given the chance, she wanted the experience of Margo. But she should avoid her if she was to stay with Angela.

Angela was lying on the couch smoking and watching *Happy Days* on the TV that Jefferson's parents had given her last Christmas. Jefferson laid her books on the dining room table, shook herself out of her wet trench coat, and went eagerly to Angela.

"Wait," Angela said, hand up, laughing. Jefferson waited, trying to make sense of the figures on the screen, but her mind was on the salley gardens of Yeats, which had immediately evoked her early days with Angela. Perhaps, by defending Yeats, she was admitting to being a novice. The less accessible Rilke brought to mind Margo's pouty lips. What color was her lipstick? Kind of a crushed raspberry, so that her lips looked stained rather than painted. She ignored Angela's proscription and sat beside her on the couch, craning her neck to kiss her laughing girl.

"Holy smoke," Angela said when Jefferson sat up. "What brought that on?"

Angela opened her arms and Jefferson wrapped hers around her, squeezing tight. Cold and wet after her walk from the station, she felt like she was being blown away and needed to hold on tight. The apartment wasn't very warm in winter. "I haven't seen you since seven this morning. I missed you." She wasn't altogether convinced this was true, but certainly wanted it to be and kissed Angela again, touching tongues, unbuttoning the top button of her blouse.

"Do you want your dinner?" Angela asked, stepping away. "I've got soup on the stove and Bisquick biscuits waiting to go in the oven."

"Too many dishes to resist," she said, pointedly fondling a breast.

"Not really. I got my period and I don't feel very romantic."

"Oh." The deflation was compounded by a recent history of Angela's rejections. It was no wonder Margo got to her; she was plain frustrated.

"If you really want to—"

"No, no." Jefferson felt like a half-dressed nymphomaniac on the cover of a dime-store novel. "I'll bring you a bowl of soup."

Angela's attention was caught by the television. "If you'll put the biscuits in the oven? Three-seventy-five for twenty minutes."

Later, while washing the dishes, Jefferson struggled with the sap that rose in her soapy arms. What did Margo do when she got home at night? Probably she went back out to a coffeehouse where she talked with poets about the mysteries of life—and love. Was there someone Margo loved? Or else she wandered the streets of the city, filled with the kinds of longings Jefferson had. Did she ever think of Jefferson?

Angela got ready for bed as Jefferson began her homework.

"What are you studying?" Angela offered her cheek for a good-night kiss.

"Research for a paper on the poetry. Remember, I read you some?"

"I know I'm a dummy, but I can't tell one from the other. Were they the poems about England?"

"That was Wordsworth."

"He made me want to travel." Angela looked toward the plaid drape closed tight across the window that helped keep out the cold. Was that what Angela dreamed of these days? "Do you think we ever will?"

"I'll have summers off once I start teaching. Angie, Angie," she said, excited, "I know what we'll do. We'll train someone to run your shop by then."

"What does all that poetry have to do with phys ed anyway?"

"Literature is part of the curriculum. I have to take it."

Angela was gazing at the drapes. "Seriously, let's start dreaming about where to go, all right, baby?"

She slipped an arm around Angela's slender waist and pulled her close, nuzzling her belly with her nose.

Angela stepped back, her voice tight. "Not right now, baby. The cramping."

"I'm sorry." Jefferson turned to her books to hide the tears that leapt to her eyes. Maybe she was near her time too. There was no reason to feel rejected. Angela was sick tonight, wasn't she?

At the bedroom doorway Angela stopped. "Jefferson, are you going to your grandparents' for Easter?"

They'd be playing the newest opera recording they'd bought. The house would smell like honeyed ham. The dessert Jell-O would shimmy on a flower-patterned plate. She tried to keep a wary tone from her voice as she said, "You know I have to spend the afternoon there."

"Just checking. I'll go to my parents'." Angela closed the bedroom door almost too carefully. Jefferson had complained about the violence of doors slammed in anger.

She'd heard the hope, then disappointment, and finally surrender in Angela's few words. They went through their tug-of-war each holiday, Angela ready to make a partial break from her parents, Jefferson too full of guilt. Would there ever be a time they could stay home, cook their own turkeys and hams, maybe next fall go in to see the Thanksgiving Day parade together?

She sighed into her cup of coffee. How could they love each other, be each other's family, be all they could be to each other and to themselves while their parents were still alive? The cloud sat so heavily on her she stared at her books more than she worked on her report.

CHAPTER EIGHT

When Thanksgiving came and Angela arrived back from her parents' place on Cannon Street, she fell crying into Jefferson's arms.

"I can't stand another holiday with them, Jefferson! I won't do it. If I have to stay here alone Christmas Day, I will."

"Ange, my sweet girl, what happened?"

"My mother, with her matrimonial campaign. I tell her I'm happily married and she bites her lip and looks away like I stabbed her with the carving knife. Don't they know it's 1976, not 1906? I can't stand it."

Jefferson held Angela closer. She couldn't let her stay home alone Christmas Day. Yet she couldn't refuse to go to her grandparents'. She couldn't show up with Angela. "I know, I know," she said to comfort Angela. "I get the silent treatment. Maybe it's not as bad, but it doesn't feel good either. They don't want to hear about anything that has to do with you, not even what a fine cook you are. Night school, that's all I can talk to them about."

Nothing was wrong with the way her parents had raised or treated her. She was too different, like one of those babies stolen from their beds and replaced by changelings.

She stroked Angela's hair, trying to exude strength. This would pass, she reassured herself. It had before. Angela would never refuse to go to Cannon Street, especially for Christmas. Would never make her choose between families. She kissed her hair, then her cheek, her neck, saying, "I love you, Angie, it'll be all right."

Angela went stiff, thrust her arms straight out, and pushed her away. "I don't want to be kissed right now! The last thing I want is that. Leave me alone."

The bedroom door slammed and Jefferson sunk to the couch, stunned.

They'd gotten through it. The next week brought snow. From a window at the little print shop where she worked, she could see that the few boats bobbing against the marina docks were covered in it. She scrubbed at the deep ink stains on her fingers in the shop bathroom, then jogged through the splashing slush toward the station. At the beauty college, she leaned in the doorway and waved. "I'm late," she called over the roar of dryers, glad there was no time to face Angela after last night. The big-eyed little baby dyke, Tam, who hung around the shop, totally crushed out on Angie, was out of high school for the day, sweeping the old wooden floor with her push broom. She waved, and Angela lifted shampoo-lathered hands from a customer's hair in greeting.

The conductor was used to Jefferson's wild dashes to catch the 3:22 and held his departure signal until she'd flung herself aboard. As soon as she hit her seat she opened her German text and began to translate. Would Margo be around to practice on today? She noticed a fingernail she hadn't gotten clean and worked at it with Jarvy's old penknife, which she'd found under the boards of their motorboat up at the lake.

Her monster cloud was with her, so she kept active, but it was bit by bit enveloping her. Between classes she stood on some steps under the overhang of a building and watched the snow fall. The city, she breathed. She drank in the movement of the streets, wide and narrow. Now that the weather had slowed everything, the music of the city seemed louder. She seemed to hear it rush through her veins. It was crazy, she knew, to love such a large anonymous entity, but the sounds of motors, of horns, of beckoning whistles, of the thrumming power plants of huge buildings—these, with the soft, nearly constant backup of her parents' record collection or the classical WQXR, had been her lullaby before they moved to Dutchess and when they came back to see a show or to shop. She'd never heard rain on her roof while growing up here, but watched the shine of its wetness transform the streets into winking pools of reds, yellows, greens. The sight was both exciting and comforting, full of promises that could not be kept elsewhere.

She ducked into the student center to remove her soaked shoes and socks and warm her feet by a radiator. Dinner was her usual special-of-the-day bowl of cafeteria soup, with a roll and butter, spiced by the growing thrill of being back in the city, of feeling as if she belonged in college, and of her daily allotment of independence. She loved having her Dutchess nest and loved Angela, except for how quirky she was being these days, but plunging into Manhattan four days a week had ended her exile. The city would keep its promises now. She would find a way to balance dejection with joy.

She stifled yawns through an introductory education course. Out the fourth-story window the snowflakes seemed larger and faster. She'd never had trouble traveling to Dutchess after school, but it hadn't snowed like this for years. If she made it, would she be able to return for Margo's class tomorrow night?

She wasn't inventing an excuse to see Margo as she galloped down the stairs and into another building. She needed the assignment for the weekend in case she got stuck.

As always, a few students waited after class to speak with Margo. Jefferson caught her eye. Did Margo stop dawdling then? Jefferson wrote the assignment in her book and they walked together into snow-muted streets, ankle-deep in the cold, wet stuff.

"Do you want to stop for coffee?" she asked. Always before they had gone for coffee with a group of students.

Laughing, Margo clasped her arm. "I must get home to feed Hermann."

"Hermann?" Jefferson asked, fearing the worst.

"My marmalade cat. Want to meet her?"

"You mean now?" She felt about twelve in all her self-conscious awkwardness.

The street was so brightly lit a spotlight might have been focused on it, yet its shadowed doorways were deep, as if hiding secrets.

"You are worrying about your train," Margo said, and gave a liquid shout of laughter that seemed to climb toward the rooftops. "I thought you had heard the radio reports. A train derailed. Penn Station is filled with people who should have been whisked home hours ago. Come, we'll call the railroad from my apartment, find out if you're stranded."

So Jefferson walked through the unreal city at Margo's side, making herself slow to match small Margo's pace. She felt rudderless, knowing what she should do, but having no will to do it and no one to help her turn away from the blooming, doomed excitement inside her. Cars and trucks had all but disappeared. It was as if a party had been cancelled and no one had notified her and Margo. They were the last revelers, looking for a celebration. She should go to the station at once, call Angela, but being with Margo lifted her mood, and the snow would not stop decorating for the party. She let its dreamy spell embrace her.

Margo lit a candle, then another, using a streetlamp to find the way through her apartment. "I like this lighting better than electric bulbs, don't you?"

The shadows danced around them on the walls. "Really?" she asked. "You live in this light?"

"Not to grade papers." Margo walked close to Jefferson. "I don't think I'll be grading papers tonight."

Margo was tiny. She played with Jefferson's fingers. Jefferson said nothing, but her blood pumped and rushed and heated her unbearably.

"The phone is over here," Margo said, leading her to the kitchen table. The apartment was not a bad size for the city. Except for stacks of books and folders, it was neat. The dark furniture looked well cared for, though far from new, all light blues and greens. Margo leafed through a phone book and read her the number. It was busy. They looked at each other across the table. Jefferson dialed again. Busy. Margo. Busy. Busy. Busy. Margo. Margo.

"Maybe Angie will know."

"Angie," Margo said, as if weighing her chances against the unknown woman.

"I'll call collect."

"I'll go see a man about a dog."

When the bathroom door closed, she dialed. She had never called home collect before, and Angela accepted the call with a panicked voice.

"I'm fine," Jefferson said immediately.

"I was afraid your classes were canceled and you were on the early train! Do you know about the derailment? Where are you?"

"One of my teachers lives near the school. She let me use her phone. The radio says the railroad schedule is a mess."

"You make her let you stay there, baby. There hasn't been a train into Dutchess since the 3:06, and it was two and a half hours late. Even if you can get on a train in that mob scene you won't get to me until morning. Stay where it's safe and warm. I'll call the shop for you. I don't think anything will be open tomorrow anyway. The beauty school cancelled classes."

"You're okay?" She rubbed her jaw, as if that would muffle her lies.

"Snug. Except I miss you. Dutchess lost power for a while, but it came back on. Will she let you stay?"

"I don't see why not. She has a comfortable-looking couch."

"I'm so glad you're safe. We'd better get off. This must be costing a fortune. I love you."

"Me too, Angie." The needle on her moral compass flickered every which way.

She hadn't felt so cold since that last long summer in her grandparents' house. The birds. She hadn't thought of them in a long time. Did they ever stray from their own nests? Maybe, once in a great while another tree looked so appealing—what a silly thought. Angie was fine. Whatever happened here was completely separate from what they had together.

Margo reentered the candlelit room. She had changed into a light green peignoir and richly blue robe. At home, both Angela and Jefferson wore pajamas.

"Angie said no trains are coming into the station at home."

"I'd be glad if you would stay the night, Ms. Jefferson."

Seeing Margo like this, heavy-breasted, at least ten years older than her, the apartment flickering like some den of seduction, fresh makeup giving Margo the florid face of a temptress in an opera, Jefferson said, "But I don't want to lose my job. I'd better try to get back."

She could see the all-too-familiar cost of rejection, quickly hidden, cross Margo's face. "What do you do?"

"I work in a small print shop."

"Ah," Margo said, with her charming smile. "Always around books, this one."

"Oh, no. Nothing like that. Pamphlets, business cards, once in a while a small gardening book or a guide to the river. Like that." Still, it was gratifying to be thought of as a book person. She did not want to lose Margo's friendship. "You have a big library."

"Literature," Margo said, a hand sweeping across the room, "is my life."

Was she saying how lonely she was?

"I teach it, read it, write it. Dream it."

"You write?"

"Of course. Don't you?"

"No. I mean, I used to, a little, in high school. But things changed. There's no time for that."

"Stories? Poetry?"

She nodded, eyes down. "Poetry. Not very good."

"Love poetry."

She nodded again.

"To Angie."

Was she crazy to admit this? She gave a half-nod, watching Margo.

"Let me show you something." Margo found a file on her desk, looked at a few sheets of paper and extracted one, a poem, which she gave Jefferson to read. She was embarrassed to get this glimpse into a teacher's private life.

"Margo, it's real poetry, you wrote this?"

"We were going to America at last. Our husbands had sent for us. Beirut was a nightmare. Marthe and I learned to take comfort with each other while our husbands were making homes for us in California. I wanted to keep flying, with Marthe, right over their heads and around the world back to Europe, nightmare or not. But war makes one practical. And impractical. I left him as soon as I could. Marthe felt too bound and stayed with her husband."

For some reason Jefferson imagined, at that moment, thousands of women all over the world leaving their Bogarts behind, confessing their love for one another and coming together in desperate, weeping relief, in want, in an erotic camaraderie against which she knew she had no resistance. She loved her own small world, but tomboy that she was, she also loved to explore.

Without seeming to have moved her hand, she found Margo's breast cradled in it and she was kneading it. She tensed in anticipation of rejection. Instead, Margo's mouth opened and her breathing became audible, wetly rasping.

Winning an Olympic medal could not have made this more of a defining moment in Jefferson's life. It was the moment she learned the power of her longing and the power of her lesbian hands. Women, from now on, would come to her for touch. She didn't know if that was how it was for other lesbians, but for her—her mind leapt to the reality that she had a magnetic heat in her fingertips that pulled them to her.

At the same time, she didn't want to make love to this greedy gnome of a woman; she didn't want to betray Angela. Margo, though, was all the allure of the city and held the mystery of her future. She was desire come to life. Jefferson abhorred her and couldn't resist her, was compelled to embrace Margo, the exotic night, even while longing for the daylight of Angela.

Despite herself, she would be nothing in the world at times but a flammable longing for each woman she desired. If one wanted more she couldn't give it to her because the longing would not stop with her. The longing would be an entity all its own, not attached to a specific woman, never satisfied. She would bring her desire to her lovers like a gift packaged up in herself, tied up with the velvet ribbon of her hands. Their coming together would be the climax for her, orgasm no more than a physical release, each woman's response her reward.

Jefferson silenced Margo with an open, wet mouth. Her rushing blood blotted out all but their sounds and the candlelight and thoughts of anything but her desire. Her whole being was centered in her hands, and the only sensation in the world was her pounding blood and the raging heat. No feelings of despair would dare assault her now. It was so good to have the heat back after Angie's recent coldness. Nothing mattered but pressing this soft new body, her first adult woman's body, to her own. Margo thrust her hips forward and Jefferson ground her pelvis into Margo's. She was crazy with hunger for this woman of the city, her fingers full of the poetry they'd recited, immemorial sap rising until she no longer could distinguish Margo's cries from her own.

CHAPTER NINE

In September 1977, the nineteen-year-old Jefferson stood at the dormitory's back door, watching her father lift his now-heavy body behind the wheel of his Cadillac. After cramming all summer to finish her first freshman term as a commuter, she was a second-semester freshman moving into a dormitory well after the rest of her class, and her parents had driven her, with all her luggage, past the still-green leaves along the roads, down to school. On their way home, they would stop for dinner and her father would have his first drink, then a second, both doubles. He'd excuse himself, and on the way to the men's room he'd pass the bar, order another, and quickly down it before returning to the table, where he would order a fourth. That might be enough to get him home to Dutchess.

Emmy came back to the dorm door to hug her one last time, as if to make up for all the missed hugs and misunderstandings between them. Jefferson didn't expect her mother to understand her. How could a straight parent imagine what went on with a gay kid, how could a mom like hers get it when her daughter's only interest was sports, when she didn't date boys or chatter or giggle or indulge in long fashion talks? The poor woman had no idea she'd been living with a husband who fooled with men and a daughter who loved girls.

"What is *wrong* with you?" Emmy had many times demanded to know, as she'd demanded the same of her husband, but much less often and much more timorously, when the evidence of his runaway drinking compelled her to confront it. Jarvy never went to the opera or the theater with Emmy these days; Emmy went with her mother. Jefferson remembered so clearly how her parents had doted on each other until the last few years when Emmy stopped drinking. Their doctor found liver damage in both of them. Jarvy ignored it. Before that they'd had their own world of two, and Jefferson had felt in the way more than she hadn't. How old were they? Maybe Jarvy was having his midlife crisis, what with his thinning hair and wide waistline and his rendezvous at the railroad station. Today, this last buffer between Emmy and her problems was vanishing.

Jefferson accepted the hug stiffly, although one part of her wanted to cry out in terror, "Don't leave me here alone!" But evidence of dependence on her part only upset Emmy and, of course, they weren't going to coddle her more than they ever had.

What *was* wrong with her? Part of her believed in her strength and talent, and was certain of success; the other half cowered, consumed by fear and self-doubt as she listened to Emmy chatter about how hard she'd find college because she was such a poor student and only wanted to play children's games; how difficult she'd find being away from home after her failed attempt to live on her own with that hair person; how ill-equipped she was for life—hard, hard life—why hadn't Jefferson listened to her warnings? She felt like the whipping boy for whatever Emmy was going through with Jarvy.

While she'd still lived with them, Emmy's words had battered her till she was heavy with fear. She'd watched every nuance of every move either made—how he drank, how she feared his drinking. She'd done a lot of cowering that last year of high school, hoping he wouldn't pound down another drink, and scared, so scared that when he did, Emmy would protest and bring on the blowup, the final confrontation. Prayed, though she didn't believe in prayer, that Emmy never found out about the men he saw. And cowered finally, in terror of her life, in the dark backseat of the car, knowing that neither she nor her mother could control their fates with Mr. Jefferson at the wheel of the box of steel, weaving his way between the dotted lines as if they were his only guides through life. Would her mother make it to Dutchess tonight?

"If you need to, Amelia, you can come home to us. There are lots of good schools in the area."

"I'll remember," she assured Emmy, thinking, you have lost your ever-loving mind to suggest it, wanting to shout, Stop it! Stop feeding my fears with yours!

If only... All her life she'd treasured the memory of the nurse at her pediatrician's office holding her against her soft pillow of a bosom while the doctor gave little Amelia one shot or another. She had never felt anything so comforting. If only it was a mother like that nurse—not this woman, leaving her among strangers—she could take on anything.

She treasured her talented body, but her parents were suspicious of women athletes—weren't they all, or most, homosexual? Jefferson had the normal teenage disdain for the ignorance of parents and despised her father for his hypocrisy. Not only was it wrong in their eyes for her to be an athlete, her error was compounded by being gay. She couldn't defend the one or ignore the other, and she endured their disapproval as if it were a blow, sometimes longing to obliterate the body that gave her joy yet caused her so much grief with its willful ways.

She tried to stand tall against their disapproval, against Emmy's dire predictions. Still screaming inside—I'm not afraid! Why would I want to return to you?—she stared at the ground until her mother reached the car. Like Jarvy, Jefferson would not show her fear. She would not cry. She would not breathe. Fear could eat you alive. Look at Mrs. Jefferson, too scared to admit something was wrong in her marriage, scared she would lose her husband every minute she was in it, no idea of what had happened to destroy the bubble of love that had sustained her. The heritage of her mother's, and father's, fears could eat Jefferson alive too.

The car pulled away and Jefferson waved. In a minute she would breathe. In a minute she would cry. Soon she wouldn't feel the fear. It would leave with those who'd taught it to her, who'd depended on it to keep her in line, keep her from disrupting their lives. As the car turned the corner her father honked, twice, cheerfully free to head toward a drink. He must, she thought, drink to blot out the knowledge that he was gay and the guilt of his betrayals. Her mother, she knew, was smothering tears, riding back toward life alone with her alcoholic, leaving behind Jefferson, their strange failure, afraid that if she cried Mr. Jefferson would only stop sooner for dinner to shut her up.

Jefferson felt as if the scream she'd muffled before was slipping from her body. A scream of protest at the life they'd go on living and that, in growing up with them, had become part of her. A scream of abandonment. They had taught her to live in the world only as they had. How could they leave her with so little? She hadn't been able to keep things together for Angela, who was rooted in Dutchess, while Jefferson had discovered that Dutchess and Angela were too small for her.

But she didn't scream. Or cry or breathe much differently or lose the fear. She felt a flash of excitement, sheer triumph that she was free of them at last. She tried to give herself to it. She stood tall and moved to shrug off the fear and silence, but both had been with her much too long, and once more her shoulders sagged. The city roared around her like a lion after her blood. The only sounds here were of dogs barking, mothers calling. It didn't smell like fall here; there weren't enough trees. It smelled like busses and perfumes and the nearby trash basket. Angela wasn't home waiting for her like a devoted puppy. That life was gone and she needed to learn the new rules. She was glad to be away from the moldy riverside apartment where one thing or another was always on the fritz. She'd yearned for the adventures she imagined the city would supply. Here it was okay to be herself, to be gay. She knew she'd be good at both. She lunged up the stairs to her room.

The dorm was two blocks from what would become her favorite coffee shop, the Lunchbox. She got in the habit of having lunch there, sometimes crunching along the packed-snow sidewalks, partly to avoid dining-hall food, but more because she could soak up the affectionate informality of the crew.

"Another adopted daughter," Sam the cook and owner said one day not long after she moved into the dorm. He was smiling down at Gladys. At six-foot-six, he had all the appliances in the Lunchbox kitchen built to accommodate him. "What would you do, Glad, without your educated orphans?"

"Get a job someplace decent."

Jefferson felt special, privileged to be Glad's new orphan and a part of this cheerful semi-family. Gladys was lavish with praise and admiration. Her banter with Sam would have made a good comedy routine at one of the local night spots.

College began to acquire the comfort of routine. Sports brightened her days. She had found the bars where, instead of fighting off her monster depression alone at the dorm, or calling Angela up and apologizing for hours for not being what she wanted to be for her, she could drink with gays at night. The morning after, Glad was usually there with that smile.

One of those mornings, Jefferson stumbled in with a very black eye.

Glad raised an eyebrow. Her youngest, Gus, in a Yankees cap, was hanging around the restaurant shooting at customers with a toy rifle. "Out," she told him when he'd worked himself into a noisy frenzy. "Go shoot the tourists." He seemed to like that idea and rushed through the door. Jefferson had stayed at school for the break, to play ball, and carouse, and to avoid Angie and her parents' world. "Well?" Glad asked.

"Would you believe I got mugged?"

"No," Gladys said, sweeping away to another customer.

Jefferson had dreaded this moment for months. She could not truthfully explain her eye without talking about her gayness, but what good was this connection with Glad if she couldn't? She watched her clear a booth, noticed the wrinkles going deeper and deeper into Glad's skin. Glad's age touched her. She couldn't think about losing her some day. At the thought, fear, magnified by last night's liquor, grabbed hold of her.

"Glad, I didn't mean to and I'm not really like that, but unfortunately I got in a fight," she said on impulse. She'd learned to blot out her fear, sometimes with liquor, sometimes with recklessness. If she pushed Glad away now by coming out to her, she wouldn't have to fear losing her later. Like when she drank, she couldn't turn back. Her hands reached to Glad, but she pulled them back. No touching, she told herself. She was coming out to Gladys—she couldn't choose a worse time for her lesbian hands to touch a straight woman. Was this why her father drank, to ease the tension of continual self-control, to keep the monster of his gay self in a cage? She wouldn't live like that. She clenched her fists and plunged on. "I was drinking in a gay bar."

Glad didn't bat an eye.

Jefferson's smile felt like melted wax hardened across her face. She rubbed her tight knuckles against the pale blue coffee mug. "I've been hanging out with this girl. Her high-school girlfriend showed up drunk. They're from Staten Island. The little slimeball started shouting and shoving. I told her to calm down. Before I knew it she popped me one."

"I hope you popped her back," Glad said, eyes twinkling. She massaged one of Jefferson's hands and opened it, finger by finger, till it relaxed.

Jefferson licked her dry lips, let herself breathe. "You don't care?"

"Who, me? Why should I care who you're screwing?"

Jefferson felt herself blush to hear it put that way, with Glad's usual bluntness. Her acceptance was so simple, like a gift; so natural, like a mother's love. Not for the first time in this coffee shop tears came to her eyes.

"Jef, poor Sam's going to go broke supplying you with napkins."

"Hey," she said, gulping. "I never cry."

"You could have fooled me, kid."

"Except here," she corrected herself, giving Gladys an embarrassed little smile.

CHAPTER TEN

M argo was unlike anyone Jefferson had ever known. A year after they met she was exciting, an exotic foreigner, intellectually challenging in a way that had never before interested Jefferson, sexually demanding—and knew more than she had imagined could be done with a body. She felt like she could do a master's thesis on lesbian sex after the first few months of stolen nights she spent with Margo. The woman liked everything and anything and then some. She had porno pictures and a deck of dirty tarot cards and books.

Yet more and more Jefferson felt sick to her stomach after leaving Margo's infrequently washed bed linens to attend a class. She was nostalgic for Angela's loving and considerate desire, while Margo was all about exciting herself to orgasm as often as possible. Margo made her feel like a fantastic lover, and it was true that she was learning a lot, but, geeze, Margo, she wanted to say, could you call me by name now and then so I don't feel interchangeable with every other dyke in New York? Once in a while she had to go out with girls her own age, if only to show off what she now knew and to enjoy their relative innocence.

It was a relief to spend time with her new friend Lily Ann Lee. They could talk for hours about anything in their still-young universes. Lily Ann was the one she went to when she felt too down to function. Lily Ann showed her a nearby playground. She taught her real handball, not the kid stuff she was used to in the Dutchess parking lot against the wall of a furniture store.

The two of them were so different: Lily Ann in dresses and makeup when she wasn't playing ball, Jefferson in slacks, tailored shirts, and snazzy vests; Jefferson well-off, Lily Ann poor; Jefferson from Dutchess County, Lily Ann from Harlem; Jefferson Caucasian, Lily Ann African

American; Jefferson gay, Lily Ann straight, or so Lily Ann thought. Lily Ann hadn't figured herself out yet. Jefferson teased Lily Ann about it, but the woman was steadfast in her attraction to guys. Something in Jefferson made her want to save Lily Ann from a het life. The very thought of her with a man seemed so wrong that she was tempted to bring Lily Ann out herself, but she feared losing her friendship by making a move.

One fall Saturday night Margo was out of town, lecturing at a Canadian university again. She couldn't help but wonder if Margo had a student in every port. As it happened, Lily Ann's date was a no-show. They went downtown together through an autumn chill as crisp as a McIntosh apple, to see an old movie in a Fred Astaire retrospective.

"Hey," she said with some excitement as they exited the building, her fists in the pockets of her quilted down vest. "I had no idea you were an Astaire fan."

"One or two of you pink folks can dance pretty fairly."

"Kind of you to notice," she replied, then, as they turned onto Greene Street, hunched against some lively breezes and spurred with enthusiasm brought on by the dancing in the film, she flung her arms out and swung around and around, singing "Isn't This a Lovely Day?" She danced the short way to the corner, then back to Lily Ann and bowed.

"Lovely day? I am freezing my ears off, you fool," Lily Ann said, stamping her feet and breathing puffy clouds from her mouth as she spoke.

Jefferson said, "I have a solution for that."

"What, a pair of earmuffs?"

She put her always-hot hands over each of Lily Ann's ears and sang "Dancing Cheek to Cheek."

Lily Ann laughed until Jefferson thought she was a bit hysterical, so she danced in front of her, leading her friend by her covered ears. Lily Ann laughed herself into Jefferson's arms. It was only a minute before their cheeks really were pressed together, with one of Jefferson's hands still warming Lily Ann's free ear.

"Ooh, you're toasty," Lily Ann exclaimed.

Jefferson put her arms around her and swayed them to the music right there under the lamplight of Greene Street. When she let Lily Ann go, they hurried to the subway arm in arm.

Jefferson had no plans, but she couldn't think of anything to say to break their silence except, "You want to see our place in town?"

"You have a place in town and you live at the dorm?" asked Lily

Ann, who had been fascinated by Jefferson's description of her parents' and grandparents' large homes in Dutchess.

She felt guilty about her family's financial comfort. "Really, the place is small and they don't want me around when they come to town."

Lily Ann stretched out her long legs. "Sure. I'd love to see how the other half lives, J."

"We need to switch at Times Square to go up to the West Side."

"I was going to have to do that anyway to go on home. I'm surprised your place isn't on the East Side."

"It's my grandparents' apartment. They got it before World War Two."

The train hummed beneath them. The subway stops were fluorescent possibilities. The intense anticipation that thinking of making love instilled in Jefferson was beginning to bud. Nothing brought her into focus more than a woman who wanted her. Something about being desired, having someone want her gay self made her light up inside like the Christmas tree at Rockefeller Center. She was sexual energy incarnate by then, driven to give Angie or Margo or whoever appealed to her the greatest pleasures of her life.

What would Lily Ann be like? She imagined her to be a passive powerhouse who could go as long as she could and give as much as she did—a passionate woman of few words, like herself. Margo always wanted to talk about how a new position felt, what they should do next. She had the *Kama Sutra* and showed Jefferson pictures. She wanted to try everything, by the book, and to experience things inside her that Jefferson, if she could have bought them, would not use. Margo was queer, she said, because she didn't like the way men were made.

Why was Jefferson so sure Lily Ann wanted this? She couldn't say. She'd had the same instinct with Angela and Margo. Her breathing was shallow. She felt a little sick to her stomach again, but more like she was scared or overexcited. Nothing else in her life gave her this sensation. Was it some kind of lesbian chemistry? Was she afraid Lily Ann wasn't reacting the same way? Was she thrilled to death that she would be making love again? Did it matter who with? Did other gay women experience this state of excitement? She couldn't ask a lover. She'd tried to find information in books, but no one had written anything, and she had no lesbian friends to question.

By the time they shuttled over to the A line, the next symptom of seduction appeared: she was trembling. She was physically uncomfortable but never felt better emotionally than at moments like this. Her storm clouds vaporized. Her anticipation was better than drinking, better than the actual sex. She was a wire pulled taut, strung over the canyons of the city, vibrating. She wasn't trembling so much as vibrating.

Her mind shut down. She was only her body. Out on the cold street again, as they strode, two strong, tall, free women, she caught Lily Ann's handball-callused hand, larger than her own. Lily Ann let her and she wanted to crow. They shared no nervous chatter, no hesitation. Lily Ann seemed to know Jefferson was hers that night and she was Jefferson's. At one point Lily Ann stopped and pointed up. The moon was a bright half circle with one star its companion. Jefferson breathed so deeply the cold air tore at her throat. She pulled the scarf from around her neck and wrapped it around Lily Ann's. When they walked again she didn't need to take Lily Ann's hand, but as they turned the corner, Lily Ann slipped it into the crook of Jefferson's elbow.

In the elevator, she smiled at Lily Ann, so they wouldn't lose the connection. She couldn't read her face, but her eyes were golden with some kind of light she'd never seen in them before.

The apartment was dark. She lit only the small lamp in the foyer. She hung their coats in the closet, weighing the risk of putting an LP on the hi-fi. She didn't know how committed Lily Ann was to what they were about to do. She had to avoid missteps or the mood could vanish.

Lily Ann had moved through the dark living room to look through a window at the corner of moon that peeked above the roof of a new high-rise.

"Lil." She used her softest voice. "Shall we dance some more?"

Lily Ann wore a soft-looking sweater the shade of fiery orange sunsets. She held out her arms. She was light and followed Jefferson's hummed rendition of "Dancing Cheek to Cheek" as if an orchestra was playing. It was amazing how feminine a six-foot woman could be.

Jefferson danced them to the big bed in her parents' room. The moon seemed to be craning over the high-rise to light their way. Jefferson, both of Lily Ann's hands in her own, guided them into seated positions on the edge of the bed. She'd never had to reach up to kiss a woman before and was very aware that Lily Ann was probably used to men taller than herself. Certainly the men she'd seen her with on campus were at least her height.

With the tips of her fingers, she felt the bones and soft flesh of her friend's face. Lily Ann tipped her head back, eyes closed, and moved slowly into her fingers until the palms of her hands cupped Lily Ann's cheeks and she could pull their faces toward each other. Lily Ann's lips were wide, soft, infinitesimally responsive to her own hot but restrained kiss. And then they fell back onto the bed, legs immediately entwining, breasts to breasts, lips to lips.

She hadn't realized how very much she wanted Lily Ann. Bits of their nearly all-night conversations came to her as they kissed, barely breathing, then gasping between kisses, for a marathon amount of time. She remembered how intense their communications sometimes became, how they'd laugh together until they were immobilized with mirth, their eyes running tears. And now, as always when she first made love to a woman, a kind of exaltation brimmed up in her. The people who thought gay love was awful would never imagine how spiritual she felt at these moments, how outside herself yet merged with her lover and with some universal power that dwarfed them and gave them love's energy.

During lovemaking, Jefferson still tended toward silence. Margo got boisterous; sometimes the neighbors banged on the wall. Angie had been chatty, joking and laughing during foreplay and immediately after orgasm. Jefferson's own silence came from focusing on them, on the ecstatic dance of giving them pleasure.

Lily Ann was silent too. There was only the sound of kissing and, now, the rustling of sheets as Jefferson guided her into a more accessible position. That was when Lily Ann hesitated.

"What's going on here, J? I think I like this. It never occurred to me that I might."

"Kind of surprised me too," she answered, meeting her eyes.

Now that it was happening, who else, she thought, but a best friend would she be drawn to? Lesbians might have greater access to women, but men did not have to make a secret of being who they were and for sure didn't have to hide their desires. It was expected, demanded, that a man make a play for a woman who vaguely appealed, and men seemed to desire them all, including Jefferson, who turned down requests for dates with incredulous laughter.

Society, she thought, says I'm not supposed to have these feelings. How can anyone dictate what feelings I should have? Lesbians, she concluded, could be parched, perishing of desire, and were compelled to lock their longing inside themselves where it ricocheted around, bruising heart, ego, and soul until, she thought, it was no wonder so many killed themselves or went a bit nuts.

It hurt to swallow her own desires. They became toxic and she felt guilty all the time about them, as if she were contemplating something enormously more appalling than attraction—mass murder, perhaps, or matricide. Not love. The feelings were immutable and had been there long before she had a name for them.

She remembered, again, the excitement of watching Emmy prepare for evenings out with her father and the thudding of her heart as she sat in the tunnel of bedclothes she'd made with Cynthia before their mothers forbade it. So when something like this happened—Margo, Lily Ann—the emotional release, though shallow with Margo, was powerful enough for her to confuse it with her hormonal drive. She thought she was feeling love, but sometimes suspected that unbearable desire was a trickster in love's clothing.

Was she in love with Lily Ann? Was she doing her harm? Was she put on earth to introduce lesbians to themselves? One by one, the bodies were piling up, and she carried both great guilt and great pride that she had been chosen to be gay, each emotion engaged with the other in unceasing warfare inside her.

"Does this mean," Lily Ann asked, "I'm, you know, queer?"

Jefferson smiled, still not touching her. "That remains to be seen."

"You know I'm a virgin."

"You never told me, Lily Ann."

"Are you?"

"You are gorgeous, Lil. You know that?"

"It sounds to me like someone is changing the subject."

She laughed and smiled in her confident way. "It's not something I ever cared about. I wouldn't think so."

Lily Ann laid her head on the pillow. "Can someone lose her virginity to a woman?"

"You're asking if my fingers can go that far?"

Nodding, Lily Ann avoided her eyes.

This time, her lack of experience was like a punch in the gut. Who, who could teach her? She couldn't bring herself to look like a kid in Margo's eyes by asking questions; she wanted to be her Casanova, her Valentino. A minute ago she'd been in heaven; now she struggled not to thud all the way back to earth. "I honestly don't know. But we don't have to do that."

She watched Lily Ann struggle with herself. Half an hour ago virginity, a husband, and chastity had been, from what Lily Ann had shared in their long talks, important to her. Now she had to make a decision. The heat rising from her body told Jefferson that Lily Ann Lee was about to complicate her own life beyond what she could imagine. Brown skin and a woman lover, was it fair to put this burden on her friend?

She began to straighten up, planning to stand, selfless, and withdraw, but Lily Ann's cry of "Jef, Jef," like warmed maple syrup, full of sweet promise, announced her decision very clearly.

Lily Ann tried to pull her down and Jefferson resisted slightly, briefly, her own desire returning in a rush stronger than she'd ever experienced before.

They grappled more than caressed each other. She learned the meaning of tearing her clothes off.

"Go inside me with your fingers, J. Do it now, quick, I want that."

It took Jefferson a moment to find her opening. In doing so she brushed Lily Ann's little hooded area and the woman gasped. From there Jefferson knew where she was. She was inside a Lily Ann so wet she had to smile to herself in the dark. Oh, yeah, she thought, talk about being ready to come out. In a flash, first with one finger, then with three, she plunged and twisted her hand to feel every wet surface and to give Lily Ann the sensation her quivering, twisting, sweating body demanded.

At one point, Lily Ann tried to touch her. Jefferson deflected her hands. "It's most exciting for me," she said, "to see your excitement. If you turn the tables, I feel less of a lover."

Lily Ann, as if in compromise, left her hands on Jefferson's breasts the whole time Jefferson's fingers, at a gallop now, filled her, withdrew, filled her again. Without warning, Lily Ann was squeezing her nipples and drawing in air like fire, growing large around Jefferson's fingers, then clamping down on them as if her walls held them in a passionate embrace. Lily Ann was as much a woman as Margo, while Angie, sweet Angie, had been no more than a girl.

With that recognition came the knowledge that she, with Angie, had been a girl too and that now, fingers being sucked into yet another woman's vagina, she had entered her own womanhood, had started her own, fully lesbian, life. In a moment, Lily Ann had her on her back and was kissing her, tongue roving her mouth, right hand exploring her amazingly wet self and bringing her to the climax that Angie and Margo, as many times as they had tried, had never given her. She thought she would explode into a million star-like pieces, all over Lily Ann's strong, dark, sweat- and juice-slicked body.

"Oh, my God," was all she could say, over and over, as she kissed Lily Ann's bumpy nipples and learned with gentle, slow fingers how tiny and delicate a tall, broad-boned woman's genitalia could be.

CHAPTER ELEVEN

Jefferson at nineteen had the kind of thick, unruly butterscotch-twisted-with-brown hair that most people got out of a bottle. She also had the androgynous, well-defined cheekbones and jawline of certain models. Her nose was slender and straight, perhaps a little long, with a decided, but not unattractive, little dip at the end of it. Lovers liked to play with the slightly pointed tips of her ears. Her eyes looked lost in dreams until, drawn up in a smile, they seemed hardly able to contain some secret impish jubilance that only intensified when a woman smiled back at her. At the same time, Jefferson's eyes had a slant of sadness to them, and it was that contrast that made them so memorable.

As young as she was, Jefferson's was a graceful, proud figure with an air of competence worn lightly: command without effort and easy, easy laughter. It was obvious why she'd always been selected captain when she was on a team, yet when crossed, or troubled, her silence cowed everyone around her. She was slender, but solid; she was not masculine, but you couldn't picture her in a dress or nightgown. She wore her clothing loosely, but it was well cut for her body and tended toward muted solids and subtle stripes with jeans and, at work, shorts that did not hide her powerful thighs. She did not walk, she strode. She neither flaunted nor hoarded the money in her family.

Jefferson loved to dance, and disco was at its height. She would have liked to wear a white suit and black shirt and be the star of the dance bars, but that would require time away from school and sports. Angela came down to the city about once a month to see her arrogant older girlfriend, Frenchy, a tiny butch woman in black jeans, a button-down shirt, and a denim jacket, with her hair cut like Elvis Presley's, who played a miniature John Travolta, but danced so well with Angela no one laughed at her. After Jefferson finished breaking up with Angela completely, she spent more time with the German professor, but Margo wanted Jefferson at her side or on top of her every minute she wasn't in a classroom so Jefferson made herself scarce.

Ginger Quinn was a junior in physical education when Jefferson was a sophomore, so it wasn't until they roomed on the same floor that she really noticed Ginger. The woman might or might not be gay, but she obviously lived to dance—and danced to live too. She was putting herself through college by teaching kids at a dance school in Washington Heights, not far from where her family lived in the Bronx. The more Ginger didn't notice her, the more she watched Ginger: in the lounge, at the dining hall, in the gym, and at modern dance performances around town. She'd go up to Ginger after each show and compliment her.

The third time she went to a performance, she'd been so down, she almost couldn't get herself together enough to don a clean shirt—white with light blue stripes and a starched collar from the laundry down the street—and black cords. She pulled her leather bomber jacket off as she entered the storefront art space where Ginger was dancing in the West Village. The minute Jefferson saw her, her gloom lifted. Ginger did a dance choreographed for a poem set to music, by that guy Yeats again: "The Lake Isle of Innisfree." Jefferson remembered it from class and got tears in her eyes again because it reminded her so much of her family's vacation cottage in New Hampshire. She wanted to introduce Ginger Quinn to her lake.

When Jefferson approached Ginger afterward the woman seemed to snap awake, as if she'd been in a trance. "You go to Hunter?" she asked Jefferson.

After a little chitchat she said, "Ginger, there's a women's bar a few blocks from here." She gave the smile that won over, she'd learned, not only the mothers of her friends, but the young women to whom she found herself attracted. "Come have a drink with me."

Ginger hesitated.

"I'm your biggest fan," Jefferson said. "The poem you danced to made me cry."

That had been the right thing to say.

She never forgot her pride the first time she walked into a gay bar with Ginger. The fact that they weren't yet together didn't matter because they would be, and soon. Heads turned at table after table. She knew they made a knockout couple, both tall and in charge of their bodies, Ginger in black tights under a short black jumper and mint green turtleneck. She nodded to two classmates and accepted hugs from three women she'd met at the bar and danced with once or twice.

A small corner table magically emptied once she had her drink and Ginger had her Tom Collins. She pulled out a chair for Ginger, who didn't seem to think it odd that she, a woman, would do so. They talked about their favorite music—Jefferson's devotion to Liszt and Queen and Ginger's to Granados and Kraftwerk. She got Ginger to tell her about her kind of dancing.

"I saw a performance on TV, I was maybe five. Women and men, a rainbow of leotards, it was so beautiful."

"So you had lessons."

"Sure. Ballet. That was as close as I could get, but it was good training. In high school I had a teacher who was into modern dance. She helped me audit classes at Hunter, which is how I got in. I wasn't much of a student otherwise."

"So, you want to be a famous dancer? Do this for a living?"

Ginger's face was flushed talking about her passion, and light from the bar's neon advertising signs sparked in her eyes.

"I guess I'm trying to say I don't care," Ginger said. "So long as I'm dancing."

Jefferson rubbed her chin and listened hard while Ginger talked about dancers she'd seen perform and music she wanted to use and how she was saving money to go to Europe—

"When?" Jefferson asked quickly.

Ginger looked at her, copper-colored eyebrows drawn together.

Had she guessed Jefferson's quick anxiety? A trip overseas did not mesh with her plans to be with this woman. She covered, saying, "I want to go over there too. Some day."

"That's exactly my plan. Some day. It'll be a long time before I can save enough."

Would Jefferson's parents pay for two? Her grandparents had offered to send her to the Salzburg Music Festival. She slowed herself down. First things first. She imagined herself kissing this woman, stroking the strong muscles in her thighs, in her calves, as she pressed her mouth between Ginger's legs, as those legs extended over her head, quivering with tension, as they hugged her shoulders. She wanted her for keeps. This, she thought, higher than drinking ever got her, was the woman she intended to marry.

Ginger was asking her about herself.

"I'm a PE major too. I'll probably teach."

"Here, in the city?"

"Where else can I play handball?"

"Handball."

"Handball is more exciting than field hockey, basketball, and softball combined. Kind of like a poor man's racquetball."

Ginger was looking at her with more interest now. "My brothers are big players. They've been in tournaments all around the city."

Jefferson caught the waitress and asked for a refill. Ginger pulled some of her drink up through the straw, but was only about a third down.

"The other reason I want to stay here is for the life."

"The life?"

"The gay life." She watched for Ginger's reaction.

"Sure," Ginger said quickly. "The gay life."

"Well, come on, you're a PE major. You didn't notice the department is crawling with us?"

"Not so much in dance. I mean, some of the guys, sure."

"You don't go out much, do you? I mean, except to dance."

"There's only so much of me. I work, I go to school, I rehearse, I set up performances, and I dance. Plus I serve in the dining hall to earn my board, and I'm an RA to earn my room. I go home to see my family a lot. Plus, the guys at school are, I don't know, childish, I guess."

"Do you like this kind of dancing?" She indicated the jukebox. Natalie Cole was singing "Our Love."

Ginger listened intently for so long the song ended.

"That would be fun to choreograph, but the rights would be really expensive."

"Ginger, listen," she said, putting her hand on Ginger's arm. "I wasn't talking about that kind of dancing." Abba came on, singing "Take a Chance on Me."

"Do you want to dance, now, with me? Here? For the fun of it?" She gulped down a big swallow of her Irish whiskey, all of a sudden more nervous than she could ever remember. It was as if her whole future depended on Ginger's answer.

Ginger looked at the people on the dance floor, possibly seeing grown women dancing together for the first time in her life. She studied Jefferson, her face beyond serious. "I'm not gay."

"That doesn't matter. I want to dance," she pleaded.

"Sure. Why not?" She reached for Jefferson's hand. "Hurry, before the song ends."

Jefferson considered herself not a bad dancer, but Ginger was terrific. Forty-five minutes later, they had danced to Eric Clapton's "Lay Down Sally," Billy Joel's "Just the Way You Are," and Yvonne Elliman's "If I Can't Have You," among others. Jefferson, ebullient, wanted to go on forever, but Ginger looked at the clock and said she had to leave.

"That's set fifteen minutes fast, to get us out of here at closing."

Ginger shook her head and started toward the table, but Peter Frampton started singing "Baby, I Love Your Way."

"This is your song." Jefferson caught Ginger's hand. "I'll deliver you to school in a cab. Stay for one more song."

"A cab? All the way to the dorm? Are you insane?"

"Yeah," Jefferson answered, dancing to Ginger.

"I've never danced slow with a woman before tonight," Ginger said, her body taut, but following.

"And I've never danced slow with anyone as beautiful as you before."

"If you were a guy I'd think that was a line."

Jefferson smiled. "Ah, but it is. Are you going to have your brothers beat me up?"

Ginger let loose with an unexpected sun-ray smile. "Maybe beat you at handball."

"I'll get Lily Ann Lee for doubles."

"I know Lily Ann."

"See? We have friends in common already."

Ginger slowly shook her head, smiling. Jefferson did something a little faster with her feet and Ginger followed step for step. This match began to feel like a dream to Jefferson.

"Would we be as good together in bed?"

Ginger brought them to a stop. "What makes you think I'd go to bed with a woman?"

"Instinct."

Ginger was looking into her eyes. They swayed as the song came to an end. Still, their eyes held. Jefferson imagined Ginger's surprise, her denial, her growing feeling of fascination. Jefferson suspected that

Ginger would never have been intimate with a boy—too busy, too disinterested, too naïve to know she was a lesbian.

When Carly Simon's "You're So Vain" came on, Ginger stepped into it and Jefferson found herself following. Something about Ginger's boldness in taking the lead got her juices flowing. A lot of women were watching them. She felt four-footed compared to Ginger, but inside, she was flying. Best, Ginger was dancing with her eyes locked on Jefferson's. No matter how Ginger turned or dipped or which way she directed her body, those green eyes held hers. She was so high on this girl she forgot to drink.

What was Ginger thinking? Feeling? Was dancing her way of evading Jefferson's interest—or of connecting? Maybe she was buying time. After a game of handball, Jefferson sometimes realized she had the answers to whatever she'd been trying to work out.

What was Ginger's body feeling? Herself, she was sweating and aware of some muscles she didn't use playing sports. The restraint, the care she employed to move with Ginger were taking a toll on her. She wasn't used to that.

What could she make Ginger's body feel?

"Come with me," she said, fitting her hand around Ginger's wrist. Ginger looked at the hand, at Jefferson's eyes.

"My parents are at our place in New Hampshire."

"I didn't sign out at the dorm."

"We'll call."

"No. I have to be there. I'm the RA."

"And RAs get single rooms, am I right? No one would know."

"What if there were a fire? This is nuts."

"I've been nuts about you for a long time."

"About me? Why? How didn't I know?"

"You haven't found out there are other ways to dance?"

She could hear Ginger's startled intake of breath.

"What?" Jefferson asked.

"I never dreamed—"

"You're full of dreams."

"But not of this—of—"

"Your knight in shining armor being a woman?"

"Sure. There was never a woman—"

"In your dreams." She pulled Ginger to herself, pressed her cheek to the side of her coppery hair, and experienced something she didn't recognize. She'd been in love before, of course. Angela was still like ivy entwining her heart that some day would leave impressions, fossils of love, but her sensations now moved inside those ivied walls. She smiled as she pulled away from Ginger.

Ginger raised one eyebrow, gazed on Jefferson.

Jefferson told her, "I'm having a heart attack, girl. You're attacking my heart."

"I don't know. I don't know. Who are you? You make me wonder— who am I?"

"Come on home. I'll show you."

Ginger looked around again. "Do I belong here?"

She saw what Ginger saw. A small, crowded room where cigarette smoke was as loud as the music, the frequent laughter sounded brittle, as if alcohol was parching the drinkers, and the women looked strained, like this was all such hard work. Her gloom threatened to reappear. She was relieved when Ginger followed her outside, relieved that she didn't see any cabs, relieved at the silence and the darkness and the cold that caught and intimately mingled the vapored breaths from their mouths, relieved to be with Ginger Quinn, the woman she would make it her business to be with until, she clearly remembered thinking that first night, death do us part.

CHAPTER TWELVE

Jefferson stood naked, feeling strong and powerful. The curtains of her dormitory window were parted slightly so that she could see the morning beyond them. It was her junior year. The fall light was golden, buoyant, the day so intensely clear that everything shone with the remnants of the night's moisture. She could hear a few cars out early Saturday below on the street. In the suburbs of New York leaves would be burning; here in the city chestnuts roasted in a cart somewhere on the avenues. Was it possible winter wouldn't come this year? The city seemed to waver before her eyes, so magical, so full of promising corners and storefronts and signs she felt confused and excited at all the choices, like riches, before her.

A day to celebrate, she thought, full of her cheerfulness, her youth, her powers. She jogged down the hall to the communal bathroom. It smelled of mint toothpaste and disinfectant. The tile floor of the shower stall was cold under her bare feet, but she bore this discomfort stoically, like all others. Under a sharp hot spray she lathered and shampooed her athlete's body vigorously, roughly, from short hair to well-fleshed but neatly formed breasts, to solid muscled legs.

"Jefferson!"

Ginger's voice filled her with a warmth as steamy as the shower. They continued to spend hours in each other's arms imagining their lives together after graduation, recordings of music she borrowed from her parents' collection playing softly, music that Ginger loved but had never owned, music she'd heard while learning dance. Over and over Jefferson dwelt on how perfect Ginger was for her, how lucky she was to have found her. But at times she'd feel frightened at how irritable she could be with Ginger and by her own compulsive flings with other women. Today she felt so good she only chuckled. Marriage, as she thought of moving in together after graduation, would cure her of those urges, she was sure of it.

She turned the shower off. "This is going to be one damn fine day, Ginge."

She could hear Ginger's toothbrush.

"You want to climb the Empire State Building with me?" Jefferson called out. "Or how about taking a boat trip around Manhattan?" Dry, robed, she joined Ginger at the sinks. "What a face," she told her. "You know you're my princess, don't you?"

"Oh, Jefferson."

"Did I make you blush?" She stepped back and bowed, robe and all. "Would my princess accompany me to the park so I can count your royal freckles?"

Ginger smiled broadly at her in the mirror, green eyes filled with light. "Again?"

"I didn't finish last time." Her spirits were so high she had to bounce up and down. Shoot baskets into the toilet booths. Surely her blood was being carbonated with excitement as it coursed through her body. It'd call for a lot of wine to level her out this day. She wished she could hug Ginger hard, but they'd be drummed out of the PE Department in an hour if they got caught.

Ginger turned to her, brushing her shoulder-length coppery hair, a long-fingered hand curved around her brush. The occasional, prized touch of those hands was a gift Jefferson had found in no other woman, including those more generous with touching. Ginger shook her head, eyes amused and sad at the same time. "You've forgotten midterm exams are next week."

She had. "Hell, we're upperclassmen, we don't have to study." She kept smiling and began to clip her nails. She enjoyed her hands and thought they looked solid and capable. She didn't want Ginger to worry about her grades, didn't want Ginger to think she was no good, and last night was to have been the final party before she buckled down. She had to get her grade-point average up this semester if she wanted to graduate on time.

"Sure we do. We'll make it fun, Jef. We can go study in the park. I'll help you."

"No, baby, you have your own work to do. I'll get by. I always do."
She gave Ginger what she imagined was her most reassuring, charming
smile.

Ginger, from a working-class Bronx family, had come to college
with hardly an ounce of self-confidence. Jefferson, who'd grown up with
well-to-do parents almost two hours north of the Bronx, had learned to
exude confidence and prosperity whether she felt them or not. And she
knew her own self-possession always reassured Ginger.

Half an hour later Ginger was in Jefferson's arms. Always, Jefferson
thought, hands firmly, familiarly caressing Ginger, the touch of this
woman was like winning the World Series. "You take my breath away."

Ginger moved her face for a kiss. "I love you."

"Open the window." Jefferson reluctantly let her go. "Tell me you
can resist a day like this."

Ginger pulled a long Hunter T-shirt over her head and crossed to
the window in nothing but that and her flip-flops. Jefferson had been
astonished to see the floor of Ginger's closet covered in rubber beach
thongs of every hue. Ginger had explained about foot freedom, as she
called it. When she was in her room, not dancing, not walking far, she
loved to treat her feet to barefoot freedom and at the same time protect
them from harm. Hence, the flip-flops. She massaged her feet with
perfumed lotions, soaked them, and decorated them with flip-flops of
every color and design she could find in Woolworths, Kresge's, May's,
and corner drugstores. Ginger pressed her forehead against the screen
while Jefferson admired her profile. She could see Ginger inhale a deep
breath of the air. "It's gorgeous."

"Your accent's showing," she said, moving to Ginger.

The occasional harshness that remained in Ginger's accent grated
on Jefferson, who'd been raised to sound like a class, not a location, but
she thought she was good at keeping the irritation from her corrections.
Ginger wanted to succeed out there in the world, after all.

"Sorry," Ginger said quickly. "Gorgeous," she repeated, this time
in open tones.

A warm breeze seemed to swirl into the room and wrap around
them both. Jefferson was dressed in a faintly pink oxford cloth shirt, a
red V-neck sweater, sharply pressed white slacks, and white moccasins.
She stepped behind Ginger and pressed herself full-length to her back,
reaching around to touch her breasts. "We could go out to Long Island
Sound and rent a sailboat."

Ginger turned and moved her eyes down her lover's body. "You're irresistible, that's the problem."

"Am I pressuring you, baby?" she asked. "I thought it would be something you'd like to do."

"It would, Jef. I'm not convinced it's a good idea this weekend."

"We won't go." She was disappointed—crushed—but unwilling to upset Ginger.

"Oh, Jef. Does it mean that much to you?"

Jefferson slumped, body and mind quickly swallowed by gloom. She laid her head on Ginger's shoulder. "Not if you're going to worry all day."

"You feel so small when you're sad," said Ginger, her tone remorseful, her arms comforting, her hands, those magical hands, soothing. "You turn sad so suddenly."

Jefferson snuggled against the beloved body, feeling, for the moment, safe and free from her own demanding will. At the same time, she realized she was clutching at Ginger. The power of her love was also the power of her need and that, she was learning, frightened some women.

"I wouldn't worry all day," Ginger said.

Jefferson straightened, still holding her. "You mean you'll go on a holiday with me?"

"I didn't say that," Ginger warned with a laugh. "I guess I'm trying to say I don't want you thinking you can wrap me around your little finger."

She began to twist away from Jefferson, but weakly. They tussled, then fell laughing onto the unmade bed.

Jefferson's good cheer returned as she realized that Ginger really would spend the day with her. But was this so important? More important than grades and Ginger's peace of mind? How many days like this did one person get in a lifetime? Ginger's gentle fingers were in her still-wet hair, her lips soft, nibbling, biting her own lips, tasting like mint.

"Ginger, Ginger, will you play hooky with me?"

"Lock the door," came Ginger's dry-voiced answer.

"Will you?" she repeated after she returned. She knelt at the edge of the bed, Ginger's feet against her shoulders, and rubbed her cheeks along those soft inner thighs. "I could die happy here."

"Not quite yet," Ginger whispered, rubbing back against her. "Not till you finish what you started."

Her lips pressed against Ginger's soft mound, still moistly hot from the shower. She parted the cleft slowly with her tongue, then asked against her, "Will you?"

"Ohh, I like that," said Ginger, pressing back. "But Jef, I want to graduate with a three point five—"

"I'll give you a four point oh—"

"Oh, Jefferson, oh." Ginger cleared her throat as if to gain control of herself. "I'm not majoring in sex."

"You should. You're real good, baby."

She loved Ginger's spicy yet sweet taste. No matter how many girls she went out with on the sly, her moral code insisted that she go down only on Ginger. If Ginger ever found out about the others, maybe she wouldn't be as hurt.

As Ginger's thighs hugged her head she pictured herself, this beautiful woman proudly on her arm, standing on the sidelines of a field-hockey game. Her old team would be more spirited because she, a school hero, watched. Ginger would be happy and secure, holding her hand. Always, Ginger would like visiting with the coach and teachers, like being her girl where that counted most. And Jefferson, all in white, a white crock of wine in her hand, would feel that mellow high only Saturday afternoons on a playing field and a few drinks could give her.

She rose, fell with Ginger's hips, her tongue no longer roving, but strumming the slick full flesh over and over on the same spot. She'd check the schedule, maybe there was a game today. Ginger would have a great time. She'd make certain of that.

They drove to the suburban Westchester County town north of the city where Jefferson's old team was scheduled to play that day. The golden light was softer and spread a romantic haze over the oranges, reds, and yellows of the trees, over the light greens of the playing field, and over the young women in short plaid skirts, intent on their game. Jefferson filled her lungs with balmy air that carried on it the scent of dozens of backyard leaf piles gloriously, briefly blazing. The thwack of the girls' wooden hockey sticks as they clashed to defend their goals stirred more than prayers or anthems. This was winterless fall, sweet nostalgia; this was living at its best.

"Having a good time?" she asked Ginger, her heart celebrating.

"Sure. I love sharing this part of your life." Ginger's face was flushed, her absorption in the game obvious.

"Want to come back to the parking lot with me?"

"Jef, don't you care that your team is losing?" Ginger clapped as the Bluejays made a goal and cheered with the other bystanders. The coach, an old classmate of Jefferson's, ran to hug the scorer.

Jefferson watched the players a few more minutes. They seemed distanced by the hazy light, as if they were ghosts floating back and forth across the field. This could all be a pleasant dream. How could she explain to Ginger that it wasn't the winning, the losing, or the playing? It was the feeling of well-being that was important. The ease of a day blessed by such indulgent light that she felt free of the strictures a normal day would bring. Wasn't it like getting drunk? Life stopped being so hard.

She strode toward the parking lot in her whites. Inside her old Mustang were a picnic basket and supplies. Before leaving the city she and Ginger had stocked the car with rolls, cold meats, and a cooler full of cheesecake, soda, and wine. She lowered the car's tailgate and pulled out her whiskey bottle with stealth, pouring a slug into a paper cup and downing it, then replacing it and grabbing one of the white crocks of wine. This was not an Ivy League football game, and tailgating, especially with drinking, was not a custom. But she'd thought it would please Ginger to invite the team for a snack after the game. And the teachers were always glad for something convivial to pour into their cups of soda.

"Hi, Taffy," she said, and lounged against the car with her white bottle.

She remembered Taffy from other games, a cute little senior from the Academy who'd always been especially attentive.

The girl reached for the bottle. Team manager, she wore her short-skirted uniform like cheerleader garb. She definitely hadn't reached drinking age. Taffy fell, laughing, against Jefferson's chest as she wrestled for the bottle. Jefferson regretted three impassable years between them. But it didn't matter anyway. *I know right from wrong*, she reminded herself. *I have a will of my own.* Sometimes she seemed compelled to do crazy things, but she wouldn't let herself today. This would be a perfect day for Ginger.

"I'm eighteen, Jeffy, honest."

"Since when? And don't call me Jeffy." The nickname came naturally to the private-school crowd. They seemed to mock her with it, watering her down so they could tolerate her half-hidden gay self. It sounded like something they would name a pet Labrador retriever.

"Since last week. I started school late."

"Looks like everything else was on time," she commented in a wry tone, surveying the body bursting with adolescence. A few years from now the girl would still be pretty, but nothing like this—the shoulder-length bouncing hair, the large breasts newly full, the face without makeup. And she spoke easily, in Jefferson's unaccented tones. They could have been raised in the same family. Jefferson gave in, handed over the bottle.

"Thanks, sport," Taffy said, and drank.

They sat and talked, legs dangling from the tailgate. The cheering receded. She was deeper into this dreamy day. There wasn't harm, surely, in flirting with this kid?

"I really thought Jody would break your record this year, Jeffy."

Jefferson tried not to show her pride that no one had scored more goals in one game than she and moved to rest her back against the inside of the wagon. She was aware of her pose as she raised her knees and held the white crock between them, her gold ID bracelet hanging loosely from one wrist, on the other an expandable watch band glinting in the sun.

Taffy reached for the bottle again.

"I don't want to get you in trouble," Jefferson said, withholding it as Taffy's smaller hands played at prying hers off. She should have brought more.

"I have gum to cover the smell."

She surrendered the bottle. There were plenty of liquor stores nearby.

Taffy bragged, "I've been drinking since I was fourteen."

She clucked her tongue against the roof of her mouth, trying to be disapproving. "Me too," she admitted with a smile, proud of her precocity. "What else did you start at fourteen?"

Taffy threw back her head and laughed. "Don't tell me you mean boys. I only go out with them to please Mom and Dad."

Their eyes held. It seemed to Jefferson as if the worshipful little girl in Taffy was doing battle with the seductive woman. She knew the woman had won out when she felt lured by her gaze. She tried, for a while, not to look at Taffy's breasts or her swinging, nearly naked legs, not to touch, with her unquiet hands, the young siren body.

Ginger joined them. It was the end of the game. All three worked to set out the food.

"Why don't you two stay up here at my parents' house tonight?"

Taffy suggested. "I'm going to a bar with a bunch of the kids after the game."

"A bar, eh?" Jefferson envisioned a long night's laughter and dancing. She wouldn't have to come down from her high.

Taffy's eyes narrowed with challenge above her raised chin. "You've heard of the Cliffs?"

Jefferson shot a quick look at Taffy, trying to hide and at the same time reveal a knowing grin. The White Cliffs had been a gay bar when she was in school. So Taffy was definitely out. Still she fought against acknowledging, aloud, that she was gay. Oh, everyone knew it, but it seemed to be one of those unwritten lesbian rules that the minute you admitted it, you might as well disrobe and hold out your arms. For herself, coming out to another woman was a line.

She told Taffy, "I guess it wouldn't matter whether we went back tonight or in the morning."

While Ginger hesitated, assembling sandwiches, Taffy said, "Please stay. I'll go call Mother and tell her you'll be there for dinner. She's been asking to meet my charming friend Jefferson."

She noted that Taffy hadn't called her Jeffy in front of Ginger.

"My famous girlfriend." Ginger laughed. She fastened the leather thong that held her hair, never looking at Taffy, and raised her eyebrows.

Jefferson stood relaxed, legs apart, arms folded, hoping hard to extend this glowing day. Her mouth tasted brackish with sweet wine and old whiskey. She reached for the bottle. "What do you say, Princess? Shall we?"

Ginger blushed again before she spoke. "Sure, Taffy." She leveled her eyes at Jefferson. "As long as we start back to the city early."

She raised her arms as if to pull both women to her. "Come with me, my pretties. The day is ours." Her heart was alive again with excitement. "We might as well stay. Unless you'd rather go home?"

Ginger rested one delicate hand lightly on her forearm. Ginger's touch always made her light-headed. The smell of burning leaves mingled with Ginger's scent, both warm and familiar in the afternoon sun. Ginger whispered, "I'm only home in your hands."

"Thank God," Jefferson replied.

Taffy leapt up and hugged Jefferson, then hugged Ginger too. Jefferson watched them: the smaller, alluring Taffy, the back of her thighs showing as she stretched up to Ginger; the elegant-looking redhead, gracefully, lightly holding the girl. No comparison, she thought, smiling into Ginger's eyes, full of the warmth Ginger induced in her, certain that she was the woman for her. There is no way I'm going to lose that gem for some good-time kid who regards me as a notch in her belt.

She pulled out the whiskey again and tipped a quick shot of it into a cup of Coke, then tipped it again.

When they arrived at Taffy's home, the early winter dark came as a shock. She stayed on the porch while Taffy smoked a cigarette. Except for the black chill through a light jacket, she felt dulled by a cocktail and wine with dinner on top of the afternoon's drinking. Ginger was inside watching a televised ballet with Taffy's parents. Out here high hedges obscured all but hints of neighboring lights. She felt enclosed. Her skin crawled. A blueness, the last sign of light from her perfect day, seemed to seep out of the night into her. She needed to run off the threatening thunder of her mood. Would it never be time to go to the bar?

She sat heavily on a hanging wicker love seat. "What's the matter, Jeffy?" asked Taffy, sitting beside her. Taffy had changed to tight, cuffed jeans, a lime-colored shirt open at the throat, and a madras jacket. They swung gently.

She sighed after a while and, looking across the yard, spoke toward the hedges, to the specks of light that promised a world beyond her blues. "The day's over, that's all. I got up and the world promised me something. It staged a spectacular: trumpets, dancing girls, glitter, and song. But it was a sham. Look—the curtain's down and it's gone, every bit of it." She held out empty hands.

Taffy picked up one hand and laid it palm up across her own. She traced the lines of Jefferson's palm. "No one with hands as beautiful as yours should feel bad," Taffy said. "Look how strong, how sensitive. I'll bet Ginger loves these hands."

A little thrill of pleasure pierced her fog. She was still so numb she ignored the sentry voice inside her, warning, warning of this beckoning stranger Taffy. But Taffy was touching her, liked touching her, and she'd become so addicted to touch, it was as if she'd been starved for it her whole childhood, as if the magic of touch could by itself lift her heavy mood.

"Every day's like that, Taffy. You wake up full of purpose, thinking this will be the day, and it ends, and it wasn't. Someday I'll have been shot down so often I'll lose the ability to feel excitement."

Taffy's face looked like the hockey players' had, so intent on winning that no emotion showed. Nor was there a note of concern in her voice when she asked, "The day for what?"

"Maybe if I knew that, I'd find it."

"Find what?" persisted Taffy.

"Fame, fortune, success? An end to the search? Home?"

"I can't wait to get away from home."

"That's the problem. I'm always trying to get away from what I think of as home too. Why do I feel so excited when I think I'm there, then lose interest?"

"What are you talking about, Jeffy? Ginger?"

Jefferson looked down at her hands, at Taffy's small fingernails, daintily shaped and polished, ever moving across her own. How could these big hands ever make a home for Ginger when they were so restless, so uncontrolled themselves? What was wrong with her? She closed her hand on Taffy's without considering consequences, to see how it felt.

"Jeffy, Jeffy," the girl said in a low purring voice. "I knew you wanted me."

"But—"

Taffy had pushed Jefferson back and lay half on top of her, her lips assaulting Jefferson's.

She pulled her head away. She hesitated to reject Taffy, not wanting the girl to dislike her and, senselessly, not wanting to act in a way that would confirm that they'd been flirting.

"Shh, Jeffy. I know." She rubbed her breasts against Jefferson. "Ginger's right inside. I don't want to get you in trouble either." Taffy moved off her and sat upright. "Wasn't I smart? I didn't wear lipstick, though I wanted to look great for you."

She knew that sparkle in Taffy's eyes. The animation bred from winning. And certainly the touch of her breasts had been exciting. She moved to the rail as Ginger, with her graceful, spirited walk, came out onto the porch.

Part of her resented Ginger's entrance; the rest of her was relieved to be saved from her own wavering impulses. "I need to stop at a liquor store on the way," she said, cheered by the feeling of escape, by the rush of adrenaline Taffy's advances and Ginger's arrival had stirred.

She drove, bought more wine, and, house by house, filled the station wagon with half the hockey team. They flew through the clear star-sparkling night to the bar where once again there was promise in the air thick as the cigarette smoke. She kept close to Ginger, brought her drinks, danced with her, brashly elbowed a path to the bathroom for her.

She was raucous, overbearing, and tried to quiet herself, to assume the air of a dignified alumnus. But, as she'd told Taffy, she was rushing to get to somewhere, and she shouted, and drank, to drown out the space between here and there.

Then, all at once, as if she'd quaffed a magic potion, she arrived. The golden day had returned. Life was hard no longer. She moved with ease, laughed low, and talked quietly, with an air of amused tolerance.

Taffy came to the table, eyes glittering like the loud jukebox. "May I dance with your girlfriend?" she asked Ginger.

Jefferson saw Ginger—dear, trusting Ginger—assent.

"Hey," she said, one hand closing around Ginger's where it lay on the table. Her lips seemed to burn from Taffy's earlier kiss. "I'm home." It sounded, of course, as if she meant being close to Ginger, but really she was talking about the state, short of unconsciousness, where one movement sends the drunk toppling from her chair, from her peace, with the weight of her passions and will.

"Time to go, Jef," Ginger said a moment, or hours, later.

She listed heavily toward Ginger as they walked to the car.

Someone handed them coffee.

"Can you drive?" Ginger whispered.

In answer, Jefferson got reckless and kissed her full on the mouth, ignoring the way Ginger pulled back from her.

A chorus of wolf-calls came from the back of the wagon. Jefferson began to drive smoothly, fearlessly, grinning crookedly, back to Taffy's town.

Once she'd delivered the tired gang, she drove to the hedge-walled house. At the sight of it her blues returned.

Taffy showed them to a room. "Sorry about the single beds," she said.

They undressed in the dark, each collapsing into her own bed, as they did at the dorm. She heard Ginger drop her flip-flops to the braided rug between them.

"Thank you for a fun day, Jef," Ginger murmured, reaching for her hand and squeezing it.

She lay, stupefied by liquor and exhaustion, the space between their beds a chasm. Taffy had caressed Jefferson's hand furtively as she showed them her room. She'd pointedly told Jefferson, while Ginger was in the bathroom, "I could have stayed with Jody tonight."

Now she lay on her back, wearing only her white slacks, sleep nowhere in view, and reached down to the floor for the last crock of wine. Ginger slept, as always, deeply, peacefully. The peace wine had brought Jefferson—where had it gone? Where was her golden day? She couldn't stand to lie alone, awake, empty-handed all night. Should she wake Ginger? No. She'd worn her out with her impulsive adventure and should let her rest.

She could visit Taffy. To talk. It would fill the long hours. She reached for another drink. They said people who drank alone were alcoholics.

"I'm only home in your hands," Ginger had said, trusting all that talent, all that beauty, all that ambition and grace to her.

She opened her eyes wide. Was she having nightmares? Why all these troubling thoughts? A chill crept through her like the sudden night earlier on the porch. She stared into the dark, horrified at the thin line between staying in bed and leaving Ginger's side; between talking to Taffy and—

Once again, she reached for the bottle, felt its round solidity in her grasping hand, drank. The wine trickled down between her breasts. She sat up, drank again. Ginger didn't stir.

She rose, heart thudding with excitement and fear. The braided rug cushioned her movements in silence. Trembling, she pulled the white V-neck over her head, picked up the bottle, and crept out to the hall. Taffy's door was ajar, open on yet another promise.

CHAPTER THIRTEEN

After winning the intramural golf tournament, graduating from Hunter was a letdown. Playing golf, Jefferson had gotten a kick out of the hush of the onlookers when things got tense on the green. She'd been such a devoted team player, but somehow, with the friends in her life, with school, with required sports and hitting the bars and Margo, then Lily Ann, then Ginger and those in between—she had nothing to give a team. What does the team player do when her team is gone? Mope, she discovered, until she went out for golf. Shining in sports was like food to her, not something she could give up. Her solution, in her junior year, was to hike down to Brooklyn on the subway and play the Dyker Beach Golf Course with a woman who commuted to Hunter from the area. Rain or shine or snow they played or met at a driving range to practice.

Graduation, in comparison, was noisy. Between her and Ginger, they filled a whole row of seats. They'd had to scramble for extra tickets, which the out-of-towners and international students had been willing to share or sometimes sell. Ginger's three older brothers were there because Jefferson had bought their tickets, and her dad and mom and her Aunt Tilly, who lived with them. Jefferson's parents and grandparents were there—she was the only grandchild—and also Gladys from the coffee shop had arrived with a bunch of flowers, which Emmy now held.

Angela had asked to come. Her beautiful, lively Angela, who was now hitched to another Dutchess girl from Jefferson's side of the tracks, Tam Thorpe, a distant cousin of Jefferson's. Somehow, despite Tam going to school, they had gotten the money together to buy the Snip'N'Shape beauty salon. Angela, of course, had lots of customers because she knew everyone from her father's candy store. Tam was a Dutchess Academy graduate and was an object of fascination for the wives of the movers and shakers in town. Jefferson remembered, as she watched Tam and Angie approach, that rough time after she moved to the dorm in the middle of her freshman year and gradually stopped seeing Angela. She hadn't had the decency to break up with her, but kept telling Angie she was too busy to see her.

One night, the fall after she and Ginger became lovers, they had, for once, been at their dorm-room desks, typing papers. Ginger had called, "Come in," at the knock on the door. It was Angela. Jefferson introduced Angie to Ginger, and that was when Angela first introduced them to Frenchy. Angela hugged Jefferson while Frenchy posed in the doorway, tapping a Marlboro out of a crushproof box and lighting up with a silver Zippo, engraved with the initials F.T. They had stopped by, Angela told her, because Frenchy wanted to check out Angie's first girl. Later, she guessed Angela visited to let her know she wasn't home being a sad sack, that she had another lover and didn't need Jefferson. Anyone could see, Ginger had said, that this Frenchy person was too hung up on Frenchy to stick with any girl for long.

Tam was a better match for Angie: bright, good-looking, as good a dancer as Frenchy, and a little on the sulky side, her eyes never leaving Angie. Jefferson hoped they'd make it, like she and Ginger would. After all this time, though, she couldn't say what made her split up with Angie. Maybe she was a little like Frenchy herself, but this time she would be true to the vow she'd made herself, to be a one-woman woman.

The truth was, Angela's tactic worked. After the visit to the dorm, Jefferson did call Angie up now and then to talk, and she did visit her at the shop whenever she went up to Dutchess. She loaned some of the money that she came into when she turned twenty-one to Angela and Tam so they could add stations in the shop to rent to other hairdressers. Tam had been hired for Jefferson's old job and was doing the part-time college, full-time print shop route too. Her parents had money, but her dad was a boot-strap kind of guy and liked Tam's approach—leaving home, moving in with a friend, supporting herself while her family paid her expenses at Barnard. Jefferson's guilt over leaving Angela was eased by introductions to the lovers who followed.

Angela and the coffee-shop waitress, Gladys, who were meeting for the first time, hugged Jefferson and cried and told her they were proud to watch her graduate. Jefferson wanted to crow: she liked making them proud. Her parents were hanging out with her golf buddy's family, and she could see her father demonstrating his swing for them. He was sober today—so far.

She went over to Lily Ann, whose mother was on her arm and smiling widely at everyone. She was surprised at how little Lily Ann's mom was.

"You take after your father?" She raised her hand flat in the air as if measuring Lily Ann's height.

Lily Ann introduced her to Mrs. Lee.

"Congratulations," she said. "You've got a smart, hard-working kid here."

"Oh, don't I know it," said Mrs. Lee, who launched into an obviously often-repeated series of smart things her daughter had said and done since she'd been one month old.

Jefferson had managed to become friends, maybe best friends, with Lily Ann. They'd had some hot and heavy months together, and it had been more than sex, but Lily Ann was smart about them too. She knew they weren't meant for each other and told Jefferson she wanted to get into the gay social life now so she could eventually meet her dream woman. "Probably," Lily Ann said, "she'll be like my mama: small and made of steel. And," she teased her, "though you're a hunk, J, she probably won't be a white girl."

"If she's a woman of steel, Lily Ann, she won't be a white girl," she joked back.

They said all this in front of Mrs. Lee. Back in freshman year, Lily Ann couldn't wait to tell her what she'd discovered with Jefferson. Lily Ann and her mom were that close. Jefferson marveled at someone who didn't have to hide what she was. All the time she was marching in the graduation ceremony she wanted to be marching up to her parents to come out to them, but her makeup really did not include steel. While they all waited for the "Pomp and Circumstance" moment, she pulled out a pink Spaulding ball and got a game of hit-the-nickel going. The graduating class had been told not to wear jeans or sneakers, but she'd never understood where they got off telling her how to dress. She'd chosen her black hightops and darkened the white soles with a charcoal pencil she'd bought for a sophomore-year art class. If her parents hadn't noticed, the muckety-mucks on stage wouldn't.

Margo was in the crowd of teachers. She'd managed to get through one term of German class with her and then switched to Spanish with a

Beggar of Love

male instructor. She'd used her high-school Spanish, which was pretty good, to meet the prerequisites. Margo didn't speak to her, nor she to Margo, for the next three years. Now, with graceful, gorgeous Ginger in her life, she wondered how she could have become entangled with the plump, permed professor.

It was Margo's staring silence that distressed Jefferson. The silence reproved, described abandonment, maybe envy of her evident happiness. There she was with young, lovely Ginger and not with Margo. She thought Margo might complain aloud, attack her verbally, or make it clear that she felt betrayed. That might have been better, she thought, better than the cold knife of disapproval in Margo's gaze and in her frozen lack of expression, verbal or in gestures. When Angela felt she'd been denied her due, she'd whined, cajoled, complained, and accused, but that was unusual for a lesbian, Jefferson realized. They were more like Ginger or even herself, who tended to avoid confrontation and the risk that the closet door might swing open. A grown woman who had revealed herself so fully to a freshman as Margo had was a walking accusation and needed no words. The things she'd asked from Jefferson for her own pleasure—Margo was now facing down Jefferson's memories. Was she wondering if Jefferson despised her? Probably, but really, she thought, Margo despised herself for trusting someone who now might share Margo's secrets with the slim, graceful dancer by Jefferson's side.

If there was a punishment on the books for allowing another woman to be that vulnerable to her, it was this silence and Margo's loud gaze. And the memory, not of the acts of pleasure, but of the suspicion that something about herself was broken. How else could she have walked away from Margo and Angela, vanishing from their lives with no explanation? She didn't even want to think the woman's name today; the sight of her reminded Jefferson of the revulsion she had felt.

Something had gone too far, something had gotten out of hand. Again, it wasn't the greedy lust of the woman or the touch of shame she felt at complying with her more imaginative requests. Something had been taken from her, perhaps by her own doing, her own complicity in cheating on Angie, sleeping with a teacher so much older than herself, learning to lie to someone she loved and who trusted her. In high school, they'd loved with the complete trust of children. She worried not only that she'd destroyed that part of herself, but that she'd done the same to Angie. Now that she knew she was capable of betrayal and inflicting pain in order to have what she wanted, she suspected everyone else in the world was capable of the same thing. She'd discovered that she couldn't trust herself to honor what she'd thought she'd believed in. How could she now trust anyone else?

Or had she only lost her innocence, a perfectly natural loss that would have happened eventually with or without Margo?

It didn't seem to matter; she realized that she was angry at Margo. No, she thought, running her fingers back through her short hair, she was experiencing a rage that befit being raped. Despite Margo's passivity when they were lovers, Jefferson had been interfered with, not Margo. She'd certainly lost some possibly nameless quality. She sensed its absence. There was something she was not giving Ginger now that she'd known how to give Angela before Margo.

She returned Margo's glare, the two of them in their ridiculous black robes, and curled her hands into fists. She left the safe circle of her friends and family to step toward Margo, then watched as Margo shrank back very slightly and peered around as if for protection before she turned and wove her way through the other professors, who were still milling around, as if finding their places in line was beneath them.

She turned back to her family, but they were looking past her. She felt the dean approach before she turned.

"Excuse me, young lady," he said. "What do you have for footwear?"

Margo, she thought immediately. Margo had spotted her gym shoes and spoken to the dean. That's when it hit her: Margo had always had this power and had always used it to control her. That annoying Everly Brothers hit, "Kathy's Clown," popped into her mind. Margo was getting her revenge by trying to make a clown of her.

She came to something like attention. "Sorry, sir. I'm a PE major. I don't own anything else." Lying came so easily now.

"Young lady," the dean ordered, "find yourself footwear in compliance with the dress code or you won't be accepting your diploma onstage."

She saw that too-familiar look of her mother's, the expression she wore at horror films. The Jeffersons had paid for this day and she knew they wanted their moment in the sun.

Gladys's feet were almost Jefferson's size. She swapped her sneakers for low pumps. Gladys coached her in walking for about two minutes, making a joke of it, making it fun. Jefferson swept across the stage in her clown shoes, in front of Gladys, her parents, Angie, Ginger, and Margo, with her head high. Instead of giving in to humiliation, she treated this wearing of the ridiculous heels for the first—and last—time as a gym exercise. If she could win a tournament, certainly she could meet Margo's mean challenge.

Chapter Fourteen

During the next few years after college, Jefferson was no less in love with Ginger, no less determined to live her life with Ginger. She still went though the horrible doldrums that had followed her out of childhood. She drowned the awful sinking of her moods at the bars and, sometimes, with the excitement of the chase. It had started with Taffy, but then, still in her junior year, Jefferson had found Patti so cute, and a senior, already out at school. Patti had slipped love poems to Jefferson in their history-of-music class. Jefferson had already known that material inside out from growing up with the parents she had and had been bored.

Drinking coffee together after class, Jefferson told her she was involved. Patti ignored this. Patti had a car. She was a golfer too and drove Jefferson and her golfing buddy to the course where they played as a threesome. Ginger, with her jobs and rehearsals and performances, could never go and had never played golf.

One day, Patti had a flask with her and by the time she pulled into a spot down by the water, deserted in winter, Jefferson was raring to get her into the backseat. She made love to Patti quickly, but would not let Patti under her clothes. The thing with Patti was over within weeks, when Patti, infuriated that Jefferson wouldn't split up with Ginger, tricked her into getting out of the car at one of the old stone-faced gas stations on the Henry Hudson Parkway and drove off. Jefferson had a flask of her own by then and, high on a combination of the half she drank after their game and her new secret freedom from secret Patti, she bounded through the streets of Washington Heights until she found the A train.

Jefferson got off at Ginger's stop and rented a hotel room. It felt so good to have Ginger in her arms that night. Her naked back, the firm curve of her waist, her undemanding desire were all so familiar and right that Jefferson knew she would never be attracted to another woman again. She was twenty-two by that time and much better at knowing what she wanted.

In her senior year, that Thanksgiving night when Minerva Castle, the little Englishwoman who helped Grandmother Jefferson, led her to her live-in room to show her the awkward but flattering sketches she'd done of Grandmother, Jefferson was drunk, like her father and mother and grandfather downstairs.

Minerva offered her more wine. She knew where that would lead; it always led there. Women were so hungry. Especially the mousy ones like Minerva, who she would never associate with sex or guess would be interested in being gay. Yet they were the most wild for touch and release.

"You're gay, aren't you?" Minerva Castle had asked. This was a woman in her thirties, exotic with her British accent and disproportionate breasts, kind of a lightweight in the brain department, but earnest and kind. "Me too," she said when Jefferson came out to her.

She missed Ginger, but of course neither could present the other at home for the holiday, like a straight couple. They hadn't even talked about the possibility. Jefferson found herself being made love to in Minerva Castle's twin bed. She didn't like it this way, preferred giving pleasure to receiving it, but Minerva was determined. The woman's clammy hands and oily facial skin had put Jefferson off, but the experience was exciting and she couldn't help responding. Minerva preferred penetration, so she didn't have to reciprocate orally and felt as if she hadn't been unfaithful. Minerva also liked a little anal penetration, just with Jefferson's pinky.

"Where did you learn that?" Ginger asked, breathless, when she used that trick at home.

"Honors Sex 300, Princess," she'd responded. "Miss Parsons teaches it on Saturday nights."

"Miss Parsons?"

Jefferson gave Ginger an exaggerated wink.

"Sure. You're kidding. I'm so gullible with you, Jef."

"Miss Parsons would wet her gym shorts. I can't imagine her—I mean, can you?"

They laughed, then Ginger tried it on her, but Jefferson couldn't come. She never could with Ginger, as if her emotional excitement was on a different track from her sexual response. She didn't let on to Ginger, of course. She never wanted to hurt Ginger.

She looked forward to seeing Minerva Castle on holidays. The woman made no demands on her time or company outside of bed, but one day in Jefferson's senior year Grandmother teased Minerva about her boyfriend the gardener. Minerva, usually as pale as Grandmother's chicken broth, turned the same pink that orgasm gave her. Jefferson was repelled. Every time she saw Minerva after that she wanted to drench her in bug spray.

Ginger lived with her parents the year Jefferson was a senior. She had already graduated, but couldn't find an apartment she could afford and still survive. It was tough because they'd been so happy rooming together at school. Jefferson fought with Emmy and Jarvy to live off campus at the family's city apartment, but they wanted her to wait until she had a job so she didn't get used to depending on them. They did agree to buy her a car, a 1971 Chevy Nova.

It had been Uncle Stephen's, then Cousin Raymond's. It was old and smelled of cigarettes, but Jarvy had the transmission replaced and the engine overhauled. All that year, it carried Jefferson and Ginger back and forth to the family place on Saturday Lake in New Hampshire, through the depth of winter in the snow and ice. Ginger had to drive what they called their chariot of ashes then because Jefferson had a horror of losing control of the car in weather, and Ginger, though Jefferson had to teach her, was a born driver and sailed through the worst storms, fearless, as if it was high summer.

After Minerva, there was no one but Ginger her whole senior year. She and Ginger had three seasons of love by the fireplace at the lake, three seasons of isolation on the long drives, during the long nights and on Saturday Lake after the tourist season, then in early spring as soon as the lake thawed. Classes were a dream to be slept though when she got back. Ginger had been able to find only part-time work during the week, teaching dance at the Neighborhood House, and without college performances, her gigs were few. They planned for her to give private lessons after Jefferson graduated and after they went to France and the British Isles that summer. Jefferson had already been offered a job teaching at a classy private school in the city through someone her mother knew. Her parents planned to let her live in her grandparents' apartment then. Ginger could move in and only have to help with utilities. She could rent a loft space for lessons.

When they visited the house in New Hampshire that winter, they learned to keep their clothes on until Jefferson got a fire started and

Ginger made up the Castro Convertible in the living room. They lived on deli food and takeout that they'd gather on their way out of the city. She made sure she scheduled classes offered only Tuesday, Wednesday, and Thursday so almost every week they would have four days together, a nine-month-late honeymoon on the lake, watching the red oaks lose their leaves, the bright red winterberries arrive, ice fishers suited up for the freezing air, and lilac bushes bursting into lusty bloom. Sometimes they hiked or boated or ice-skated, but mostly they stayed in the knotty-pine house with nothing but their nubile minds and splendid bodies to entertain them. Jefferson had never been happier.

Despite the way dance displayed Ginger's body, she had that Irish-Catholic shyness about moving around the house naked and shocked Jefferson the first night she donned a granny gown. Now she knew why relationships died. Someone put on a granny gown or one quit drinking when the other didn't. A curtain closed and shut one person out, or a curtain opened and revealed too much. The first time she saw Lily Ann Lee's breasts with the moles on them, it shouldn't have mattered and didn't for a while, but now they were friends instead of lovers, partly because Jefferson could live without ever seeing that body nude again. Everyone, she thought, has a right to her own aesthetic.

Ginger's body was beyond compare. Jefferson could spend days, weeks, years of her life watching Ginger walk, bend, reach, scratch her bottom. The gown smothered the fire in her, but there was so much more to Ginger and to what they had together. With praise and encouragement someday Ginger would get over that self-consciousness. Would it be too late by then? Or would she automatically pull a granny gown over her own eyes, look away or not see what she was looking at?

When they were together they were by turns comfortable, playful, sexual, but mostly asleep. During the week Ginger was all about dance. As much as she adored Ginger, as close as Ginger came to being everything she could want in a woman, sometimes she felt like she was married to Tinker Bell.

In those early years, they didn't have sex, they made love. Ginger was open, eager, easily roused and satisfied. She followed Jefferson's lead as pliably and as gracefully as she danced. Ginger professed her love, collapsing like a telescoping cup into something like a loving little animal, warm, so close she might be under Jefferson's skin or curled around her heart. She whispered her ardent feelings and passionate promises of forever. Ginger made it clear that she knew their bond was beyond breakable. She used the term "soul mates" and Jefferson agreed that they were, although she had somehow imagined a more consistent devotion on both sides.

She would get out of bed while Ginger slept—afterward—and sit down with the bottle of Jameson. She'd sip it over two ice cubes and replay the way tall, willful Ginger went all soft and yielding in her hands that night. The contrast excited her beyond anything she'd ever experienced and she felt like a top-of-the-line lover—creative, sensitive to Ginger's every desire, as if she were an extension of Ginger's perfect body, as if Ginger was some other self she could please.

Yet the next morning she could find little sign of her fiercely loving Ginger. With Ginger's mother's disappointed coldness—she'd gotten her first job as a chorus girl on Broadway when she became pregnant with Ginger—and her father's work-above-all ethic, where could Ginger have learned that sweetness can carry over into the daylight hours? She probably had all she could do to save the loving little kid she must have started out as from withering completely. With Ginger turning to a will-o'-the-wisp come daylight, Jefferson felt a little less guilty about her own absences, like she was entitled to them, damn it.

Ginger worked hard and spoke of quitting performance, opening a dance school. "I want to earn my keep here," she told Jefferson, though with Jefferson's teaching wage and her family's deep pockets, they weren't hurting. Ginger picked up money giving dance classes, especially after school hours and on Saturdays, when Jefferson was off.

"Keep performing," she urged Ginger. "Princess, it's your dream, your mom's dream too, and I'd miss watching you dance." In truth, she'd been bored at the last few performances, but Ginger didn't have to know that.

"Sure. As long as I have a steady income," Ginger had answered.

"But you're a dancer. How could you cut that off? If I had a talent like yours and didn't use it, I'd fade away."

"Teaching is a talent too, Jef. And coaching."

"Teaching is a job. Maybe some day there will be gay softball teams to coach and I'll love what I do, but right now, it's part of my job. A fun part, but nothing like your name up in lights."

"I can't get satisfaction out of dancing unless I know I'll have solid ground under my feet, like you do."

"I can coach till I go blind and deaf, Ginge. You won't be able to dance that long. Now is when you need to be performing."

"I don't know." Ginger moved away from her and crossed her arms. "Of course I want to perform forever, but I'm an ironworker's daughter from the Bronx. I know my limits. Do you see my brothers getting all artsy? Joseph can draw like he was born to make a living doing portraits on Sixth Avenue in the Village. He and Kevin followed my father into the union. It's their best shot in this life. We're not in with the people who go places. Maybe if I'd been a tiny bit more talented, well connected, more of a hustler, more outgoing, maybe I could reach the big time and earn enough to keep me for the rest of my life, let a husband support me—"

"I'll support you, damn it."

"I know you would, sure, but I couldn't live with that. You've got your own way to make. Your family may have money, but you're not the idle rich. If you supported me I'd feel like a failure. I need to prove I can succeed in the dance world, and if I can't do it as a dancer, I'd like to do it as a teacher. I have to ask myself, too, how long can I realistically keep up performing? What will I do when my body gives out?"

"You don't believe enough in your own talent," she said, not asking the hard question: why did Ginger think it was all right to be financially supported by a husband, but not by her?

"My biggest talent is work. I watched my dad rack up the overtime year after year, with no life beyond work except a beer, the TV, early to bed, never a complaint. He was my model, his are my values. It's how I earned college and paid my way through. It's how I got his respect. I couldn't believe it the other day when he said he'd borrow on his retirement to invest in a dance school when I'm ready."

Had she been attracted to Ginger because she thought Ginger would be some kind of star? Okay, a little bit. Maybe there was a spot of tarnish now, but it wasn't like Ginger would have to give up dance to be a used-car salesperson or something. She'd seen Ginger teach at the Neighborhood House and she was good. She had the nine little ones in her beginning tap class moving like mini-Rockettes. Even the really heavy teenager in Saturday-morning modern dance was learning to carry her body gracefully, thanks to Ginger. She couldn't knock it. Ginger clearly delighted in giving away what she knew and loved, just like Jefferson got into it too when she was teaching.

"I have a girl in one of my classes," she told Ginger. "Gilleberta Konic, tall, so skinny you think her stick legs might snap out from under her. Gilleberta's the daughter of someone at the UN. I watched her learn to dribble a basketball, weaving this way and that, lunging after the ball, tripping on it, bending so low it was rolling, not bouncing. I figured she'd be okay when she started pulling herself out of one of her rolls by lifting the ball like it was glued to her fingertips. I felt so damn proud to see Gilleberta out on the gym floor doing double-ball power dribbling. I knew I was doing the right thing, teaching PE."

"I don't know which way to go, Jef."

"Yeah, you need a compass." She considered saying aloud that she'd like to borrow it when Ginger was through, but how do you tell your lover that you need a moral compass?

Ginger was in her thirties before she did throw the towel in on her performance career and accepted her dad and Jefferson's offers to help start a school. The Neighborhood House had wanted to hire her full-time, but she would have had to take on all kinds of recreation classes other than dance. Once Ginger made her decision, she got to work. She went up and down probably every block in Washington Heights, where she'd been working, looking for studio space. Jefferson had scored a job as a swimming instructor for the parks department that summer, but got off at three and would go look at the spaces that appealed to Ginger.

Once they found the spot, a second story on the edge of West End Avenue with level hardwood floors, a plate-glass window across the front for natural light, and wall space for mirrors and bars, she helped Ginger clean, paint, and polish the floors. This would be the most time they would spend together for several years. Ginger opened her little school and not only taught, but marketed, did the bookkeeping, the cleaning, grant writing, scholarship research, and kept up some classes at the Neighborhood House. The hours by the fire were gone, as were nights without the granny gown. Jefferson yearned for her as intensely as she had before she'd introduced herself at Ginger's performance. She felt like something left to mold at the bottom of a barrel.

She wasn't surprised to find herself in bed, spirits again high, with a younger dancer, a woman physically like Ginger who was rehearsing for a Broadway show called *Dancin'*. The woman, Alexis, had grown up in Alaska, of all places, adopted by an evangelical minister in Palmer. Alexis had learned to dance at church camps. The woman was wild with her New York freedom, drunk every night after performing. She'd almost thrown herself at Jefferson in a bar and led her back to an apartment she shared with four roommates. Alexis paid the least rent and got a convertible couch in the living room for her space. When they opened the bed they would move two folding screens to shield themselves while they went about their business fervently, but in absolute silence. Two of the roommates, gay men, turned up the TV and occasionally called jokes about springs squeaking. It didn't seem to bother Alexis. She taught Jefferson about multiple sequential orgasms and practiced what would have been exhibitionistic lewdness had the screen fallen down.

Other women were golf and softball. Ginger was her first love, field hockey her second. Jefferson was her own goalie.

A bit ashamed of herself, Jefferson invited Ginger to see *Dancin'* soon after it opened, using two tickets the dancer gave her. She could understand why Ginger wasn't up there. She couldn't see her performing these rote audience-pleasers night after night. Ginger and modern dance fit a lot better; Ginger and Jefferson fit a lot better. She never saw the Broadway woman after the show and was pretty clear that she wouldn't get stagestruck again. She relished having elegant Ginger on her arm at the theater, the cock of the walk.

The neighborhood hadn't had a dance school for many years, and enrollment was so crazy good the first year that Ginger hired her spinster great-aunt Tilly as clerical help. Aunt Tilly had retired from her lifelong job as a public-school clerk, so not only did she set up the office in a more professional manner, but she was tickled to get out of the house and back into the world again, as she put it. She was a big, boisterous florid-faced Irishwoman in voluminous, dark polyester dresses. Her hearing had declined with age.

The first time Jefferson stopped by Ginger's school after Aunt Tilly was installed, Tilly eyed Jefferson. "So you're Jess. The roommate."

Jefferson froze. She knew, like she knew when a puck would make it straight into the net, that this woman had caught on that Jefferson was gay. She decided not to correct her name and flashed her winner smile. "Glad to meet you, ma'am. I'll bet you're Aunt Tilly."

Instead of answering, Tilly said, "My niece has a big family, Jess. Lots of strong men and willful women. None of us would be pleased to see our little Ginger hurt. By any one. For any reason."

"Not by me." She answered softly and seriously. She would never hurt Ginger by seeing these other women. Ginger didn't have to know, just as her mother had never known about Jefferson's father. At least, she didn't think Emmy had found out. If she had, Ginger would play it the same way: she'd live with it rather than divorce. Probably. It would never come up, though, so that was a moot point.

The six- to eight-year-olds came clattering out of tap class then, and Ginger formally introduced her to Aunt Tilly. All three joked and laughed together, as if no smoldering warning had been passed, as if Jefferson had no reason to quake inside every time she ran up the loft steps two at a time and saw the harridan at her desk, guarding Ginger.

It was hard to get time for the two of them in those early days, but whenever Jefferson returned from straying she would insist. It was the best antidote as well, she hoped, immunization from doing it again. If they didn't go to New Hampshire, they might find their way to Fire Island or Provincetown. Once she booked a hotel off Broadway and they saw two shows, lingering late at an after-theater restaurant and getting into bed at the same time, something they could seldom do at home because of their different hours.

Skin to skin with Ginger, she remembered all over again that Ginger smelled like home, tasted like home. She'd be touched with a comforting familiarity more satisfying than some frenzied orgasm brought on by a stranger's fingers. After their days together, she felt cleansed and refreshed, ready to swear off the bars and the drinking, to get up early enough to eat breakfast before school and to come straight home.

This would work for the first few nights. She'd get the laundry done, mop floors, peel cobwebs from the corners of ceilings, all while singing along with her Eagles albums. On the nights Ginger had no classes she'd have a pot of stew or baked chicken ready, and they would wash and dry the dishes together, smiling in their contentment, Ginger sometimes doing a few silly dance steps to celebrate new flip-flops Jefferson had spied outside a bodega.

By Thursday night Jefferson would be half in the bag at her favorite bar of the moment, as likely as not dancing with her old standby Shirley or, if she'd caught enough hell at school for being late or smelling like last night's alcohol, she'd be in the bar bathroom making out with some new woman in town for a convention, a fashion shoot, a news assignment. Her despairing moods pursued her. She would barely make it home before they felled her, and she'd topple into bed before Ginger got in from work. She would will herself to forget the feel of her fingers plunged to the hilt inside the roomy secrets of the suburban mother of three she'd entertained that night. She'd lie in bed, wanting Ginger until Ginger came to her, hugged, nuzzled, and turned on her side to sleep.

CHAPTER FIFTEEN

The first time Jefferson was fired from a private school had been the department head's doing.

Right out of Hunter College, she'd started as a swim coach for the school. Swimming was not her favorite sport, but she was mostly able to stay out of the water and dry as she demonstrated strokes and acted primarily as a lifeguard at the school's indoor pool. She was hired to teach the next school year and found herself surveying groups of girls aged six to thirteen, clad in despised one-piece green gym suits, while they dropped off ropes and jumped short of minimal marks as they tried to meet the guidelines of the newest fitness program. She wished there was more interest in competitive sports and volunteered to coach or referee almost every game that came up.

It never occurred to her that enthusiasm wouldn't make her popular. Two of the other teachers, who apparently counted on after-school fees to make ends meet, weren't used to sharing their after-school pay. Mrs. Dove, the department head, said she liked the breath of fresh air Jefferson brought and expressed intense interest in her career, to the point of taking her out for coffee after work. Then it was a glass of wine at the chair's apartment a few blocks away. She stayed for dinner, with wine during the meal, and met the husband, an insurance-claims adjustor. She and the chairwoman drank more wine when she stayed after dinner while the husband went to his chamber-music rehearsal.

That was the night Mrs. Dove put "Moonlight Sonata" on the turntable and set it to repeat. Their talk became more intense—about sports they both loved and the classical music they'd grown up with. Mrs. Dove shared her philosophies on not having children, on the plague of men in the world who were the cause of war and destruction, and too much information about what her husband demanded of her in the bedroom.

For all her swaggering lesbian ways, Jefferson knew nothing beyond her own experience. The romantic headiness of Beethoven, the intimacy and eroticism of Mrs. Dove's revelations, the apartment lit only by the lights of the city outside were too much for her. She was still learning how hungry women were for butch hands, her butch hands. She thought Mrs. Dove was the most desirable of women, a sort of conquest. She didn't pretend to herself that she was in love with her or particularly attracted to her. She was flattered that so urbane a woman, more conventional than Margo had been, a woman in her forties, would be, as Mrs. Dove said, fascinated by her. Although Jefferson had not come out to her, Mrs. Dove confessed, with a tipsy slurring of words, that she was attracted to her.

They were sitting knee to knee in the dining alcove, wine low in its green bottle, a vase of flowers perfuming the furniture-heavy apartment, and Mrs. Dove was fingering the tips of Jefferson's collar with the index fingers and thumbs of both hands. Jefferson knew the chairwoman had freshened her lipstick and perfume on her last trip to the bathroom so she, half in fear that she would lose her job but emboldened by her share of the bottles of wine, her hands itching with the need to touch, without actually deciding to move, reached under Mrs. Dove's skirt, past her garters and the tops of her nylons, while the piano gently bumped along its notes, carrying their hot sighs into the air.

Mrs. Dove had also taken off her panties. Jefferson slowly moved her hand from vertical to horizontal, thus prying apart Mrs. Dove's thighs, and pushed her middle finger forward to lightly touch her clitoris. Mrs. Dove's legs fell open, and right there, on their facing chairs, Jefferson brought her almost to climax, then almost again, and then let her come. Such a roar of pleasure rushed from Mrs. Dove it was all Jefferson could do not to jump and to keep her finger in place.

She ran it down to Mrs. Dove's wetness to tease inside. Mrs. Dove, nimble phys ed teacher, lifted her legs until both feet were flat on her chair and let Jefferson move fully inside her. The woman moaned and moaned with the "Moonlight Sonata" until she collapsed on Jefferson, who went to one knee to catch her and found herself facing that hot wet place that begged for her tongue, but of course that was not something Jefferson would do except at home with Ginger. Mrs. Dove climaxed this time with her legs tight against Jefferson's ears, rocking her head side to side, three of Jefferson's fingers inside her. This was exciting, but Jefferson was glad she'd numbed herself with so much wine; they hadn't so much as kissed and she felt a little soiled.

"He's due home soon," the chairwoman said when they were done, her voice deep as a man's.

Jefferson went into the bathroom and scrubbed her face and hands, feeling none of the euphoria that went with making love with Ginger. Instead, she imagined herself possessed of the thin strength of a badminton racket, the tools of sports: the exacting edge of an ice skate's blade and the arc of a golf ball. She looked at the dexterous, sensitive hands at the end of her slender wrists and marveled at their mature authority in the ways of pleasure.

Mrs. Dove was dressed and putting the dinner plates in the dishwasher. She'd cleared the table, replaced the chairs, straightened her clothing. Jefferson, sobering up, sensed that something inside her had changed irrevocably.

"May I help?"

"No need!" Mrs. Dove answered in a high voice that reminded Jefferson of glass wind chimes. "That's why I have a dishwasher." Mrs. Dove still had her back turned when she said, "I know you must have lesson plans to review and papers to mark. You probably want to be on your way."

"Well, no, I—"

"That's all right. Scoot along. I'll finish up here."

The woman sounded like she was working up to a scream.

"Are you all right, Mrs. Dove?"

"Oh, my, look at the time. Mr. Dove will be here before you know it."

So that was the problem. Time to clear out before hubby came home. But why wouldn't Mrs. Dove look at her? She backed toward the door, waiting for some sign, some acknowledgment of what they had shared, but saw nothing, not even a meeting of the eyes. And Mrs. Dove would be like that every time they were together, as if she could connect with Jefferson only in the ever-decreasing conversations before sex and then through her erogenous zones, not with words or fond looks. At school, Mrs. Dove never looked at her, not to supervise, not to praise, not to criticize. Jefferson had a lot of freedom, but she'd expected a little help in her first year of teaching, so she would know if she was doing it right. The chairwoman invited Jefferson to dinner every week that April and May, then stopped.

At the end of the year, her contract wasn't renewed. Mrs. Dove told her the school had decided they needed someone with a master's degree in her position.

"We'll give you an excellent recommendation." As she said this, Mrs. Dove handed Jefferson a sheet of paper. It was a job announcement at a school in the city. "I know the chairman."

"Hey—"

"You do want a good recommendation?" Mrs. Dove's cold eyes held a clear warning. "Really. It's a step up for you. I only have your career in mind."

She was hurt and confused, but who could she talk to about it? What recourse did she have? No one, none. She got a summer job with the city parks, teaching little kids to play tennis. Come September she started all over again, working for Mrs. Dove's friend, another middle-aged married woman. This time, when Mrs. Gatlin invited her to dinner with her husband, before he left for his stage-managing job, and bragged of the excellent wine they'd bought at a vineyard upstate, Jefferson declined. She had to start on her master's so she could keep her job, she explained, without sarcasm, and expressed regrets that she had no time at all for a social life. She felt as if she were being passed around like a plate of hors d'oeuvres at a dinner party. No more older women, she swore. At least never again with a boss.

CHAPTER SIXTEEN

During her graduate school and early teaching years, Jefferson kept up her visits to the coffee shop where Gladys the waitress worked with the cook, Sam. Since she wasn't close to her parents, she gave Glad pink roses every Mother's Day and slipped Sam a cigar with each of her new achievements. The first time Gladys came to visit, Jefferson and Ginger had moved into Jefferson's grandparents' apartment in the west eighties.

"I've lived in my Mott Street neighborhood all my life. This is the first time I've been in a place this far uptown," Glad said when she handed her a birthday present one year.

"You look like you've entered enemy territory," Ginger said. "And the villains are out to get you."

"At least you're not on the Upper East Side."

Jefferson popped open the pinot grigio that Glad had brought for them and smelled the acid of the cork. "My grandparents are more about value than prestige, and they're the ones who bought this apartment originally when it was dirt cheap."

Gladys exclaimed, "My place is three times this size. Which is why I waitress, or we couldn't pay for it."

Ginger laughed. "It's the size of our first dorm room, plus bathroom and kitchenette. We're used to it."

"My parents don't know I'm living with a girl yet," Jefferson said. "They think it's exactly my size."

Ginger said, "Oh, sure. You really think they haven't figured it out, Jef?"

Ginger's hair was short and bouncy now around her bright freckled face. Jefferson adored her dancer's legs—as long as her own—and her elastic body. Jefferson shrugged. "Without paying rent," she explained, "we can afford to run the dance school."

"If they ever ask, we'll tell them I sleep on the hide-a-bed. They think my clothes in the closet are Jef's school clothes."

Gladys looked shocked as she laughed. "They don't know you at all, Jefferson, do they?"

She shook her head as she set out a plate of cheese and crackers. "Never have, never will."

"Doesn't that make you sad? Your own parents?" Gladys asked.

"I never thought about it. Should it?"

Ginger had a pitying expression as she said, "That's all she's known. Her family isn't loud and scrappy like Irish families."

Gladys nodded. "Or like my Italian relatives."

A gray loneliness approached like fog. She finished her wine, topped off Gladys's, and poured a second glass for herself. "This is excellent."

"I told you about my wine guy," Gladys said.

"And Jef is so jealous that you have one."

"I can have him put aside two when he finds something."

"Sure. Give me a call and I'll make a trip down there." She turned to Ginger, who was working a crossword puzzle, legs crossed, one flower-patterned flip-flop dangling. "We never get downtown to see the kids at Café Femmes anymore," she lied. "Would you mind if I went without you?"

"Of course not." Ginger looked up at her. "They're mostly Jef's friends anyway," she told Gladys. "They never liked her having an artiste-type girlfriend."

"Don't be crazy," she said. "They never said anything against you."

Ginger raised her eyebrows at Gladys, whose expression revealed nothing about all she knew. Gladys reached into the shopping bag by her side and pulled out a big box.

"It's Jefferson's birthday, but these little things are for both of you."

Ginger was not one to get excited over gifts, but she sat on the couch and watched as Jefferson opened Gladys's big gift box.

"A garlic press!" said Ginger.

"You are a winner, Glad. Look at this red spaghetti drainer," Jefferson exclaimed.

"Look at this unique cheese grater." Ginger held it up.

"A real Italian spaghetti bowl. Look at this design. Surely, Glad, you're not hinting that we should ask you to dinner?"

"And serve me what I'm used to," Glad replied. "I'm going to turn you two into good Italian cooks."

"Not me." Jefferson jumped up for refills. "I'm the bartender."

Ginger sighed. "Not me either. I only cook frozen dinners or nuke deli."

Gladys came back every couple of months over the years. At one of those jolly communal dinners Glad announced she was going in for a mastectomy.

That night she and Gladys got drunk on Jefferson's Irish whiskey. Her insides had turned as cold as her ice cubes at the news, but she managed not to show her alarm and sorrow. Smoothly, but in a voice that sounded tinny in her own ears, she said, "You'll be fine, Glad. We'll pickle you before you go in. You won't feel a thing."

"Ernie says he's tired of these old things anyway." Tears were falling over her smile as she outlined her abundant breasts. "He says it'll be like before the kids came, when I was a flat-chested broad." She laughed. "Like you."

Jefferson couldn't help but blush before that pointing finger. She was hardly flat, but didn't advertise her breasts.

Ginger held up her bottle of Coke in a toast. "To all you wonderful, flat-chested broads."

Soon after that, Ginger left for a performance.

"So," Jefferson said, "how are you doing with your news?" She refilled their glasses and sat next to Glad on the couch, hip to hip. Glad put an arm around her shoulders and squeezed her tight.

"I liked that wine you served earlier," Gladys said. "I have to write down the brand before I leave. I'll get us a bottle for Ernie's birthday." She went quiet. "I think I'll still be around for Ernie's birthday."

"Of course you'll be around." Jefferson tried to find something cheerful to say. The cloud of doom was back; if Glad could die, then… "I remember the first time I tasted whiskey," she said. "I thought I had swallowed fire. I was with one of my teachers—"

"The one you had an affair with? Margo was her name?"

"You remember her?"

"I even saw her once. At your graduation."

She ducked her head, embarrassed. Margo hadn't been much to look at, not compared to Ginger. She cleared her throat. "We were in a restaurant and she had her usual wine. I was feeling young and inexperienced so I ordered what sounded like a grown-up drink, whiskey on the rocks. It was all I could do to keep the tears from flooding down my face. The last thing I wanted was for Margo to see I really was young and inexperienced."

They laughed at that and all the other stories they'd been repeating to each other over the years of their friendship.

"You're such a great person to laugh with," she told Gladys.

Gladys laid one hand on Jefferson's arm. "You've turned into a good buddy."

She felt such warmth toward Gladys. She really loved the woman. Were she and Glad meant to be together, not with Ernie and Ginger? Life was such fun with Gladys and she was so comforting when Jefferson was a little down. And now, what if she lost her? Cancer! Not her Gladys. Blindly, drunkenly, she reached for Glad to kiss her.

Gladys turned her cheek in time.

Jefferson gave her a quick, tight hug. "Sorry. I got a little maudlin there for a minute."

"S'okay," Gladys said. "It's what I should expect, being with the gay Don Juan of the West Side."

"It wasn't like that, Glad. I don't go around seducing every woman I like." Ginger hadn't found out about that one-night fling with Taffy or the other drunken infidelities, but she told Glad about most of them.

"What was this, then?" Gladys asked, pointing to the spot on her cheek where Jefferson had kissed her.

"The truth is, I never meant to be lovers with most of them. No, the real truth is that I never went after even one of them, except Ginger—and Angela—and that hit me by surprise. I didn't know I was queer till that first kiss with Angela."

"Don't put yourself down."

"Am I?"

"That word, queer."

She thought briefly. "I kind of like it. I'd rather be a queer than act the way a lot of these straight people do. Not you, of course." She decided to tell Gladys about her father.

"You have a point."

"I was saying something though. Something I wanted you to know. Can't remember now."

Gladys was not quite as drunk as Jefferson. "About not really wanting the others? I guess you mean the ones you bring to the shop."

"Some of them I bring. The ones I can stand to see again. I've gone home with some doozies, Glad." She shook her head.

Gladys laughed. "I'll bet you have, Jef, if the ones you bring are the good ones!" She moved her face closer to Jefferson's, as if to see her better through the blur of the liquors. "Tell me. Why do you do it if you don't want to?"

"It's hard to say. Hard to say." She repeated, "All I know is that Ginger is the only one I ever pursued, except for the puppy love with Angie, and I didn't have words for what I wanted then." Dizziness started coming on and she grabbed her glass. The cold ice cubes helped shock her out of it. "I don't know how not to. I don't know how to be a friend without sex."

"Kind of like guys can't help seeing women through their hormones?"

"No. Not at all. Guys want the sex. I'm after the friendship, and it comes out all wrong. I don't know how to tell a friend I love her without coming on to her."

"Like what you just did."

"Yeah."

"Wouldn't it simplify your life to hug someone?"

"How do you hug? The next thing I know, my hands are running up and down her back or she's confessing she's been in love with me since the first day she saw me. Like it or not, we end up—well, you know."

"Aren't you the hot stuff." Gladys pinched her arm.

"It's not me, Glad. They actually say that."

"So you step back and tell them you're sorry, you didn't mean it like that."

"And hurt their feelings? I don't have the heart to say no."

"And when you never see them again after a night together you think their feelings aren't hurt? People know not everyone is going to be their true love."

"I know. It doesn't make sense. It makes me feel crazy. It's easier to do it when they're not in front of me. At least we had a nice time together."

"Always?"

"What do you mean? Oh, the lovemaking? Yes, always. I don't get complaints in that department. I tell them they're great like that. And a lot of them are. Listen, maybe you don't want to hear this kind of thing, but it's the only way I can finish."

"You mean, come?'

Jefferson looked hard at the floor. The rug's rectangles seemed to be warping under her sneakers. She put the icy glass back against her cheek. "Yes. It never happened with Ginger."

There was a hesitation before Gladys spoke. She knew Glad was shocked. "Does she try?"

"She did. Sometimes. But I could tell she wasn't really into it. Either you're passionate about making love to a woman or you're going through the motions. These pickups, they mostly get passionate. There's a lot more give-and-take with them. It boils up from inside me."

"Then I'd say you and Ginger have a problem."

"She doesn't know that. I never told her."

"You pretend?"

"I guess I did. I didn't want to hurt her feelings." She decided she might as well tell Glad how it was. "When I went with Angela, Glad, she was all about touch. We learned about love by loving each other." She realized she was searching Glad's eyes for a sign of comprehension.

"None of us had tutors, Jef."

"Don't tell me that. You had movies and TV and books. They were depicting straight people wanting to have sex with one another or having sex with one another. Angela and I thought we were the first ones, the first girls to feel like that about each other."

"It's that different?"

"We didn't know. We didn't know anything is what I'm trying to tell you. So what I learned with Angie was that a girl likes to be touched and touched a lot, all the time, but Ginger wasn't like that. Ginger wasn't a hugger or big on kissing unless we were officially doing it. If I could touch her five percent of the time at first, by the last few years it was minus five percent."

"It sounds like making love is something in the past." Gladys was shaking her head.

She patted Glad's hands. "What was your first clue?"

"Oh, Jefferson, I know you're hurting, but I have to tell you, you're the biggest coward I've ever met."

"Coward? How?"

"It's not their feelings, or Ginger's feelings, you're trying to spare, it's your own."

"I don't get it. Nobody's hurting my feelings."

"You're protecting yourself too well to be hurt. Making love to these strangers is like giving them a present so they don't feel bad that someone else got the prize. You want them to like you, but listen to Auntie Glad. They're going to like you more if you say no right off the bat. You're giving them something you have no right to give away because it belongs to Ginger. You know that, don't you?"

She had her head down and was massaging her forehead with her fingers. Glad was practically yelling at her. "I never thought of it that way."

"You have to talk to Ginger about what you need from her. And you never will as long as you think you're getting what you need elsewhere. And you're not getting it. Not really. Being with Ernie that way, it's like walking through a gate to each other. You're never going to get the gate between you and Ginger open this way. You'll always be chasing her. Ginger will never feel truly connected with you."

"Because I couldn't come with her? But I love Ginger, not all the others." She offered her open hands, knowing her face was full of appealing innocence and acknowledging to herself for the first time that the status quo suited her fine. She loved being a Don Juan and she loved having Ginger. She simply wasn't terribly interested in a marriage deeper or more devoted than the one she had. But she didn't know if she'd lost interest because of Ginger's innate way of distancing herself—the critical comment, the quick disapproving grimace, the long hours at work—a distance that more and more felt like rejection. "I swear, Glad," she lied.

"You don't love her enough to tell her what you need."

"It's not that big of a deal, Glad."

"Yes it is, Jef. I promise you it is."

CHAPTER SEVENTEEN

For their fifteenth anniversary, when they were thirty-three, with what Gladys said still on her mind, Jefferson and Ginger decided to fly to Florida. One of the women from Café Femmes, that arrogant little butch Frenchy, who'd dated Angela way back when, talked up the Clearwater Beach area where she had family. Florida in February sounded like a great idea: no slush, no freezing temperatures, no heavy jackets. She and Ginger had never traveled together except to dance festivals like Jacob's Pillow in Massachusetts and the Jeffersons' summer cottage in New Hampshire.

"Girl," Lily Ann Lee told her the night before they were to leave, which happened to fall at the same time as their monthly dinner, "you are excited out of your mind."

She swallowed a forkful of fra diavolo. "It's more than a vacation, Lily Ann."

"Rekindling the flame?"

She pondered that a minute. "How can I explain without—I mean—"

"Spilling the beans about Ginger?"

"That's kind of it."

"How long ago did the romance leave?" Lily Ann kept her eyes on the fork and spoon she was using to lift linguini from her plate.

"Since she opened her school." Shame rose to her face in a blush.

"That was what, six years ago, J? And you put up money for her damn school?"

"Some of it."

"Like half. Some repayment."

"It's her first love, Lily Ann."

"And you think a trip to the white sands of Florida will change that?"

"Let me tell you something. But it's between us, right?"

"Everything is, J. You're my best friend."

She smiled at Lily Ann, then cut her pasta into smaller and smaller pieces. "You know how, when you're going to be with someone, you maybe do an extra shower before bed or sponge off the important places?"

She snuck a quick look at Lily Ann, who was, as she expected, regarding her with amusement. Doing sex was one thing, talking about it was embarrassing.

"Kind of like a magic charm?"

She took a long sip of the dry red house wine. "I've been doing that at home every night for no reason ever since Ginger opened her school."

"Oh, J." Lily Ann's face was a quick display not of pity, but of tragedy observed. "That explains a lot."

She laughed, her gaze not leaving her plate. "My wayward path? Margo read me a poem once, about a picture on a vase, back in Grecian times, about how hot it can be to want without getting. The line that stuck with me was, 'For ever wilt thou love, and she be fair!'"

"I'd be seducing every femme in the city too."

"If you were butch."

"Which I'm not."

She smiled. "I'll drink to that," and drank again.

"But seriously," Lily Ann asked, "you know how you've told me Ginger kind of likes guys? Do you think that might have something to do with it?"

Although she shook her head no, she couldn't look Lily Ann in the eye. She was in the grip of that lightless place where she was filled with silent screams. She reminded herself that she always lived through it and opened her eyes.

Lily Ann asked, "Is it a worse betrayal because it's with a man?"

"All I know is I want to kill any man who touches her, even innocently. Not that I believe a man could touch her innocently."

"Don't think about it."

"It's her sacred body, you know? I never touched her without, what—awe, amazement, the beauty of her, like the best sunsets, the sweetest bird song, poetry." It had been a long time since she'd dared touch Ginger even casually. She couldn't stand to see her shy away. As much as Ginger liked sex, Jefferson's desire seemed to disturb her. Ginger was just going through something, she told herself. Although Ginger denied it, she suspected she'd been touched in a bad way as a kid. Or something. Sometimes she would lie there sick with desire for Ginger and hope. Hope was the killer. She felt like a fool for hoping and she cherished it like a last embrace of her beloved.

Lily Ann pursed her lips, looking disapproving.

The conversation didn't dampen her enthusiasm for the trip. She always dreamed that this time things would be different.

While Ginger spent the boarding wait on a pay phone with her dance school and her family, Jefferson pictured the two of them wading in green-blue shallow waters and holding hands as they walked the white sands at twilight. In the heat of the afternoon they'd be in their room at Don Cesar's, a baronial pink palace of a place that, from the brochure, looked like it had aged well and was posh in the lobby and well-appointed in their room overlooking the beach. She imagined the luxury of Ginger's trim body, her long red hair spread as it used to be across the fine linen pillowcases, ready for Jefferson once again.

And it was like that.

The first afternoon they were in swimsuits. Jefferson had a little flab around her body, from all the whiskey, she supposed, and swore she'd cut back, maybe suggest she and Lily Ann have Chinese instead of Italian food. Sprouts and veggies and bean curd would be good. She could quit drinking if she wanted to, but why? Life was more fun with it.

She didn't wait for an excuse from Ginger, but stepped boldly up to her and slid her bathing-suit straps off her shoulders, leaving the wet suit across her breasts so the mound of them was half exposed to her kisses and their covered heft was in her hands. There was a radio in the room. She'd found the classical station earlier. "Afternoon of a Faun" was playing. Perfect.

Ginger said nothing, only let her do what she wanted. She waited for some response, but Ginger stood there as if deciding whether to give Jefferson the gift of herself.

No, Jefferson thought, unfastening the top and swallowing as much as she could of Ginger's left breast, partly kneeling to capture it, moving her tongue around the nipple hard enough to rouse a statue and playing with the other nipple the way Ginger had liked when they were first together.

Finally, Ginger sighed, and she rolled her swimsuit down her belly and bottom, down her legs, waiting for Ginger to step out of it while Jefferson paused, crouching at the tops of Ginger's long legs.

"Baby," she pleaded, coaxing Ginger's legs apart, then parting her outer lips with the fingers of both hands. She ran her tongue from top to bottom of her open and, she discovered, cream-covered labia. "Baby, you're dripping."

Ginger, silent as always when they made love, moved one foot sideways and bent her knees to give Jefferson more access. She kept her tongue in motion while supporting Ginger at the hips. Dancing as always, Ginger lowered, then raised, then lowered herself against Jefferson's tongue, varying the pressure until Jefferson stayed with her clitoris, circling while Ginger shuddered above her, knees akimbo, hands on Jefferson's shoulders in the most erotic stance Ginger had ever assumed with her.

"It's been too long," Ginger admitted as Jefferson stood, sliding her hands up Ginger's sides. Ginger's calves had been pressed against the king-sized bed. Jefferson stripped off the spread, blanket, and top sheet, then stood at the edge of the bed and beckoned her.

Ginger said, "I didn't know I'd missed this so much. There's never time."

She reached for the buttons of the shirt she'd thrown over her old Speedo.

"Let me," Ginger said, swiftly unbuttoning and slipping the shirt off. As Jefferson had, she loosed the straps and pulled the Speedo down, pressing her lips against Jefferson's, opening her mouth, inviting Jefferson's tongue inside.

Jefferson really let loose then, years of desire flooding her senses. She touched all the parts of Ginger she'd loved and been denied for so long. She was excited, as Lily Ann had said, out of her mind and took Ginger again, her finger thrusting into the beloved narrow wet burrow of her lover slowly and gently until she had Ginger meeting her every move, chasing her finger, as if they'd never stopped making love together.

She knew she had Ginger then, had reconnected with that primal part of Ginger that wanted nothing but pleasure and release. Elated, she withdrew her finger and positioned her hand to insert three fingers. "I love you, woman. I'm giving you my love. Can you feel it?" Making a triangle of her three fingers, she reached as deeply inside Ginger as she could, no longer as gentle, her one desire to drive Ginger wild.

If the old hotel had thinner walls Ginger's cry of pleasure would have brought security.

Ginger slept then, and Jefferson watched the reflections of the pool below dance on their ceiling until twilight. She dropped off too and was only awakened by the feather touch of Ginger's hands on her. She opened her eyes and smiled at Ginger. Ginger's fingers were circling her tummy.

"Kiss me," she'd said.

Ginger kissed her. They touched lips and tongues for a long time. Desire overtook Jefferson again. She led Ginger's hand back to herself, hoping she was ready. Ginger used one of her long fingers to manipulate her. She focused all her concentration on that one spot and moved her hips to their rhythm. She badly wanted to come for Ginger. Ginger lifted her pelvis to get the touch she needed from Jefferson. Jefferson's thighs tensed. She was so near, about there, when Ginger stopped.

"Did you come?" Ginger asked.

"Not yet, honey. A little longer?"

"Sure. My tongue?"

She still always refused oral sex from other lovers, saving that for Ginger and being completely frank with her lovers about why. She could only groan and nod. Ginger missed her cue and obviously interpreted her response as a no. Her finger went to work again, but she wasn't otherwise caressing Jefferson or kissing her, or saying longing words.

She gave up after a while and pulled Ginger to her. She held her. Why hadn't she ever tutored Ginger in lovemaking? She'd never been with a woman so incapable of following the signals of her partner's body. Why wasn't her deep love and desire for Ginger enough by itself?

She got up to go to the bathroom. Ginger was watching as she returned. She smiled and anticipated Ginger lifting her arms to bring her close.

"Stop doing that to your hair," Ginger said.

She had a habit of running the fingers of both her hands through her hair to roughly comb it back from her face.

She stopped.

"It doesn't make you look attractive."

As she got under the covers, she touched Ginger's shoulder with one hand.

"Cold," Ginger said. It was true. In her hurry to be with Ginger she'd washed, but hadn't waited for hot water. Her mistake. Ginger pulled the covers over her shoulders as she turned away from Jefferson. "You wiped me out."

Hesitantly she curled against Ginger's back and met no resistance. She held Ginger with a tenderness no one else since Angela had inspired in her, softly kissed her lovely hair, considered herself fortunate to have this much contentment with Ginger. She drifted off to a fantasy of mutual passion, mutual orgasms, mutual declarations of eternal love, but awakened with the question that haunted her always: why had Ginger, a dancer, never learned to be a lover? Was it because she'd been with no one but Jefferson? Or was it the worst reason: Ginger couldn't feel passionate about another woman, about Jefferson—maybe about anyone.

Each day of their vacation was the same: sleep late, breakfast at the hotel, swim, make love to Ginger, nap, have drinks before, during, and after dinner at the hotel restaurant, which was an elegant affair. By the fourth day, Jefferson persuaded Ginger to explore another beach and they walked hand in hand, in warm, ankle-deep water as far as they could. Ginger smiled at her a lot. They talked abut everything but work, about which they had agreed not to speak, and sex. Why didn't Ginger ask her if she was okay with what they did? Or explain why she never wanted to make love at home? Lack of time was a lame excuse.

On the last day of their vacation she resolved to bring it up. Ginger had become entirely passive in bed. Her receptiveness was thrilling, her responsiveness exciting—and Jefferson couldn't stand it another minute physically, never mind emotionally. If she could work this thing out with Ginger, maybe she'd leave the other women alone. She reached for the glass on the bed table, sipped her whiskey, then took a long swallow. She'd confess that she had never had an orgasm with Ginger. It would either destroy them or make things better.

"Ginger," she said while Ginger rested in her arms after several orgasms. She told her what hadn't been happening for her, though she didn't say it had never happened. She described what she needed from Ginger, looking in her eyes while she did, asking if Ginger was okay with what she was saying.

"Sure. I'll do better, Jef," Ginger said in a sleepy voice, and reached up to her.

It was a simple, autonomic response that led her to initiate lovemaking once more. Ginger had a less-than-wild orgasm, then lay there smiling.

"Ginge," she said when Ginger stopped moving. "Ginge," she whispered, not for the sex, but to escape the unavoidable journey to her dark place.

In recent years Ginger had started snoring as she slept, in a very quiet, ladylike way. She snored now.

Chapter Eighteen

The day of Gladys's funeral it was the bright hot summer of 1996, but Jefferson felt cold, so cold. At thirty-seven, she felt stooped and worn out. She emerged from the dark subway into all that radiance, hoping that the black of her blazer and pants, let out at the waist since her grandmother's funeral, would draw sun rays to her and blanket her with warm comfort. She remembered that funeral, how tranquilizers had been the wrapping around her grief till liquor was served back at the big old house she'd grown up in. She'd finally passed out on top of the guests' coats in the front room, never having shed a tear.

This church was grand, ornate. How often had Glad set foot in it, living? Other mourners climbed the wide, stone steps; Jefferson didn't know these people and hoped no one would notice Glad's lone queer friend. She imagined that customers seldom attended waitresses' funerals. There was Sam, though. Glad had worked for him half her career. Glad told her that some students returned after graduation with pictures of their wives, husbands. Jefferson had escorted Ginger those many years ago to meet Glad, as if taking her home to meet mother. Some brought baby pictures; Jefferson offered winning team shots from whatever job she currently held. Of course she'd introduce some of her side-dish lovers. After each of these disappeared, Glad would ask, "How's Ginger?"

"Ginger's fine," she whispered now, pausing in the sunlight before she mounted the steps. "Ginger's as fine as ever, Glad," she said gratefully, feeling Glad's presence in the warmth, like a stream of herself from heaven. "She had to work today," Jefferson went on, "rehearsing her students for this season's big recital. I'm sure she loves you encouraging me to stay with her." As she said this, she thought about her reservations and hoped she wasn't telling Glad a lie.

"What did you expect?" she could imagine Glad asking. "You run around on Ginger, you're pouring the booze down your gullet like you've lost all interest in living, and you've never held a job for more than three years at a time."

The first time Ginger left her, when they were in their mid-thirties, she hadn't gone as far as moving her things from the apartment, but Jefferson left too, sleeping for over a week on Gladys's couch. It was painful to be in the apartment without Ginger, though Ginger was not often there. That's actually what she'd been counting on when she'd brought Taffy home with her, the one day Ginger managed to leave work on time.

It was a silly thing to do. She didn't like Taffy, that spoiled preppy jock who'd grown up to be a fund-raiser for some big foundation, but some piece of Taffy was a magnet for some piece of Jefferson. She suspected that Taffy was someone she could have been, someone she might have liked being with. Taffy was more comfortable in the world than Jefferson. She drank a lot, but had matured into one of those women who could juggle people successfully. No matter who was actually hosting a gathering, or if there was no host at all, Taffy kept the conversation going and the drinks flowing and made the introductions. She knew how to connect people, which ones would hit it off, and how to retreat gracefully once she could see they would be fine without her. Jefferson admired that skill.

Moreover, it was hard to deny a professional beggar. Taffy never stopped chasing her. And she never stopped succumbing to Taffy. That day she'd gone, after school, to one of Taffy's soirées. When Taffy had an education project, she liked to have some teachers around to show they were engaged in the process, as she'd told Jefferson. To thank her, Taffy treated Jefferson to drinks afterward, on top of the cocktails they'd already been served. She introduced Jefferson to Russian vodka. It was only when Ginger walked in on them that she realized how badly her judgment had been impaired—by Taffy as well as the vodka. Ginger arrived in time to see her on the couch, nude, licking Stoli from between the reclined Taffy's shockingly superior, golden-hued breasts.

Ginger's quick departure both woke her up and stunned her. She was too drunk to respond quickly. She let her go. Taffy seemed annoyed at first, as if the surprise had been Jefferson's fault, but she recovered more quickly and Jefferson found herself lying with her head in Taffy's still-naked lap, Taffy soothing her with reassuring words as she stroked Jefferson's hair.

"She'll think I've been sleeping with you all along," Jefferson said, groaning at the irony. Her sad monster was threatening to engulf her.

"Jeffy, you have."

She groaned. "What am I going to do?"

"If you want her, Jeffy, you crawl back on your knees. You stop drinking and stop fucking me and whoever else's bed you share, and you promise her all the things you're incapable of giving her: sobriety, fidelity, stability. She'll risk giving you another chance and you'll be more careful." Taffy sighed. "And you'll stay away from me for the rest of your life."

"No, Taff," she cried, contrite now to two women. She felt so out of control, kind of crazy too. She held on to Taffy, afraid that she, Jefferson herself, would disappear altogether.

Taffy, who had retrieved the Stoli from the freezer after Ginger left, offered it to Jefferson.

She downed a swig, two swigs, a third and suddenly remembered what it felt like to be master of the universe. She parted Taffy's thighs and enacted a betrayal Ginger would never know about. Taffy fell back, legs excitingly open, her own hands spreading her center, an icing of opaque moisture decorating her persimmon-like parts. Jefferson really liked this Russian vodka. She'd never made love so effortlessly or so effectively. Taffy responded with all the athleticism she'd displayed on the hockey field.

When she woke up, at about one thirty a.m., Taffy was gone. Slowly, she remembered that she was home and Ginger wasn't. She was still fairly drunk, but sober enough to know she'd chopped the bottom out of her boat. She wished she were in the family boat up on the lake, hauling water-skiers or racing across the water, slicing the lake in half with a line of white, like the line of Taffy's cream. Shame engulfed her. She tore the covers and sheets from the bed and washed them, load after load. She raised every window in the apartment to air out the scents she and Taffy had left. The bed remade, she showered and went to the living room to await Ginger.

Ginger called, midafternoon.

"Is she gone?"

"Yes. I'm so sorry—"

"My love for you is a curse and a blessing, Jefferson. I guess I'm trying to say, you're working hard to make your love nothing but a curse."

"Princess, it wasn't love, like with you. It was stupid drunken fumbling to prove—"

"What? That you're as good as a man?"

She was taken aback. "Why would I want to prove that? Do you think a man would be better?"

"I don't know what else you're trying to prove."

"No!" She was insulted that Ginger would think to compare her to a man. She didn't think before she said, teeth gritted, "That. I. Was. Wanted."

There was no response on the other end of the line. She ran the pads of her fingers along the light down on her jaw.

"Are you coming home, baby?"

After a silence, Ginger answered, "I don't know."

By eleven that night, she knew Ginger was gone, maybe for good. She wanted Ginger to be able to come home. More to the point, another night in the apartment, images of her life with Ginger warring with carnal images of herself and Taffy, was unthinkable. She jumped on the subway down to Gladys's.

Gladys took one look at her and said, "It's bad this time."

She hung her head.

"What did you do?"

"Russian vodka. And Taffy," who she had introduced to Glad. She told her about Ginger, hanging onto one of Glad's arms with her two hands. "May I bunk on your couch?"

"I should probably say no. I'm pretty disgusted with you, Jefferson. But you're sober at the moment, aren't you? And you know you made a mess of things."

"You know what, Glad?" She rose and went for her coat. "I can get a room at a hotel. I don't want to be a bother to you, or at home. Waiting."

"Sit down," Gladys ordered.

"Why can't I get it right?" she asked, complying. "Other people, you and Ernie, lots of people get love right." That's when she started crying. Glad persuaded her to try AA.

Today, outside the church, she pulled the damn tissues from her pocket, remembering that Glad had gone to get her a box of tissues that first time Ginger left. Other times she'd cried on her shoulder, Glad would hand her napkins from a dispenser on the counter. How could she go into that cold mausoleum of a church? *I don't want you to be dead, Glad!* If she didn't go inside, she could think Glad was out of touch for a while, that was all.

A cloud passed over the sun and then moved on, like a gentle warning. She straightened from her stooped posture and pushed back her hair.

"Okay, Glad, I get it. It's the only way I can visit you now. In sunbeams." A breeze, so rare these last few days, blew back at her. She smiled. "And breezes." She stepped inside the church.

Her suit did hold a little warmth and she huddled inside it through the cool vestibule, into the still, high-vaulted church. Mourners filled the first nine rows, then straggled back to where she settled. She shuddered. Church was another place where silence was more valued than truth. She recalled going with her parents to hear the careful, empty sermons, as if those would teach her about life. She'd sit perfectly still, *yearning* to be outside practicing her softball pitch. "I hope you appreciate this," she silently teased Glad.

The organ played. There were flowers, sermons, hymns. She tried to think of Glad, to remember her, but the other mourners distracted her. She didn't want to look at the coffin. Then someone stood up in the family pew, made his way to the front, and bent to an instrument case. It was Gus, Glad's youngest, a man in a full beard now instead of a boy in a baseball cap, readying a French horn instead of a toy rifle. So Gus had become a musician. How she'd envied Glad's kid growing up with such a woman. She let her mind wander back, back to the days when they'd met.

She shivered in the cool church all these years later, watching Gus prepare to play. Glad had come through that first operation, but there had been others, and Jefferson never knew the last few years when she'd gone away—for golf tournaments, an alcohol cure, for the women between times with Ginger—if Glad would be at the Lunchbox when she came "home."

Yet she never went to Glad's apartment and didn't know this son who would honor Glad or the other children or Ernie. She'd been afraid she wouldn't fit in on Mott Street, that the friendship couldn't be the same there. Glad had been proud to be her friend, but both of them knew that Jefferson belonged where she was in Glad's life.

Gus lifted his horn to his lips and began an excerpt from "Finlandia." She could sense Glad beaming and proud, watching how he filled the church with breath and emotion and sound for her. She felt elation at the way he returned to Glad the gift she had given him with his life.

Her thoughts drifted even farther back to her freshman self on the dormitory steps. Stricken with grief—and yes, it had been grief—to watch her own mother go, to watch her take off with the gifts she'd never given and to leave the heritage of fear. Of silent expectations. Of alcohol.

She bowed her head, not bothering to wipe away the tears. Glad's persevering acceptance had finally sunk in. Too late for Jefferson's athletic career, but not too late to succeed at being Jefferson. "I'm really not afraid to be me now." She fixed her eyes on the sun ray stealing in through the stained-glass window, sighing with the breeze that entered when someone opened the church door. Glad and Ginger, between them, had been there when Jefferson was finally finished with drinking and on her feet again. It had been over a year now. She'd go from Glad's funeral to another AA meeting. And cry for a week if she had to.

She whispered hoarsely, "I want to cry loud enough to fill this church with sound for you."

Were tears the only gift she could give to Glad, the woman who first loosed them? She envied the boy with his horn, who had found his own voice, and who'd had a mother who'd heard him all his life. But her tears would have to do: the wrong gift, to the wrong mother. And Glad would accept them, as she always had.

The last of the music faded. Now, she thought, Glad would be at peace.

She left the pew, finally, but a hand touched her elbow as she reached the church doors.

"Here," Sam the cook said, eyes wet with his own sadness. He thrust a handful of napkins toward her. "I knew she'd want me to bring some for you too."

CHAPTER NINETEEN

I'm forty-one, Jefferson thought as she watched the twenty-year-old pitcher wind up. Once she'd been on the pitcher's mound, her body tall, powerful, no gray in her thick sandy hair, proud muscles in her arms. Now she was coaching. *How in hell did I get to be forty-one?*

The batgirl trotted across the park's newly mowed grass carrying water. The hot sun felt good, heated the grass scents, made the spectators' encouragement sound languid, undemanding. Jefferson drank, remembered to smile then into those adoring batgirl eyes. If this kid only knew, if those eyes had seen her at her depths, high on whatever combination of drinks she could get.

The opponents got a hit; Jefferson tensed, ready with her signal talk to guide the Lavender Julies up the last step from their two-year slump into winning the citywide series. Inside, she clicked, in perfect tune with her team. And they clicked with her. At last they were playing in unison, not like the beginning of the season when she'd agreed, once more, after a first year of failure and a season off, to coach the "Lavender Losers," as everyone had taken to calling them. "You're our only hope," Sally the bartender had pleaded for the team she and Liz sponsored.

It had been twilight outside Café Femmes. Soho was shutting down for the night. A few lingering art-gallery customers had been sitting outside sipping cappuccino or Irish coffee at the new sidewalk restaurant Liz had added to the bar around the time the team was born. Some of the gay kids who worked in local garment factories burst in, joking and laughing and jostling one another. Gabby was garnishing salads the customers had ordered; she had taken over the food preparation from the start, as if she'd at last found her passion in life.

Jefferson, whose mood frequently resembled thunderclouds these days, had replied, "You're pretty desperate, then."

She was seven months into her third attempt to live sober.

Teaching again, commuting to the Academy she'd attended as a kid. They'd taken her when no one else would give her another chance, taken her at least partly on the word of her AA sponsor, an old woman who'd taught there herself when Jefferson was the school heroine, breaking records, leading the field-hockey team to victory after victory. Her memories had not led to a kind comparison with who she'd become.

"Yo." Gabby nudged her with an elbow as she settled her chunky body onto a stool next to Jefferson.

"How's my favorite daughter of the American Revolution?"

Once something like that got out, that her family had been in New York practically since Peter Stuyvesant, she'd never heard the end of it. The kids were always kidding her about having "come out" twice. She shook her head, smiling, though she had neither grown up in the city nor been in the kind of family that would come out. They liked the idea of having a fallen blue blood in their midst, even if she wasn't a blue blood and had experienced no more introduction to society than matching chugs with Angela between kisses at the first gay bar they'd managed to get into with fake IDs.

"Tell me I'm not under duress," Jefferson had answered, gesturing to Sally, who was filling beer mugs.

"You finally finished your master's degree, didn't you? You have more time now."

"I don't know if I can handle it, Gab. Coaching—losing."

Gabby laid a hand on Jefferson's shoulder. "It was too much for you last time, I know." She paused. "But when you were sober, were you ever good."

As always, Jefferson's heart warmed to this praise. She placed a hand over Gabby's. "Can I buy you a Julie?"

"You like my concoction," Gabby asserted. She assumed full credit for the drink the team was named after, although Sally was the one who painstakingly created it to tempt Gabby away from liquor. They both watched Sally pour the grape juice and seltzer over crushed ice, then add an orange slice, a lime, a cherry. "Hey," Gabby protested, and Sally snapped her fingers, apparently remembering only then to add another cherry. Gabby toasted Jefferson. "To a winning season."

"But I haven't said yes."

"Listen, Jefferson," Gabby said, "it's the Julies. A magic team. If they win, so can you."

"What if they lose?"

Gabby looked at her appraisingly. "I'm betting you can lose one thing now without losing everything." She pulled noisily on her straw. "Customers," she had added then, bustling away to a sidewalk table.

The other team called a time-out; the Julies kept their energy high, as Jefferson had taught them to, tossing the ball back and forth. She turned and saw Sally, tall, lanky, blond, blushing, probably at something outrageously flirtatious Marie-Christine, the outfielder's girl, had said. Jefferson pictured Gabby downtown tending bar so Sally could be at the game. The winning game. Maybe.

Three teenaged boys stopped, jeered the teams, made clucking sounds at Marie-Christine. Jefferson tensed again. Once she would have laughed at the boys, but recently, she wanted to rave and rage and pummel. She turned away. Sober, she knew the team was her business. Marie-Christine and Sally could take care of themselves.

The other team got back to work. The Julies' pitcher, maybe drowsy from the sun, threw the batter an easy one and the ball rose high, every head following it. The outfielder, Annie Heaphy, caught this third out and jogged nonchalantly toward home, while Marie-Christine cheered wildly, tossing words—hero, savior, champion—like flowers toward her.

But Annie had always been cool to work with. When the team had seemed to band against Jefferson, Annie supported her, worked to convince the others that Jefferson could be trusted now and wouldn't let them down.

The way she had Ginger. That was about the time the Jeffersons put her in rehab, hoping to stop the drinking. She'd laughed at them, aware that her father would be stewed by dinnertime, but, engulfed by the heavy cloud of her newly diagnosed depression, she'd gone. Her memory of those years was like one of those gummy erasers, crumbs of events and women and jobs and students piled like rubble in her mind. Receiving her release after a few months, thinking she was sober and fit and raring to go again, she hadn't gone back to Ginger. No, Ginger was behind her. Then, having recovered from a drunken car crash, Jefferson decided to forsake team sports. She'd play golf again. She'd be a victor again, like in college golf, like in prep-school field hockey. Her parents paid for a coach. Rusty at first, she soon played local, then regional tournaments. She pursued the golfing ladies, gay and straight, and maybe that diversion contributed to her ever-falling rank.

Her age, her years out of golf, and liquor hadn't given her much chance to become a scratch golfer by a long shot. By the time she landed the local lady golf celebrity, wining her and winning her into bed, she'd begun to drink wine—so no one would feel uncomfortable—and eventually returned to Jameson, her first liquid love, a taste she'd acquired under her father's tutelage. That led to the horrendous accident, to losing her driver's license and drying out, yet again, in the hospital where she stayed for ten days with a compound fracture of the ankle. There hadn't been a hint that she could succeed on the tour, and her parents, who had been supporting her financially, gave up. She'd double-bogeyed her life yet again.

The huge lightless affliction that had bedeviled her off and on since childhood settled on her in the hospital. A drink would have lifted it like a magic potion, or always had when she was younger. It had grown less and less reliable in recent years. After she got out, she didn't want to drink, but her moods had been gray. Had she been medicating herself for something all those years—dejection? That free-fall thing that happened to her sometimes and left her scared? Where had that come from?

Thank goodness Ginger hadn't given up. She'd been at the uptown bar, frequenting the place after dance recitals and the ballet, as if waiting for Jefferson—who sought her out, pretending not to, and allowed her to escort her home, not letting on what she needed. That had been the second time she'd dried out. Cold turkey. Out of sheer determination. And she'd begun to teach phys ed again, had stayed with Ginger.

During that period Lily Ann Lee introduced them to Café Femmes. Sally was an old college teammate; others in the bar remembered or had heard of Jefferson. And in the last few years together Ginger would always find Jefferson there, grumbling that it was the only place in the world where she got respect. Ginger would call a cab—assuming she found her at all that night—and escort her home. Until one night Ginger didn't come to Café Femmes and the next morning Jefferson found Ginger's note at the apartment: *I've got to help me now. I know I can't be with you until you do something for yourself.*

The women at Café Femmes who had watched all that had been on the softball team that first year when Jefferson, still drinking, had failed them so badly as a coach. Not a few had fallen for the still-powerful

Jefferson and hoped to win her from the memory of Ginger, had tried to cure her addictions—and had ended up being hurt themselves.

But it was Ginger who still had Jefferson's college cap. The cap that had, at least partially, drawn Jefferson back to the woman who'd kept and treasured a hat worn during the winning of so many games. If only she'd been able to work things out with Ginger. Why had Ginger waited so long, too long, to try and help? They'd been no more than roommates for so long. Why had she even wanted Jefferson back? Not that it mattered: that cap and her memories were all that was left of Jefferson's glory days.

Shielding her eyes with one hand, she watched the Julies get a hit, a strikeout, a walk. They'd learned to trust her, despite the way she'd been. They'd learned, too, what she'd taught. And they were up a long time before the umpire called Millie out on strikes. They hadn't gotten another run. The score was two to two.

"You're good, Coach," Annie said as she prepared to jog to her position in the outfield.

"Thanks, Heaphy." But what, Jefferson wondered, am I doing here at forty-one, coaching a dinky little amateur softball team? What in hell did it matter if they won or lost? She'd called Ginger when she hit six months' sobriety. And called her monthly since then, to talk, to update her and maybe… She didn't even know why she wanted career-obsessed Ginger back.

Out of the corner of her eye she saw Liz arrive. Sally's partner at the bar and at home, Liz worked the night shift. She must have gotten out of bed and come directly to the game. She reminded Jefferson of Ginger: very feminine, yet tough and devoted to her woman and her dream. She'd told Jefferson that she saw Café Femmes as much more than a gay bar, as a place where gay kids could be together whether they drank or not. She watched Liz and Sally hug, smile into each other's eyes. Their passion never seemed to die, Jefferson thought as she turned back to the game. Like hers for Ginger. If only she hadn't treated her so badly. In AA, they said not to start a new relationship in the first year of sobriety. But she didn't want a new woman; she wanted the warmth and comfort of Ginger in their early days. And not because she knew her from back when. She wanted to be worth something to Ginger now.

She could see Liz focusing on the game, holding Sally's hand. It mattered to Liz that the Julies won. That night last summer, after Ginger had left, when Jefferson was the only one in the bar and Liz apparently thought she was too drunk to notice—that night came back to her vividly.

Behind the bar Liz was sobbing in Sally's arms. No-nonsense Liz, sobbing. She could see Sally's hand stroke Liz's thick, dark hair.

"We can borrow more money," Sally was saying.

"No," Liz mumbled. "We're not going under because of my dreams. Look what happens." She gestured toward Jefferson.

With no one else there, Café Femmes had felt like a cold cave. The jukebox was silent; the electronic game, like some night bird, beeped only occasionally; no sounds came from outside. There was no place in the world but this refuge, and its darkness seemed to thicken before Jefferson's eyes, shadows gathering to blot out her life, her world.

"The bar is still healthy." Liz had dried her eyes. "I won't sacrifice it for some iffy sidewalk café the kids might not come to." She supported herself against Sally. "Half a dream's better than none, right?"

"Wrong," Sally had said quickly. "We'll make it."

"How?"

"Faith. You believe in what we're doing. I believe. We have to have some faith that our instincts are right, that this is exactly the right time for a space where gays and straights can mix. The right place for a gay bar the neighborhood can be proud of."

Liz's tone was bitter. "Next you're going to tell me the Lavender Julies can win the tournament."

"Yes, I am. They're only three years old."

Liz laughed through her tears. "You're a hopeless optimist." She blew her nose.

"Not hopeless," Sally said. "You know, I always thought we had to hide away in a dingy neighborhood, come and go in the shadows. I never expected Soho to take off like this. And you taught me to hold up my head here. To put that fancy lavender awning out front. To spill our dirty gay selves onto the sidewalk. To get those blatant lavender-and-red uniforms for the Julies." She pulled Liz close. "You, baby. Maybe the neighborhood's not bragging about us yet, but I feel better. The kids do too."

But Liz had been looking at Jefferson. "They do? They sure don't bother to show it."

It was that night, that very moment, that she began to fight her way up. Dreams, she thought now, as the Julies fought not to lose.

Dreams. She savored the word in the bright daylight, as coach of this bright lavender-and-red team. Every woman out there was dreaming of winning, as she once had. And for all her awards, had she really ever won yet? Won like Sally meant when she spoke of Liz's dream? Won something for herself by winning for everyone? Was this a dinky little team she coached? Hell, no. She'd learned what they'd taught her too. They were quick and smart, skilled now; she'd made certain of that. All they'd needed was a leader. And what did their leader really want? To be a sad has-been all her life? Or to give them something to hold their heads up for?

She watched the batters on the other team more closely. The one up now would freak at a curveball, she decided, and signaled the pitcher to throw one. As the pitcher struck her out, Jefferson saw it all in her mind's eye: the Julies, in bright red and proud lavender, at the street fair next month, behind the Café Femmes booth, under a big sign: ALL-CITY WINNERS! The Julies, shaking cans at people to collect funds for block improvements, block gatherings, for pro-gay political candidates who wanted the Soho vote. They'd carry the red-and-lavender banner through the streets, representatives of the community. And on Gay Pride Day they'd march, they'd parade, they'd storm the city, waving at the cameras. Shadows? Never again, Sal and Liz! They'd lead the damn parade, triumphant, all-star champs: the players and their lovers, fans, mothers, fathers—their coach. Yes, she could use a little glory too. Not glory like it used to be but, shit, who remembered that now? Except herself. Except Ginger.

It was the last half of the last inning. Annie Heaphy stepped up to bat. The teams were still tied. The sun was a little less hot. The grass was strewn with intent lesbians. She could see that the teenaged boys, passing back through, seemed gripped by the tension. Marie-Christine had begun a cheer:

Our Lavender Lovers
Are Lavender Winners!

Jefferson remembered the very first time her own team had won, they'd been playing field hockey up in Rye. She'd been very together, in tune with her teammates, and had pushed and wheeled her way toward the winning point. The cheers sounded—the cheers that were, for that glorious moment, the only sound in the world.

She'd thought she'd never hear them like that again, and here they came now, rising, swelling as Annie Heaphy hit the ball with all the power in her middle-aged arms and it sailed over the pitcher, sailed over second base, sailed over the outfield, toward the roof of the Plaza Hotel, and Annie came running, running, no longer nonchalant, around every base till she was home. Home.

Jefferson didn't care who saw her. She stood crying in front of everyone. Crying to see the batgirl twirl in excitement, to see Liz smiling and crying all at once, to see Sally leaping with delight, to see Marie-Christine dance Annie around and around.

To see Ginger.

Where had she been? Watching out of sight?

And holding Jefferson's cap. Her winner's cap—looking faded, worn, but with a good stiff brim to it still, bent in the middle, where she liked it.

"I thought you might need this again," said Ginger, always ready with the right gesture, a weary compassion in those green eyes that looked like home.

Chapter Twenty

By the time she was forty-four, Jefferson had developed the habit of grabbing two cold ones on her way home from work. She'd quit alcohol for three years and knew she could handle a drink again now and then. She always stopped at Jogi's, the little store that kept its beer colder than the others on her route home. Tipping the beer back and pouring it into her mouth relaxed her from a hard day of teaching these crazy public-school kids. She was glad to get on with the city school system; the commute to Dutchess Academy had become a grind. When she left work now, the noise of the kids' excited shouts and her shrill gym whistle faded from her ears; the iced liquid soothed the raspy feeling in her throat after a day of yelling instructions. The act of chugging right out on the street felt like bursting the bonds of bureaucracy that tightly taped every muscle in her body.

The first can would be empty when she got upstairs, and she'd stick the second in the freezer while she changed her clothes. Ginger taught afternoons and evenings, so Jefferson's time was her own. This was when she'd pay her bills, clean the counters, correct hygiene-class papers—whatever needed doing—while she downed the second beer. She was still into whiskey, Irish whiskey, and after her chores were done she drank it with a short dash of water to open it up. If the beer was her bridge to life after school, whiskey and water was what mellowed her out.

She was aware that she'd developed a ritual over the years, but she considered it better than going from school to the bars downtown. This was her parents' ritual, the way the adults in her family relaxed in the evening. It felt natural. When Ginger was home, Jefferson drank no more and no less. Ginger might have nothing with her but one wine cooler. Every now and then they would share a bottle of wine with dinner or celebrate an anniversary or New Year's with champagne, but Jefferson drank most of it and was proud that she could hold her liquor while Ginger got giggly and silly on a couple of glasses. In the early years it had never failed: alcohol made Ginger amorous. They'd had some good times getting Ginger tipsy.

It was Friday night. The usual crowd would be at Café Femmes, but she felt too tired to go schlepping all the way downtown. Spooners was a hushed little bar around the corner. They played old rhythm-and-blues and left her in peace. They also served Jameson, which was all she really wanted from a bar.

Spooners, ironically named for its original owner, Walter Spooner, was a mixed non-gay/gay male bar. She felt safe from temptation there, but comfortable. She slipped into her bomber jacket and walked the two blocks, feeling good. The night was soft, the traffic was light. Neon came and went in the windows. She felt a little neon herself, lightly buzzed, shimmering, an adventuring shadow. A couple of drinks, she thought, looking forward to joshing with Neal, the bartender, then she'd go home and watch a TiVo of *Will and Grace* with Ginger. Ginger had left her only once since that second time; Jefferson hadn't slipped up and gotten caught since then.

She loved the sound ice cubes made when warm whiskey cracked them. Inhaling, she smelled the Jameson and knew life was perfect.

She didn't understand Ginger and knew she never would, no matter how many gay boy bartenders she unloaded to about her. That was okay, she thought. What she wanted to know was why she loved her so much. The older Ginger got, the more she withdrew from that warm, playful part of herself that Jefferson kept hoping would come back full force.

Gladys had noticed it too. She'd asked, not long before she died, "What's come over your girlfriend, Jefferson? Would a smile make her face fall off?"

"She gets more like her mother every year," she'd told Gladys, rubbing her shoulders. "More silent, more frowny. My playmate is just about gone."

"Maybe it's some sort of inherited illness," Gladys had suggested, letting her head fall forward. "Or maybe—"

"Uh-oh. You're going to blame it on me. I hear it in your voice."

"No." Gladys's voice was lower and slower from the massage. "But did your dad pull on your mom what you do on Ginger?"

She tried to keep the pressure of her hands steady on Glad's shoulders. She'd never told anyone else, not even Ginger, about Jarvy's extracurricular activities. Angela never mentioned it either. It was too unreal, even to herself. Wow, what if Glad was right? It had never occurred to her that she was acting like Jarvy in her own way, or that Emmy or Ginger had been shaped by her spouse's behavior.

"Or early Alzheimer's."

"What? No! Not my Ginger."

"I read where there's a personality change first."

"That's crazy, Glad. There's nothing wrong with Ginger but a little stress."

"Which you add to."

"Stop being a pain in my butt, Glad." She'd changed the subject.

Here at Spooners, no one knew about Ginger, and Neal was always trying to fix her up. He couldn't understand why someone as hot, as he called it, as she was didn't go home with a woman every night instead of hanging around with the boys. She didn't tell him that this was as safe a place as there was for her: few women came in, and if one did and she felt compelled to stray from Ginger, it wouldn't be with a lesbian from their circle of acquaintances.

"You're no fag hag," he once told her. "Did you get your little heart broken?"

One of the regulars had suggested, "She's Mrs. Jameson. Married to the bottle. It's sort of like being a bride of Christ, only your savior is liquid."

"You'd think I spent every night in this bar," she'd answered. "I have a life, you know."

By then a new arrival had taken the men's attention. She'd been troubled ever since by the impression the regular had of her.

Tonight, Neal, the forty-something balding flirt, was in a matchmaking mood. "The babe in the back booth with Alvaro? I'd almost give up boys for her."

Jefferson glanced that way and found an impish-looking, animated, slim white girl crowded into a booth with three large queens, who, in an unqueenly way, seemed to hang on her every word. Jefferson could hear the woman's Southern accent rising and then falling to a hushed hoarseness. Oh, yeah, she thought, and sent a round to the booth when she ordered her next drink. She felt less bummed out than she had in a week. She was on a new SSRI for the depression, but it didn't do much more than take the edge off so far.

The girl was probably straight, she was thinking, when she felt the little hand on her forearm.

"I wanted to thank you in person." The woman got closer to Jefferson. "That was so sweet."

She could see now that the woman hadn't needed more to drink by a long shot, but then she didn't either. The woman also looked older close-up, perhaps early forties or a hard-lived late thirties. Her eyes, besides being slightly unfocused, had a shocked hardness to them, as if something terrible had happened to her and she'd never recovered. It was a look she associated with straight women. They accepted such horrors, some of them, at the hands of men.

"My pleasure." She pressed the delicate hand that was offered but, inside, turned away. All women are good, she thought; they're just not all good for me.

"May I sit with you a while?" the woman asked. "I'm Delia. My cousin and her friends are getting a little much."

The part of her that wasn't excited by these slumming straight women felt apprehensive. They can come and go as they please, she thought, taking from the gay world and scuttling, titillated, safely back to their own. She was angry at their invasion of her sacred ground. The woman was already settling on the stool next to hers, and she already had a friendly arm around Delia's waist.

It turned out that Delia had never been to New York before, was staying with her cousin, one of the queens, and had divorced her third husband. Delia was a driver for a linen service and gave Jefferson an earful about running a sales route.

"Aren't there gay bars with more women in them?" she asked Jefferson, but when Jefferson started to write out a list of addresses in her whiskey-sloppy hand, Delia insisted that she couldn't go alone and bought Jefferson another drink. "Unless," asked Delia, "I shouldn't be buying? Is that some kind of insult to you?"

She was at the stage of inebriation where it was so easy to shrug off qualms and Delia was so brashly cute, she said, "I'll chaperone you to one women's bar, but then I need to go. My partner will be home waiting for me."

"I'd wait for you too, sweetie." Delia's words were a little slurry.

At that moment Jefferson experienced the transition from the world of gravity, atmospheric resistance, and common sense to being high. Delia was no longer a confection of makeup and alien experiences, but of womanly grace and a commanding desirability. She steered Delia out of the bar. They were barely out of sight of the bar when they began groping each other, staggering into doorways, tilting against gates as they kissed, and coming to dead stops on the sidewalk for long clinches.

"I was never with a girl before."

"We need to get off the street before someone sees us."

"I have my cousin's key."

Finally, they reached the subway.

Delia read an address in Bay Ridge from a scrap of paper she found in her purse.

"You're kidding."

"Is that too far?" asked Delia, her face expectant, her eyes roaming Jefferson's face and body.

"For you?" she replied with a smile and once again slipped her arm around Delia, pulling her snug against herself as they navigated the stairs and turnstiles to the platform and keeping her close once they were seated on the nearly empty trains. How could she deny Delia now? She'd committed herself with that first round of drinks. She could be home in a couple of hours. Why, she thought with drunken logic, disappoint this woman who needed badly to come out?

They were over the bridge, it seemed, in record time, and outside a tan apartment building near the Eighty-sixth Street subway stop. There was no camera visible on the elevator, but Jefferson had come down enough to refuse to fool around. She also didn't want to miss *Will and Grace*. Ginger would be home soon and wondering where she was. In the cousin's apartment, Delia immediately poured Old Mr. Boston whiskey over rocks and added soda. Jefferson drank, chasing her high regardless of the fact that this brand would give her a horrible hangover in the morning.

While Delia was in the bathroom, Jefferson wandered the living room of the one-bedroom apartment. The queen had filled his walls with posters, photographs, and framed headlines from gay-pride parades and political protests. Jefferson wondered if he had attended all of these events or was a collector of memorabilia or both. This year, maybe she and Ginger would march. It had been a while for her; Ginger never had.

Delia's body surprised her. Thin though she was, she filled out her lacy black nightgown admirably. Jefferson, starting on her second Mr. Boston, admired the woman from the bedroom doorway. Although she'd told Ginger how negligees got her motor running, Ginger consistently opted for her flannel nightgowns.

"Aren't you ever going to come touch me, Jefferson?" Delia asked in that hoarse, husky voice.

Jefferson, back in mellow mode, smiled and started unbuttoning her own shirt.

"Oh, boy. I never thought this could be so exciting." Delia's drawl had become more pronounced with each drink.

Jefferson lounged against the door frame, shirt untucked, hanging open, both covering and promising. She wanted to go to Delia, but no, she didn't want to. She remembered the last time and how she'd sworn she was through with strangers. Wasn't it time to show some respect for what she had with Ginger, despite how little they had? When she wasn't blaming Ginger for her absences, both literal and sexual, she was blaming herself for giving Ginger such sparse allegiance and violating their love, if that's what it still was. They hadn't had sex since Florida. No, they hadn't had sex since she told Ginger what she needed. Boy, had that backfired.

While she wondered whether love without desire on Ginger's part was still love, Delia, on the bed, ran those delicate hands down her nightgown and Jefferson felt herself stir. Delia raised one hand to her right breast and rubbed the nipple. Jefferson's eyelids became heavy. Through her narrowed vision she watched Delia pull at the lace that lined the bottom of her gown and inch it up her thighs. Jefferson responded as actively as if Delia had been going down on her. Then Delia reached under the covers and brought out a vibrator. She started it and moved it over her gown. She could see the outline of Delia's other hand, under the gown, moving one finger. Jefferson was throbbing and drank deeply to slow her reaction, fascinated and at the same time saddened.

What got into these women's heads? Why would it be so exciting to have another woman, a complete stranger, watch from across a room? Had Delia been fantasizing all her life about a moment like this: the drunk butch lesbian in the doorway, shirt open, excited by Delia's excitement? Jefferson had never imagined anything like it, but it fed something in her.

Not a sexual need, something a little dark. Something that got a minor kick out of being the one standing and in control of herself while this woman wriggled on the bed. She had her period anyway, so this suited her fine, but what had happened to the high-spirited kid she'd been?

"Somebody's got to," Delia said, her voice barely there. She pulled her gown up to her waist, spread her legs until her heels overhung the mattress, and replaced her fingers with the vibrator. Jefferson's impulse was to go to Delia and put her fingers inside her while the vibrator stimulated her. She knew the woman would push her shirt aside and touch her breasts while Jefferson made her come, but before the impulse made its way to her slowed-down brain, Delia sucked in one loud breath and squirmed against her hand, saying, "Oh. Oh, oh, oh, Jesus."

Jefferson drained her glass at the sound of the queen's key in the front-door lock, thinking, for the thousandth time, if I never drank again, would I still go prowling for strangers? She quickly buttoned her shirt as Delia fled the bed for the bathroom. The queen, his makeup a mass of fissures like bleached, dried mud, looked puzzled, then scared, then knowing, all in the moment that Jefferson fled past him. She bounded down seven flights by swinging over two or three steps at a time, grasping the rails. At the second floor she missed a step, almost went down, but caught hold of the bar. All her weight hung on her twisted wrist for a long, painful moment. She tackled the next flight more slowly. Outside it had begun to shower, and the cool raindrops splashed against her face as she jogged to the subway stop, ignoring the misery of her wrist.

She caught the R train back into the city, cradling her left arm in her right, angry that she would have to play handball this way for a while. She knew what sprains felt like and this was a sprain. Tomorrow, she promised herself again, she would drink nothing, not even a beer. Sordid nights like this were not how she wanted to spend the rest of her life.

CHAPTER TWENTY-ONE

Jefferson paced under the hotel canopy. She moved away from the gray building, out to the curb, back along the red mat to the glass double doors. The doorman, about sixty, whose uniform sported golden brown shoulder braids that almost matched his skin, watched her with a scowl on his face. At first, she'd explained that she was waiting for a guest. That had been half an hour ago, when she was fifteen minutes early. Now she scowled back at him.

What was he going to do? Call the cops because she wanted to make amends to Shirley and was a little bit anxious?

She looked quickly up, but saw only a family leaving the hotel. The sharp scent of the father's lime aftershave hung behind him in the wet air. A tiny girl in a hooded red rain cape held his hand. He lifted the girl over the water in the gutter and set her in a waiting limousine next to her mother, then waved until they were out of sight.

Jefferson recombed her wet hair. "Amends, Jefferson," she told herself. "You're making amends to the woman, not seducing her all over again." Then why had she put on cologne? Why the new burgundy shirt she'd been saving for a special occasion? Why her brown leather jacket and her softest cords? Why was her heart doing the tango, double time, inside her chest?

Again, there was activity in the lobby. Again, it was not Shirley. What would she look like after ten years on the West Coast, writing comedy in movie land? Would she be harried like some of the LA career women Jefferson had met? Or her zany old self, cracking jokes with every breath, unable to relax long enough to make love decently, despite having come on like a hurricane, despite acting like a mini-sex goddess?

Why in hell had Jefferson been obsessed with getting the woman to bed?

Because that's how she'd been in those days. It hadn't been Shirley, it had been all of them. And for what? What was left? She should at least have good memories. When it had come time to sort through what she'd done, and to whom, she'd found that the histories of all those beloveds, not to mention the details of the relationships, eluded her in a way the women never could. Now she was tracking every one of them down. She had to clean up yesterday to make today work.

Damn. Where was Shirley? It was half an hour past their meeting time. Jefferson felt clammy, chilled through by the late fall rain. Did she get the day wrong? The time? The hotel? Should she go up? No. That was the last thing she intended to do. She'd already spotted a coffee shop around the corner where they could talk safely. She'd even purposely left her big black umbrella at home, the one she'd used so often as an excuse to pull a woman near for the first time. Had she used the umbrella with Shirley? Would Shirley be expecting it? In any case, she herself would not fall into any of the traps she'd set for others.

For a moment, Jefferson stopped pacing. She stood at the edge of the canopy, peering through the downpour at the yellow cabs, the black cabs, the mail jeeps, the limos, the beat-up economy cars that jammed Broadway at the end of this crosstown street. Rain seemed to trap the exhaust smells. A few people with umbrellas squeezed through the gridlock, then turned up Broadway at a furious pace, as if to make up for lost time.

Lost time. Jefferson jammed her hands back in her pockets and whirled into her pacing again. Almost thirty years she'd lost in her games of sodden pursuit. Because it was true, what her new AA sponsor had said, that as soon as Jefferson stopped drinking, she had also stopped whoring around. The same sponsor had practically promised that her depressions—and she'd finally admitted to herself that's what they were—would lift if she practiced the twelve steps. Obviously, she'd have to practice harder.

She thought of Ginger, left at home, burying herself in work, left without a whole lover, or plain left. That feeling of guilt was compounded by all the guilt she carried around about the rest of her little love-them-and-leave-them liaisons.

What could they have had if Jefferson had stayed home? A little of the peace she sometimes experienced now? A feeling of freedom, like she could do anything, go anywhere, and it would be good without fighting or tears or conflict? Without the feeling that some malevolent creature lived inside her and busied itself tearing her up, so that everything demanded a hundred times more effort because first she had to stitch herself back together again?

Jefferson pulled her hands out of their hiding places. She stood, half under the side of the canopy, half in the rain, looking at them. First the backs, pale and chafed from early tastes of winter. Then the palm, callused a little from working out recently. Her right palm collected rain in a tiny puddle at its center. These were the hands that had stopped dragging themselves, one over the other, up an endless rough rope. She licked the rainwater in her palm. Its taste was metallic, almost bitter, and snapped her right into the present, into this moment of waiting to make another apology for being such a creep in the past.

A cab pulled in front of the hotel so quickly that Jefferson surmised it had been stuck in the Broadway traffic. Without seeming to move, the doorman was beside it, sweeping the passenger door open. A leg appeared, high-heeled shoe first, then a long calf with the edge of a dark, clinging skirt at its peak.

LA had been good to Shirley. Jefferson smelled her own sweat and the tango began again. Had Shirley changed so much, or had Jefferson forgotten the poise, the warm smile, the arms that hugged as if they were made for welcoming back old lovers? Didn't Shirley remember how Jefferson had dumped her, abandoned her in that sleazy bar for a quickie with a woman she'd had her eye on for weeks and who'd finally returned Jefferson's interest that night? She couldn't hug Shirley back, so consumed was she by the old guilt.

"Come on up, handsome. The years have seasoned you nicely." Shirley offered her arm.

Jefferson didn't so much hear and see as feel the cab pull away, leaving a vacuum she suddenly had to fill. Instead of being in the hotel waiting for their meeting, Shirley had been out living her own life and caught Jefferson off balance. And she hadn't expected Shirley to have this presence, this woman-of-the-world air of command.

"Jefferson?" Shirley said after a moment.

Quickly, Jefferson answered, "I thought we could go to the coffee shop around the corner."

"Oh, God, Jeff. I am so wiped, I have to use the little girls' room, and I long to change out of this monkey suit. You can wait in the lobby if you want, but I promise not to bite."

The doorman was watching the sky, hands behind his back. Jefferson felt like she was at the tail end of a tug of war, pulled forward under the canopy by a need to put an end to a past that shamed her, pulled back by temptations of repeating that past. In the few seconds she needed to make a decision, Shirley's face adopted a look of concern; the doorman's, one of even deeper suspicion.

"Jefferson?"

She linked Shirley's arm with her own and steered her into the lobby.

It was hot in there and smelled like the steam heat of old New York buildings. As they crossed the lobby she could see herself, Shirley's elbow cupped in her hand, in a mirror. The floor was a huge black-and-white checkerboard, and Shirley's heels clicked across it.

"What's the story, handsome?" Shirley asked. "This isn't kidnapping at my age, you know."

Jefferson managed a smile. They sat facing each other on a faded couch. Cream-painted columns dotted the lobby like elderly guests half-snoozing the afternoon away.

Shirley's arm burned against Jefferson's palm. She had always touched women like lovers, she realized. It was as much second nature to her as worrying about how she looked. Was it too late to learn how to be friends?

"Do you mind if we don't go upstairs?"

"Since when is Jefferson afraid of the big bad wolf?"

"Aw, hell, Shirley. That's the problem. I *am* the big bad wolf. If I went up there with you I might act like I used to, and that's not what I want." She felt about as debonair and in control of this situation as the three little pigs.

"What do you want, Jeffers?"

Now she remembered what had sparked her desire for Shirley. Those vivid blue eyes, like a splash of cold water, a surprise every time. As she always had, Jefferson stared into them, withdrew from their intimacy, but went back for more. She made her hands crawl inside her pants pockets where she fingered a heart-shaped stone Ginger had found on the beach during their trip to Florida. There would be no casual touching of Shirley, no touching at all. "I want to apologize."

The blue eyes looked shocked. "For what? For being the prettiest butch I ever beguiled into my bed?"

"You beguiled me into your bed?" It had never occurred to Jefferson that the campaign might have been mutual.

Shirley lifted wavy hair back from her eyes. "Don't you remember? I interrupted the great chase. You wanted what's-her-name, that siren everybody was after. What was her name?"

"Cindy?" Jefferson asked, guessing.

"Yes. And the last time you and I went out together—well, you got drunk again and I decided Cindy could have you. So what are you apologizing to me for?"

Jefferson sat straight up and ran her fingers through her hair. Shirley had let her go. "For disappearing on you at the bar. For going off with Cindy."

Shirley was still toying with her own hair. She shrugged. "That's the way it was back then. Or the way I was. Trying out this one and that one. Not that you didn't measure up the nights we spent together." Shirley looked up into Jefferson's face from under her hair, her laugh like melting chocolate.

Jefferson struggled to get out of the past, the bar, the guilt of having abandoned this woman. "What did you do?"

Shirley narrowed her eyes and cocked her head. "Are you serious? What do you think I did? We did?"

"I didn't mean the nights we spent together, Shirl. After I left you. In the bar."

"Actually, I'd rather describe our nights together. But who can remember a bit of it? Why?"

Jefferson pulled herself back on track. "Because I need to apologize for a lot of things. It's part of getting well for me."

Shirley relaxed against the couch now and seemed to study Jefferson. "Okay," she said after a while. "Thanks. I appreciate you caring after all these years." She smiled. "I like you better this way, you know. Undrunk."

Nodding, Jefferson smiled. "Yes. Me too."

"Whatever happened to that fancy dancer you lived with? Was she really the love of your life like you claimed or your perpetual chase? You butches do like your conquests—especially the straight ones."

"We're still together." She added in a mutter, "No thanks to me."

Shirley reached over and ruffled Jefferson's hair. "You look like a drowned rat. You want to come up and dry off, you charming big bad wolf? My promise still holds."

"Your promise?"

"That I won't bite."

Jefferson filled her lungs with air and exhaled very slowly. The tug of war had started again. Couldn't she spend some time getting acquainted with this woman she obviously didn't know at all? She almost pulled her comb from her pocket, but stopped herself. How she looked didn't matter. "Okay."

"Good." Shirley stood and started toward the elevator. Jefferson watched her, her hips, from across the checkerboard floor. The rain still poured down loudly outside the windows on the other side of the lobby.

Shirley whirled at the elevator, cocked a hand on her hip as if presenting herself for Jefferson's inspection, and asked, "Because tell me the truth, Jeffers, am I really your typical Red Riding Hood?"

She remembered that tiny girl in the red cape who'd come out of the hotel earlier. She laughed, shaking her head. "No, you're not. But I liked being the big bad wolf so much I thought you were." She joined Shirley and, as the elevator lifted them, could almost see the old wolf in the lobby below, waving good-bye.

CHAPTER TWENTY-TWO

While Jefferson was still in the city, she had watched a lot of crime shows, starting with *Missing Persons* in the 1990s. At first it drew her because Jorja Fox, who'd been on *Ellen*, was in it, but more recently she'd gotten into *Without a Trace*. One night, as she watched, she realized that her life was an episode. Should she have reported Ginger missing? Had Ginger's parents done so?

"So call her parents," her enduring best friend, Lily Ann Lee, urged. They were at Jefferson's apartment on the Upper West Side. It had the luxury of two small bedrooms, and she and Ginger had filled it up nicely together. The monthly maintenance fee was hefty, but she could cover it without help from Ginger. It had been their home for decades.

Lily Ann had come over to help her move Ginger's belongings into the second bedroom, which Jefferson had been putting off, unable to bear the finality of packing Ginger away.

"I did call Ginger's parents. Four times." She rested her forehead on Lily Ann's shoulder. "They hung up on me."

Lily Ann patted her on the back. "I thought you all got along."

"So did I. But now she's with a guy and they must be in pig heaven."

"Still no reason to be rude to you."

"At least they were clear."

Lily Ann closed a cardboard box and labeled it. "I don't think they would have hung up on you if she was really missing. They have to know she's okay or they would have called you."

"Exactly what I've been hoping," Jefferson said, taking the box from Lily Ann and moving it across the hall. "I think we're going to get about everything in the closet," she called back, opening the closet door.

The sight of Ginger's fanciful shoes filling the closet floor startled her. It was like finding Ginger's ghost. Some nights, instead of plumping her pillow for the dozenth time and trying yet another position with which to lure sleep, she got out of bed and prowled the ghost of Ginger through the house. She would plunge her hands into Ginger's dresser in hopes of finding something she hadn't yet discovered, something with associations so vivid it would bring Ginger alive before her, a living, walking presence she could almost pull back on the bed with her and engulf herself in pleasure.

Lily Ann came to the door. "Jef," she said. "Why would you want someone back who would do this to you? I mean, it hasn't always been heaven on earth, has it?"

"That was my fault."

"Yet she didn't leave until you stopped drinking and settled down."

"I guess the damage had been done by then."

"And I'd guess the blame isn't all yours."

"Ginger never pulled the stunts I did."

"You know this for sure?"

The very idea startled her. "You think, while I was running around on her, she was—"

"Wouldn't be the first time, J."

"That's crazy!"

"What else explains why she tolerated you hooking up with anything that moved?"

"Lily Ann, I think someplace in her understood."

"Understood what? That you were a good old-fashioned cad?"

"That I so welcomed being wanted—as who I am—for my queer self, that I couldn't say no to any woman who cast her eye my way. Sometimes I think I wanted Ginger because she hadn't wanted—never did want—me, but responded, like I did, to being wanted."

"Wow," Lily Ann said. "You about lost me there. Whatever, there was something you weren't getting at home, Jefferson, and you know it. I'm not saying it was sex." Lily Ann held out a hand to stop Jefferson's protest. "That much rabbiting is not about sex."

"You never liked Ginger."

"I never exactly understood what you saw in her."

"She was—"

"And I don't need to know. That woman lived behind a vault door and nobody got to spin her wheel, if you ask me. But knowing you, that's what you liked about her. With Ginger, your chase never ended, and nothing you can tell me will convince me that it's not the chase that turns you on."

She reached to stop Lily Ann, holding her by the arm. "Lily, you're my best friend, what brought this on?" Had Lily Ann been jealous all these years?

"You want to know what I think, J? I think, when you stopped drinking and running around on her, Ginger got bored with you. I think there was something in that woman that needed you to be a bad girl. I want you to see what was what clearly. I don't want you beating yourself up over it or getting jaded about love."

"She's my girl, Lily Ann." She knew she sounded pitiful and unsure, but no one had ever told her these things before. Did she really know what she was doing? "She might not have loved me anymore, but ever since Ginger—she was the only one who wanted to be with me. The rest, since you, have wanted sex: sex from my fingertips, pleasure from my hands, praise of their beauty, admiration for being on my arm."

Lily Ann looked at her as if deciding whether to tell her something. Was there anything left to tell?

"You think she was different from the others?" asked Lily Ann. "It was no coincidence, you know."

"What?"

"The hotel. Shirley. Ginger finding out."

"You're not saying she planned it."

Lily Ann shook her head. "No, but she was waiting for an opportunity to come along and make up her mind for her."

"So I handed her the bat and she hit the ball out of the park? Is that what you're saying?"

"Or she choreographed the dance."

"How?"

"She had to get away to find out if you'd defined her correctly."

"Defined her?"

"You told me she'd never felt attracted to women before you."

"It wasn't in her frame of reference, never occurred to her."

"She has to find out if she's living her life or one you made for her."

Lily Ann was right, she decided, remembering the women she'd been with who hadn't known they were gay—until she came along.

They were sitting together on the sofa now. Jefferson was holding Lily Ann's hand tight.

"That," Lily Ann explained, "is one reason why this is such a major blow to your ego. You failed to keep her and also failed to keep her gay, J. By defining her you defined who you are and what you can do in the world."

"Are you saying I wanted to control Ginger?"

"She's proof of who Jefferson is."

"You've got to be kidding me. Since when are you the expert on Jefferson, not me?"

"If you were a thinker, J, or a noticer or even stood still now and then, you'd be teaching philosophy, not PE."

But she wasn't really listening anymore. Her eyes got all glazed and her ears filled with an Abba song she loved to dance to. This analysis stuff was fluff. She just did what she did.

"You still want to find her, don't you?" Lily Ann asked.

She was surprised at the question.

"What about writing to the family, asking if you can take them Ginger's things, or if they want to pick them up?"

Jefferson felt like the floor was falling out from under her. "Give away Ginger's stuff? Her first tap shoes?" She held them up. "The green leather sneakers she found in the trash?" She knew she must look silly, the large bear Ginger had won at a street fair under her arm, the tap shoes dangling from one hand, a long slinky black dance skirt draped over her shoulder.

"Give them up, J. Go face-to-face with the family. They'd have to tell you something then."

"Lily Ann, I don't think so. I can't imagine."

"Okay, don't twist yourself inside out, girl. I can see how it could smart a bit."

She let out a painful breath. "You know what really makes me break down? Folding sheets by myself." She remembered the time, folding laundry together, she'd wrapped Ginger in a sheet and spun her out, then collapsed on the clean linens with her. She gave a happy laugh at herself. "Thanks for listening to me obsess, Lil. Come on, let's get the dresser in here."

The weirdest change for her wasn't Ginger's absence; it was the absence of the despair that had haunted her all her life, until the last several months. Listening to someone else talk about her family in an AA meeting, she'd realized that Jarvy was an alcoholic. He'd been a happy drinker through her childhood, but at some point that had changed. She remembered how moody he was and wondered if he, too, had suffered from joylessness. If he, too, had tried to escape it with whiskey. If his dalliances at the railroad station in Dutchess were attempts to shake off frightening funks like, she'd figured out with her sponsor, her womanizing had sometimes been.

They had drifted back to the furniture. "Ginger left this beautiful dresser?" Lily Ann asked. "It's gorgeous and in such great shape."

"It was her grandparents'."

"I'd use it, myself."

"No, Lily Ann." She bumped Lily Ann's arm with her knuckles. "If it belonged to your ex you wouldn't want to wake up in the morning and have it be the first thing you see."

Lily Ann hefted her side and they walked a few steps, Jefferson backward.

"But it isn't my ex's," Lily Ann said, setting the chest down. "Neither is Ginger's family. I could call them, J. I could say me and my husband are coming to town for the weekend—"

"You'd do that? Pretend to be straight?"

"Why not? I could call right now."

"They might have caller ID."

"Tonight then."

But when Lily Ann called Jefferson that night, before the *Murder, She Wrote* reruns came on, she said no one had answered and promised to try again the next day. "I'm not leaving a message, J, in case they think it's strange of me to be too persistent or decide to get hold of Ginger about who I really am."

"What if they know, Lily Ann? What if they give you a number to call? I'm not going to call it and have to talk to them."

"We can Google the number. Or use a reverse phone directory, Jef. I have some resources at work."

Jefferson closed her eyes and saw Ginger and Mitchell in the back of the cab again. "Do I want to know?" she asked, flipping the hood of her sweatshirt over her head and crossing her arms in a defensive pose.

"You want to know she's all right."

"Mitchell wouldn't hurt Ginger."

"But what is he doing with her?"

"Lily Ann, you're talking like he kidnapped her for ransom."

"For all you know, he might have. Or worse."

"What're you talking about? Mitchell is our friend."

"Friends don't ride off into the sunset with your partner."

"No call. That's what gets to me the most, Lily Ann. Ginger would tell me something, wouldn't she?"

"If she could."

"You're scaring me."

"What's worse, J, her running off on you with a man or foul play?"

"Worse for Ginger or worse for me?"

"Gee-jus, Jefferson."

"Well, it's the truth. I assumed she and that turncoat wanted to be together. I may not deserve better after all the years I ran around on her, but I'm sober and faithful now." She knew she was whining.

"She got bored? She did like you better wild?"

"But if Mitchell was up to no good, then when she comes back, we still have a chance."

"You mean it saves your ego."

"What's left of it." She looked at Lily Ann. "You don't get it, do you?"

"I get being left, J. College. Remember? There was me, there was Ms. Big Hair—and goodness knows who else."

"I was a kid. She was the bartender. And femme. I was swept off my feet."

"Again."

She touched Lily Ann's short hair. "I wish I hadn't treated you like that, but at least I didn't leave you for a man."

"Gets you where you live, doesn't it?"

"She always said she could be bi, but a lot of women hang on to that idea, especially femmes. Like they have one foot on shore and can bail if the going gets rough."

"So you're saying it's worse because she's not leaving you, she's leaving the gay life."

"Something like that."

"And you take that personally. A double rejection."

"Everything I am. Everything I stand for. Everything being with me means, from the intimate stuff to her knowing how I brush my teeth."

"It is not a failure for you, J. You're such a catch."

"It's my failure. I've failed us all."

"All like who—lesbians?"

She nodded. When was she going to find someone who really, down to her roots, understood, somebody queer enough to know the depth of what Ginger had done?

"It sounds like you'd rather she was dead."

"Dead? Who said anything about dead?"

"That's what it sounded like to me."

"You've been watching too many cop shows."

"I don't watch cop shows. I hang out with some cops, though. The things they tell me."

"You think I should report her as a missing person?"

"I don't think you can. Not with her family refusing to talk to you."

"That confirms what I think—she's still with Mitchell. Why else won't they tell me anything?"

"He could have threatened them."

"And Aunt Tilly?"

"That's where he grabbed Ginger from, her school, remember?"

"So you think I should go looking for her."

"If you insist on wanting her. You've heard that Jamie Anderson song, 'Her Problem Now'? Well, she's his problem now."

"But," she said, looking for the words she needed. "It's not even Ginger. It's that sweet thrill of longing. No, that's not quite true, but the two are bound together. With Ginger there's the permanent pleasure of seduction."

"I swear, you need therapy, girl. Even if she left to be with him— and the suitcases, unless they're a smokescreen, might confirm that. But even then, J, wouldn't you expect Ginger to come after you if you'd been gone this long with no word?"

"I never thought of that. She might be waiting for me to make a move."

"She might have gone willingly with him and now be stuck."

"You're not thinking she's gagged and bound somewhere."

"I never trusted Mitchell. He was always showing up places with straight girls, like he needed to show the world he wasn't as queer as the rest of us."

"Where are you going with this, Lily Ann?"

"What if he—they—went to one of those fix-the-gays groups?"

"Ginger would never go along with that."

"She might not have known what she was getting into, J."

"But her parents might have."

They looked at each other.

Lily Ann said, "A cult kidnapping?"

"Which would mean the family isn't talking because they're shielding her from me. They finally got her away from the big bad wolf."

She sat thinking for a while, confused. This made more sense than anything else. Still, it didn't sound like Ginger to go into some kind of cult deprogramming situation. She'd always scoffed at them. "Why would Mitchell have dragged Ginger with him to something like that? Why not work on himself?"

"He's the type of guy who needs a prop."

"He could have told her anything. That she needed to get away for a while. Or that they were going to a dance workshop and to let me stew because I'd done it to her enough. No, that doesn't make sense. It's not Ginger."

"You don't know what makes sense for other people, J."

"For Ginger?"

"It's midlife-crisis time, J. You had a soft landing. Ginger may be taking off."

"I stepped back, didn't I? I respected her choice and even expected her choice. I thought I deserved this. I thought if a man was involved I couldn't fight back."

"No, you assumed you'd lost."

"Maybe I have."

"And maybe you haven't."

CHAPTER TWENTY-THREE

The next spring, she waded, twice, through fallen white blossoms in one of those delightful pocket parks hidden in midtown before she completed a trip to Café Femmes. This was the first time she'd gone to the bar without Ginger in her life.

She sat with Gabby and Lily Ann, started to tell them how good it was to see them, and found herself crying. Her companions went dead silent.

"I'm sorry," she managed to say over a blast of rap out of the jukebox. "I don't know where this is coming from. I never cry."

"Du-uh," said Gabby, who had taken off her apron and closed the food side of the bar. "It's your first time back since—"

She could hear Lily Ann sock Gabby in the arm. She looked up. "It is, I know," Jefferson said. "I was thinking about it. I mean, I came here so often without Ginger."

"With good reason," Gabby said.

Jefferson asked, "You mean you didn't like Ginger either?"

Gabby looked embarrassed. "It wasn't that I didn't like her, it's—"

"That you didn't like her," Lily Ann finished for Gabby.

"She was kind of a cold fish, I always thought," said Gabby. "You loved her so much and Ginger—I mean she'd laugh and joke around and all with us, but it was like she was always playing a part and ready to leave the minute you would. If she was like that at home, no wonder you ran around on her."

She scraped her fingernails through her hair. "So all those years I was trying to measure up and there was nothing to measure up to?"

Gabby shrugged. "Some things are too tough to do."

"Or we make them tough," Lily Ann amended. "You held that girl up on a pedestal and then couldn't meet the expectations you thought she had."

"But she didn't have them?"

"You have to care to have expectations of a person," Gabby said.

"She didn't care? That's ridiculous!"

"She couldn't care," Gabby said with finality.

"Why are you ganging up on her? I didn't know none of you liked Ginger."

"She wasn't so good for you," Gabby said. "She maybe wanted to be, but I would think about not going after her, if I were you."

That was because she didn't know the little girl in Jefferson. Only the lover knows the little girl who lets herself be held in the night and laughs at silly things over breakfast and admits it when she's scared. She scooped petals from her pockets and drizzled their wilting whiteness from her hands to the table. "If I knew where she's hiding. I don't want to stalk her. I wouldn't even try to talk to her, but this knowing nothing— she could be in trouble. She could be wanting to come home. I feel like she's been gone for a lifetime and that she's coming right back."

"Ah-hem," Gabby said.

"What?" Lily Ann asked.

"I heard something."

Jefferson looked up. "Gabby," she said, reaching for her. "About Ginger?"

"About Mitch."

"Speak," Lily Ann commanded.

Gabby picked up a second napkin to shred. "This trick was in his apartment last summer. He saw a brochure."

"What trick?"

"A guy I run into because of work."

"How well do you know him?" Lily Ann wanted to know. "Is he reliable?"

"What kind of brochure?" Jefferson asked.

"You know, one of those cult things."

"A Kool-Aid cult?"

"No. Where they brainwash you straight."

She stared at Gabby. "You're kidding."

"It was a brochure."

"Did he say anything about it?"

"Who?" Lily Ann interrupted. "Who are we talking about? Somebody making this up to sound in the know?"

"No. I see this guy like, daily, when I pick up ingredients. He sells pestos and garlic spreads. Like that. We've been doing business for centuries."

"What's his name?"

"Nuncio. He's cool. Really."

Jefferson asked, "Do you think he made her go to one of those groups with him?"

"He said he and Mitch talked about it, about Mitch wanting to change, being tired of tea rooms and tricking, and being scared of HIV. He said Mitch thought he might find some, you know, calm and serenity. Like that."

"And he needed a partner in crime," said Lily Ann.

"My partner," Jefferson replied.

Gabby asked, "Did Ginger ever say anything about that kind of thing?"

She thought back. "No," Jefferson said. "She used to say she could go either way, but she happened to love me."

"Oh, that's an old tune," Gabby countered. "I'm not gay. I only happen to have been with my girlfriend Muscles since 1953."

They all laughed. "Maybe Ginger was a little like that, but I thought she'd gotten over it. As you said, it's been a long time."

"Mitch must have worked on her."

"They were really good friends. I thought we all were, but he performed with Ginger sometimes, playing flute."

There was a silence. Lily Ann asked, "Did Nuncio remember the name of the place?"

"There was more than one," Gabby said. "And no, he didn't remember details. I asked that."

"We can find them," Jefferson said.

"Do you really want to?" Gabby asked.

Jefferson said, "You'll never get information out of one of those groups."

"Oh, but I could," Gabby suggested. "I could pretend I'm interested, get a tour."

Lily Ann laughed. "They might have a wax museum—famous conversions."

"The Gallery of Gay Conversion Failures: Ellen, Rosie, Sir Elton," Gabby added.

Jefferson had to smile. "Sounds like fun. How's Sunday for you?"

"Seriously," Lily Ann said with a sigh that sounded like resignation. She reached under the table and pulled out her laptop. "A little Wi-Fi and we might get a handle on this."

"But," Gabby interjected, "Mitch might have gone there first, gotten fixed, and then dragged Ginger off."

"How could she," Jefferson moaned. "She might as well have stabbed me right through the heart. Not saying a word—it feels like an attack."

Lily Ann reached for her hand. "No. It's a retreat. This has been building for years, J."

She stopped herself from whining. "You're my friends. You've never criticized me for my acting the way I do. I hope you know me well enough to understand that I accept full responsibility for being an out-of-control dog. But I always came back. And never—how could she—"

"A man. Disgusting," Gabby said.

To hear another butch say that was soothing. She nodded to Gabby in thanks. She felt such shame. It wasn't something she could explain to anyone. Even Lily Ann didn't understand how deep it went. Another woman was one thing, but this…

Lily Ann came up with a list of groups in the metropolitan area that Mitch could be working with. "They must go back for follow-up. We could get schedules."

Gabby shook her head. "Five places. What are they, churches?"

"All but one," Lily Ann answered.

"That's the program then," Jefferson said. "Mitchell is Jewish."

"Observant?" Lily Ann asked.

"He didn't keep kosher or anything, but he did a seder every year and was into cooking. He made a mandelbread you wouldn't believe. Maybe if I'd cooked more—"

"J," Lily Ann intoned. "It isn't your cooking. It's who you cooked with."

She nodded. That truth was inescapable.

She had slowly realized that she'd never been hurt before. She'd skipped away from other women as she would from a drinking buddy, which some of them were, or a work friend when she changed jobs. Or she got too deep into their egos or dreams and they didn't want to let go. Not one had walked away from her.

Now that it was her turn, she was stunned by her pain and jealousy; she had never learned this side of love and was completely defenseless. She might have to move. The city had become Ginger, pirouetting around her in long skirts, long hair, and tights, her colors always somber and her occasional bright laughter all the more startling.

Even if she'd been hurt back in her drinking days, she'd been too pickled to feel much or to remember. She'd started drinking in her teens, and her sponsor told her that might be where she was stuck: her feelings all these years like a teenager's.

That Sunday they actually went to the small box of a building in New Rochelle where Straighten Out held its seminars. Lily Ann Lee was driving and Gabby sat in back. There was a seminar scheduled for three o'clock. They were watching for Mitchell's black Hyundai SUV, but the small parking lot was almost full and there was no sign of it. A row of forsythia bushes blazed yellow in front of them. She still saw their brightness when she closed her eyes to dim the spring sun and the sting of salt in the tears she refused to let fall from her eyes.

"This feels humiliating," she said.

Gabby agreed. "What are we going to do, grab her back?"

"Jef wants to know where she is and if she's safe. Seeing her here would give that to you, Jef, wouldn't it?"

She nodded, eyes closed, one hand on each of her friends. "I could sit on the sidewalk with a tin cup, begging for information."

"Maybe there's a secretary inside—"

"What I was thinking," Lily Ann said. "I'll go in, say I was supposed to meet Mitchell here."

She gave Lily Ann an encouraging push toward the door. "You go, girl."

Gabby handed her a bottle of green tea from the cooler. She held it against her hot cheek, watching the doorway for Lily Ann now. "You guys are good to me."

Gabby harrumphed in the backseat. "What the heck. Amaretto's working today, there's no games on the tube. It's a nice ride in the country."

"This is what you call country?"

The street was all but treeless, the pavement littered. A vacant lot stood to the other side of the yellow bushes, and across the street was a storefront church, abandoned after the morning services.

"New Rochelle was country when I was growing up."

"No secretary," Lily Ann said when she returned. "But there was a guy smoking outside the back door. Tried to register me. Told him Mitchell Para had recommended them. Nada. Not a flicker. He either really doesn't know Mitchell or he's a good poker player."

"Thanks for trying, Lil." She squeezed Lily Ann's upper arm. "You're too good of a friend for this old sad sack."

Gabby rolled her eyes. "So what's Plan B?"

Lily Ann started back toward the city and suggested, "Jef, I think you should leave a message asking Ginger to call you."

"I already did. Three times."

"Hoo, boy," Gabby commented.

"They can't stay away forever," Lily Ann said. "We watch Mitchell's apartment."

"We have jobs," Jefferson said.

"Yo—what about where he works?"

"I don't want to see Mitchell, Gab. I want Ginger."

"So you follow him."

"Home?"

"Maybe he's not going home. Maybe they're staying with friends. You know, till they think they're safe at his place."

"Maybe he moved," Lily Ann said.

"So now we have three places to watch? His apartment, if it's still his. His work, if he still works there. Someplace new, if we can follow him to it."

"Right," Gabby agreed.

"Listen," Lily Ann said. "It's not like this has to be twenty-four-hour surveillance. We stop by and watch a while on our way to and from places. We check in the night before to see who goes where."

"What about me?" Gabby said. "I live a block from work at the Femmes."

"Hey, right. You keep listening. Maybe he'll show up in the bars. Or contact someone in the community. Put the word out. These are our people. We all hate these make-'em-straight groups."

Jefferson said, "I should be making these plans, not leaving it to you."

"J, that's like saying somebody burned in a fire should heal herself. You're injured, practically critical. You need to let us be your nurses."

She shrugged. "Okay, but I get to feel guilty."

"Have at it."

"You femmes are much stronger than us butches. And more honest."

"No doubt about it."

"Hey," Gabby said, "you're supposed to argue about that."

CHAPTER TWENTY-FOUR

Mitchell Para's day job was in a building on the West Side. Instead of hanging around it, risking a return of the despair inactivity brought on, Jefferson decided to storm the office. Mitchell had explained that it was a small food-brokerage firm called Faster Foods that had been founded by his straight, cigar-chomping brother Morton. No one was at the front desk, so she peered around the paneled partition that screened seven men at desks clumped so close together she couldn't imagine they'd be able to hear anyone on the headsets that clung to their heads. Every one of them was smoking. There were two doors with frosted windows, both closed to the warm spring air. Her heart beat faster to think Mitchell might be inside one of those offices.

One man looked up from his computer screen. "Help you?"

"Mitchell Para?"

He motioned to the office behind him on his right.

Jefferson threaded her way through the desks, waste baskets, and electrical wiring. Classy place to work, Mitch, she thought and buried her hands more deeply in the pockets of her hoodie. The men barked into their phones, punched at keyboards, yelled questions at each other. She breathed in so much cigarette smoke she coughed as she knocked on the door.

"Yeah!"

It wasn't Mitchell, but a shorter, heavier look-alike who had adopted the shoddy day-old-beard look.

"I know you?" he asked.

A trembling started inside. "Jefferson. I'm a friend of Mitchell's. Is he here?"

"What kind of friend doesn't know he's on his honeymoon?"

Her face went cold. Now she was trembling all over. "Honeymoon?"

"Might as well be. Shacked up with a woman, no phone, announced he would be gone two months."

"Where?"

"The Caribbean? Brazil? Who knows with my *meshugana* brother? Why? He owe you money?"

"No." She'd tried to come up with explanations on her way there, but not seriously, half expecting to see Mitchell, to hear that Ginger was staying with him until she found her own place. "Who did he abscond with?"

"The little *faigele* finally got himself a woman. What's her name, some Irish redhead."

She reached to the desk to steady herself.

"You want to leave a message?" He was watching her. "Hey, wait a minute. You're the two-timing girlfriend. The one she was leaving, aren't you?"

When Jefferson didn't respond, Mitchell's brother said, "You people. I don't know what's wrong with you. Sleeping with anything that moves. You girls are as bad as the guys."

"Where did they go?" she asked again, refusing to break eye contact.

"I need this like *loch im kopf*. I can't tell you. Mitch would break my neck."

"I want to know she's safe."

He gave a disgusted-sounding laugh. "With my brother, believe me, she's safe."

She placed her hands on the desk and looked down at the man. "I can go to the police, tell them I think she's been kidnapped."

"What are you doing? Threatening me?" He carefully chose a cigar. "You think the police would rescue a woman who went willingly with a man and bring her back to a creature like you? They would laugh you out of the station."

She thought of a hundred things to say, but they were all lame. He was right. She wanted to threaten him, to hit him until he told her. Why not? What did she have to lose?

"Are they here in the city?"

"Maybe."

"I'm not playing games, Para," she said, her anger building.

"Good. Then why not leave before me and my brokers decide to play games with you."

"You're a real sweetheart, aren't you," she said, poking his arm hard with an index finger.

"Did you say you're leaving?"

She moved abruptly away from his desk. Did he cringe? There was an old wooden desk chair behind her. Its springs creaked as she sat in it. "I'd love to leave, but I haven't gotten what I came for yet."

"All right already. They're in the city. At Mitch's place. You have the address?"

"Don't bullshit me. They're not at Mitchell's."

"Okay, okay. They're upstate. The family has a cabin up in the Catskills. That address I'm not giving you. Not that the address would help. It has an electronic gate and a stone wall twice your height, topped by shards of glass. If you found it, you'd never get in."

With a feeling of great exhaustion and that threat of returning despair, she sat back in the unsteady chair and folded her arms, silent, thinking she'd need a ladder and some blankets to protect her from the glass. "I'm not leaving until you give me what I need. And I don't mean lies."

"Fine. No big problem. You sit there while I tell you what I think. God made us to mate with the opposite sex. What you and my brother do is a perversion. Your lives are filth. Your whole existence is about satisfying your basest physical urges, like animals, and you never produce children, the whole reason behind those urges. You spread disease and you lead children into ugly lives like your own because you can't stand being alone in your ways. This Ginger was probably a very normal person until you debased her."

Instead of telling him to shut up or walking out, she listened. So this was how straight people thought of her. She wondered briefly if they could be right and if losing Ginger was her punishment.

She sat there like a weighted punching bag enduring its blows as Mo went on.

"It's sick, this hang-up you people have with the same sex. You know it can be cured, yet you do nothing. Mitchell has gotten help. Our rabbi sent him to a group that cures this curse and he's now his natural self. Too bad he didn't cure him of his love of goyim, but I won't go into that."

She kept her eyes down, hugging herself. The more Mitchell's brother talked, the closer he was getting to spilling the beans.

"Our congregation is supporting my brother in every way," and he named a large synagogue Jefferson had heard Mitchell mention.

She shut out Mo's words as she searched her memory. It was in Brooklyn where Mitchell had grown up. He'd driven them past the beautiful old building and told them how much he wished his family, conservative Jews, would wake up and smell the coffee. More and more the conservative movement was turning toward acceptance, but not his family, he had said with a curse of disgust. Now she was getting a taste of what Mitchell had gone through. And Ginger's Catholic family must have preached the same general disapproval, though she had never come out to them. "Why break my mother's heart?" Ginger had asked, while Jefferson wondered if Ginger's stony mother even had a heart that could break. "They'd think I was going to hell and that I would never meet them in heaven."

Jefferson could say nothing. She had never come out to Emmy and Jarvy either; it hadn't seemed worth the effort. She figured they knew and didn't want to get into it either. Since Ginger always had to go "home" for holidays, she went to her family alone too, if she went at all.

Mo was still lecturing when she decided that he wasn't letting anything else slip out. Without a word, she rose to go.

"Here," Mo said, thrusting a pamphlet at her. "You can get help too. My people can refer you to your own groups."

"What is this?" she asked, and read aloud, "'JONAH is a nonprofit international organization dedicated to educating the worldwide Jewish community about the prevention, intervention, and healing of the underlying issues causing same-sex attractions. JONAH: Jews Offering New Alternatives to Homosexuality.'"

She banged the rolled-up pamphlet against the desk and looked at this man, sick to her stomach. "What is their problem? What is your problem? This is none of your business—their business." She looked at the back, which referred to something called NARTH, National Association for Research and Therapy for Homosexuality. "You're nuts," she said. The address for JONAH was in Jersey City, practically on the other side of the Holland Tunnel. They'd been watching the wrong place up in New Rochelle. Honeymooning in Jersey City? Not my Ginger, she thought, and smiled at Mo, poor obsessed Morton Para. Feeling taller than when she arrived and more hopeful, she stomped in her best butch manner out through the clutter of barking men and their electronics.

Chapter Twenty-five

Whenever she thought about Ginger with Mitchell, which was endlessly, Jefferson felt as if she was the burning wick of an explosive.

Dry-eyed for the most part, shriveled with regret, she waited for the suicide bomb in her heart to go off. Only the routine of teaching and being with her friends kept her intact. She battered herself with questions: How could she have been so stupid? The drinking, the chasing, her silent sulking because she never came with Ginger and Ginger didn't really try, never asked. She should have talked about it with Ginger instead of letting it become her wedge between them—she had driven Ginger away. Glad had been right. It shouldn't have been a big deal. Orgasms were wonderful, when they came, but not as wonderful as the rush of pleasure to hear a lover cry "Oh God!" or call her name over and over: that was love!

At the same time, Ginger was so absorbed in her work, had for so long spent all her spare time on performance. Ginger, she thought: named for a dancer. Ginger had spent her whole life living up to that name. It was how she begged for love, by giving her heart to dance, the only way she could earn her mom's smiles and brags. They'd had this in common, the way they spoke with their bodies. She tried to put her feelings into words, but she'd never been articulate enough. She'd always spoken to women through lovemaking and still wanted to express herself with her hands. That's when she knew, instinctually, how to say what she wanted; that was the language she spoke.

But she couldn't blame anything on Ginger. Dance was her work, her passion, as Jefferson's seemed to have been that constant search for love, or what passed for love. Maybe Lily Ann and Gabby were right: it was as if she was making up for Ginger's inattention by finding substitutes. Filling up on cake because all she got of steak was the bone. It was so hard, though, to admit she'd chosen wrong, that Ginger had been bad for her. She tried now to remember the good parts, but they were overshadowed by the harm—the harm to both of them.

She'd been about to ring Gabby's buzzer. They were driving across the Hudson to nose out the group Mo had told her about. They would attend a meeting. Lily Ann had refused. She was afraid she would lose it.

What had occurred to her was the coincidence. Ginger had given up her occasional performances because her body hurt too much and she'd be depleted for days afterward. Then this thing with Mitch. Were they related? Of course they were related. But how?

Because something was missing in Ginger's life? In Ginger?

Could it be that Jefferson chose Ginger because Ginger couldn't give her what she needed? It sounded like it really was the search she loved, more than Ginger or the other women. Like she really was in love with the seduction, with getting rejected over and over and repeating all the exciting feelings with someone new. What would she do with love if she got it? Be satisfied? Turn it down? Look for more? Even her body, she thought, refused to let go with Ginger. There was a safety in holding back. Now, she saw, she'd let herself in for the biggest danger of all, losing almost thirty years together.

She was doused in a sadness as pervasive as spilled cheap perfume. She'd never needed Ginger to love her; she'd wanted only to be a beggar of love.

During the long nights of her sleepless solitude, she realized that she didn't know whether Ginger had tried and she'd repulsed her with her wandering, or if Ginger was incapable of loving her. Of loving another woman, a man, anyone. If she found Ginger, if Ginger ever came home, could they be fixed? While they were still together, a part of her had looked forward to the blameless end of a relationship so tangled she didn't see a way to unravel it. She should be grateful that Ginger walked out. Then there was the other question—could she even stand to touch Ginger after...after a man. It disgusted her, what men and women did. Would Ginger allow that to happen to her? She didn't even let Jefferson go inside her because it hurt and brought her no pleasure.

On Sundays, long ago, Jefferson would open her eyes toward the bedroom window and the bright or pewter sky over the city. It was morning, it was New York; all she had to do was roll over to Ginger and she'd know she had a perfect life.

She would roll over. Ginger would stir. Jefferson would make sure her hand was warm, then cup it over the ridge of Ginger's hip bone, one of the sexiest parts of a woman's body. She'd learned that if Ginger moved into the palm of her hand, the signal was green. She'd press herself to Ginger's side and move her hand firmly across her belly, then up to the far shoulder and guide her until they were mouth to mouth. Sleepy Ginger would pout into her kisses while Jefferson's hands traveled her body. Biggest morning thrill? When Ginger's light fingers found her back and dug in, encouraging her. Nothing like it. Nothing like it on earth. Were they still on earth?

The long dancer's body was the earth in itself, and Jefferson the explorer. She never wanted to lose this pleasure and always stayed open to new ways, new heights where she could lead them. She heard the music of the night before and let its beat move her. Stroking today, stroking Ginger's face, her arms, her breasts, stroking till that hip bone rose and she met it with her fingertips, stroking down, down the hollow.

Sometimes Jefferson wondered about these magical feelings. Why was she so hung up on giving them to women? What in her makeup brought lovemaking to the forefront of her life? It wasn't orgasm for herself; something in her erupted when she made a woman come, maybe a kind of emotional orgasm.

Ginger wasn't one to get all mushy after sex like so many women seemed to do. Declaring life-long devotion, undying love—all of that. Jefferson was, but never let it out to the other women. That was part of the reason she wished she could finish with Ginger. A feeling of closeness and devotion might wash over her, might take. Would Ginger be repelled by an emotional declaration? As much as she revered Ginger now, it was always a little dicey, knowing where Ginger's boundaries lay. Ginger could be a miser of love.

Some lesbians, she'd found, were so afraid of her passion she had to hide it. She didn't know if they'd had bad experiences with men—or with other women—but she'd had to temper expressions of desire around them, had to move slowly and watch for their eagerness or apprehension. Ginger had no problem with sex, when she allowed it, but emotion sent her scurrying deep inside herself.

She'd have no plan to put her mouth where her hand was, but

would find herself burrowing in, getting her cheeks as wet as she could, breathing in Ginger's sweet-tangy smell, tongue reaching into her as far as it could go. One day she indulged in something she'd never imagined doing, but Ginger's digging fingers told her it was a right move. She thrust to the beat of the music in her head, wondering what Ginger was thinking, aware the roots of her tongue were tiring, wondering if Ginger thought at all at times like these.

She'd asked her what she thought when she was all alone on stage dancing, and Ginger had told her she was high, high, high. Her thoughts were in the heavens. Her thoughts passed way out of words. And that's what she sounded like now, humming, keening real low, little blips of surprise at the sensations, and then it all combined into a resonant, deeply satisfied sound that made Jefferson smile against the soft, relaxed pulp of her girl.

"Orange juice and eggs for a sunny-side-up day!" she'd cried when she entered the kitchen, showered, naked, dry white towel wide like a cape so she could wrap naked Ginger and dance her to the shower. Ginger laughed when she got high-spirited like this, although she had a limited sense of humor; she wasn't good at making laughter, but did give in to it. She'd step in the shower again with Ginger, soap her up, rinse her while Ginger did her own glorious copper hair with green Prell, French-bunning it, ponytailing it, and they'd hug and laugh, slick against each other.

Sundays shone always, even when the weather tried to dim them. She loved crossing town to walk in the park with Ginger. Glowing light shirt, blue jeans, Ginger in loose purples and blues. Years and years of Sundays ahead of them, exploring, lolling, part of the scene, happening on festivals, ball games, lovers. Sunning on the rocks, lesbian reptiles, they called themselves in their early years. Jefferson would climb a tree, Ginger would run off, she'd race to catch up and usually find her at the zoo. They'd buy ice cream, spend a while talking to the animals, everyone smiling around their streak of youth and beauty.

And dancing. Humming and dancing on the paths, on the Great Lawn, Sheep's Meadow. Dancing past the cabs at Eighty-sixth Street, dancing on the bridges, dancing in the fountain, dancing with the Alice in Wonderland statues. It felt like they were still making love Sundays when they used to go out, wherever they went. It was always summer on Sundays, even when they ice-skated at the rink.

She tried not to think about that weekday she came home early and the lovely light-skinned boy Ginger danced with came out of the bedroom. He'd been trying on Ginger's outfits to dance a women's part in a drag ballet. She wouldn't go to see the ballet with Ginger. She'd felt something wrong there. Felt some airy attraction between them. It was the curse of infidelity, she learned that day, to suspect, to worry, to have adoration turn to jealousy in a moment and never go away.

She thought she wanted no walls. But she put them up as often as Ginger, and she didn't know how to knock them down. Clouds over their park, spoiled juice on Sundays. She'd block it from her mind till she saw Ginger flirting with the fairies at a bar. What did she expect? Ginger's father and little brothers doted on her growing up—she still liked the attention of men. That didn't mean she wanted to be with one, that Jefferson wasn't enough.

She'd given Ginger everything she had. Except for the times she frittered it all away.

Maybe she should give it up. Let him have her Ginger. It was obvious that's what Ginger wanted. She shook her head, buzzed the door for Gabby, or Amaretto, to let her in. In the elevator she thought that what Ginger wanted wasn't obvious at all. She had known this woman—if she had known her at all—for thirty years, and nothing about Ginger had signaled this move. Unless she was looking for someone who would—could—appreciate being loved. Unless she was tired of Jefferson's resistance.

Gabby's partner Amaretto was a nonstop creative person, a costume designer by trade, and she had run out of room to display her crafts in their Brooklyn apartment. The walls were hung with masks, the floors dotted with costumes on dressmakers' forms, the furniture draped with patches of remnants that would have made great selections in a fabric shop. Gabby had a big blue recliner and a wide-screen TV. She aimed the remote at a Yankees game and turned the set off, lowering the recliner at the same time.

Amaretto and Gabby had both grown heavy over the years of inventive cooking they did for each other and for their friends. They were known as the gourmet cooks of the crowd. They had a warm, indulgent, laughing relationship and were always bubbling over each other's words and stories. Gabby had stopped drinking before Jefferson—maybe that had made a difference.

"Is that new?" she asked Gabby.

"No," Gabby replied. "I bought it when it first came out in '97. Amaretto had it framed for my birthday."

They stood arm in arm under a NY Liberty Team Show Stoppers poster.

"This is almost as nice as the Lavender Julies Softball poster Angela's Tam made up at the print shop," she teased.

Gabby laughed. "I don't know how you stand to look at that thing on your wall."

"What a roster," Jefferson said. "Sophia Witherspoon, Kym Hampton, Teresa Weatherspoon—Rebecca Lobo!" These were breathtaking athletes. "Too bad our team is—"

"Sucky."

"That's not true anymore," Amaretto called over the kitchen counter where Jefferson had heard her loading dishes and glasses into the dishwasher with an occasional clink. Now Amaretto switched on the dishwasher and the apartment filled with the sound of rushing water.

"They were losing for so long," Gabby complained.

Jefferson had to stop herself from saying, "They're not the only ones." She was remembering all the times she came home from teaching or coaching and Ginger was home too, working in the kitchen, lying on the couch listening to music, or even watching the evening news. Each time it had given her a sense of permanency and rootedness she longed to hold on to forever. Her grand nemesis, her Achilles heel, was herself, so unable to give up cheating. What could she do to make up for that? She had offered more than once to support Ginger. She had the interest from her grandparents' trust fund to supplement her teaching salary.

Of course Ginger had declined. She had always clung to her independence as if afraid that Jefferson wanted to quash it. She thought she loved Ginger's independence. Maybe Ginger had sensed something about her that she didn't know.

She almost laughed to think of all she didn't understand about Ginger. How she adored wearing fancy flip-flops at home. And god-awful plastic shoes to parties or the bar. They were still in Ginger's closet, an exasperating part of Ginger she'd never understood, but loved. Ginger had taken to sneaking new shoes into the house because Jefferson always laughed at the sight of them. Pinks and purples and lime green and coral. Flowered and strapped and sometimes rhinestone-studded. She'd tease

Ginger about having drag-queen feet, but she shouldn't have. To her, the shoes were a femme decoration that filled her with amused appreciation, but to Ginger, this must be the way she coddled her feet, treated them for their gracefulness and coordination and pain. A dancer's feet were her glory and foundation.

"Yo, Jef, where'd you go?" Gabby said.

"Sorry. I was remembering."

"Lunch is made," Amaretto said. "Enough for all of us."

"Thank you." She gave Amaretto an enthusiastic hug. "But I don't know where we're going."

"Not Jersey City?" Gabby asked.

"There's an office for JONAH, but I couldn't find a street address."

Amaretto said, "That leaves us with the Paras' summer place."

"Up the Hudson. In Treadwell."

"We'll ask around," Amaretto said. "If we don't find anything, we've had a nice picnic outing up the Hudson."

"I checked an online phone book. Nothing listed for Para. Who knows if that's even the parents' name."

She'd rented a car for the day, and Gabby had to explore it thoroughly before getting in. "You think we're going off-road?" Gabby asked.

"I have no clue. I rented the SUV in case."

"Man, I hope so. We're ready for it. Am, can we have one of these some day?"

"Sure, after you drag me to Cartier to buy me a diamond ring."

"This would be more practical."

Amaretto laughed. "In Wyoming."

"Isn't that over the county line?"

"Yo, did you catch my girl Mariska on the tube this week?"

Amaretto laughed. "Here comes the *Law and Order:* SVU fan club," she said.

"Hey, Gab," Jefferson teased, "I could watch Hargitay all night, every night, but D'Onofrio and Erbe are sooo much cooler in *Criminal Intent.* They actually think." And the two were off on their usual running argument about the merits of the shows.

Bantering with these friends made the drive very much like going on a picnic, and Jefferson actually found herself taking pleasure in the ride—when she wasn't worrying about what they would find in

Treadwell. If they learned where the Paras' place was and if Ginger was there, then what? Would she barge in to interrupt them in bed? Her girl's hands on someone else? No, she didn't want to see that. Sit in a living room talking about it? She would be speechless. Slit Mitchell's tires and leave hate notes?

She remembered the night she went to see a performance Ginger was producing. Ginger was taking money at the door. Between sales, Jefferson said, "You told me I'd have to stop drinking for you to stay. I've stopped. Come home with me tonight."

Ginger had slept at her parents' apartment all week. Jefferson couldn't even remember now which transgression it had been that had driven Ginger out. Jefferson had been spending her evenings at AA meetings and going out for coffee with other alcoholics.

The pain in Ginger's eyes was wringing her heart. She'd been about to say something and Jefferson saw her curl forward over her pain. She was going to say no forever this time. "I don't want to live without you, Ginger. You're the one I'm supposed to be with."

She'd thought the man who'd approached them was trying to slip past Ginger. He put a hand on Ginger's shoulder and Jefferson tensed, ready to throw it off if Ginger gave the slightest sign of fear.

The man spoke. "Who's this, babe?" He turned Ginger toward him with his big hand.

Ginger's look of pain turned to sadness, a vast and agonized sadness that offered no hope for Jefferson.

"Oh, no," Jefferson said in a hoarse voice she'd never heard herself use before. She'd been standing on a fragile cliff and now fell. Her heart, her soul, her hopes were far from the safe branches she sped past. Ginger bent her head in confirmation and walked off with the man.

Still in free fall, Jefferson couldn't look away from the sight of Ginger and the man, willed her body to be still, the body that only understood movement. If she did move, it would be true and the fall would go on and on. She'd rather live with this paralysis than live without Ginger, go on into life with the knowledge of what Ginger might have done, an incurable anguish that led her, once again, to the comfort of Irish whiskey.

Later, Ginger assured her that the man was one of the backers of the performance, a friend and a dance instructor like herself. She believed Ginger, but she knew what she'd seen, knew that Ginger had been a dance step away from trying to find with the man what she had not found with Jefferson. She blamed herself and had no idea how to stop her cycle of transgressions.

"Jef," Gabby said sharply. "The exit." She turned to exchange a glance with Amaretto.

"No, I'm not avoiding the exit. The memories—I don't know how to block out the memories," Jefferson told them with a small laugh. In truth, her hands were cold and her jaw a little sore from tension. She hadn't wanted to relive that scene today, or ever. She'd gone back to AA and Ginger had returned to her again.

Treadwell turned out to be a town built on recreational pursuits. Between the river and a state park, there were boat ramps, bait shops, and summer bungalows; a few motels and bed-and-breakfasts, campgrounds and trailer parks. The summer traffic was like driving in a pot of glue— they couldn't get out of it. The downtown consisted of four blocks ranged around a small square of green with a playground. They spotted a hardware shop, a T-shirt store, three real-estate offices, a tiny post office, several antique shops, a drugstore and gift shop, and a gas station and convenience store combined.

"Where's the sign, 'This way to the Paras' summer place'?" Gabby asked Jefferson.

It was a weekday. Jefferson had taken off because Gabby and Amaretto both worked most weekends. They found the town hall on the other side of the gas station, but the whole place was shut down for the noon hour. While Jefferson and Gabby discussed what to do until one thirty, Amaretto walked into the nearest real-estate office and chitchatted the guy into telling them the Paras had a small place overlooking the river north on the main street.

"You're the femme," she told Amaretto. "You can charm them, can get the job done. I don't see why you stay with us."

"Butches are irresistible," Gabby said.

"Obviously that doesn't apply to all of us."

Gabby sighed beside her as Jefferson went around the block and headed north.

"We're kind of nice at home anyway. Out in a crowd, sometimes I feel bad for Am, having to introduce me instead of the handsome hunk she could have on her arm."

"Take that back, sweet-butt. You are my handsome hunk."

Gabby smiled. "All I'm saying is, you femmes could have it easier if you switched to their side. Maybe Ginger, you know, wants to take the easy way out for a season or two."

"Hey, Gab, Gab," she said, tapping Gabby's thigh. "That's not how you treat the people you love."

"I know. She must be crazy. I mean, really, like a screw came loose." Gabby peered at Jefferson. "I never would have thought Ginger would do this in a million years. I can't get over it. I mean it makes me think if she would, then—"

"No," Amaretto assured Gabby. "Not if you beat me. Not if you ran around on me. Not if you insisted on doing all the cooking."

"I don't guess we'll have to test you, then," Gabby said. "But, listen, Jef, whatever pushed her over the edge, I am so sorry."

She sighed and nodded. Tears threatened her eyes.

"He said to watch for the super-tall hedge along the road—there," Amaretto said, pointing left. Jefferson drove slowly past, unable to see anything beyond the wall of green.

"These people are into privacy," Gabby noted. Jefferson had pulled ahead of the traffic and now slowed at a driveway. "Not as much privacy as Mitchell's brother described. I don't see a gate or a glass-topped wall. What a liar," she said, coming to a stop. The driveway cut back on the other side of the thick and carefully barbered hedges. "We would have seen more if we'd rented a boat."

"And a periscope," Gabby added.

"Do I have to do everything for you two butches? Drive up the driveway."

Gabby loudly sucked in her breath. "What if they're there?"

Amaretto twisted her neck to look at Gabby. "Honey-baby, what if they're not?"

Jefferson turned in and followed the graveled drive.

"Can't you stop that crunching?" Gabby complained. "They'll hear us."

But the house was perched half a lot away, right over the river, and a raucous helicopter made its way upstate, following the course of the water. The noonday sun highlighted the house, making even its forest green siding bright. She stopped the SUV before rounding the next corner. Did this place remind Ginger of their times on the lake in New Hampshire? Did this man make life half as sweet as it had been for them in the early years? Did Ginger know she was tearing the skin off Jefferson's heart?

The lake had been a still place, peace radiating. The river here never stopped. It was tidal this close to the Atlantic, running north, south, north again, running, running, running. Like a dancer, like an athlete, the river was all about movement.

"Jefferson?" Amaretto asked.

"In a game," she answered, "you have to know when to run for the base, the basket, the ball, and when to stop and watch." The pain was incredible, even worse than 9/11. She'd have to go. Leave the apartment, leave her job, leave the city, leave her friends behind and go where thoughts of Ginger weren't as common as streetlights.

No one was at the house. There was no garage, no car in the driveway. A phone book lay on the porch in its dirty plastic wrapper, and last fall's leaves were bunched against the front door where it looked as if they'd huddled all winter. She put the car in reverse. She was both relieved and disappointed. "Let's find a spot by the river and have our picnic there."

CHAPTER TWENTY-SIX

Was there anyone lonelier than a lesbian on her own at a men's bar on a cold night, Jefferson wondered. Then she answered herself: yes, there was. It was a lesbian listening to the hum of a microwave oven, glass platform rotating under a Lean Cuisine for one. She'd had to get out of the apartment.

She'd managed to get the last stool at the end of the bar where she could see this whole room and the entryway everyone would have to pass through to get to the dance floor upstairs. She didn't know how many men's bars there were in the city, or what her chances were of finding Mitch, or someone who knew Mitch, but her friends had found nothing. She'd been cruising for him nearly every night for the past two and a half weeks. He wouldn't be able to stay away from other men, no matter what was going on between him and Ginger. Mitch adored men, spent every penny he had on them, and talked incessantly about his heartthrobs, current and past.

She'd tipped the bartenders well with each soft drink she ordered, but none had opened up about having seen Mitch. For a while, her search had kept her hope alive, but tonight she questioned why she was bothering.

Because you love her, she told herself. Because you want to catch him, she heard her mind admit. Catch him and, what, expose him to Ginger? When she really examined her motive, though, she knew it had more to do with some kind of ownership. Ginger was hers, body and soul. She would find her and get her to return. She needed Ginger. Without her Jefferson feared becoming a cipher in the city. For all of her absence from Jefferson's life, Ginger was central to all she did. Sure, she was free now to do anything or see anyone she wanted to, but Ginger had acted all of these years as a springboard, the home fire, an anchor, her main point of reference.

She might have done her laundry alone, but some things of Ginger's were always mixed in with her own. She might have eaten dinner alone, but she always cooked extra for Ginger to eat when she got in from work, or she ate what Ginger had not. Ginger was the center of her life. She'd considered posting her picture among the others at Ground Zero, because that's still how she felt, like a disaster had hit.

The next bar was no more promising so she changed tacks and went back out in the bitter cold to a mixed place on the East Side. For all she knew, Ginger and Mitch both went to the bars. Or were into threesomes. Or never went out at all.

She slopped some of her soda when the guy said hello. Looking behind, she confirmed that she didn't know this short, pudgy, older African American man.

"Don't look at me like maybe you should call the bartender for protection," he said. "You look like you need a friend. My name is Ellis."

She found herself telling him the whole story.

"Gay Pride was the worst for me," Ellis said. "We lived in a medium-size city and we'd been working to put together a pride day for-ever. Then he fell in love with one of the other organizers. All three of us wanted pride to happen and we made it happen. But to see him marching hand in hand with someone else—girl, do you know how that tore out my insides?"

"This is the first time I've wanted a drink in a long time," she said, fingering her chin. "I want to cry into my beer and get stinking drunk with you."

"Naughty, naughty," said Ellis. "I didn't come over here to knock you off the wagon. How about if I put you in a cab and out of temptation's way?"

She reached over and gave him a little touch on his collar. "How could you not know Mitchell?" She described him.

"Oh," Ellis squealed, "you mean Mitch the Bitch!"

"He looks like I said?"

"Yes. I heard he was experimenting with a woman. He used to have the wildest parties at his place upstate."

"Did you ever go?"

Ellis laughed. "Go? I'd stay for days at a time, hon. We used to call it gayboy Para-dise."

"Do you know where he is now?"

"You think he's got her up there?"

"No. I went and checked."

He was gazing at her as if sizing her up. "I'd guess you can take care of yourself, but honey, Mitch the Bitch can turn mean in a heartbeat. Why do you think we call him that?"

"All the more reason to find him."

"All right then. But be careful."

"If I had a gun I'd tote it along—"

"Tote it? What are you, Cowboy Jefferson?" Ellis said. "Can I change your focus a bit? I want to introduce you to someone—I saw her come in."

She crossed her arms in front of herself as if to ward off a vampire. "No! No matchmaking."

"Matchmaking? What do you take me for? I have a social life to keep up and she looks like she's free for babysitting."

She shook her head, but she was smiling.

Ellis hugged her. "I know what you need, girlfriend, so you sit back and let your Uncle Ellis make it happen."

She was surprised to see that the very young woman Ellis brought back with him was wearing a skirt and even more surprised when she felt herself snap right out of her funk.

"This is Brandi. Brandi, this is Jefferson."

"How old are you?" Jefferson asked. She was being tired and peevish, but really wasn't in the mood to charm an eighteen-year-old into bed. Let someone else teach the kid the ropes.

"Ta," Ellis said, and swept away like a lady in a skirt with a train.

"Twenty-six," Brandi answered.

"You sure?"

Brandi said she was. Jefferson told her to sit down, then went and got Brandi another drink. It was polite to do so, she told herself. How much money could a twenty-six-year-old have?

As it turned out, Brandi had no reluctance to tell her about her cool job at a start-up software company for $55,000 per year and many other details of her life, her family, her inner thoughts, her sexuality, and all of her past lovers' names. She invited herself home with Jefferson, had a cab called, and snuggled close to her on the drive.

Brandi was little and cute and funny and aggressively worshipful. How could she resist? Upstairs the woman peered at everything, as if to memorize the details of an older dyke's magical life. Jefferson emerged from a quick shower to find Brandi stretched naked on the bed, smiling and waiting.

Jefferson sat on the edge of the bed and stroked Brandi's face. "Was I ever this soft?" she asked aloud.

"You're still soft," Brandi said, and gave a quiet laugh, then placed Jefferson's hands where she wanted, rubbing against them with an arrhythmic excitement that felt fairly frantic to Jefferson. Brandi's rhythm seemed out of sync with her own. Was it possible that Brandi had no rhythm? Could she dance?

Still feeling tired, Jefferson made a few half-hearted moves to get control of the situation before she gave up and let Brandi arrange, then rearrange them as if to some feng-shui pattern, making little chortles and mews all the while. She hated the term, but once in a while she'd found herself with a woman who had to control what was happening, who ran the fuck from the bottom. Was anyone more frustrated than a butch thwarted in her lovemaking?

Brandi moved two fingers inside her. Jefferson stayed her hands and said into her ear, "I'm more your outside-stimulation kind of woman."

When Brandi put tongue to her and manipulated her at that jagged irregular pace, she felt no pleasure, but Brandi came within seconds after Jefferson's middle finger made contact. Came with a kind of shimmy, saying, "Mmm, mmm, mmm," like she'd discovered a particularly good flavor of ice cream.

"Jefferson, Jefferson. That was so good."

Jefferson felt like a giant vibrator, set to high speed. Surely now, after her release, Brandi would chill out, stop fussing over Jefferson and let Jefferson make love to her. It's what turned her on most. Or maybe, she thought with a growing panic, Brandi was always like this. How could she get her to leave tonight? Leave now? Brandi was one too many in a long life of one too manys.

She was going to tame this one before she left, though. She kissed her and touched her and let Brandi do her thing, but this time, when Brandi had found a height of excitement Jefferson recognized by her sounds and moving hips, she gently encircled Brandi's wrists with her hands and held them down above the woman's head. Brandi squirmed and wiggled in pleasure, as if she'd hoped Jefferson would be at least this forceful. Her last act was to lower herself onto Brandi's mouth. The girl whipped Jefferson's clitoris around with the point of her tongue until Jefferson, by meeting the tongue at her own rhythm, flattened it into a soft round shape she could rub against until she came, no matter what Brandi wanted.

After Brandi left, a few hours later, Jefferson felt empty, empty, and wandered around the apartment. It too felt empty, empty without Ginger.

CHAPTER TWENTY-SEVEN

She couldn't imagine Ginger sitting with the women in a synagogue. Surely she wouldn't go so far as to agree that Mitchell was better than her because he was male. He didn't even have the courage to stay gay.

Her mind played with this question and with all her questions about Ginger the same way her tongue toyed with the space in a tooth left by a dislodged filling. She couldn't even fill the space with other women. After that irritating night with Brandi, she'd lost the desire for them.

Three times her phone had rung in the past week and the caller had hung up. Could that have been Ginger, interrupted while trying to reach her? She refused to let her escape next time and, as a consequence, felt like a fool more than once when she announced abruptly that she would meet the caller at their bench that Saturday at one o'clock. Ginger would know she meant the bench by Morris Park in the Bronx where they spent so much time together when parted for the school holidays. Gabby, Lily Ann, and a fellow teacher had all been confused at her desperate shouting into the cell phone when they called.

It had been a magic, welcoming bench. Back in college, Jefferson would ride the train up to Dutchess, do Thanksgiving or Christmas or Easter dinner with her parents and grandparents, then take off for the city as soon as she could. She'd stay in her grandparents' Manhattan apartment. When Ginger was able to get away from her family for only a little while, Jefferson would hop the subway and they would meet at the bench in Morris Park. She remembered one day when they sat there in heavy coats, boots, gloves, and hats, lifting their feet to offload snow and brushing it off each other's shoulders. While gay lib had touched their world, it hadn't made them feel like they could do anything but hold hands if they didn't want to get beaten up. She had probably heard every anecdote Ginger could remember from her childhood during those rendezvous. And to this day she could re-experience the deep, but romantic melancholy of their partings, the sight of Ginger walking away though the snowflakes, apartment buildings ringing the island of their park, the twilight fading and lamplight spotlighting her until she was gone.

She went up to the Bronx on the next Saturday morning and treated herself to pizza at Patricia's, some of the best in the city. She was glad to be doing this. Inaction left her feeling helpless. Feeling helpless risked a mood of disaster.

By twelve thirty she was on the green wooden bench, a black iron-rail fence at her back, the *Village Voice* dance page open on her lap. In her brown bomber jacket, the leather worn to tan in some spots, cracked beyond the help of regular applications of saddle soap, she skimmed the paper for Ginger's name as she skimmed the street for her face. Did she really think for a minute that Ginger would show up? They'd had such fun here during college, sneaking around, stealing touches, scanning passersby for other gay women. What had they thought? That they could follow them to some secret meeting place? Something like that. Back in the 1970s there was still a thrill to the whole being-gay thing, like they were some kind of outlaws clothed in nothing but their sexuality.

She waited, nodding greetings to walkers, especially the kids, some of whom might have been in her classes if her school was in the Bronx. The neighborhood was still heavily Italian and they had always felt relatively safe from observation here, an area seldom visited by the Quinns, who lived several blocks away. On Saturday afternoons the neighborhood was hopping. In the three hours she spent sitting, pacing, remembering, and dreaming, she searched hundreds of faces. None of them was Ginger's. As the sun moved lower in the sky, she became chilled and paced back and forth in front of the bench to keep warm, as miserable as she had ever felt in her life. When the streetlights popped on, she left her station and walked back to Patricia's. She got two more pizzas, packed in dry ice, then rode the subway back to Manhattan, feeling like a nitwit. She'd gone all the way into Manhattan and was halfway through walking to the apartment, snow flurries making the sidewalks a little slick, before it occurred to her that she might not have been alone. Had Ginger driven by in a cab, a bus? Had she approached from behind and withdrawn? Maybe, if she did this every week, Ginger would come forward. And maybe she had lost her mind.

There were no more hang-up calls. She'd e-mailed Dutchess to confirm that neither Angela nor Tam was trying to reach her. They concluded the person on the phone had probably been a complete stranger, misdialing and frightened away by her mad invitations to the bench. Nevertheless, the next week she went back. It rained that second Saturday and the wait was even gloomier than the first, except for the pizza breakfast. Sometimes she thought she was acting out a fantasy, a screwed-up lesbian version of *An Affair to Remember*, and sometimes she felt the pull to that bench so strongly she knew it had been Ginger trying to reach her.

Why was she even doing this? She'd tried so hard to be what Ginger wanted that she'd lost herself along the way. She shook her head. What Ginger wanted was, to Jefferson, a moving target. As if, she thought, as if I knew—could ever know—how to make Ginger happy.

She developed a cold after the trip, which seemed stuck at the bottom of her throat, deeply rooted, both itchy and painful. Cough as she might, she couldn't dislodge it. Tonight she'd use Vicks, but not today, not when she might see Ginger. She'd had caller ID installed on her phone at home and call forwarding to her cell. She held the cell in her gloved hand, inside her jacket pocket, ready in case Ginger phoned.

She was at the bench over two hours that third Saturday, using tissue after tissue to staunch the runny nose she'd finally developed, when Mitchell Para, in a long black overcoat, jaywalked toward her.

Rage made her stand; she almost left, but she felt so weak from being sick and, really, what choice did she have?

He stood in front of her.

"Where is she?"

"Home. With her family."

She didn't know how to respond.

"She's sick, Jefferson."

"Sick? How?" An icy bitterness spread through her chest. She hated what he was saying, hated that he, his history with Ginger so relatively recent, knew more than she did. She grabbed the lapels of his fancy coat. "What did you do to her?"

Mitchell pulled back. "Chill, girlfriend. Let's not get into recriminations. She needs us. Both of us. She doesn't want to die in her childhood bedroom in the Bronx."

"Die? She's going to die?"

Why did it seem like Mitchell got some satisfaction from telling her, "She's been very sick."

"There was nothing wrong with her when she was home. Nothing," she emphasized.

"Don't look at me like I gave her something." Mitchell wrapped his hands around his upper arms. "It was an aneurysm." His teeth chattered when he spoke.

She was trembling with anger. She wanted to hurt him with her fists. "And it didn't kill her?"

He sat quickly next to her on the bench, his coat pulled close around his thighs. "Listen, Jefferson, it's not what you think. Nothing happened between Ginger and me. We thought it might, but no, it was a last struggle with our own natures. Meanwhile, she'd been holding her stomach off and on for weeks, and I thought it was because of the fight she was having inside. Finally she admitted to a tremendous pain in her gut and down her legs. She was nauseous and I could hear her in the bathroom throwing up violently in the night. I knew it was no little bug. A few nights ago she said her heart was doing a NASCAR. She felt all cold. I didn't even call an ambulance, broke every speed record getting her to the hospital. They did the surgery immediately."

"Did it hit her brain?"

"No. It was…" he said it slowly, as if the words were foreign to his tongue, "it was an abdominal aortic aneurysm. They said she can recover completely."

"And she wants to see me?" she asked, furious that she had to ask Mitchell what her Ginger wanted.

He looked away. "Not exactly, but I know Ginger's miserable in her parents' apartment." He seemed to take a deep breath before asking, "You want her back, right? Couldn't she move back home with you?"

"I can't believe I'm standing here talking to you like you have equal stake in Ginger. I've been with her almost thirty years and you, next to that, you're nothing to her."

His look seemed to hold both pity and disgust. "It wasn't long, but I was absolutely with her. Focused on her. Faithful to her in every way."

He knew that wasn't something she'd been able to give Ginger until recently. Or maybe gotten from her. What had Ginger given Mitchell?

"You need to understand," he said. "Ginger's a performer, like me. I know her through and through even without your thirty years."

"Right. You're Mitchell the elusive. I remember. A typical dancer. Focused on yourselves, your careers, only half there for us mortals." He arranged his face into a look of deep regret. "You want to bail," she said.

"Not at all. Ginger needs you. Needs us."

"Any particular reason she's not moving in with you?"

"Jefferson, she doesn't want me. I was, I don't know—her midlife crisis, I suppose. When she heard you were seeing some woman again she lost it."

She pounded her fists on her thighs. "I wasn't seeing anyone. I was making amends. It's part of living sober. It was something I did to be more well for Ginger."

She remembered practically begging Ginger to get checkups, and Ginger, who never did want to pay for health insurance, promising to go and then, caught up in student rehearsals and performances and all the administrative details of running a school, neglecting her health year after year. A memory was coming back to her. Hadn't Ginger once told her about aneurysms running in her family? Someone—her grandfather had dropped dead of one, and an aunt, really young too, younger than Ginger. She was lucky to be alive. And now, out of nowhere, Jefferson had the choice of nursing Ginger back to life or never seeing her again. Some choice when she was trying to accept that Ginger didn't want her.

She shook her head. "You wanted Ginger enough to lure her away from me, but not enough to give up your sweet little career for her."

"You're right," he answered. "I'm as self-absorbed as Ginger. It goes with the territory."

"Self-absorbed? No, my Ginger isn't that bad."

"Yes, she was, Jefferson. Is. And has always felt guilty about it, about not giving you enough of herself."

"She told you that?"

Mitchell nodded and rose as if to go.

She was stunned by the news of Ginger's feelings of guilt. Ginger knew she'd been holding back from her. They'd both held back. Poor Ginger. Was that something they could fix? She realized that hope was raging in her heart again. And she hated it. Hope was a golf ball. Too much of the time you lost it in a sandpit, a pond, or the woods, but once in a lifetime you swung a crazy long shot and got a hole in one.

Almost to herself she said, "When I was younger I swear I had no clue what was right and what was wrong, but now, Mitchell," she looked up at him, "I think you and I both know exactly what we need to do."

"You're right, Jefferson. I've learned where I belong and who I'm really responsible for."

As Mitchell darted away through the traffic, she wished she carried a stash of poison darts to fling into his back. Damn Ginger. She could have said something, could have tried to work it out. How many times had she berated Ginger in her head for letting her get away with sleeping around on her? Now she knew Ginger was so involved in herself she simply hadn't been paying attention. It was funny how much she was like Jefferson's mom, both there and not there: the perfect lover if you didn't mind getting your love at arm's length.

Mitchell had taken the path; Jefferson leapt the iron rail and jogged to the street. Finding a cab near the Quinns' building would be nearly impossible, but Ginger was going home with her. Today, if she could swing that hole in one.

CHAPTER TWENTY-EIGHT

Ginger was still able to get around without help when Jefferson took her up to the lake. It hadn't happened right away, but then the pain returned. Ginger thought she had cancer because she could feel some sort of mass inside, unlike before, when she'd only had pain. Why hadn't they taken out the tumor when she'd undergone surgery, she asked Jefferson by phone. Ginger was still at her parents' apartment, trying to get strong enough to go back to work. She refused to move back in with Jefferson, who was working full-time, when her mother was home all day and could help her.

It was May before she agreed to go to the lake with Jefferson for a week or two. Away from the city, who knew, Ginger said, she might be 100 percent again. The damn city doctors didn't know what they were doing. There was a ball of something in there, she could point to the exact spot, but she was damned if she'd go back to a cutter. That's all they wanted to do: cut, cut, cut.

She knew Ginger well enough to see that she was in denial and that her anger at the surgeon came from fear, but she'd gone online and researched her condition. She had to agree that it sounded like a simplistic diagnosis, but she was no doctor. Maybe blood-pressure medication and getting away from stress was just what Ginger needed. It couldn't hurt.

As for being together, they hadn't talked about Ginger's little getaway, nor had Ginger been in touch with their friends. She had no clue what was going on inside that gorgeous head. They had only seen each other in luncheonettes near the Quinns' apartment on Saturdays, but they talked on the phone a lot, hours at a time some nights. With Ginger so removed, she was in full seduction mode again and had no interest in going anywhere else to be with anyone else.

On the way to the lake, where Jefferson had taken no other woman, Ginger insisted that Jefferson let her do some of the driving. It might tire her too much, but it seemed important for Ginger to see herself without limits, so Jefferson stayed out of it. She watched Ginger's hands on the steering wheel now, her fingers as thin as they had been when she'd gotten together with her in college over twenty years ago. They'd lost the classical station a while ago and were listening to an NPR blues show. These were a dancer's hands, deliberately expressive when Ginger moved them; still as sculpture otherwise. Movement had always been Ginger's language as well as Jefferson's; she wasted neither words nor motion. So they were quiet on the ride north. Five wordless hours by Ginger's side was more pleasure than five years with anyone else.

They hadn't been lovers for such a long time, hadn't even touched. Jefferson couldn't stop herself from sighing. She had messed up one time too many. She didn't like to think about the gap in her life between Ginger's desperate exit and the diagnosis that brought them together again. She'd cried about it in their doctor's office, while Ginger was dressing in another room. Dr. Fried had offered to prescribe something to make it easier to help Ginger through her recovery, while emphasizing that recovery wasn't certain with this illness. Jefferson had always quit taking meds before, refusing to admit that her blue times were something she couldn't handle on her own. This time, she started taking Zoloft and could feel its buffering effect.

Ginger drove them out of Laconia and north along Lake Winnipesaukee. Jefferson noted all the changes since she'd last visited. The lakes region, once protected by the old money that had developed it as resort communities, was selling out to the condo-hungry and the manufactured-home retirees from Massachusetts.

"There it is," she said. As always the pleasure of her first glimpse of the vast blueness of Lake Winnipesaukee licked right up through her innards like attraction to a new woman. One breath of this air and she seemed to breathe out the worst of her awful spurts of despondency.

"How far to Pipsborough now? It's been so long since I was last here," Ginger said.

Jefferson reached to Ginger, touched her gently, and pointed. God, she loved this woman still. She could touch everyone else she cared about, but she'd ruined Ginger and her for touching, for much of anything. "We're on the outskirts. Go up over the hill. I was thinking that it wouldn't need much flooding to make Saturday Lake part of

Winnipesaukee. I wonder if global warming will do something like that. Make the lakes region one big lake."

"Oh, I remember that restaurant. They forgot to thaw the lobster tails," Ginger said with a little laugh.

She laughed too, but remembered how cranky Ginger had been over the lobster. She'd slept out on the cold porch, leaving Ginger fussing in the bed in the then-unheated cottage. "Fine dining is not the lake's forte. That's why we brought groceries."

"And bakery. What did you get?"

"I went to that Austrian place on Ninth Avenue. They had the Viennese cake you like."

"Sure! The Sacher? With chocolate ganache?"

"That creamy icing."

"I can have all the chocolate I want, but you'll have to eat the icing, Jef, you poor thing. The doctor said fat-free food or die. You can't imagine, anyway, the nausea I felt when it happened. At least I know the symptoms now."

"Poor Ginger. I'm so glad, so glad…"

Ginger looked at her and gave a nod as she turned her eyes back to the road.

Jefferson pressed her hands together, words pooling just behind her tongue, enough words to drown her. She remembered where they were and said only, "Oh, hey. Go to the right after that frost-heaves sign."

Bad choice of landmarks, she thought. She hoped the cake wouldn't make Ginger throw up, as more and more foods seemed to. Ginger still talked in terms of food sensitivities and allergies, but Jefferson suspected there was a bit of food anxiety going on. She was talking about a macrobiotic diet. Was she afraid of sex too? She longed to reach over and touch Ginger's hair as she always had, but she'd done it once and Ginger had flinched enough to notice. No, she'd hurt Ginger too many times to expect touch. But once. If they could make love once, she knew it would knit up some open sores. Could love ease Ginger's blood pressure? Strengthen other weaknesses in her arteries?

Then she remembered how long it had been since they made love. As she struggled to stop drinking, her mind wasn't on sex. Ginger had never been much of an initiator. When Jefferson emerged from her fog, filled with energy and a new enthusiasm for life—how could she have missed the everyday pleasures of baking a cake, reading a big fat book, sitting through a whole Yankees game on TV and talking with

Gabby about it later? Her body seemed to cry out for Ginger's touch, but Ginger, she realized, had always been sparing with her touches, and now—did Ginger like the sober Jefferson? Had it only been the inebriated, chemically altered Jefferson she found attractive?

Ginger turned into the driveway to the Jefferson family's bungalow. The ground was all pine needles. Jefferson opened her window for the spicy fragrance. The sight of Saturday Lake made her feel like she had arrived home. Ginger turned off the engine. Somewhere below them, far out on the lake, a boat was speeding. Otherwise there wasn't a sound. For several minutes, they sat in the car. Silence was a luxury after the city.

She looked over at Ginger and saw her eyes were closed. "Gi?" she said.

Ginger started, as if she'd been asleep, and smiled with her eyes still closed. "So peaceful."

Jefferson instructed her, "Stay put. I'll carry things in and get a fire started in the woodstove."

Ginger stirred. "I'll help."

In her best gym-teacher's voice, a voice she'd perfected through decades of teaching and coaching, Jefferson repeated, "Stay put."

"Yes, teach," she agreed with what sounded like both resignation and weary pleasure.

Jefferson was surprised, and this was the first sign that she should be as worried as she was.

Later, she settled Ginger on the couch under one of her grandfather's old green army blankets, smoothing back her hair. She realized she was studying Ginger's face, looking for signs of illness. She had to stop that. The blanket's smell brought back the feel of itchy warm wool on chilly New Hampshire vacation nights. God, she loved it here, especially with Ginger, regardless of the reason. She pulled the door quietly shut behind her, walked out from under the trees and down the sloped lawn to the lake. It was that golden time of late afternoon when sunbeams fanned like spotlights through the branches along the shoreline. She sat on a boulder at the edge of the little cove, the sandy beach at her feet no bigger than the floor of a two-man camping tent, and listened to the lake water lapping at her toes. The summer people weren't up yet, it was too late for anybody but wild-turkey hunters, and the fishers seemed to cling to the full rivers and streams in spring. The neighbors on one side, behind an old low stone wall, would return from Florida after Memorial

Day. The year-round people on the other side were the town veterinarian and his wife/receptionist.

Jefferson had taken time off work to pick up Ginger. She had been afraid that Ginger would change her mind about coming up. She wished she could keep her here with her forever—which didn't promise to be a very long time—but she wanted Ginger near the city hospitals, and Ginger had gotten tight with one of her hospital nurses. Three of her old dance students helped with the housekeeping, while Ginger's many relatives from the outer boroughs kept her supplied with casseroles and stews and baked goods. Once a week Mrs. Quinn did her special "Ginger shopping" with the younger brother, who still lived at home and carried the shopping bags of food. They got Ginger out for exercise and fresh air. If that meant walking to the nearest bench in the park and watching the Rollerbladers, dog walkers, and joggers rush by while Ginger and her mother, eighty-three, rested for the three-block trip back, that was fine.

Jefferson hated to cook and wasn't very good at it, so for the trip north she rented a car and stocked it the way Emmy and Jarvy always did: ordered a ham with scalloped potatoes and vegetables from Trimmings to Go. The fragrance of the honeyed ham had made her long for dinner despite—Ginger laughing at how wicked she felt eating fast food—getting drive-through Dairy Queen for lunch.

The lake water was still. The green trees, lawns, and white cottages that lined it were interrupted here and there with trees in various stages of maturing: hawthorns, hickories, maple, oak bunched together like femmes dressing for a pride dance. Wooden oars knocked against metal oarlocks as two kids in fleece jackets, collars up, rowed an aluminum boat along the shore. She was chilly and needed a nap herself. She and Ginger could walk back down to the water tomorrow, in the bright of day. Inside, Ginger's flip-flops flapped.

It was five thirty that evening when Ginger said, "You snore now."

Her back was to Ginger as she hung her bomber jacket on a hook. She was glad Ginger couldn't see her smile. Ginger had been pretty loud herself. Had Mitchell snored, she wondered, a dull pain entering the area of her heart.

She'd woken in the soft leather easy chair that had been her grandfather's, doing that—snoring through her nap. She turned to Ginger and explained, deeply embarrassed, "It's this extra weight I've put on." Since she didn't sleep with anyone these days, she hadn't known. The truth was, she didn't even sleep with herself. A premenopausal insomnia had fallen on her, and lying awake through much of the night had become yet another problem to solve with an early retirement. She closed the curtain in the window next to her chair and pulled the floor-lamp chain. The room was luminous with a warm yellow blush. "Did I wake you?"

"No. I got chilly."

She sat up to tend to the fire.

Ginger startled her again. "I put more wood on."

Through the stove window she could see flames working at the wood. She wanted to hold Ginger, to make her warm. "I need to bring in a supply for the night."

Ginger picked up the book that she'd set facedown on her chest. Would Jefferson have time to finish it before Ginger—no, of course she'd finish. After dinner she planned to read aloud to Ginger from *The Hitchhiker's Guide to the Galaxy*, a book Ginger had raved about ten years earlier, one of the times they had tried being together again. She'd heard that laughter was healing. Could more laughter, or less cheating on Ginger, have prevented the aneurysm?

She rose quickly—before she did something crazy like put her arms around Ginger and keep her close forevermore—and grabbed the barn coat hanging at the door. Outside, she dragged the lake-chilled twilight air in through her nose and pushed it from her lungs, hard. How did anyone get through the mishmash of hope and finality that was a brush with death? Would she talk about it? Would Ginger remain in denial and pretend it hadn't happened?

One minute she was thinking that maybe Ginger would get back with her, and the next she was imagining the world without Ginger in it.

Her father kept the wheelbarrow upended against the front row of wood in the shed. She slammed firewood with satisfying whacks into the wheelbarrow until it was piled high, then pushed it to the porch steps. Ginger opened the door for her and held it while Jefferson toted in armloads of logs. She thought she might as well get enough for Saturday night too and went back to fill the wheelbarrow again, gentler with the wood this time. When she returned, Ginger was sweeping up fallen bark and log dust, as she had dozens of times before when they'd spent time in New Hampshire. Why did Ginger have to get sick? Had all Ginger's shut-down feelings corroded her arteries? If only Ginger could let go, be loving and cuddly like she'd been at first, before she'd opened the school, back when she still had dreams of performing, when the world was filled with promises instead of late-night bookkeeping, parental demands, kids' fickle attendance, all the bottom lines of being grown that had robbed them of the childhood of their love. Ginger got too serious on her.

She berated herself. It wasn't Ginger's fault, but her own. All the heartache she'd caused finally burst open inside Ginger and almost killed her.

Jefferson didn't sleep much that night. A splinter in the palm of her hand throbbed. Every time she woke up from the discomfort her brain got back on the why-Ginger track, with links to the it's-all-my-fault siding and the Ginger's-going-to-beat-it station stop. Instead of getting up to serve Ginger breakfast in bed as she'd planned, she didn't awaken until the sun was high outside her bedroom window and Ginger sat on the porch wrapped in the army blanket, sound asleep, quietly snoring, a mug and a saucer with a smear of cream cheese and some poppy seeds from a bagel on the porch rail. The smell of coffee had not wakened her because Ginger was sticking to herbal teas, which were better for her blood pressure. They'd brought a whole braid of garlic because that was supposed to be good too, and they had to replace salt. Ginger was adding brewer's yeast to everything but the chocolate cake.

It was noon by the time they strolled down the hill. Gentle, regular exercise, like walking or swimming, had been prescribed, and Ginger had to avoid going out in very cold weather, which they'd be unlikely to get on a spring morning. She found herself monitoring Ginger for signs of pain.

"I wish I could bottle this day," Ginger said. "It's the perfect mix of balmy and breezy, sun and shadow, blue and green. And I feel wonderful!"

Hope washed into Jefferson's heart. The surgery had worked! She touched Ginger's hand with a quick, soft gesture. "We can get the canoe out of the boathouse and paddle to Two Oar Island."

At Ginger's nod, she ran back up the hill for the key and grabbed bottles of water, chocolate bars, some almonds, and beach towels, stuffing it all in a rainbow-striped beach bag. Ginger helped slide the canoe into the water, but Jefferson wouldn't give her a paddle. "Pretend you're Cleopatra on the Nile."

"Sure. Complete with a built-in asp."

"Don't talk that way."

"I need to face it, Jef."

She held out the wrist where she wore her plastic hope bracelet. "You don't need to assume the worst."

"Okay, I won't. From here on out," Ginger said, "you can call me Miz Sunshine."

She felt like a flower yearning toward the sun. She would love Ginger back to superb health if it could be done. Otherwise what good would it have been to finally have learned to be faithful? Faithful unto death was not her idea of happily ever after. "Would you prefer I park on the shady or sunny side of the island, then, Miz Sunshine?"

"Surprise me."

She smiled. How long had it been since Ginger had challenged her with that phrase? Her heart wasn't the only place hit by a flood of hope this time. She hadn't brought Ginger north with designs on her body, but an invitation wouldn't be unwelcome. She wanted desperately a last cautious, beleaguered lovemaking. She pulled the paddle through the water steadily, rhythmically, remembering Ginger's scent, the give of her flesh under Jefferson's fingertips, that incredibly stimulating narrow tuft of red hair she loved to play with.

The little island was shaped like two crossed oars. She drew around to its sunny side and entered the V between the oars, aiming at a sandy patch. This cove was a sacred place. She'd motored out here a lot the summer before college and been back several times over the years. There was plenty of tinder and it was easy to find fallen limbs for a little fire.

She pulled the boat onto the beach and helped Ginger out, gratified that Ginger let Jefferson help her, sad that she needed help. Today they sat, skimming rocks, Ginger talking little, as if she was too tired even for words. She told Ginger about work, how she missed the new equipment and decent playing fields that had gone with a private education, including for the girl athletes, but her students needed her so much more she had no regrets about the path that got her to them. They'd mobbed her last September, two telling her that they'd only come back to school because they liked her class so much. She had hopes of convincing a few to try college.

"Why is it that the teachers liked by students are always the ones butting heads with the administration?" she asked.

"Jef, you've always been in trouble no matter where you taught."

She scoffed. "That was because I kind of had attendance problems. Since I stopped drinking, I seem to, I don't know, get all contrary when they tell me what to do. It's like they're in it to make themselves feel more important, not to teach the kids."

Ginger closed her eyes and smiled. "I'm glad I had enough saved to indulge in this long vacation."

"And health insurance through your group."

"It's almost time to go back to work so I don't lose it. Not to mention that there are so many people on our waiting list for classes I may never get to all of them teaching till I'm eighty," Ginger said, with a sad look on her face.

"And you will," Jefferson said with a smile of certainty. There had been all kinds of cancer in Ginger's family, but only one uncle who had, as her parents put it, dropped dead. They'd never known the cause for sure, but now thought he must have had what Ginger was having, this aneurysm thing. The family saw one another through the tough times and went back to work. Her father and brothers thought they were invincible. Ginger liked to say that anyone who had survived her mother, a stiff, pert-looking, sharp-tongued woman, had to be invincible. Her father, as good as his word, had snuck into their retirement fund to get Ginger the rest of the seed money she'd needed to buttress Jefferson's investment, to start her dance school. When Mrs. Quinn found out, she went and stayed with her sister's family in Woodside for six months, leaving her husband and her bachelor son to cook and clean and shop for themselves. For sure Ginger had inherited her mother's unbreakable will.

On the trip back to the Jeffersons' house the afternoon breeze broke the water into a million moving facets of light, like diamonds floating everywhere. They didn't speak and there was no sound but wooden paddle and water. Although it felt more like she was stirring a thick pudding than pulling through water, she knew it was she who was stirred up. The Jefferson place came into view, set like a monument in its nest of great cedars, balsam firs, sugar maples, and white pines at the top of the green slope of lawn. The sight always made her think entering heaven could not feel better.

The cottage, really too large for a cottage, but that's what her family had always called it, was freshly painted white with a screened-in front porch and gray roofing. It had two bedrooms, although in the summer, Jefferson usually used the cot on the porch. The sun would wake her, its rays reaching between the trees to touch her face and eyelids. If she had to define happiness, it was a place, this place, for her. Finches and sparrows sang early morning songs. Whenever she came up here she wondered why she lived in the city, but of course she knew why. The lakes region was short on gay life. There were no Café Femmes softball teams to coach. No gay friends she'd known forever.

She guided the canoe into the boathouse and held it steady while Ginger climbed onto the wooden walkway that lay between Mr. Jefferson's powerboat and the racks where they stowed the canoe and the kayak. She attached hooks and touched the switch. Pulleys hoisted the canoe out of the water. She rolled the lake door down, then hurried out the dry door and locked it. Ginger sat on the brown wooden bench, her long hair wavy, thick, still mostly copper against the shade of the pines. Jefferson stood before her, offering her hands to pull Ginger up.

Ginger seemed to hesitate at the bottom of the hill as they reached it, caught her breath, and started up. Jefferson lagged a half-step behind, slowing herself to Ginger's decreasing pace. They'd gone about two-thirds of the way when Ginger stopped, swaying in place. Her voice was thin when she said, "Jef. I can't. I can't make it up this little hill."

"We can do it together," Jefferson replied, all hope rolling back down the hillside, like a golf ball after a weak chip shot. Ginger had been so strong—why was this happening? "Or else," she joked, "I'll stick you in the wheelbarrow!" She put one arm around Ginger's waist, the other under her elbow, so that she pushed and supported and steered. Resting a few feet on, she looked to the treetops and asked the goddess, her higher power, the universe—whatever—to give Ginger back her life, but she knew now, as they started their last awkward dance uphill, that Ginger was a step away from being wholly spirit. The touching they were doing at this moment was nothing like any she had felt before with Ginger, only with Glad.

That night she lay in bed on the porch with two army blankets over her sleeping bag, yearning for Ginger. She wanted to crawl into bed with Ginger, who slept inside, and have Ginger hold her, hold her and maybe say something soothing or how sorry she was to have gone off to look for happiness in the wrong place when Jefferson came home to her once and for all, how she'd miss all the years they could have had together now, how she'd miss Jefferson and longed to stay, stay, stay, and then Jefferson would roll out of Ginger's arms and hold her and say, but we have now, we have this minute, this night, and maybe tomorrow for perfect closeness, as close as I've ever been to you, to anyone, as close as I'll ever want to be with anyone, and I can carry this time all the rest of my life and feel I've lived and loved well.

But she never crawled into Ginger's bed and Ginger never held her, never held her at all the way she'd longed for her to. Had Ginger been ready for that all these years and Jefferson not there to receive it? Ginger was her heaven, her afterlife, her universal love. Ginger had only been able to love her by staying through it all.

On a drive the next day she told Ginger she had enough years with the school system and planned to retire. Whether she helped Ginger to live or to die, these last days or years would be Ginger's and Ginger's alone. A long time ago Ginger had told her she wanted her ashes spread here, under the pines. She would ask Ginger to stay at the lake with her, sell the dance school and live off the interest. Maybe they both could find some peace by the serene water while Ginger was alive. After that, well, she would have planted the shadow of the flower that was Ginger at the lake.

CHAPTER TWENTY-NINE

To Jefferson's surprise, Ginger agreed to stay. She wasn't ready to sell the school, and it paid her enough that she felt she was contributing to the household. Jefferson mailed in her resignation; her young substitute was a good teacher and wanted full-time work. They went back to the city once a month to see the doctor and so Ginger could claim she was teaching part-time and managing the business long-distance. Those trips wiped her out.

It was as if Ginger was preparing herself for a final stillness and the quiet of afterward. She slept a great deal, of course, and when she was awake, Ginger lay motionless a lot of the time. She wanted no music and seemed perfectly content to walk slowly to the bench overlooking the lake on the cooler summer mornings. She said the green lawn and the blue lake water soothed her. Every night, Jefferson went to bed excited about their walk to the bench. She enjoyed every moment with Ginger; loved looking at her, loved helping her, loved making her life better, loved Ginger's touch when she held on to Jefferson's arm. How many more moments would they have?

At Ginger's insistence, she called Webbers, the local funeral parlor, in case. Ginger had explained what might go wrong post-surgery—loose stitching, not enough of the artery resected, a new aneurysm. If that happened, Ginger said, she might go very quickly. Russ Webber came out and made arrangements with them. All Ginger wanted was to be cremated before her parents got hold of her body and buried her in a box with some priest mumbling over her. Ginger had sent a copy of the paperwork to her brother Joseph and told him to say she loved them, but Mom and Dad were not to stop Jefferson from carrying out her wishes.

Only once had the subject of Ginger's time with Mitchell come up.

"I'm sorry I caused you pain," Ginger had offered. "I never had sex with him."

She nodded. "I thought—"

"Oh, please. I could smell his men on him."

Her mouth filled with the taste of bile, and she got so hot she could feel sweat at her hairline. She could say nothing, only shook her head.

"I felt sick and weak and disheartened and didn't know it was this illness. I was afraid I'd been wrong all those lesbian years. I was sick in spirit. Then I realized that you were so much of my spirit I was even more sick without you."

She nodded in response. "It was my fault, Ginger."

Neither of them could say more. They went back to watching television, an old William Bendix movie neither had seen before.

Mr. and Mrs. Quinn drove up one Saturday—the two brothers and their wives, the stay-at-home brother, and Ginger's parents—with the five nieces and nephews, all somehow stuffed into Joseph's old Suburban, the whole big Irish family. Ginger rallied and instructed Jefferson in roasting chickens and mashing potatoes. The frozen vegetables went into the microwave, and dessert was ice cream with fudge and marshmallow sauces out of jars. It had actually been fun, but Ginger got too tired. After that, Jefferson couldn't imagine Ginger dancing again and knew Ginger wouldn't want to live without dance.

The third Friday of August, they went outside after Ginger's afternoon nap. The pines shaded them while the sun scattered silver sequins atop the wind-chopped lake waters. She led Ginger to the bench and stood behind her, hands on her shoulders. Ginger was getting a gray streak off to one side of her hair. When Jefferson commented on this, Ginger raised one hand, slowly, and laid it on Jefferson's. It was four o'clock. They were in the long, sad decline of the day. Afterward, Jefferson wondered if Ginger had been practicing saying good-bye with that brief, cat's paw of a touch. When Ginger moved her hand away she asked Jefferson for a little water. Jefferson had learned to keep a six-pack cooler iced on the porch and stepped inside the screen door to get a bottle.

She moved around the bench to place the straw at Ginger's mouth. A red bubble was growing between Ginger's lips.

"Ginger?"

Ginger was staring toward the lake.

"Ginger," she insisted. "Oh, God."

Ginger gave a gurgling sort of cough and blood leapt from her mouth, down her chin, onto her lap.

Quickly, without thinking, Jefferson grabbed Ginger under the arms and laid her on the grass, turning her head sideways to keep her from choking on the blood. She touched Ginger's cheek and asked, "Ginger, are you still with me?" There was no response. Her other hand had already pulled out her cell phone and, despite all her practice out of Ginger's sight, she fumbled and dialed 999, then 411, and finally 911 and heard herself yell for assistance at her address.

"Hold, please. Stay on the line."

The pause seemed so long she was about to hang up and call back.

"Is that the Jeffersons' place?" the operator asked when she returned.

"You know it?"

The operator gave instructions to the ambulance, then answered, "I've been to parties there."

Oh, great, she thought. Who knows what went on. "Can you get me some help? We're around back."

"What's happening?" the woman asked.

"Ginger—she's recovering from surgery for an aneurysm. She vomited blood. Her abdomen is really swollen. I think she's going."

"Passed on?"

Without me, she realized. She's sending me away and bowing out without me. Jefferson knew she deserved nothing better, but hadn't she made up for some of the grief she'd caused Ginger? Ginger had left her again. She was gone for good.

She stopped herself. This was not about her. Ginger was dying here, or was she really already—

Her voice was dry, rasping. "She's bluish and cool to the touch."

The operator wanted to know if Ginger was breathing. "But don't do CPR."

She couldn't, with the blood continuing to run out of Ginger's poor soft mouth. "I can't find her pulse."

"Do you have a blanket? She'll be in shock."

It was so hard to look into Ginger's eyes and think she probably saw nothing now. "A lap throw. I've got her lying on it on the ground. Wait, I'm lifting her legs up to the bench. She's so cold and clammy."

"The medics are on their way, hon."

She felt as alone as she'd ever felt. "Ginger? You're the love of my life. You fill my world. You—" Why hadn't she found these things before? "You'll always be with me," she whispered. "It's okay to go now. What if you couldn't dance?" So fast she almost didn't know she'd thought it, she considered all the time and energy Ginger would have to give her if she couldn't dance, but said, "I'll love you wherever you are."

She caught sight of the mail boat on its way into the harbor. Ginger's eyes stared toward it. They'd always talked about taking a ride on the bigger mail boat over on Winnipesaukee, but never had, and here was the little Saturday Lake mail boat, a reminder of everyday life going on and on without Ginger, without time to be together the way they could have been and no one on the boat aware that Jefferson's world was shredding.

A siren wailed, coming along the curve of the lake.

"Any sign of life?" the operator was asking.

"No!" she yelled toward the phone, which lay on the pine needles next to Ginger. "Sorry, Ginger. I have to see what's going on inside your mouth again." It sounded silly as she said it, as she heard a vehicle approach. It was that she wanted, wanted, wanted her girl. She mopped more blood out and set her lips to Ginger's, tasting her dear lips tinged with metallic blood, thinking that this was the last kiss, their death kiss.

Two medics rushed to Ginger. "Is there someone who can be with you?" one of them asked, after confirming that Ginger was gone.

She only wanted to be with Ginger. "No."

She lingered over this task, crying as she worked, cleaning Ginger up as best she could after the medics had taken her inside and laid her on the red-and-black checkered bedspread. They told Jefferson to call Webbers.

This was going too fast, she thought. "Can't I keep her tonight?" But she knew that was senseless. In the silent vacuum of the emergency vehicle's departure, nothing was left but Ginger's paisley flip-flops, splayed on the ground where they had fallen.

What would be good about now would be a drink, but she'd lost her taste for drinking altogether. Her drinking had killed Ginger, hadn't it? She wondered if Ginger had found out who she really was: a creature of Jefferson's definition or some new butterfly never before captured and too fragile to survive.

Jefferson called Joseph. He would go over and tell the rest of the Quinns. She set out Ginger's new dance outfit, the black leotard and sparkly blue gossamer wrap, before she called Webbers. She and Ginger had picked it up on one of their trips to the city, an unspoken understanding between them of its purpose.

That night she called Lily Ann and asked her to tell their friends. She had the wild thought of calling Angela, back in Dutchess, but didn't, of course. She didn't want to tell Emmy and Jarvy. Not tonight. What she wanted was to tell Ginger. To have Ginger say, "There, there, there," and hold her, rock her, make love with her until sleep melded them together with the contentment only warm, sated bodies and glad hearts can know. Wasn't that all she'd ever wanted?

Chapter Thirty

Jefferson wouldn't let her friends help her finish her move north. "Wait till I get settled in and then come to visit," she insisted. She drove up on a Monday. Wet fallen leaves, gold and brown, green and red, lay everywhere on the parkways. Ginger's belongings were still in the guest room at the apartment. A small moving truck was bringing what she would need. She preferred the simple camp furniture at the lake to most of the pieces she and Ginger had collected, but her computer, iPod docking station, clothing, photos, sports gear, and books, her bicycle—she could not live without them. Whew, she kept saying to herself as she little by little decided what she'd need and what she could let go. She'd wondered if dying was something like this, letting it all go, offloading the heavy accumulations of the years and drifting away.

Retiring at forty-eight was the craziest thing she'd ever done sober, but she knew she was right to get out of Dodge. Ever since she'd stopped drinking and started on the depression medication, the same old same old wasn't doing it for her. She'd probably partly bored Ginger into leaving. No more impulsive excursions out to the bars, no more disappearing all night, no more skulking around the apartment hungover and cranky.

Before Ginger left with Mitchell, their lives had become serene and routine. They had gone to Café Femmes together, but with only a bottle of sparkling water in her hands, she'd felt left out. All those dykes downing alcohol, content to yell at one another over the music, to dance dirty in front of the whole world—had she lived like that? As the women got more and more drunk, they seemed to become different people: the loud ones got louder, the quiet ones more withdrawn. And young! Had she and her friends ever looked this young? There was something ugly about the sight of these children playing at adult activities. Ugliest of all was the sight of a young lesbian blitzed out of her mind. She'd thought of herself as suave, urbane; au contraire, she realized, she'd been a bleary-eyed, stumbling drunk, slack-smiled, and, like these tipsy butches, boring beyond belief. Some nights when they bestirred themselves to go downtown and see their friends, she started to yawn before she left the house. More and more often she and Ginger veered into the video store on the way to the subway and returned home with a chick flick, made popcorn, and fell asleep thirty minutes before the end of the movie. Was she still Jefferson without Irish whiskey?

That first official night after she moved into the cottage, she made a fire. Grandfather Jefferson had built the fireplace with the help of a local stonemason, using small slabs of granite, a couple with embedded smoky quartz, garnet, and crystal gathered from nearby fields when the cottage was built back in the 1930s, others brought from her grandparents' Dutchess land. When people started building around them, the accessible rocks had mostly been used, so Grandfather had put up a four-rail fence with bracing, low enough for the deer and moose to get in and out, open enough for the bunnies and other little guys to pass under.

The great-room walls were the original tongue-and-groove wood paneling, stained and shellacked to a shine, and the floors were made of wide wood planks with big, old-fashioned blue braided rugs. When they replaced the outhouse with a bathroom, they made it large enough for a toilet and shower. Originally they used the antiquated, red hand pump out front. An enamel sink hung on the wall outside the bathroom, supported by metal poles and skirted with old oilcloth-enclosed storage.

Only the kitchen had been updated. The pine open shelving and single wooden counter, patches worn in its varnish from use, hadn't changed, but in the 1950s, the icebox had been moved out back to store tools and garden implements. Her grandparents had put in a stark white Frigidaire Kelvinator, which whined now. The repair guy from Mailboat Harbor, though long retired, still came out to work on it and the Tappan range they'd bought at the same time. Only the clock at the top of the stove was not working. It stuck with a click every time it passed 3:18. She'd see if she could get that fixed and find someone to blow insulation into the walls.

There were two bedrooms off the great room, with knotty-pine three-quarter walls and, over them, an open loft where she'd slept as a kid. The climb up the vertical wooden ladder to the mattress under the attic window had been a highlight of her childhood. From the foot of her bed she could see the rafters over the living room and glimpse the grown-ups talking, smoking, and drinking on the deep screened front porch, its floor painted blue. Now the big bedroom downstairs was hers. The red-and-black checked bedspread and matching curtains at the screened windows must be at least as old as she was. There were no doors on the closets in the house, just rods and blue muslin shower curtains. The cottage, dotted with floor lamps, had always felt more like home than her parents' big, dark, ungainly house in Dutchess.

Her things weren't due until the next day, so she had little to keep her busy. She'd brought their blue-and-purple-striped comforter and wrapped it around herself on the old overstuffed couch. How many times had they made love on this very couch when they were first together? How many times sat touching shoulders, hips, feet, with their legs resting on the cherrywood-slab coffee table, watching logs burn in the fireplace? The mantel was made from a piece of the same cherry. They'd talked about work, their friends, their plans, growing old together, foolish bits from the local papers, their favorite TV shows, the old framed nature watercolors hung on the walls. It seemed they could talk about anything for hours, for days, for whole vacations. The more history they had together, the more there was to talk about. The silence got to her now, but she couldn't bear to cover up the quiet with music or TV. It was their silence, the vacuum in her life Ginger had filled, that she hung on to. All she had left was the very present absence of Ginger, which at least affirmed that there had been a Ginger, had been love, and she hugged the shadow of who they had been as tight as she could.

After a week of unpacking and setting up, Jefferson thought it would be good to be face-to-face with people someplace other than the grocery, hardware store, and post office. There was a bean supper at the Methodist church in Gramble, twenty minutes north and east along the lake. She'd always wanted to go to that bean supper as a kid, but that would have interrupted her parents' established cocktail hour, and the church didn't serve liquor. Ginger, brought up Catholic and turned off by the priests' child abuse, had made a face and exclaimed, "A church?" Now Jefferson was a free agent, like it or not, and no one could stop her.

Truth be told, aside from feeling like a length of herself had been severed, she kind of liked kicking around trying to figure out her own agenda with nobody else's itinerary or baggage tripping her up. Life, pain and all, had become an adventure again, and she, the real sober McCoy, was the greatest source of surprises.

Once past the gray stone doorway, she could see the long tables waiting for the crowd. They were covered with sheets of colorless butcher paper, not the brown of the crab shacks in Maryland where she'd taken Ginger one wonderful long weekend. They'd traveled to Washington, DC, on Amtrak, then rented a car to get around. The dinner had been fun, but the strongest image she had of that weekend was of Ginger's long, muscled dancer's legs in the air while Jefferson made love to her. The memory was so powerfully erotic she had to force herself to tune back in to this small-town church where she stood beside the children's leaf tracings, feeling awkward, and looked for an empty seat.

And there they were, a small knot of lesbians clustered at the end of one of the tables. One more chunk of home fell into place for her.

The first one to spot her, a hefty woman with curly short hair who looked like she might get familiar with a six-pack pretty regularly, glanced away, then did that mumbly thing dykes do when sharing a spotting on their dyke radar. The second one, thin, with short bleached hair and a Xena sweatshirt, checked Jefferson out and alerted the slight woman across from her, the only femme—or straight girl—in the group. Bangs made her look very young, but the rest of her hair, straight and feathered at her shoulders, was laced with gray. The gray, with her light makeup, made her look both mature and alluring. She had high arched eyebrows that gave her a questioning look, but beneath them were calm yet merry blue eyes. The woman gave her a quick smile, then looked again, as if realizing Jefferson was gay. The fourth woman never stopped talking.

Of course they would all be at the bean supper, and they all would go together. They were probably locals who had been going to bean suppers since infancy. Or one of them, the femme, she imagined, had been dragging her friends for years. She forced herself to keep eye contact with them and not get shy about this. They were the first gays she'd seen in Pipsborough. She was at least ten years older than the youngest of these women, but they would know others—if there were others. She might not get a chance like this again.

How she had always loved the hushed defiance of being gay, the underground of secrets and shared knowledge that ensured their survival in the face of physical danger and psychic extinction. She didn't know if she could appreciate coming out now, when coming out meant a public declaration, a not-so-shocking rebellion before an audience of parents, peers, and employers. She thrived on doing lesbian things in the dark of night, of society, of her soul.

The woman with bangs was addressing her. "This is family-style. Come join us. I'm Dawn Northway." Her smile was now wide and open. She wondered who in the group Dawn Northway was hitched to. She looked happy. Jefferson pushed her sweatshirt hood off her head, picked up a folding metal chair, and inserted it between Dawn and a palsied woman in a flowered fleece cardigan who looked near ninety. The old woman grinned and nodded her permission.

"I haven't missed a bean supper in forty years," the old woman whispered. "I was a server until the shakes got so bad. Harry and me, we helped start them. When Harry died nineteen years ago this month, I still came to the suppers." She winked. "I knew he'd be here in spirit."

"Are you bragging again, Kathy?" Dawn Northway asked.

Jefferson put a hand on Katherine's arm and exclaimed, "Heaven forbid! Katherine's way too young to have anything to brag about."

Katherine bent forward in her seat to see past Jefferson. "Your friend is right. You get to be my age, you have a right to brag," she told Dawn. Then she whispered to Jefferson, "She's our librarian. Ed Northway brought her mother over after the Vietnam conflict. Word is, he saved her life. There must be a dozen Viets on the Northway farm now. Ed and the Mrs. brought out all the family left living." She lowered her voice. "It was a scandal at first, but I say, what harm have they done? They stay to themselves unless they're doing something civic-minded. All of the men volunteer with the fire department."

Jefferson waited for more, but Katherine turned to her other neighbor.

"Our lucky day," said the talky dyke when Jefferson met her eyes. "Usually we get to sit with Republican retirees."

"Hey, troops," she said, relapsing into her old coaching jargon, "how do you know I'm not?"

Dawn touched her shoulder as she laughed, as if they were already old friends. She kept her hands smooth-looking and nicely manicured. "This is Rayanne," she said. "Don't mind her and her sarcasm, she's harmless. We went to college together. Which makes her one of my oldest friends."

Rayanne gave Dawn an annoyed look and told Jefferson, "That's oldest in years, not age."

"That gets her every time," Dawn confided, with a grin at Rayanne.

Jefferson guessed the two had been more than friends at some time. She asked, "What do they do, bring the food to the table?"

"Eventually," said Rayanne, settling her chin in her hands with a loud, discouraged sigh.

The thin woman craned her neck toward Jefferson and said, "It's worth the wait. Things get a little backed up in the kitchen at first. It's all volunteers." She reached across the table to give Jefferson's hand a brisk shake. "Shannon Wiley, present and accounted for," the woman said, wincing as she stretched. Back trouble, Jefferson noted.

After an inward chuckle at Shannon's soldier-like formality, she turned to the hefty mumbler. "Jefferson," she offered.

"Yolanda Whale. And I already know my name fits me."

"Hey," she replied, hands up in front of her. "Never crossed my mind."

"Keep it that way," Yolanda advised, "and I'll turn you on to the best ale in the world."

"Sorry, I don't drink any more."

"One of those twelve-steppers?" Yolanda asked. "Nothing worse than a—" Yolanda looked around and whispered, "than a dry dyke. Except for a slogan-slinging dry dyke."

"Poor me...poor me...pour me another drink," Jefferson recited.

"Oh, I like that one!"

She saw looks pass between Shannon, Rayanne, Dawn, and two men at the table.

"I'm Drew Blaine and this is my partner Ryan," one of the men said.

Again, she shook hands. "What a nice surprise." She hadn't realized the two men were part of the group and gay.

"We come to protect our town librarian against Mrs. Green."

"Is she crushed out on someone?"

Dawn Northway laughed. "Fat chance!"

Northway was wearing pink lipstick and light eye makeup. "You don't look like my image of a librarian," Jefferson said, which only made Dawn laugh harder. She'd never seen blue eyes in an otherwise Asian face. She was curious about Dawn.

Ryan explained. "Donna Green thinks *Huckleberry Finn* should be banned from the library."

"Among other innocent books," Drew added. "The whole Harry Potter series, for example."

She told them, patting one of Dawn's hands, "That's ridiculous. Can't you get rid of her?"

"Tell me how," Dawn pleaded.

"I'll handle her," Shannon said, glowering. Jefferson couldn't help but think Shannon's bleached, surfer-boy haircut would make her butch of the month back at Café Femmes, especially, given her sweatshirt, with the fans.

"No, Shannon," Dawn said. "You'd only make it worse."

Shannon put on a sulky face.

"What would you do," Rayanne asked, "put sugar in her gas tank for the next meeting?"

"I've thought of that," Shannon said, "but she'd get a ride with some other wacked-out gay-hater."

"They're scared," Dawn said. "We need to find a softer, kinder way, or it will come back to bite us."

"This smell is killing me," said Yolanda. "We could get the bitch in here and starve her to death. Where's the food?"

Katherine glanced their way. "They got started late," she explained. "Corbin Adams had the key and he got stuck t'other side of the lake."

Jefferson sniffed the air. "You're right. That smells fantastic. I've never been to one of these before."

"Hang around with Miz Dawn and you'll be here every month," Yolanda said.

Dawn, who seemed to laugh every time she spoke, and not a nervous laugh, but the laugh of someone who genuinely enjoys herself, protested. "We lined up early to get in with the first sitting. If there was a decent restaurant around, we could get together there."

"Or if one of us cooked," Rayanne said. "Do you cook?" she asked Jefferson and, without waiting for an answer, went on. "The boys cook. We need a girlfriend who cooks. Or are you a tourist?" She said this last as if it was a curse.

"I moved into my family's cottage. I'm here to stay."

The swinging kitchen doors bounced open and the rich, sweet smell of baked beans rushed out with them. Middle-aged and old women served up huge bowls of beans, brown bread, cole slaw, and what looked like red hot dogs.

While they waited for their server, Shannon said, "I had to drive

Yolanda's truck over because Yolanda wasn't too steady." She explained to Jefferson, "I visit my folks in Laconia on Saturdays and get a ride with Yo. Except when I chauffeur her. We won't let her drive home till she's sober."

"Can't get the supplies I want in Pipsborough," Yolanda explained.

Shannon, her look full of concern, said, "Meaning Golden Loon Ale."

Yolanda said, "I drink Golden Loon. You're a Xena fanfic addict. If you couldn't get your Xena fix anywhere but Hollywood—"

A smile stretched Shannon's mouth, and one deep dimple showed up on her right cheek, then a second on her left. "I'd bike the whole way."

"Fangirl," Yolanda said to Shannon in a teasing tone. "You'd think they could at least serve local beer or wine at these suppers." Jefferson remembered sounding like her not all that long ago, alcohol her first concern.

"I have an idea," Dawn said. "I'll accept that job in Concord and you won't have to go to these suppers."

"No!" Shannon, Yolanda, and the two men cried.

Rayanne rolled her eyes. "Forget it. You're not going anywhere. We found you a nice, eligible bachelor. You are an eligible bachelor, aren't you?" Rayanne pointed a speared chunk of hot dog at Jefferson.

"Well, yes and no."

Shannon was looking worried.

"That was clear," Rayanne said, sarcasm getting past her mouthful.

"Stop, Ray," Dawn said.

"It's okay. I'm a sort of bachelor, but I'm not eligible."

Shannon stared at her, fork halfway to her mouth, like Jefferson should go on.

She shrugged and told them, "It's not over till it's over."

This time it was Dawn offering comfort with a touch of her hand on Jefferson's and sympathy in her eyes.

A silence followed. Yolanda broke it, saying, "They're still upset because I started crying while we were in line. I mean, life would suck if Dawn went to Concord. She's the life of the party."

"Life is a party with Dawn around."

"There, there," said Drew, patting Yolanda on the head.

Jefferson felt like she was intruding on a family quarrel, and at the same time, this affectionate feud felt familiar. She could be at Café Femmes. This was promising, she thought, as, from a host of homemade pies a server offered, she chose the apple with a big slab of sharp cheese.

It was crazy, but right this minute she was extraordinarily happy. She loved living at the lake. Sometimes she got the incredible feeling she used to have when she was winning a game. It filled her up and she was a walking smile. But how could she—without Ginger?

Dawn Northway was smiling at her, nodding in approval when Jefferson raised her eyebrows to indicate her pleasure in the food. Their eyes held, forkfuls of pie midway to their mouths. She reminded herself that she had to get out of the habit of thinking of femmes as prospective bed partners. She'd been wondering if it was possible that she'd given so much of her heart away she had nothing more to give; certainly no forevers. She'd had her forever.

By the end of the dinner, after she declined to go drinking with Yolanda Whale, escaped Rayanne's detailed history of the town of Gramble, New Hampshire, since before the Europeans arrived, got a sweet hug from Dawn, hired Shannon, the surfer-dude Xena freak some girl was going to find delectable, to do some work around the cottage, and accepted the offer of a driving lesson in the snow that winter from Dawn, she knew she was making some friends. These people were hungry to add to their community. She was elated.

CHAPTER THIRTY-ONE

There was no getting away from the snow. She had to drive across it, so she depressed the accelerator on her new Toyota Avalon, heard the wheels spin, the engine strain. She inched forward, then threw the shift into reverse, pressed, moved back, pressed—and she was finally moving through this slick little snow dune.

Dawn gave a cheer.

"You know what's funny?" she told Dawn. "Toyota calls this car's color Blizzard Pearl. If I get us stuck we'll blend right in and not be discovered till spring." Then she plowed into more snow and powered out again.

"Go, girl," Dawn cried as Jefferson broke through.

"Getting stuck's not what scares me," she told Dawn as she slipped along the parking lot, past piles of rain-pocked snow and refrozen melt. "And don't you tell anyone I'm scared. I'm forty-eight—too old to be such a sissy."

"Oh, the big bad butch girl who can fix anything and is never scared."

"Hey, I can power through most anything. It's the skidding and spinning that gets me in a stew."

"Don't be such a control freak," Dawn said. "A little four-wheel cross-country skiing is fun."

She scowled, gripping the wheel as if she could keep the car from flying. "For daredevils like you, maybe."

"Jefferson, you live in New Hampshire now. Either you let me teach you to drive in snow and ice, or you might as well move back to the city."

"Good gravy," she said, and got ready to send the car into a spin again. "Maybe I should have gotten an SUV."

"Are you kidding? These Avalons are tanks."

"Bless stability control. Drew said a sedan would be better for hauling around retirees who couldn't get into anything high off the ground. He also suggested a little elegance, so I got the heated leather seats. And the GPS, of course, to find these places."

Jefferson's grandfather had taught her to drive a big sedan in Dutchess when she was ten. Up and down the long driveway, around the old house, in and out of the garage. That man trusted her with his shiny black Lincoln, but when she got her license her parents didn't let her drive in snow or ice. They weren't far enough upstate for it to be a problem very often, and in the city she bussed or took the train if there was a chance of bad weather, or asked Ginger to drive.

"Wow," she said.

Dawn looked at her. "What?"

"I bought a grown-up car. And I hate snow now. When did snow lose its magic and become my enemy?"

"That," Dawn said, "is what we're doing here today. Taking the sting out of snow."

"Good. I want it to be magic again."

"Okay, brake hard."

She did and her tail end spun out.

"Don't brake again yet! Steer into it. Yes. It was almost automatic this time, wasn't it?"

"Automatic heart failure," Jefferson said. "I'm beginning to see that learning to drive in the snow is like learning to dance sober. You stumble a lot. It's easy to feel out of control."

She braked on her own this time and brought herself out of the skid without coaching, then crunched into a small snowbank a plow had left in the parking lot. She turned off the car and held up her hand to keep Dawn from talking. The world around them had become a perfect picture of peace. The evergreen boughs hung low under inches of snow. There was no sound other than the ticking of her cooling engine. She couldn't see the lake, but she felt its calm, perpetual presence, icy-coved, harbor-bound, icicle-ringed. Here, she thought, she slept well.

She recalled that Ginger, whose life was about movement, had loved the stillness of winters at the lake. She would carry a plaid car blanket down to the dock and sit cross-legged on it, stillness herself, like an ice sculpture. After a while her breath would become invisible. Jefferson would make hot cocoa when she got back. They'd sit in the warm kitchen, refrigerator whining, icicles cracking off the windows, with her family's red stoneware mugs, and grin at each other, plan dinner, share thoughts, some perky Schubert on the stereo, nap in each other's arms. Thirty years had passed since that winter before they were roommates when Ginger drove the old Nova up to the lake most weekends so they had a place to be together. And now Jefferson had to learn to drive in New Hampshire winter weather. At least the car had safety features Chevrolet hadn't dreamed of when they made the Nova.

The Avalon was fast losing heat. She started the engine, but the tires didn't move.

"Not to worry, Jef. This time depress the brakes a little to get both wheels turning, but not enough to lock them. That back-and-forth business we tried with the car may be good in bed, but it's hell on a transmission."

She laughed. "Where did you learn all these Hints to Heloise on Wheels, Northway?"

"Oh, I learned from Drew Blair. Did he tell you his dad was a mechanic and his older sister, dandy Andy, the gay one, was an absolute artist at fixing up cars? She has her own shop in San Francisco now. Drew says he used to follow her around and she'd let him polish hubcaps and hood ornaments. He's taught me a lot."

Jefferson laughed. "She raised him right—the woman fixes the cars and the man washes up after her."

It turned out that Dawn was comfortable to be with. They'd laughed together all afternoon, Jefferson banishing pangs of missing Ginger when they cropped up.

"So what makes a city gay girl choose conservative Pipsborough?" Dawn asked as Jefferson practiced driving.

She told Dawn about her family's ties to the lake and her cottage.

"A cottage on the lake," Dawn responded, sounding impressed. "I'll bet it's no cottage. More like a lodge?"

"Maybe a small lodge. I spent summers as a kid swimming, waterskiing, and boating here. My father drove up weekends and Emmy's reins were looser than they were in Dutchess, so Pipsborough always felt like freedom to me."

It still did, she thought, and now she was beginning to be part of their little gay community, hanging out at Dawn's, taking what she called a dyke break before returning to work. She had to get over to some woman's house with a for-sale sign and paperwork. So far, she was only an assistant realtor, but she'd taken her agent's test last week and knew she'd aced it. She'd been as scared of the test as she'd been driving on snow, scared she was too old to learn the minutiae required. She'd had to put in a lot more studying than she ever did in school, but she really wanted her new life and her new job to work. She'd thought about quitting teaching and selling property for years, anticipating that real estate could give her a freedom she'd never have in a classroom. New York was such a tough town to break into, though, that she'd never done it. Pipsborough was a whole different ball game.

She'd managed to get enough years in with the public-school system that she had a small pension. The interest from what her grandparents had left her when they died gave her a little more each month, and she'd socked away the $10,000 Emmy and Jarvy had been giving her every year for Christmas to save on inheritance taxes. She'd planned some day to buy a little condo at the lake. When she'd taken the leave of absence to bring Ginger to the lake last summer, her parents had surprised her— they wanted to trade the cottage for the apartment in the city. They went there so seldom now, they'd explained, and to tell the truth, Emmy said, her father wasn't up to hauling wood and keeping the place shipshape, the way he used to. He wasn't sober enough, she'd thought at the time. She knew they were furious about what the terrorists had done to their country and especially to their city. Moving into Manhattan afterward was the way they struck back and reclaimed their territory. Their minds were made up: the cottage was hers for the cost of taxes, insurance, and upkeep only.

Innisfree, she'd immediately dubbed it, after the poem Ginger had introduced her to all those years ago. Of all the dances Ginger had created, she'd most liked the one set to the song made from Yeats's poem. She'd immediately recognized the spirit of Saturday Lake in the poem. Now, she remembered only one line, but it was enough: "And I shall have some peace there, for peace comes dropping slow…"

If she'd loved the place as a kid, she grew even more attached as an adult. In summer breaks from teaching she'd come up for days at a time. She'd liked to watch the visiting grandkids of retirees belly-flopping off the end of docks as she once had and launching Sailfish from the beach. Old folks waded, skinny-legged, in the warm water or swam laps out to the raft and back.

Now she planned to overhaul her grandfather's boat. She didn't need one that powerful, but it was a beauty, an old Hacker Craft Runabout from the 1930s. It needed about forty coats of varnish to keep the mahogany looking good. Her father had everything rebuilt over the years—a total restoration from the frame out, with new gauges, new windscreens, and a 1994 six-cylinder engine. The boat, the *Maggie J.*, after her grandmother, could go 45 mph, but she only wanted it for tooling around the lake, exploring with more than a canoe as she'd longed to do when she was a kid. Her parents had been more interested in wine parties and the Barnstormers Summer Theater over in Tamworth than in entertaining a child. Now she could get a dog and train her to go boating. They'd pull into uninhabited sandy coves and swim in the warm water, then share lunch on the beaches. She'd throw sticks for Merry-Go-Round; she'd already named her, thinking if she gave her a fun name, she'd be fun. She had a heck of a lot of catching up to do on fun, now that she was here. Without Ginger.

Here—at the lake! She bathed her eyes in the vision of placid blue water and the green that outlined it. She'd never understood how stressful it was to live in the cacophony of urban life until she moved to the lake for good. After the horror years, as she thought of them, from 9/11 in 2001 to Ginger leaving in 2005, Ginger's death in 2006, and quitting alcohol in the midst of all that, she needed a safe home. Nine/eleven had definitely started the whole sequence. She'd thought the whole city was going to blow, thought they'd been bombed and was waiting for the next attack. She'd shepherded the kids from her high-school hygiene class who hadn't been picked up and escorted home to the auditorium, where many had waited into the evening, crying or giggling senselessly from nerves and fear; the teachers grim, holding themselves together for the students, but terrified, she learned later, every last one.

Jefferson and Lily Ann Lee had had plans for dinner the night of the attacks. Only when the last kids had gone home and she'd been walking the mile and a half to her apartment, looking around at the dazed people, some of them dusted with the fine light gray ash that she later saw blanketed Ground Zero and which she only recognized then had been more than incinerated structures, had also been the ashes of the dead; only on her long trek did she manage to understand that Lily Ann wouldn't be meeting her for dinner. Her job was to procure whatever the crews needed. Jefferson hadn't heard the news by then of all the trapped firefighters, hadn't had time to start a vigil or to wait for news of

Lily Ann. Her answering machine was miraculously blinking when she arrived home. Lily Ann, always thinking of other people, had arranged for her mother to call to say Lily Ann was fine and would be working as long as necessary so wouldn't meet her for dinner that night.

A week after the attacks, on September 18, they met, mightily tall Lily Ann looking haggard and bent. Jefferson, by then aware of the extent of Lily Ann's loss, had begged to do something to help. Lily Ann wanted to be held, so they got their lunch to go and went back to Lily Ann's place, where she cried in Jefferson's arms for almost half an hour before returning to what was by then being called Ground Zero. On the day of the attacks she'd been in her headquarters office. After fifteen years serving in station houses, and reaching lieutenant grade, Lily Ann had broken an ankle in three places. She hadn't wanted to retire so, with her MBA, she'd gotten transferred to the fire department's purchasing office. Her limp saved her life, but her guilt was a heavy pack she carried on her back instead of her gear as she expedited supplies for the rescuers day after day. Jefferson insisted on giving her a short, inexpert massage before Lily Ann left; then she cleaned Lily Ann's apartment and went down to the grocery across the street to get her some frozen dinners and fresh fruit.

It wasn't until she was vacuuming Lily Ann's floors that she let herself think about what she needed to do for herself. She hadn't been eating either. Café Femmes was open downtown, but it had been days before she had the time to get there for news of her friends. Everyone knew someone who'd been affected, and one of the kids who hung out there, a courier, was still missing. She got through AA meetings by being the convivial host, making coffee, listening, talking about how glad she was not to be drinking right now, when she'd be so vulnerable to obliterating herself with a terminal binge. Ginger's brothers had gone rushing down there on an unauthorized rescue mission, but hadn't gotten past the police barricades.

That week she'd lived through some kind of filter that made her feel far away, as if the shock of the devastating day had left her with a concussion. Voices sounded muffled, figures looked a little blurred, she made decisions she didn't know she'd been contemplating, including looking into getting certified to teach in New Hampshire.

The 2001 school year had already begun, so she'd stayed until the following June and then kept going back. She was still there four years later when Ginger left. Then she used some sick time she'd accumulated and wandered in an uninformed way, telling herself she was not looking for Ginger and catching sight of her long copper hair everywhere. Where would she start a serious search? What if she found Ginger and was turned away? Ginger and Mitchell could have returned to New York, for all she knew. If she'd only gone after them she might…

That kind of thinking drove her nuts. Over the next few months, before Emmy offered her the cottage, she had visited some friends in Connecticut, but knew their promised land wasn't hers. She'd been raised in privilege and felt drawn back to something greener, bluer, more a park-like setting than industrial towns or suburbs, more a lake than the unpredictable river up in Connecticut. She checked out Boston, but it looked ready to crumble even without a terrorist attack. The northern Maine coast was dramatically wild, but she wanted calm. Upstate New York, Vermont—neither offered what she wanted, though she didn't have a clue what she wanted.

By the time Ginger left, she knew she didn't want younger dykes looking at her like she was a troll when she danced with a silver-haired woman to a girl-group oldie. Good gravy, she was forty-six. Slack was showing around her neck, her face, and she was growing gray. Heaviness hadn't been in her plans, but it was swallowing her like a second body. Actually, she didn't see it herself. She still saw brown hair in the mirror, but her haircutter told her. She was not the lithe dyke sun god she saw in her mind's eye. And she worried, a little, about who would want her, if Ginger didn't come back; who she would be willing to expose her not-so-flat tummy to, her breasts, grown heavier. No one, was her immediate thought.

The kids were so skinny. Had she actually been as thin in her twenties and thought it attractive? They wore so much makeup now and did strange things to their hair. She'd never been particularly attracted to bleached blondes or women with frosted hair, but couldn't imagine why the baby femmes dyed their hair that dull black color or thought henna red made them what they called hotties. Green streaks or dreads, those didn't bother her; they fit better with her idea of rebellion. But the eyes of the kids, they slid away as if she were a future they would not acknowledge and a past that shamed them. She could see that they were convinced not only of their immortality, but of their superiority, as she had been of her own, back then, and, to tell the truth, now.

It wasn't that there weren't women her age out there. She never thought that no one would want her. There were enough needy single—or not single—lesbians—or not lesbians—that she had no fear she'd hold no attraction for someone. Angela had two Dutchess County femmes she wanted to introduce Jefferson to, but Jefferson fretted that she would never want anyone but Ginger. She was surprised to realize that when she saw a face on the street that interested her, it was always the face of a woman within a few years of her own age. She'd smiled—her attractions had aged with her and beauty had become something different for her.

In the spring after Ginger walked out Jefferson wandered through the lakes region of New Hampshire, in a rented car she picked up at the Manchester airport, and drove into Pipsborough without Ginger, expecting to experience all the ambivalent feelings she had about her self-absorbed parents and her lonesome tomboy childhood. Instead, she grew excited, drawn to the sites of her memories.

Snow still covered the great green lawns of estates and inns alike, but the roads were clear. Under the sunny daylight, pines and birches shed snow like women dropping pure white shawls. Instead of going to her parents' place, she checked into a large old cream-colored inn, tasting the area as a stranger might, and wanted to stay forever.

When more snow fell, she called the school to say she wouldn't be in the next day or the next. Each night she went down to the mostly empty dining room for dinner. Every morning she walked a mile to the Pipsborough Café for breakfast with the locals. Later that winter she spent another week, and three more times in the spring she came up for long weekends, once as a treat for Lily Ann, who was upset that Jefferson wanted to leave the city, but by the end of the weekend looked better for the break.

"Could you find a place any whiter than this?" Lily Ann had asked with the old snap in her tone.

"I take it you don't mean the winter snow? I'm planning to recruit some color to the area. If I move up here. If I get a real-estate license."

She'd always liked to look at other people's apartments and houses. It fascinated her the way everyone had different ideas about how to use space and how creative they could be. Pipsborough didn't offer much in the way of employment, but when she made the move to the lake, the cheerful sixty-something guy who ran the real-estate agency in downtown Pipsborough, Marion Buckleback, had been glad to talk to her. They had coffee at the café a few times, and Buck put her in touch with the state agency that administered the exam. "If you taught New York City high-school kids," he told her, when she'd confessed to having no sales experience, "you can sell a tent at the North Pole." He'd added, "You're not without charm, Ms. Jefferson. You cut a pretty smooth figure, as a matter of fact. There's something about you buyers will trust. You look young, but you talk like you've been around long enough to know a good thing when you see one."

His wife Serena was the other realtor in the office and she wanted to quit, pushing her husband to hire someone. She'd had several brushes with skin cancer, which had left her face and hands scarred. "I don't want to frighten the buyers away," she said, sadness plain in what had obviously become an old joke. Jefferson thought she sensed some resignation too. Serena Buckleback was getting ready to be sicker, maybe to die soon. Buck never dropped his salesman's good spirits or whined about having a wife who seemed to age a decade in the first month Jefferson spent with them.

Dawn broke in on her memories. "I think you've got this driving-in-snow thing down, Ms. Jefferson."

She realized she'd been completely absent as she followed Dawn's instructions. She announced, "One more run, though." Conscious of what I'm doing this time, she thought.

She eased out on the road and drove them to Dawn's house in town, maneuvering over two ice patches and parallel parking on about two inches of snow, to show off.

"Ginger would be amazed," she said.

"I'm amazed. You were like a robot in an electrical storm when we started. All charged up and currents gone wild." Dawn reached for her and they hugged.

Jefferson looked at her as she opened the car door. Something comforting about Dawn allowed her to breathe more deeply in her presence. Dawn had a Saturday Lake stillness to her. "Thanks for scraping me off the wall. Let me treat you to lunch?"

"I wish," Dawn replied. "Drew and Ryan are running over to the Home Depot in Tilton, and I need some things."

"You and this community—it's like you're married to it."

"Married would be wonderful. I so envy all the years you had with Ginger."

"Hey, you know, I did feel married. I don't think Ginger ever did. I don't know. It wasn't like that with us. We had a different kind of marriage."

"Maybe you can give us country bumpkins lessons."

"Right. Lessons. Me. Did you want all your dyke friends to run off with your gay male friends?"

"Whoops."

She managed a three-point turn on Dawn's narrow street and drove to the real-estate office quickly, as if the roads were clear. She was afraid she would turn back and ask Dawn and the boys to invite her to go shopping with them, like some lonesome little kid.

CHAPTER THIRTY-TWO

The three-quarter moon hung over a hill across Saturday Lake. Jefferson was alone in the ancestral cottage long after even the hunting camps had run out of beer and gone to bed. The lake was not known for its nightlife. Her windows were open to the cool air. The silence reminded her that the loons were gone for the winter. Not even the loons for company, she thought.

She hadn't brought all that much in the way of possessions, having been in a mood to empty her life of the old. She was spending time at the natural-food store in Wolfeboro, buying whatever would cleanse her abused liver of alcohol's abuse. Sleep came at odd times and she almost always gave in to it. Daily, she went into or out on the lake. There was something peaceful about a lake: the waters were still, the encircling land was a calming green. She loved the sounds of a boat on water and the occasional shout, slammed door, or honk of a horn on shore. The sky seemed to surround her in a protective embrace.

Her new home was larger than the apartment in New York, but it seemed easier to keep neat, with its smoke-darkened, wooden walls and big windows that looked out at water or trees on both sides. Her queen bed seemed to dwarf the master bedroom. She felt incomplete without her bouts of melancholy. Would a dog help? Its needs would give a structure to her days. Then she ran into a little kid shivering outside the grocery store who had been trying to give away six tiger kittens all day, with no luck, and expected her father to arrive soon, prepared to do away with them. He'd had the mother fixed, the little girl explained, and was picking her up now. She got to keep the mother, but these kittens were so cold. Jefferson carted them all home with a promise to return their blanket to the kid's family. So much for a dog, she thought.

Timid at first, they turned into little ruffians. My gang, she called them, and gave them the names of graffiti artists she'd noticed in the city. Little Star, Dust, Risky, Crunch, Doze, and Lionel did fill up the bed, not only with their own fuzzy bodies, but with kitten spit-up and other mistakes she hadn't anticipated. She could have had an animal back in the city if she'd been sober enough to feel she'd be there to give it enough attention, and if Ginger had been interested. Now not only did the kittens have a home, but with them around, she felt like she had one too; she couldn't remember a lonely night. Maybe this was what she and Ginger had needed, little beings dependent on them.

Dust clambered over one foot now, grabbing for the ends of her running-shoe laces. Doze lay, paws up, on her grandfather's easy chair next to the front window, where she could see beyond the porch to the lake. Jefferson loved these things right out of her childhood; better she have memories of her family than of Ginger. Like she could deny memories of Ginger. Risky was batting at the vertical blinds that lay open to the night. Lionel and Crunch were boxing on the couch and Little Star was feinting at Dust's tail. She laughed aloud. She was making up for all those kittens Jarvy wouldn't let her have, all those puppies she'd yearned for. Damn, she should have done this years ago. There was no question in her mind that alcohol had taken almost everything from her. Look how long it had been since she'd stopped drinking, and she was only now finding what she really liked in her life: the lake, the kittens, her home, her new friends. She was one of the lucky ones who'd been able to stop drinking.

Jefferson bent to pick up Crunch, the puniest cat. He'd had such a hard time eating dry kibble at first. Every bite was a stretch for his little jaw, but he'd insisted on chewing it like the bigger kittens and made the loudest crunches imaginable when he succeeded. Crunch's tail was still a little spiky, slow to fill out like the others' tails. He was responsible for putting Jefferson back to sleep when she came wide-awake in the dark, only to remember that Ginger wasn't beside her. Crunch would climb to her chest and settle at the base of her throat, almost singing, he purred so heartily.

"What kind of life are we going to have together, Crunch? Will it always be calm and quiet like tonight, the seven of us hanging out together?" Crunch wriggled to get free and she set him on the couch. "Are you my way of keeping all possible girlfriends at arm's length? Who would want someone with six cats?" She wondered if that was why she'd gained all this weight. Being attractive to women had been its own high; she didn't know if she wanted to go there again. Maybe the kittens and the weight were anchors, exactly what she needed to be self-sufficient, untempted by the liquor and sex in which she'd tried to drown herself. She had become a victim of her own myth: too many women, all too welcome in too many bars with her free-spending ways, craving the attention good looks engendered.

One Saturday afternoon she heard a rough knock on the heavy wooden front door. Little Star looked up at her with wide eyes, then vanished back under the bed.

"I came to meet the kittens," Buck said. He held out an icy-cold leather-gloved hand.

Jefferson sat Buck on a stool at the breakfast counter and filled two heavy mugs with hot chocolate and miniature marshmallows. She told him to help himself from the chipped gray pig that had been her grandmother's cookie jar. She stocked it with macaroons. Risky was already sniffing Buck's shoes, and Doze was sniffing Risky's bottom. "Chocolate. My last addiction." She raised her mug in a toast to her guest.

"If I'd known you wanted a cat, I could have given you some of ours."

"Part you and Serena from your babies? No way."

She collected the kittens and took them all, in her arms, to Buck. Only Crunch stayed on his lap, looking up at Buck's neat silver beard in what appeared to be wonder. He finally climbed up Buck's jacket and tried to cuddle with the beard, but lost his footing. Buck held Crunch against his cheek.

"How's Serena?"

Buck brushed his beard back and forth against Crunch. "You know she had another treatment this week. She's always pretty unhappy after one of those. Our oldest daughter arrived to help out. They don't think much of my cooking."

"Cooking? What's that?"

She opened the freezer and showed him her collection of Lean Cuisines. The refrigerator closed, rubber on rubber. The seals were dried out; she'd need a repair soon. Buck laughed in his neat, quiet way. He was so much like Pipsborough itself, classy without being pretentious like so many of the people who lived over on Lake Winnipesaukee, which they seemed to think was not only larger than Saturday Lake, but better quality. Properties went for less on Saturday Lake and tended to be like the Jeffersons': big enough for the family that owned it, but not a country estate or one of the newer, wasteful McMansions that were replacing so much of the forest.

There was a crash from the bedroom. Quickly she scanned the room. "Risky," she called. She got up and peered into the bedroom. The green-shaded banker's lamp was on its side on the night table, but hadn't broken. Risky charged out from under the bed and grabbed her foot.

She carried Risky in and settled in the easy chair. Buck carefully checked the couch for kittens before he sat.

"I see that the Conservation Trust is getting the Kents' land."

"Thank goodness, yes." Buck's sweet smile grew wider. "The Kent kids are keeping the house and an acre around it. They almost sold the whole piece, intending to give a percentage of the proceeds to the Loon Preservation people over in Moultonborough."

She considered. "This is better, right?" She'd always been vaguely aware of environmental issues, but beyond contributing to a fund for Central Park, she hadn't paid much attention to them. "Better than one of these second-home zillionaires who are driving out the natives and the little people and the cabins on the lakes to rip out trees and build five-thousand-square-foot homes?" Like Pipsborough, Buck was a strange mix of Republican and conservationist.

"I think it's better. The more land that's available to wildlife, the more they can thrive."

"You're a closet liberal, Buck," she teased him, kicking back in her recliner and locking her fingers behind her head.

"I can't think of anything more truly conservative than conserving nature," he said, with that winning smile. "It's a shame we have to depend on the government to protect so much of it." He had Star on her back in his arms and was scratching her tummy, but now he looked sad. "You don't know where to devote your energies or who to send money to. So much is needed. A cure for cancer would be a priority for me right now."

"Don't you think Serena will make it?"

"Serena's been making it for about ten years now. I think the cancer is catching up with her."

"You think she's going to—"

He nodded and lifted Lionel. Star spat and wriggled free. "The cancer has spread."

What had people said to her when Ginger was sick? "I'm really sorry."

"Thank you."

"What can I do?"

Buck laughed quietly. "You're doing it, coming into the business with me. I never wanted a big firm, but I do need a second agent."

She bowed. "At your service."

"And I like your lack of ambition."

His words startled her. "I do want to make sales, Buck."

Buck put a hand up. "I know, but you don't want to develop every parcel of lakefront. Some agents are so money hungry they're blind to the consequences of their greed. I see the realty business as a service, not a get-rich-quick scheme, although it's been good to us. Putting a big chunk of land like the Kents' into the Trust's hands is better for our bottom line than ten gated developments that destroy the reasons people want to live here."

"I don't need to get filthy rich," she assured him. "But I am going to have some cat-food bills to pay now." She rattled a box of treats. Lionel looked up and the other kittens came running. "Whoops. That was a bad move. Here, go ahead and give them some, Buck."

Unlike most guys, Buck didn't claim more than his share of space, but she could not imagine living, sleeping, with—oh, ugh, facial hair, and all the rest. She thought, how could you, Ginger?

Buck was talking about a commercial building in town that he had listed, and the kittens were tumbling over one another on the kitchen floor. When her cell phone rang she expected it to be for Buck, but it was her mother.

"Ginger's brothers are here, at the apartment," Emmy said.

"What are they doing there?"

"They want her things."

She'd put off going through Ginger's closet. It was too painful. "Did they say where they're moving them to?"

Emmy consulted with them and she heard Kevin reply, "Home. To our parents' apartment."

"Let me talk to him, Emmy."

Kevin was the one who gave Ginger the roughest time about living with a girl. What did the family want with Ginger's possessions? There were lesbian books and photos of them together. "Kevin," she complained, "I'd like to keep a few items."

"Calm down. They want something to remember her by."

"I'm trying to remember what's what. Leave the books, okay? Hers and mine are all mixed in," she lied. "And there's a box of photos, nothing your parents would want."

"Where's the urn?"

"The urn?"

"With my sister's ashes. Mom and Dad at least want to bury her ashes."

"Kevin, Ginger wrote the family that she wanted her ashes scattered here at the lake. I already went out in the boat and did that."

The line was silent for a long moment. She could imagine Kevin struggling with his hot temper. "Tell your mother where everything is, okay? I need to get this done before five."

"It's the things in the guest-room closet, isn't it, Amelia?"

She didn't want to sound desperate to her mother and named a few other items. "You can buy a new toaster, Emmy," she said to her mother's protests. "I'll buy you a new microwave. It's Ginger's and it's very old. Give them my number here and my e-mail address in case they need to get hold of me." She knew she was trying to avoid cutting the last ties. "Don't let them take—" She listed a few items they had bought together or she had bought for Ginger.

"They're starting to pack things. I need to go, Amelia."

"Give my contact information to Joseph, not the older one, not Kevin." She wished it had been Joseph she'd talked to. He'd been closer to Ginger and more sensitive than Kevin. He'd once given Jefferson a framed sketch he'd done from a photograph of Ginger dancing. She'd never felt more accepted by the family than at that moment.

"Everything all right?" Buck asked when she ended the call.

She'd never said anything to him about being gay. Surely he'd figured it out. Would she lose his mentorship, her job, if she was open? "I lost someone I love too, Buck," she said, waiting to see if he preferred not to know.

"It was the woman you mentioned—Ginger? Is that why you left the city?"

"Staying on alone," she explained. "The person leaves her marks everywhere. Your home, your block, your friends' houses, your favorite restaurant. Like echoes coming back from someplace you can never reach again."

"Did Ginger die?"

"Yes. Here, at the cottage."

Buck's face was full of sympathy. "I'm really sorry. How long had you been...friends?"

"Something like thirty years."

Almost whispering, Buck said, "Us too."

That made her eyes smart with tears. She turned away and got the carton of milk from the refrigerator.

"Not for me, thanks," Buck said. "I need to pick up some Kytril from the pharmacy and get home with it. The old nausea med stopped working."

She nodded, still unable to speak. She wasn't the only one not having fun. The cats scattered when Buck stood. He held out his arms and looked at her. They hugged quickly, tight.

"See you at the office," Buck said as he replaced the chair, scraping its rubber casters against the linoleum. He let himself out.

She stood in the kitchen swallowing her tears. It was always like this. Suddenly she'd find herself howling in protest and pain, having no memory of a transition from not thinking about Ginger to full-throttle hurting, usually late at night, with nothing to distract her. Bent double once more with the agony of loss, she let the tears out. Some day she would stop crying. Some day she would move on. Doze stared at her, then came timidly and rubbed against her ankle. She felt a smile break through her tears, along with an exhilarating swell of love. What could she learn about love from six kittens? Adopting them, wanting to care for them, being loved was the best decision she'd ever made.

Chapter Thirty-three

D awn, who in the city would be called a sporty femme, sat slightly inside the wide, dark doorway of her garage. If someone had asked Jefferson what a sporty, or tomboy, femme was, she would have mentioned girls' softball and basketball and power tools. She would have described a woman not afraid of a challenge, who could also fold clothes neatly, cook well, and make a butchy woman feel powerful even as she gave over her power to the sporty femme.

"What's this one going to be?" asked Jefferson.

Dawn was whittling with an old green Girl Scout jackknife. She held the carving up and laughed. "A bird. Doesn't look like much, does it? I'm trying to get the wood to curve as smooth as a woman's hip."

Jefferson raised one eyebrow, but Dawn didn't notice. Although Dawn's conversation was not without sexual references, she hadn't expected her to say something that sounded so butchy. This rural Amerasian librarian was so unique that she was fascinated.

It was a mostly sunny day. Every now and then a dark cloud blocked the light enough that Dawn set the bird down. Jefferson couldn't help but wonder if country femmes seemed butchier than city femmes because they had to be more self-reliant. Once she would have checked this notion out, but these days she was about as interested as that wooden bird would be. Her life had a certain skeletal feeling right now that both scared and comforted her. Without the complications of juggling relationships, she felt free, but she had no clue about how to live unencumbered, with only herself to consider. These new friends, like this cheerful tomboy femme—she hadn't built much history with them, had no commitment to them, hadn't made love with them. She was still a free agent.

Her cell rang. She popped her Bluetooth headset into her ear and retreated to the side of the garage. It was someone rescheduling an appointment to look at a house.

"Shannon Wiley!" Dawn said when the stringy, shambling surfer-dude dyke strode into view, pushing her bike. The sun followed Shannon, who wore a silver-and-blue Xena T-shirt.

"I got a flat a block from here," her visitor said, pulling a small tool kit from the saddle bags and flipping the bike onto its handlebars. "Here." Shannon took a bunch of forget-me-nots from a pocket inside her jacket and handed it to Dawn, cheeks dimpling in an obvious struggle not to smile too widely.

While the flowers weren't a blatant courting gesture, they were more than what most friends would do. Instead of accepting them, Dawn lifted her black hair, with its strands of gray, up from her eyes, and said, "Would you fill the jelly jar on the shelf over the sink and stick them in it? I'm feeling too lazy to get up."

Shannon always did what Dawn told her to and had the jar of flowers by her feet in seconds, then walked to the other side of the driveway and rolled a tree stump over to her bike, sat down, and started fiddling with the flat tire. Dawn looked at the flowers and shook her head, smiling at Jefferson. She held out her hands, one with the bird, one empty, as if to say, "What can I do?"

To get past her awkwardness about Dawn making a co-conspirator of her, Jefferson asked, "Where'd you get all these stumps? There must be a dozen."

"When I moved here, the back lot was full of them. It'd been logged off decades ago, from the looks of it. I hired a little backhoe and dug them out. The next year, when they were dry, I used my chain saw to flatten the bottoms. I like them for sitting and for chopping wood, for drying flowers, for sawhorses, to look at."

Jefferson had never met anyone like Dawn, so feminine yet unafraid of guys' work. "And you learned to operate a backhoe where?"

"My dad has one at the farm," Dawn replied, intensely sanding a bump on the bird's tail.

Shannon said, "Geeze, my father won't let me near his circular saw, much less heavy equipment."

"I was the eldest. I got to teach the boys when they came along."

"Are all country girls like you?" Jefferson asked Dawn.

"Why? Do you need a couple?"

"A couple of country girls?" Jefferson asked, trying to pass herself off as an innocent.

Someone laughed, and Dawn looked up under her glasses at Jefferson with a smile. "I was offering tree stumps."

When Jefferson said thanks anyway, Dawn tried Shannon. "How about you?"

Jefferson realized her hands were hot and glanced around. Who was setting off her desire alarm? It had to be Dawn. She stuffed her hands in her hoodie pocket. Dawn? Really? She wasn't ready for this.

Shannon was saying, "I have real sawhorses and real lawn chairs, thank you very much."

"How can you fit all that in that cabin you're renting?" Dawn asked, an edgy sharpness to her teasing. She wondered if they were exes.

Shannon looked down. Was she embarrassed about where she lived? "My landlady lets me have space in the old barn."

A cloud bumped the sunlight. The day was both cool and not cool, kind of indecisive, the way spring could be. Shannon was following Dawn's hands as they whittled. The poor kid might start drooling if she was deprived of those hands another minute.

"Killer carving," Shannon said. "Can I see it?"

"Not till I'm done."

"I can live with that," Shannon quickly said, pursing her lips and nodding, while obviously thinking the opposite.

They sat in silence while Dawn gently carved shavings from the bird's breast. Now and then Jefferson cupped a hand underneath and caught them. They smelled like something from her past; she couldn't name what. She could see Shannon's attraction to those delicate yet sure hands. But a librarian? Maybe the stereotype put her off, but as much as she liked Dawn, she couldn't think of her as a lover. The truth was, she didn't think of anyone as a lover. That part of her was still dormant.

Shannon's hair, Jefferson thought, must really get noticed in conservative Pipsborough. Shannon had told her she'd moved back to the lake from Nashua less than a year ago. Jefferson suspected you could be a little weird in a town that size, but not here. If Shannon stayed in Pipsborough with long brown hair for the rest of her life, she wouldn't live down the impression of wildness her current do gave. Here or anywhere on Saturday Lake. Lake people seemed to have a memory for anything different, unless you were actually from the lakes, like Dawn, who had told her that her family had a farm over near Stillwater Lake. She'd promised to drive Jefferson out to see the farm and Jefferson was curious, but very leery of getting closer. She could feel Dawn's interest coming off her like waves of warmth from a woodstove. Dawn wasn't interested in Shannon, the one who wanted her. She smiled: lesbians were the same everywhere.

Rayanne came around the corner, ignoring the stop sign. She parked her silver PT Cruiser well away from the other cars. Rayanne and Dawn had met at UNH Plymouth about a thousand years ago, Dawn had said, and had a thing going, but Rayanne was a squabbler, so they graduated not speaking to each other. A few years later, after Rayanne's agency decided to open an office in Pipsborough, they ran into each other outside the post office and got in the habit of having lunch on a bench by the water in good weather and at the Oar Stand, a breakfast and lunch place, all winter. Rayanne, Dawn told Jefferson, had turned out to be a good friend.

"Greetings and salutations, comrades," Rayanne called. "If I'm at Dawn's, it must be Saturday afternoon."

"Hi, girl," Dawn said.

"What is that article of clothing you've got on?" Shannon asked. "It looks like a cross between cutoffs and capris."

"She thinks she's the fashion maven," Dawn pointed a thumb toward Shannon, "because she's seen the world." At Jefferson's raised eyebrows, Dawn explained, "In the National Guard."

Rayanne had hips like the handles on a bowling trophy. When she walked, the hips seemed to roll her along. Her oversized T-shirt read "Olivia XXX Leisure Dept."

"They're Saturday-afternoon-at-Dawn's pants."

"Après-mowing is what they look like," Shannon said. "What did you do, fall on your butt in the clippings?"

Rayanne struggled to walk a stump into the shade of the garage. Shannon got up to help her and placed the stump between Dawn and Jefferson.

"Where's Yolanda?" Shannon asked.

Dawn answered with a laugh. "Getting the beer, probably."

An earnest look appeared on Shannon's face. "Should we be worried about her drinking or what?"

"Shan," Rayanne said, "because you and Jefferson don't drink, the rest of us aren't necessarily drunks."

Dawn laughed. "Rayanne, you and Shannon ought to be lovers. You wrangle about every subject under the sun."

"This makes us compatible?" Rayanne barked. "Not my idea of the perfect marriage."

"Besides," Shannon said, twisting something on her bike tight with a wrench, "we're both butch." She staggered a bit as she rose from her bent position. For such an active woman, Shannon must find having a bad back inconvenient.

"Speak for yourself," Rayanne countered. "That is so old-school. We're past roles now."

"Rayanne," Dawn asked, "how could you not know you're butch?"

Rayanne scowled. She really was one of those naturally scrappy women. Jefferson could imagine Dawn laughing while Rayanne tossed verbal spears at her. Jefferson could also see how Dawn might be drawn to Rayanne's take-charge attitude. She asked, "How's New Hampshire Private Financial doing?"

"Hot," answered Rayanne, who worked Saturday mornings. "Really hot. I don't know where people are getting the money in this economy and with the dollar worth shit in Europe, but they're investing. The terrorists don't scare them off. Americans can't accept that we're no longer safe in the world—thank you very much, Mr. Bush. I think more investors are using us to avoid the real-estate market. Of course, now I'm competing against the online services, so I have to give a little extra in the special-attention department to—"

"There's Yolanda." Shannon was making a transparent attempt to turn off Rayanne. Once you got the woman talking about the world of finance, Jefferson noticed, there was no end to it. She felt a sad little smile move her lips. She'd love to dish this crowd with Ginger.

Yolanda Whale drove a red, long-bed Toyota pickup outfitted for her one-woman landscaping business. She was reaching into the truck bed, inevitably, for the cooler of Golden Loon, a local ale she sucked on all day. She had two bumper stickers on the back of the truck. One was for Hillary Clinton, and Jefferson could see the part of the other that read, "and magic is afoot."

"I can't decide if Yolanda is an alcoholic," Dawn said. "She's so fussy about what she drinks."

They all looked at Jefferson. She'd told them her history, but all she could do was rub her jaw, then say, "You can't tell someone she has a problem, no matter how worried you are. She has to find out herself. I mean, you can tell her, but that doesn't do any good till she's ready to hear it."

"I'm not saying she has one," Shannon replied. "She seems so close to her beers, I don't know where she'd ever fit in a girlfriend."

Rayanne asked, "And what's your excuse for not having a girlfriend?" Of course, they all knew perfectly well that Shannon's reason was hopelessly wanting Dawn.

"Do you guys look like a meeting of the Lesbian Lonely Hearts Club or what?" Yolanda said, offering bottles to Dawn and Rayanne. Rayanne accepted. Yolanda pulled a strawberry Yoo-Hoo out of her back pocket and gave it to Shannon.

Jefferson laughed. She was re-creating the Café Femmes crowd here in rural New Hampshire. She glowed with fondness for both groups. Friends, kittens, the lake—what else could she want? She glanced at Dawn. She decided she was drawn to Dawn, to her calm, her groundedness, her acceptance of and by her family. She thought Dawn was interested, but was she?

"Oh, cool," said Shannon, opening the bottle quickly and gulping half the beverage down. "Thanks," she said to Yolanda.

Jefferson had brought the Manhattan Special sarsaparilla that she imported by the case from the city.

"I don't know why you like that pink chalk so much," Rayanne said.

Shannon answered with a gurgling strawberry chuckle. "Yoo-hoo's better than that slug bait you guys swill. Thanks, though."

Dawn's eyes just touched Jefferson's before she refused the ale.

"PMS?" Yolanda asked.

"No, I don't want to hurt the baby," Dawn replied, with a straight face.

She watched as every head turned to stare at Dawn, locked in place until she laughed. Dawn's laughter sounded so delighted, so contagious, that even Rayanne couldn't stop long enough to scold her.

"You got us," Yolanda finally managed to say before her giggles started again.

Jefferson spent another hour listening to her new friends open bottles, bicker, and joke. Sleepy, she watched as the woman across the street weeded at the side of her house, a wide straw hat shading her face. Ginger should be here, she thought again, cruising into a dream.

Early in their relationship Ginger had always been ready to stroll down to the lake, go for a swim, help with a cookout, making it all fun because they were together. But then if Ginger were still around they wouldn't be in New Hampshire, they'd be in the city; they wouldn't be with this group. On a spring Saturday afternoon they'd be watching the gang play softball. No, she'd be watching softball. Ginger would be teaching unless the game ran late. Saturday was a big day for dance lessons and recitals.

Ginger had liked to stay in on Saturday nights, the night Jefferson most liked to party. It was seldom that she could get Ginger to go to Café Femmes with her, and, to be fair, she usually didn't go with Ginger anymore to the dance performances Ginger loved. Symphony Space, the Joyce SoHo, the Kitchen—she'd been to so many with Ginger, but the truth was that if Ginger wasn't dancing, or if they weren't dancing together, she was pretty bored. The best time of year was summer, when they went to the Midsummer Night's Swing at Lincoln Center and danced outdoors to all kinds of bands with hundreds of people. Ginger gave early evening dance lessons there, and on those nights Jefferson would join her as her demonstration partner, dressed in a black shirt with cream-colored silk tie and vest. They would go to eat and return to dance for fun to swing music, salsa, and everything in between.

Those nights had been highlights in her life. Not much could compare to the high of leading Ginger, a fantastic dancer, on a summer's night, publicly, in a salsa. Ginger would wear a flared skirt and a light top— Jefferson's favorite was a sleeveless V-neck orange pullover that slipped down Ginger's shoulders as they danced. Ginger's long red hair swept across her bare shoulders. When they went home, Jefferson anticipated that she would be unusually inspired in her lovemaking, the rhythms of the night dictating the placement of her lips, her hands on Ginger's body, how she'd slide a thigh between Ginger's legs, how she'd run the arch of a foot along Ginger's calf, the pulsing of her tongue on Ginger's narrow labia and the tiny clitoris that made her feel so tender each time she exposed it. Year after year she forgot, until the cab ride home, how worn out Ginger would be, how she wanted nothing but sleep.

Now and then on those dancing nights, Ginger pinned a rose to Jefferson's vest, usually pink, for its erotic contrast with the androgynous tie. For years now, Ginger hadn't done that or wanted to make love after dancing. Jefferson felt a wave of separation anxiety, but from what? The dream? A constant hope? A habit of expectation? Every night for all those years she hoped there would be a lover in their bed.

After so many years of conflict and distress—running after women, Ginger walking out—after her drinking stopped and they relaxed into the conflict of their crazily enduring love, after hitting their stride together in so many ways, Ginger had to die?

One of the neighbor's cats came by. It was the stubby little tiger who always begged for affection. She lifted him to her lap and scratched under his chin.

"You okay, Dawn?" Yolanda asked. "You're kind of quiet."

Dawn laid her head back on the bunched-up hood of her navy blue sweatshirt and blew air through her pursed lips, a sound the little tiger stopped purring to attend. "I've been offered the job in Concord."

Yolanda looked away, her mouth open. Rayanne said, "No." Shannon looked at her like she'd announced she was going straight.

"It's a director position. More money, more variety, more challenge."

"But," Shannon said.

"Is that why you went to Concord the week before last? For an interview?" Yolanda's voice was tense with accusation.

Dawn looked at her hands, gouging little bits of wood to form a lifting wing. "I didn't want to say anything in case it didn't work out."

"You're leaving us?" Yolanda said. "But this is my family."

"How much are you asking for the house?" Rayanne asked.

Jefferson scratched the kitty behind its ears. The lake seemed to be rapidly draining, the landscape altering beyond imagination. A lawnmower droned up the street.

All the delight had gone out of Dawn's eyes. It was clear to Jefferson she didn't want to work in Concord. What was going on? She was happy in her work and had friends. Was there a problem with her family? Weren't they all, as American lesbians, hard-wired to leave their hometowns to seek romance and their fortunes?

"I don't want to leave all of you," Dawn explained, "or my family. But I'm treading water here."

Shannon's voice had a plea in it. "You love your job."

Jefferson knew Shannon would be hardest hit, because Shannon thought she had a chance with Dawn. She slung an arm over Shannon's shoulders to commiserate.

"You think you'll meet somebody in Concord? Somebody better than you'll find on the lake?" Yolanda asked.

Dawn shook her head. The sweet tan pit bull from up the street ambled by and sniffed a rosebush. The tiger spat and launched itself off Jefferson's chest, raking her skin through her shirt. She swallowed her startled cry to listen to Rayanne.

"You'll be able to retire earlier," Rayanne said. "And get a bigger pension. You're almost fifty—I can see why you've got to go. And it's only an hour and a half away."

"Thirty-eight is not almost fifty," Shannon, thirty-six, protested, as if defending Dawn from attack.

Rayanne said, "I can rent you my little guest cottage when you come to town to see us. I'll give you a good break."

"Geeze, Ray, listen to yourself," Yolanda said. "If you come back to visit, Dawn, you're staying in my guest room."

"Or in my cabin? I could go stay with my dad," Shannon offered, staring at Dawn as if willing her to stay and share her bed.

Dawn interrupted. "Sometimes you'll want to come to the city, won't you?"

"Shopping," Rayanne exclaimed. "We can do Steeplegate Mall."

Yolanda opened another ale and glugged down a good portion of it. Jefferson knew how that went—Dawn's plans were another excuse to drink more. No one knew better than she did that removing the femme from the equation would ruin everything. She could see that the four of them had a tender balance, house-sitting for one another, hosting round-robin weeding parties, meeting at Dawn's as a kind of anchor to their weeks. She'd learned, too, that Shannon cleaned gutters for Rayanne, who was afraid of heights, and had been roped into cleaning all the others' too. Yolanda hauled everyone's trash in the pickup, Rayanne did their taxes, Dawn did basic house repair.

For herself, the thought of starting out again on her own, even as a real-estate seller, still scared the socks off her. Zoloft or no, she needed these new friends and didn't want to see the foursome melt away. Then, too, there was the strange tug on her heart Dawn's announcement had brought. But look at her, the funny little tomboy. Dawn reached down to pull up her soccer socks and brushed wood chips off her knee. She wore what she'd said were her brother's old red soccer shorts and a huge tie-dyed T-shirt in swirls of primary colors. Dawn clearly wasn't interested in projecting femme allure to this group, but damn, Jefferson thought, feeling a spark of her old self, she looked inexplicably good in that getup.

Yolanda walked a stump over and sat, blowing into the neck of her bottle to make a deep, mournful sound.

"I can't deal with this subject," said Rayanne. "Did you hear Spain is making gay weddings legal?"

Yolanda sputtered. "Spain? They've got more Catholics than Massachusetts."

Dawn was clearly glad to get on to another subject. "Does that make the U.S. the most knee-jerk country on the globe?"

"Who cares!" Shannon wailed. "Is this world all about couples? The four of us get along fine single."

Yolanda drank and played a new note. "Personally, I am pretty fried with all this gay-marriage publicity. They ought to leave it alone before some straight starts killing honeymooners in P-town."

"I don't think I could find a marriage that's better than what we have," Rayanne said.

"Had," Yolanda pointed out.

"Check it out: it's not over till it's over," Shannon cried, echoing Jefferson's words.

Dawn looked as if she'd known it would be bad, but hadn't expected this. She walked to the refrigerator and poured some iced tea. "Come on, guys," Dawn said. "Tell me how I can turn my back on this job."

"Watch this!" Yolanda said, standing and turning until her back was to them. "Piece of cake."

"You jerk," Dawn said, laughing.

Yolanda sat down on her stump again. "Seriously, if I give you a million dollars, will you stay?"

She laughed again. "Make it two million and you're on."

"Hey," Rayanne said. "If that's what happens when you threaten to leave, I'm leaving too."

"Marry me." Shannon dropped to one skinny knee. "I'll support you. You'll never have to work again."

"Watch out, Dawn," Yolanda warned, "she's serious."

"No, she's not," Rayanne said. "Shannon's tired of living in her cabin. She wants to move in with you so she doesn't have to get a real job."

Dawn smiled fondly at Shannon, as if she knew the woman was serious. "Get up." She raised her chin upward. She didn't seem to mind having three butch admirers, but she also seemed real clear that she wasn't stringing them along. "Sorry, Shannon. There's nothing I'd like better than someone to marry—except being single." Was that true? Dawn didn't move her eyes from her carving.

"What are you asking Dawn to marry you for?" Yolanda asked with an affronted tone. "She's already married. To us."

"Oh, right," Rayanne said. "The world is going to love it when we demand equal rights for group gay marriages. Wouldn't some of those bigamist religions be pleased."

"I'm really serious this time," said Yolanda. "This is as good as it gets for me. We don't fight, don't get in one another's faces, can leave at the end of the day, but we know we're here for each other. That's like all the good stuff and none of the bad."

Shannon asked, her voice wistful, "Isn't there something missing?"

Rayanne laughed. "You may have a point. Romance? Sex? Are they worth it?"

"And if we were married, you wouldn't leave us. Either we'd all go," Yolanda argued, "or we'd all stay."

"Or we'd divorce," Dawn suggested.

"That's what it feels like," Shannon said. "It feels like you told us you're getting a divorce."

Yolanda opened another ale. Shannon wrung her hands. Rayanne stared at the woman across the street. The neighbor was rolling out a rumbling, overflowing weed-filled trash can. Jefferson had pulled almost as many weeds early that morning while it was still cool. Her laundry was done. Before quitting and checking in at the office, she'd groomed the kittens, who had acted like she was trying to kill them. That had helped defrost her beat-up old heart.

"What about Snickers?" she asked.

Dawn answered. "Look at him in the window watching for signs that I'm coming in to feed him his cat food." She sighed. "I'll have to find an apartment that allows pets. I won't buy anything until this house sells and I know the job's for me."

Shannon said, "I'll keep the house up. If things don't work out you can come back." Shannon didn't have a steady job. She cleaned pools in the summer and washed dishes at the inn weekends and holidays year-round. She rented a small, unheated cottage out of town and seemed to survive the cold-weather months with a space heater and an incredible number of layers.

"Oh, right," Rayanne said. "Like she can afford to buy in Concord if she keeps this place."

"I can't picture you in Concord," Yolanda said. "Where are you going to carve? I can't see you in an apartment building, with no yard work and no gang to hang out with."

"I'll check *Out In the Mountains*, that gay paper, for a hiking group."

"They folded," Rayanne said. "I used to advertise there."

"Anyone want iced tea?" Dawn asked, going back to the garage.

Shannon followed her inside and grabbed a mug she kept over the laundry tub. "Did you already accept the job?" Jefferson heard her ask Dawn in a low voice.

"They gave me to the weekend to decide."

"Come to my place for dinner."

"Are you asking the others?"

"No!" Shannon said.

Jefferson shook her head. Suddenly, shy Shannon was making her move. She was cute in a desperate kind of way. When Jefferson looked around, she saw that the others were listening too.

"Better to stop her now," Rayanne whispered, "than to build up her hopes."

"I don't think so, Shannon," they heard from the garage.

Shannon sounded like her next word hurt coming out. "Why?"

"I like things the way they are."

"I wasn't going to—"

"We won't tempt fate, okay?"

"It's because you're not over Bonnie yet, isn't it. That was four years ago!"

Drew had filled Jefferson in about the woman Dawn was with when she bought this house. Tall, sports-crazy, fickle Bonnie was what he'd called her. Drew had said that he still couldn't believe Dawn hadn't known what Bonnie was doing behind her back. That shame, he'd said, was part of what kept her from trying again.

Had Ginger felt shame when she caught Jefferson fooling around?

Why hadn't she seen what harm she was doing? It was so clear to her now.

Shannon strode from the garage and asked the others, "What good is getting the okay to marry when nobody wants me?"

Dawn had already turned her back. She seemed not to hear Shannon.

"We've decided," Rayanne said when Shannon sat again.

"Decided what?"

"You're not going," Yolanda told her.

"Of course I'm going. Don't you guys want the best for me?"

Rayanne laughed. For all her sharp words, she had a laugh like tickled wind. Dawn smiled despite herself as Rayanne said, "Not without us!"

"We're going to tie you up and keep you here, that's all there is to it," said Yolanda, taking Dawn's hands in her own and swaying face-to-face with her. "Flatten your tires, put sugar in your Subaru's tank, call Concord and tell them what a mistake they'd be making."

"Yeah," Rayanne added, "tell them you're queer."

"These days, that would probably make a library hire me so they didn't get in trouble for discriminating."

"But seriously," Rayanne said, "you are plain nuts to leave the lake. Everybody wants to live here, you know that. And to have a job here? We are living every sucker's dream. How can you think about giving it up?"

"You want to meet someone, don't you." Yolanda's voice had a new edge to it and sounded accusatory. "The lake lezzies aren't good enough for you."

Shannon was quick to say, "That's her right."

"At least," Yolanda said, "there's a couple of bars there."

Rayanne asked, "Will you still go to Women Outdoors with us?"

"Not if she has a girlfriend," Yolanda declared.

"Wait a minute," said Rayanne. "This is the best place to attract a girlfriend. Who wouldn't want to move to the lake?"

"Do I get to say anything?" Dawn asked. "I don't want to leave the lake."

"So why go?" Yolanda asked.

Jefferson could hear a robin in the tree in Dawn's backyard. Rayanne looked puzzled, Shannon looked anxious, and Yolanda said, "Maybe it's because I know my brother and I are going to inherit the shop, but I can't get all that excited about career moves that rip me away from everything I love. This is your home, Dawn."

Rayanne said, "Maybe you're ambitious. There's nothing wrong with that. It's the American way."

"You should know," said Yolanda.

"I'm not ambitious," Rayanne said. "I like money."

"Who doesn't?" asked Yolanda.

Rayanne answered, "Shannon."

Shannon grinned. "I guess I'm not very ambitious."

Dawn sighed. "All right. You find me the woman I'm looking for around here and I'll stay."

"I told you it was about meeting someone, didn't I?" Yolanda declared.

Dawn sat and began to whittle again. She had small but sensitive-looking hands, very dexterous. It was amazing that she could both whittle and keep her manicure. There was nothing as lovely as a femme's touch. Femmes somehow managed to make touch as gentle as dandelion fluff, yet exciting beyond imagination. Her voice was as light as her touch, clear, but quiet, like grasses rustling in the lake.

She was so different from Ginger—and from all the women she'd been with. There was none of the New York jangle, rushing, or ego about her. Jefferson couldn't imagine Dawn contained inside crowded buildings. She belonged to the lake and the country air. Her friends were right; she was as much a part of this place as the native trees and birds. Dawn would have fit in before the settlers arrived, when it was all lake and forest. She drifted into a dream of colonial days and walking across a village green with Dawn, courting her in a gentlemanly way.

But Dawn was telling them about her dream partner, looking at her knife and wooden bird. "She'd be on the tall side, with thick hair I'd want to run my hands through—maybe brown, but some gray would be fine. She'd be sturdily built, but not fleshy, strong-looking. Probably late forties and survived some tough times, or maybe in her fifties already. She might not sound like a New Englander, but she'd fit into this upscale resort town somehow, like she was bred to money. It would be the woman's hands that would be most striking, though. On the large side, long-fingered, younger than her face, with prominent veins that made them look stronger. And experienced. She'd have to be very experienced."

Jefferson ran through the small inventory of dykes she'd met on the lake, but couldn't think of one that fit the description. That's when she realized the women were looking at her hands. A trickle of excitement moved through her. Would her hands be considered big, her fingers seem long? Hadn't others remarked on their strength?

CHAPTER THIRTY-FOUR

Jefferson was learning that love is a hard habit to break.

"No matter how much I try to stay open to being with someone else, when I remember Ginger, there's no way."

Shannon, with her high energy and need to please, was helping her get the bottom scum and algae off the Runabout. Jefferson's parents had been there so little the past several years that Jarvy hadn't taken his usual loving care of it. She had the engine in town being overhauled.

The day was glorious: blue lake, blue sky, mellow sun, smooth mahogany. She was learning, in sobriety, that her good emotions could be overwhelming, and the bad now had blunted edges. This spring was long and lovely.

"You could have any woman in the world—even Xena—with your looks and a house by the lake. You're nuts."

She examined the kid. Shannon wore black canvas sneakers with holes at the small and great toes, camo cutoffs, and yet another Xena T-shirt with its sleeves ripped off. The bleached tufts of her hair were pointing every which way. She looked like she'd barely survived a major battle with something much bigger than herself: a hurricane, a bear, deep depression. Her eyes were big in her pale face, her cheeks as sunken as if she'd lost her teeth. Her lips were badly chapped, and her roots were growing out a dull brown.

Jefferson had been listening to Mozart, but Shannon said she needed a beat to work and changed the station to rock.

"You mean I could have Dawn."

Not looking her way, Shannon said, "I think she's stayed so far because you moved here."

"Shannon, you have Dawn on the brain." She wondered if her lack of interest in Dawn was Dawn's very availability. Playing hard-to-get wasn't Dawn's style.

"I wish that's what was on my brain."

She pushed up the sleeve of her purple, white, and gold hoodie and poked at the boat's joints with a screwdriver to make sure the wood was firm and not rotting. Without the Zoloft, hearing Shannon's troubles would put her in a bad space. "Shannon Wiley," she said.

Shannon stood up to stretch, grimacing as if pain was moving through her back. Eyes downcast, she apologized. "I've bugged Dawn and Yolanda about this so much. I have to talk to somebody else or I'll go nuts."

"Want more iced tea?"

Shannon held out her plastic glass and Jefferson filled it from the pitcher. The ice cubes were almost melted and had stopped their conking sounds. She sprayed some cleaner on the hull and waited for Shannon to open up. The woman wasn't that much younger than she was, yet treated Jefferson like an elder. Of course, Shannon acted like a teenager, with her crush, her bicycle, her perpetual joblessness, and her gamin looks. Jefferson vowed to listen and not advise. She didn't know much more than Shannon did about how to live life.

"What's going on? You look shook-up." Maybe younger than a teen, she thought. Shannon looked like a little boy, lower lip wobbly, trying to be brave and hold back tears.

"I got a letter from the National Guard. They're calling me back. I'm scared they'll send me to Iraq. I can't go to Iraq. Or Afghanistan. I'll die from the heat alone, never mind, you know, the bombs and stuff. It gets up to a hundred thirty degrees in Iraq—can people survive in that heat? I don't know where the heck Afghanistan is."

"There's no way out?"

Shannon sounded very adult as she explained. "They're not letting much of anybody leave the service, whether or not their enlistment terms are up. They could get me over there and keep me for fifteen months, eight years—if I lived that long. I was active-duty in 1998–99, and then I was in the National Guard for three years. The army wrote me a few months ago about transferring from the Individual Ready Reserve to the National Guard or reserve. They made me think I wouldn't go to Iraq if I did that. I didn't know what to do. What could I do? I didn't know if they were twisting my arm to volunteer. I stayed in the IRR because I'd be out in June. None of my old army pals knew which way to turn either."

"My brain is spinning. I didn't know there was something besides the guard and the regular reserves."

"The IRR is, like, different. We don't do a regular schedule of training. We're not paid like reservists. But we can get recalled in an emergency because we still have that reserve-duty commitment. I heard at least two thousand IRRs transferred to either the army reserve or the National Guard. I'll bet you the ones who went for it will go over too." Shannon sat on the edge of the dock and covered her face with her hands. "I am so scared."

"Would your back keep you out?"

"What the fuck? There's nothing wrong with my back."

Jefferson wasn't going to argue. She'd seen it often enough: athletes so used to living with their pain that they didn't even notice it was there. What could she say to Shannon? She'd never been much at coming up with solutions to other people's problems or comforting them. It wasn't that she didn't care—or was it? Was she learning to care more, post-alcohol? Maybe she did care about this kid. Well, like they said in the program, fake it till you make it. She scrubbed at another spot of mildew. "Not everyone goes, do they?"

"Check. Thousands of soldiers killed since 2003."

"Oh, boy."

The kid was crying now. "What would you do?"

She thought carefully. What would she do? "Back when I was your age I was drinking a lot. I would have pretended to myself that it was no big deal, gone over there, and stayed drunk as much as I could. Now, though, I can't imagine being able to pull it off. I'd see if my parents' old friends could pull any strings. They know a lot of people, including retired army and Washington insiders."

"My parents don't know anybody. My dad got early layoff as a machinist at a furnace factory and my mom works in a card shop at the big mall. They didn't want me to go into the service, but I thought I could meet some gay girls there. Pipsborough isn't exactly Northampton."

"So did you?"

Shannon was scrubbing the hull with wide, fast swipes, grinning despite the tears drying on her face. She snuffled. "Sure, loads of them. I

was seeing a girl while I was still in boot camp. It got better from there."
She dipped her rag in a bucket and wiped her nose with her sleeve. "I'd
have to leave my cat with my folks. He wouldn't understand why I left
him." She shook her head. "I guess the army wouldn't care that he's my
dependent."

"What about telling them you're gay?"

"That only matters in peacetime, unless they catch you. This gives
them a chance to kill us."

"You're kidding me, right?" She raked her fingers through her
hair.

"Hell, no." Shannon looked shocked, as if everyone should know
the deal with gay soldiers. "Each queer they send over means some
straight boy doesn't have to go. And if I tell them, then I might have a
less-than-honorable discharge."

"So you think there's more of a chance you'll go."

"I know they're still kicking some of us out, but at the rate the
enemy's blowing up soldiers? I think we'll all go."

"Have you thought about Canada?"

"I don't much want to live up there. But I got my cat's papers from
the vet in case. It was one thing when Vietnam draft dodgers went north.
Canada's not taking in AWOL Americans this time around."

She wondered what Dawn's father would say to this dilemma,
given his illness, his daughter's disability, and his marriage to the enemy.
"I don't know what to say, Shannon. It kind of sounds like you signed a
contract you can't renege on."

Shannon hung her head like one of Jefferson's kids in trouble for
daydreaming in the outfield. "Not while I'm alive."

"Hey, you could meet the love of your life over there."

Shannon's face was solemn, but her eyes looked as if she was
savoring that imagined meeting, and soon her deep dimples began to
show like little shadows on her cheeks. "With my luck she'd be Iraqi and
her fundamentalist brother would catch us in bed."

"Or you'd be with her when your company is attacked."

"I can't believe we're over there at all. I wouldn't hesitate to go if
they were landing at Hampton Beach."

What did this youngster want from her? Maybe nothing. What
could she give her? Maybe nothing.

Shannon stood, rag dipping. "Listen," she said with her brawny

New Hampshire accent. "If I disappear, to wherever, would you do me a favor?"

Here it came.

Shannon Wiley had a desperate look. "Would you look after my cat? And Dawn?"

Jefferson thought she could see the conflict flashing like a danger signal in her eyes. Would Jefferson steal Dawn? Of course not, Jefferson thought. She and Dawn Northway talked as she and Ginger never had, even in the beginning. The words, like storms of memory, that she'd never shared with anyone, poured out of her: the women, her grandparents, drinking, her bare-bones career…

She drew them all for Dawn with words. She never knew she had such a need to talk to someone. Not even with Lily Ann had she opened up this much. Something about Dawn, the feeling of Dawn, some gladness of spirit, relaxed Jefferson. Was it because they weren't lovers? She wanted Dawn to know everything about her, bad and good, before—before what? Becoming lovers? Before losing her to someone else? Before she lost her because of her terrible confessions? Before she lost the impulse to lay herself bare? Yes and no. It was because she had that same gladness of spirit. Dawn knew how to be happy. She liked being happy. Nothing had crushed that spirit.

She never felt ashamed when she shared stuff with Dawn, nor did Dawn ever blanch. Dawn responded with stories of her own, mild in comparison though they were. She might even, Jefferson suspected by the flush of Dawn's face and the quick cascade of her words, be turned on by Jefferson's lustiest escapades.

And then there were the other stories. Jefferson's and Dawn's: Jefferson's sports failures and triumphs; how Dawn's father rescued her mother's family, risking everything himself. How her mother and father fell in love at first sight, she cowering in her hooch, shielding her younger siblings with her body, he appalled by orders to shoot everyone and following the family down the tunnel in the floor of their home. Dawn said she expected the same for herself. It was as if her parents recognized each other from some forever time ago when they were locked together in some way. One day Dawn confessed that she'd had the same feeling the night Jefferson walked into that church basement, and she followed it with a quick joke about having a gene for underground love.

Dawn said she hoped that confiding in Jefferson wouldn't chase her off. She told Jefferson how much she valued their friendship and companionship above all else in her life. She asked for nothing more, would accept nothing more. Jefferson admitted that sometimes she'd gone with women because she didn't know how to say no. Dawn was looking for love, not kindness; a soul mate, not sex. If it turned out right between them, if Jefferson came to feel as she did, they'd know because they would combust in passion, there would be no mistaking it. Meanwhile, Jefferson, for once in her life, was content to wait. Talking was proving to be as gratifying as physical seduction.

"Shannon," she began to caution, then remembered that when she was Shannon's age, everything felt this important. Shannon wanted her to keep anyone from horning in on Dawn. She could see how she had fooled herself into thinking she could control anything now that she watched Shannon make the same thinking error. "Does Dawn need looking after?"

"Everybody needs looking after."

It wasn't her place to open Shannon's eyes to her ulterior motive. She wanted her to know she had no designs on Dawn. Who knew what life would bring while Shannon was away? It was very possible she wouldn't come back, or would come back missing limbs, crazed by heat and violence and fear, needing care herself. Did lesbians have a way to help their own veterans? She'd never thought of this before. Wasn't Shannon really asking Jefferson to take care of, to save PFC Shannon Wiley? She shook her head. Most of her adult life had been about taking care of women. Right now Jefferson, finally sleeping through some nights and eating better, was numero uno for Jefferson.

"I can be her friend," she told Shannon. "And yours." She thrust with her putty knife to emphasize what she was saying. "But I'm nobody's mother and I have fewer answers every day."

Shannon gave her a wide-eyed look, like she knew Jefferson did have the answers and was withholding them. "If anything happened to Dawn," Shannon explained, "I might as well go over there and let them do me in so I don't end up doing it all myself."

When Jefferson was alone again, thinking about young Shannon, she felt like she'd learned nothing in her whole life and all of a sudden she was expected to be this expert on everything. Didn't it show that she was all hollow? Shouldn't she be able to at least come up with a way to think things through? Why? She'd never thought anything through in her life. Her decision to leave the city itself had been nothing more than a reaction to Ginger's illness, maybe a belated reaction to 9/11. She was always running from pain. How smart was that? Pain hadn't beaten her yet. Her spirit was as strong as Dawn's and always would be.

"Don't try to escape the pain, Shannon," was all she'd been able to advise, gesturing to the lake with the knife. "It's like trying to drain the lake dry."

CHAPTER THIRTY-FIVE

On Jefferson's forty-ninth birthday in August when she had no prospective buyers or new listings, and to celebrate her first house sale, she went with Dawn to see her parents' farm. As she drove, Dawn pointed out her personal landmarks and told funny stories about each. They skirted Lake Winnipesaukee south, then headed west for another twenty minutes, climbing and descending the twisting roads, bouncing over frost heaves, coming suddenly on wide-open views of meadows and the mountains beyond. Dawn exclaimed at the purplish red clover and the light blue yarrow flowers. Occasionally they came to an intersection that boasted a predictably white church and an out-of-business gas station with the original red pumps or an open general store/post office/video-rental shop, also white, often peeling. Large grayed houses offered living rooms and front porches converted to antique shops or junk heaps. Between intersections the houses were rare and usually white, sometimes red or cedar shingled.

Dawn drove without haste. Jefferson, fighting to stay awake after another night of insomnia, asked questions. It occurred to her that she seldom got to know women in this way. Pillow talk had always been her style. She missed the touching and dipping in and out of a woman, interrupting life stories with lovemaking.

Women loved to tell their stories and Dawn Northway was no different. That was one of her appeals: despite everything that attracted Jefferson to Dawn—her sunny energy, her prized Asian heritage, the way she would give a sudden shout and leap to a tree limb, then climb and grin back down at her friends, her passion for women's basketball—the woman was a regular femme. She shopped at the malls and primped before going out; she could whip up a tasty stir-fry and folded her laundry in thirds, patting it even.

Jefferson's phys ed background made her sensitive to the way people moved. It hadn't taken her long to notice that Dawn's left leg was less flexible than her right. Dawn didn't so much limp as have a slight hitch to her step. This seemed like a good time to ask whether she had been injured.

"No," Dawn answered. "Agent Orange touched all of us in one way or another. One of my sisters had spina bifida. She died seven years ago because her urinary tract was malformed and there was not much they could do surgically. My brother is slightly mentally retarded, but he can do farm work. Mom had three miscarriages. The chemical can make babies more prone to infection, and that's what I had, a bone infection. They had to remove some of the bone. My left leg is shorter than the right and the leg didn't develop like it should. They said I almost died. Carrying this leg around helps me remember how lucky I am to be alive, despite Agent Orange. Both Mom and Dad were exposed to it. Mom has scars on her hands and back, and Dad has leukemia."

She whistled and touched Dawn's cheek lightly with her knuckles. "Yet you're always laughing. Couldn't have been much fun for a little girl. Or a big girl."

"Years of exercise regimes right into my teens. But I showed them. I downhill ski, I water-ski, and two years ago I learned to snowboard. Some day I'll get a wetsuit and drive over to the shore to surf. Read my blog. It's the first place I've been able talk about it."

"I don't think I could read it. Blogs make me feel like I'm reading people's diaries. Tell me why such an active person went into library work?"

"Oh, it's exciting! I've always read a lot and I think reading is the cure for all ills in this society. Look at the prejudice against gays. It comes from lack of education. If we could get books about us into the schools and libraries it could be our era of enlightenment, Jefferson."

"That simple, is it?"

"No, it's not simple at all, but it can be done." Dawn emphasized her point with a gentle touch on Jefferson's leg. "My first job was as a worker bee in the NYC Public Library. I was only a page so I had a lot of public contact, and I saw all sorts of kids looking for books about themselves."

"You were in the city?"

"I got my master's from the School of Information and Library Science at Pratt. I interned at the Yorkville Branch of the New York Public Library. It was between Second and Third avenues."

"I know it."

"Do you?" Dawn gave a buoyant little laugh. "Everyone around here seems to think I made up this fairy tale about living in New York or else why wouldn't I still be there?"

"Good question."

Dawn looked over at her. "Why aren't you?"

She thought for a moment of a way to say it all in a nutshell. "I've only known the city and our summer place. The city stopped working for me. I needed to start fresh, to leave some things behind." She paused to see if she wanted to share more, but, no, talking about Ginger wasn't in her game plan today. "I feel more alive here now than I do in the city, though when I was younger, I felt more alive there." She checked herself for the truth of this and found she felt exactly that way. "And why didn't you stay?"

"Oh," she said, with that openness of hers that made Jefferson feel like she could trust her in everything. "My parents paid the tuition on the condition that I come back here when there was an opening I liked. They don't exactly grow on trees, small-town library jobs. So it didn't happen for a while. We tend to stay till we retire." Dawn laughed again. Jefferson noticed that her blue eyes appeared streaked with light. "And on our wages, we don't retire young, us stuffy old librarians."

Jefferson laughed with her, all too aware that she was guilty of imposing the stuffy stereotype on fun-loving Dawn. She spotted a foal huddling near its mother.

Dawn cried, "Cute," and, in her chatty way, launched into yet another anecdote about growing up on the farm, this one having to do with a kitten who thought a foal was his mother.

"I haven't laughed this much in years," Jefferson admitted. How could she not respond to such open expressions of joy?

"I have to say," Dawn replied, "you're easy."

Laughing yet again, she said, "Tell me about working in the city. It must have been different for you, after," she spread her arms to indicate the farm, "this." She found herself missing the city or maybe missing her coaching days. She still had her national credentials. She'd have to think about getting back into it here in New Hampshire.

"In the city? I worked up from the circulation desk to collections development," Dawn said as they rolled past a collapsed barn. "I did materials selection, programming, bibliographic instruction, community outreach, and helped patrons with the Internet. The volume of users and shortage of staff made me feel like a production worker in a factory. I got to know a few patrons, and I still get together with some of the staff when I go to library-association conferences and when I go to the city. Surviving that crazy busy job gave me the confidence to know I could run a rural library, even a small, underfunded one. It seems like I work all the time now, going to meetings at night to keep the town's goodwill, filling in for volunteers who don't show up, but I love my job." Dawn laughed again. "If I move to Concord I'd work as much, but get paid better. And I'd be away from this board, or at least from the bitch on wheels."

"Someone's bugging you?"

"Donna Green, the book-banner. She and her husband retired and built a gigantic McMansion over on Winnipesaukee. She doesn't want a lesbian running her library. I'd rather leave than get fired for some trumped-up reason that covers up homophobia."

"I remember going through that. You're damned either way."

"You are. She's driving off other board members—they can't work with her. Why don't you volunteer for the board?"

"Me? Oh, Dawn, thank you for the compliment. They want respectable people on boards, not gays."

"Jef." Dawn used her nickname for the first time, a sign of warmth that gave Jefferson unexpected pleasure. "I hate to be the one to break it to you, but you *are* respectable. You're a home owner with roots in the area, people know your parents, you're a realtor, a volunteer coach—how much more respectable could you be?"

"It's hard to forget, you know: getting fired so much, blowing my chance at professional golf, the drinking, all the women."

Dawn was smiling with what looked like affection. "You sound more proud than worried about your sordid past."

She realized Dawn was right and grinned. "I did relish certain parts of being the big bad wolf."

"I'll bet you did," Dawn said with a knowing grin. "I think you're trying to get out of being on the board."

"I'm not much for sitting around listening."

Dawn said nothing. This, thought Jefferson, is how femmes get me into bed. "I'll give it a try," she conceded.

"It would be so terrific to have one more vote. I mean, this woman was livid when she saw my banned-book-week posters. She wanted to burn them."

"If she quits, I get to resign?"

Dawn smiled. "We'll revisit it if and when, okay?"

She shook her head as Dawn changed the subject. "There's Stillwater Lake. It's always been too shallow and mossy for swimming, but it makes canoeing interesting."

She imagined paddling with Dawn to the treed island she could see partway across the lake. But no, she had to get out of the habit of viewing every femme as a potential fling. That wouldn't do in a small town where you were likely to see the woman the next day at Food Fresh or couldn't borrow a library book without an awkward encounter.

What a bummer. She was free. She could see whoever she wanted and without guilt. Here was this lovely woman whose eyes, raised at the corners and narrow-lidded, hinted of her Viet-French ancestry.

Jefferson's hands felt so empty these days. She spent parts of her wakeful nights longing to press her body against another woman's, longing to hold her hands and to feel her lips, as she had longed for Ginger, sleeping beside her, but unattainable most of their years together. The need for a lover had an urgency like a powerful spring fever that consumed her. It had always been like this, from Angie on, and during the day her restless vision darted into shadows, searching. She felt like some sort of love missile, on fire herself, seeking heat akin to her own. She was reemerging after Ginger and was bowled over by the raging emotions and urges of a seventeen-year-old. She didn't want to leave the cocoon of her safe solitude. It's no wonder I drank back then, she thought. Was there no escape from longing?

At the same time she felt worn-out, too old for love games. Her body, once so like an adolescent boy's, was breaking down. Her knees hurt when she walked. Lifting her grandmother's heavy frying pan brought back her golf elbow. She was growing softer and rounder, but early arthritis limited the exercise she could do. She wasn't golfing these days either. Who would want to be courted by someone turning gray in all the wrong places?

Dawn was explaining more about her job. Jefferson was trying to listen, but really was deciding that she was kidding herself. Being a lover was for kids, yet she felt like a kid. What was up with that? Was it menopause coming on like an enormous fast ball, messing with her hormones so she didn't feel the urge one day and it slammed her the next? Its timing was good, given that she was going to live here, so far from cruise central, where she'd either be prowling every night or completely out of the loop, home moping. She sort of missed the edge cheating gave her. There was no getting away from it. She was still, when she was switched on, a compulsive lover and a chronic seducer. Ginger had been perfect for her: a permanent challenge and frustration. Jefferson lived in hope, always at the ready, seduction refined to something so subtle Ginger could not be offended at Jefferson's overtures. Jefferson waited and tried and went elsewhere, but always came back, burning for Ginger.

The burning had not disappeared; only Ginger was gone. Ginger was the dance of love, always dancing away, Jefferson always in pursuit.

Dawn had grown silent. Jefferson glanced at her. She really was a pretty woman. Sitting by her side was a pleasure. Dawn looked her way. They smiled. She kissed her fingertips and touched Dawn's cheek again, overcome with a shyness she'd never experienced before.

"Your farm," she said as it came into view, "is picture-perfect." They had passed miles of summer corn and now she saw a herd of hefty cattle off in the distance. Herefords, Dawn told her. The two-rail picket fence along the road was a pristine white, and the stone wall by the entrance to the driveway was in perfect shape. As they drove around to the back of the house she noticed that the kitchen garden had rows of lettuce, squash, green beans, strawberries, spinach, and more. The deer fence around it must have been eight feet high. The house glowed white with neat dark blue shutters and clean many-paned windows that looked like originals.

"Dawn," cried a small woman with rouged-looking tan skin darker than Dawn's.

"Aunt Tuyat." Dawn put her arms, black purse dangling, around her aunt.

"You stay for lunch?"

"We had lunch, Aunty. This is my friend Jefferson."

"Jefferson?" Dawn's aunt seemed to be tasting the name. "How do you do?" She looked at Dawn. "Older friend," she commented, smiling at Jefferson.

"I am very pleased to meet you, Ms.—"

"Call me Aunty, like Dawn does. Come in, come in."

Dawn whispered, "They never know who's a friend, who's a lover. She thinks you're too old for me."

Following Dawn into the house, Jefferson nodded, even as she admired the slight shimmy in Dawn's walk. Aunty was probably right.

The Northways' kitchen was big. A young boy sat at the table eating from a bowl with a fork.

"My nephew, Tong," Dawn said. The boy smiled and nodded, mouth full.

A woman very like the one who had greeted them outside entered the room with a tray of empty dishes.

"Mom, meet my friend Jefferson. Is Dad awake?"

"Yes, yes. He is still awake, finishing his coffee and his cigarette. He will sleep soon. Go see him."

Mr. Northway was in bed, gaunt, pale, his legs long under a dark green comforter. The room smelled like rubbing alcohol and was very hot. Her dad had given Dawn her height and then seemed to have run out of the tall gene, as her siblings were shorter. He smiled broadly as Dawn hugged him.

"He smiles all the time," Dawn said as she led Jefferson out a back door. "No matter how bad he feels. He treats my mother like a porcelain doll. That's their song together, 'China Doll,' the Grateful Dead song, not the old one. He's a happy man. It's like, he is still so happy to have gotten through Vietnam alive and to have found something beautiful to bring back from his experience, he's content despite being so sick." Chickens ran up to her, away from her, and under Jefferson's feet. "These are Rhode Island Whites. They're good layers and hardy in the cold, except for their combs. Come on, girls, let us through."

The barn was next, clean and modern. Dawn hugged one of the young men working there. "Another cousin," she explained. "Eric." Once outside, Dawn lowered her voice. "Mom brought over as many of her relatives from Vietnam as were left. Her family worked so hard on the farm with Dad that he was able to expand it. Now that he's so sick, there's plenty of help. Northway Farm doesn't have to sell out to developers like so many of my friends' parents have."

"This place must be as big as Central Park," Jefferson said. They were headed toward woods that bordered one side of the Northway land. She remembered the tiny space behind the candy store Angela had lived in with her parents and thought of how far they both had traveled from that first glorious kiss.

"Oh, at least twice that size. Dad and Mom own 1,560 acres and raise corn, soybeans, and hay. They have 110 head of dairy cows and a good-sized herd of sows over across the road."

"That's all the same farm? With a road running through it?"

"Happens all the time." Dawn looked to their right and said, "Race you to the wall."

Jefferson, with her menopausal weight gain, felt cumbersome running after her. "I used to be faster than that." She was laughing and out of breath, rubbing a stitch in her side.

They stepped over another stone wall, then climbed a hill. She wobbled a little going over, but caught herself before Dawn looked back. That darned arthritis again. Dawn pointed to another farmhouse some distance away along the road that split the farm. There was no mistaking that Dawn loved the place; her eyes shone with that gladness she so often saw in Dawn.

"Dad and my uncles built the other big house. The Vos—Mom's maiden name is Vo—live there. Two of my nieces and nephews are going to college, but four want to be farmers. Lan, my oldest cousin, has already bought adjacent land and is working it with Dad's equipment in exchange for her labor here. She wants to get into heritage seeds and sell to restaurants and gourmet shops."

"To each her own." Jefferson imagined the land covered with snow, the isolation of winters. Where she'd grown up in Dutchess at least had movies, local theater, concerts, and the train into the city. Here there were cows.

"Dad didn't have to marry my mother and bring her here. He didn't have to make a new home for her family. My father is quite a guy, Jefferson. He kept on being a hero even back in the States. I don't really want to move to Concord, especially with him so sick."

"Then why go?"

Dawn made a 180-degree turn and pointed to a distant house in a clump of trees. Jefferson could make out a yard littered with cars stripped of tires, an old refrigerator, and other large refuse. Some tethered goats worked the grass. "That's where I came out. In that half-wrecked manufactured home you can see back in the woods. Her name is Dee Buchman. She sits out on that back porch drinking beer all day. Walks the empty cans to the tree stump and target-shoots. Her brothers sold all the family land except where the house stands, mostly to us, and they work at the ball-bearing factory in Laconia to support their families and Dee, all living in that house along with their mother, who's in her nineties now. Her brothers probably blame themselves for their little sister Dee being gay. They fooled around with her when they were all kids."

Jefferson could picture herself in that woman's shoes, surrounded by her cats and a dog and a goat, always ready to bring someone out with her touch, her hands. She'd seen homes like that before, on rides around New Hampshire: old couches and folding chairs lining the sagging porches, antique pickup trucks gutted and rusting, always a goat munching tufts of crabgrass. You saw pictures of the South looking like that, but not of New Hampshire. These run-down homesteads were hidden alongside narrow roads tourists didn't frequent. Penniless, as exhausted as the land on their family plot, generations stayed on penniless, bitter, ambitionless, the whole clan drunk.

"She won't talk to me," Dawn said. "Or look at me, ever since I broke up with her when I went to college. What a character she is. Her hands were rough from farm work, but she always had a row of girlie tools on her kitchen table: hand lotions, nail clippers, little scissors, ceramic files, buffers, cuticle pushers—lined up like references. Since then I've seen her in town with one woman or another. She's there for the straight women who want a break from roadhouse boyfriends or old-hat husbands. Maybe, some day, one of them will stick with her, show her a better life." She looked at Jefferson, sadness—no, tragedy—in her eyes. "I knew there was no place good for me with her."

"Hey," she said. "That's pretty amazing."

"What?"

"To know what you needed before you started. I'm impressed."

"Oh, Jefferson." Dawn opened her arms as if to hug her. "How could anyone not know?"

She shrugged. "I stumbled along, tripping into jobs and relationships."

"Until now?"

She surveyed the farmland, thinking how grateful she was to have been born where and who she had been. "I knew I needed a change."

"Exactly," Dawn said. "But how do you know what change is best?"

The sky had clouded over and she felt chilly. In the city, the streets would be bustling; here only a flock of some small dark birds seemed to have business outdoors. It was a moment so low that Ginger's betrayals, both leaving and dying, felt like newly sharpened blades. She felt like screaming, but of course never would. Instead she covered the lower half of her face with a hand and squeezed her eyes shut.

Her tone all kindness and concern, Dawn asked, "Jefferson? Are you all right?"

How easy it would be to turn to Dawn, put her arms around her, and submerge herself in the woman. What was stopping her now, when she so needed the comfort? The honesty and kindness of this woman left her incredulous. She didn't know a lesbian could be this unguarded and unfettered. Now that she'd found Dawn, she wanted to keep her in her life.

"Yes, I'm fine. I'm trying to answer you, but how can I when I'm guessing at the answers myself?"

"But to move here—that was a big decision. How did you make it?"

She smiled, turning to Dawn. "I put on my ruby running shoes, clicked my heels together three times, and said, 'There's no place like home.' And here I was."

Dawn shook her head, smiling too, and, as they walked, sometimes running off to see a wildflower, sometimes leaping at a tree limb as if to climb, and leading Jefferson to highbush blueberries, the last of the raspberries and gooseberries, which she'd never tasted before.

CHAPTER THIRTY-SIX

Jefferson parked outside the Pipsborough General Store, which was also the only gas station in town. Shannon worked there part-time. Dawn Northway's car, a red Subaru with a bike rack on the back and a ski rack on the top, was out on the street next to a pile of red, gold, and brown leaves instead of in the lot, as if she'd been in a hurry.

There was no sign of either woman in the front of the store. A CD player was set to repeat Macy Gray's song "I Try," and it boomed out the door. From the back she could hear what sounded like boxes and crates being slammed one on top of another. She hesitated at a bin of cut-rate tools and gizmos in the kind of plastic packages that required an engineering degree to open and was deciding that she should leave when she heard Shannon say, "Then maybe I should go wherever the Guard sends me if you don't want me around."

She could hear Dawn's low, kind voice answer. "That's not what I said, Shannon."

Before Jefferson could leave, Dawn came out of the back room, her cheeks pink.

"Jefferson," Dawn cried, a big smile erasing her troubled expression.

She could see now that Dawn had been crying. "What's wrong?"

"It's Shannon," Dawn whispered, leading her outside. She was massaging her forearm as if it was sore. "I try to be her friend. She asked me to stop by to help her figure out what to do about the Guard."

She'd never seen Dawn rattled. "Did she hurt you?"

"No! I keep hurting her." Dawn obviously saw the puzzled look on her face. "I'm not interested, Jefferson. I only want to be friends, not lovers."

"Did she force herself on you?"

"No. Nothing like that. Not physically, but she won't accept my disinterest and keeps threatening to hurt herself. I don't know what to do."

"Okay. I know this is none of my business. Believe me, I don't want to make it my business." The thought scared her. She'd come to the lake for peace. "I'm trying to be a go-along-to-get-along kind of person."

"I'm not trying to involve you. Really. I'm venting," Dawn said, with a sad little smile. She wore a T-shirt with a rainbow that read, Rainbows Are So Ghay.

God, she thought. I don't even know how to be a good friend. She knew what she'd do had Dawn been a lover or an ex-lover, but they were friends—and she'd fallen in love with Dawn's family. She dropped by the farm perhaps more often than she should. Dawn, in the safe context of her family, had become her confidante, as had, for some subjects, Dawn's bedridden dad, a soft-spoken guy and a good listener. He told her about the lakes region, the history of the Northways and the Hills, his mother's people. He knew everyone but the newcomers. He told her stories of the houses and merchants. She consulted him about keeping up her house and who was the best boat mechanic, the most honest car-repair shop. She felt protective toward his daughter.

"Dykes get ridiculously messed up," she told Dawn, thinking, except you. "Let me talk to her."

"Would you?"

She shook her head. "Either that, or I follow you out of here."

"And you know what Shannon will think if you do that."

"I thought life with Ginger was complicated," she joked, giving Dawn a fast hug.

Dawn laughed, the sadness erased from her eyes. "Ginger and what's-her-name, and who's-a-madig, and this one and that one and all the others."

"Hey, Dawn, dirty pool. Now get lost while I solve all your problems."

Jefferson headed back into the store. Shannon came barreling from the back rolling a full dolly at top speed.

"Whoa," she said, stepping out of the way.

Shannon swerved to miss her, slammed into an end-cap display of boxed cereal, flung up her arms to protect herself from flying boxes of Life, and turned red. "Oh, bummer, you heard what we said, didn't you?"

"I barely got here."

"What's wrong with me? I mean, look at me. They all say I'm so adorable, but they don't want me loving them. Am I really that awful?"

A man came in the store and went to fix a cup of coffee.

Shannon whispered with a desperate earnestness, "I never tried anything with Dawn from the get-go. Never. I only loved her. Love her. Dawn said it nicely, but she basically told me I'm in her psychic space and should get a life." She went to ring up the sale, head down, dejection in her walk. Jefferson picked cereal boxes out of the aisle.

"Catch anything, Jim?" she asked.

"More trout than I can eat. Want one for your supper?"

Shannon's voice brightened. "That would be super. I don't have an appetite and I'm getting tired of sardine sandwiches."

Macy Gray's wistful, exciting voice repeated her combination love song and dirge, the music fanning a useless flame in Jefferson.

Shannon, feet shuffling a little to the music, turned to Jefferson. "And you're not out selling houses because?"

"On my way," she said, and looked at her watch. "I had some time to kill and thought I'd grace you with my presence."

The fisherman came in with a trout on a hook. Shannon wrapped it in a brown paper bag, then a plastic bag, and slipped it to the back of the dairy cooler. She came out yawning. "I hope I can remember to take that home. Man, I've got to get some sleep. I forget what I'm doing in the middle of doing it."

"Are you working a lot?"

"Not enough," Shannon said, turning out an empty pocket. "I'm having a heck of a time sleeping."

"That's not helping."

Shannon protested. "It's not all about Dawn. It's the National Guard thing. When I do fall asleep I dream of hundreds of little bombs falling from fighter jets and I can't find my cat to grab her and run."

The phone rang. Shannon gave the store's closing time to the caller.

Partly because Jefferson wanted to know and partly to change the subject, she asked, "Hey, how do you cook a trout anyway?"

Shannon and the fisherman, who'd been making a phone call outside, tripped over each other telling her their favorite recipes, and she faithfully wrote them down. When the guy left, Shannon was all enthusiasm. "We can have a fish fry. You want to have it at your place? Not that I'm inviting myself over, of course."

A group of kids invaded the store, and Shannon loped back to the register to ring up caramel apples. Jefferson wandered the aisles, letting the memories of the place as it had been forty-odd years ago move through her mind. When the children left, she led Shannon around the store.

"What happened to the post office? There was a little window right here and a woman who took the postcards I mailed to my girlfriend back in Dutchess."

"I remember the post office too," Shannon said with a heavy sigh. "My aunt and uncle lived in Pipsborough, and they let me open the box and pull out their mail."

"Fancy boxes too," said Jefferson. "Brass, with an eagle."

"And sun rays. Remember that?"

"My dad and I would walk from the cottage. He'd get cigarettes and I got penny candy. And a cap gun once a summer if he was feeling good."

Shannon smiled, looking at the floor. "This store had the best water guns."

"I remember," Jefferson said with a laugh. "I couldn't wait to get home to fill it. I climbed down to the stream outside." She pointed out a window to where water ran toward the lake.

"And got soaked? I did that too. Man oh man, I miss being a kid. Remember how we got all summer off?" Shannon's face changed, her shoulders drooped. She shook her head. "I should have stuck to water pistols."

"You learned to shoot in the Guard?"

"No, my dad taught me. We used to go out in the woods. He'd pin a paper target to a tree and we'd have contests between us two. I hit the bull's-eye my first try and got pretty consistent. Do you shoot?"

"No. Never appealed to me. I was more into contact sports."

"Right. Gym teacher." Shannon stopped and held a half-full case of Starburst candies in one hand. "Or are you talking about the other contact sports?"

She grinned. Was Shannon actually starting to relax that tense, stringy self of hers? "You're right. I'd rather do those too."

Shannon's eyes flashed in a too-familiar way. The woman was

sizing her up as a lover, wasn't she? That was pretty desperate. They were clearly both attracted to the Dawns and Gingers of the world.

"I'm staying away from that sort of thing. I've made some bad decisions in my life," she told Shannon.

Shannon quickly reached to pack the candy into a counter display. Jefferson caught the one that dropped.

"You couldn't actually call them decisions sometimes. My heart would up its rate and I'd be off on the chase again."

They were at the cash register, Shannon behind the counter, Jefferson in front, paying for a pack of gum. Shannon was watching more schoolkids, who were eyeing the cigarettes and Shannon in turn.

"There was this butchy senior in a high school where I taught," she told Shannon, "one of those posh uptown schools high-income parents all want their kids to get into. It was the week before graduation. The kid was eighteen, age of consent in New York is seventeen. Not that I would have taken her to bed. A student and not my type. But that's what she wanted. I figured, show her some places, let her meet gay kids. That's what I did—after she graduated.

"Turns out the parents—overprotective? Never saw anything like it. I mean, one look at the two of us, you know we're not into each other, chasing skirts together. Kid picks another butch. Mom catches her with said look-alike. Dumb kids. In the graduate's bedroom, playing at sleepover. Of course the mother wants to know. Kid tells all, dad calls the school. I have to meet with the parents and admin. Mom calls me another one of those masculine women. I get fired, like it was me in bed with darling daughter. Nothing good ever comes of mixing butches."

She'd been interrupted a few times while Shannon rang the register, but they were alone for her point.

Shannon shrugged, but didn't look at her. As she locked the register and walked into an aisle she asked, "What are you going to do about a girlfriend up here?"

"Again, I'm retired from all that. I've had enough," she proclaimed, knowing this was no longer quite true. A great sadness came at her like a hurricane of tears yet to be shed. She felt a deep pang for intimacy and for the place she and Ginger were supposed to be sharing, the place that was to have been their togetherness.

Shannon started cutting a box open. It was a case of huge cans of Hawaiian Punch. Shannon lifted the big blue cans one at a time and slid them along the wooden shelf, stopping off and on to massage the small of her back. "Pretty slim pickings around here." Her eyes were narrow as she studied Jefferson.

"We could start a lesbian inn, bring up the touro-dykes."

Shannon moved the dolly to another aisle and slid it out from under two cases of soup, then sat on them, studying Jefferson silently.

"What?" asked Jefferson, who was ready to leave.

"What? What? Didn't you hear your brilliant idea? An inn. A lesbian B-and-B." Shannon's arms waved as she spoke. Her eyes had come alive with enthusiasm. Jefferson didn't see how a femme could resist her. "Build it and they will come, right?"

Shannon held the sharp edge of the box cutter against her thumb. With the forefinger of her other hand, she was tracing the veins in her wrist. Jefferson looked at her watch. She had to get going.

"You're the realtor," Shannon said, slipping the cutter into a back pocket. "Find us one of those old farmhouses gone to rack and ruin. I'll get my dad to help us fix it up—" Shannon slumped again. "I'm not running anything from Iraq, am I?"

"I'll be on the lookout, Shannon, for when you can. You're a natural for the manager. Can you cook breakfast trout?" she asked with a smile. Macy Gray sang on.

"Cook breakfast?" Shannon reached out two hands toward her and Jefferson slapped them. "I am the waffle whiz, the superb scrambler, the bagel boiler. I can cook bacon, omelets, flapjacks, and home fries that would leave you begging for more if you weren't already stuffed to the gills. Trout is a specialty of mine. Start looking, Jefferson. Start now, okay? Give me something in my damn life to look forward to."

"I actually have a place in mind, come to think of it."

She watched the life drain from Shannon's eyes. Shannon turned away to the Hawaiian Punch. "Nothing ever works out for me. Never mind."

"I've got to go to work," Jefferson said, remembering when she'd felt that down. "I might stop by that house I'm thinking of, which is conveniently empty." Getting Shannon's mind off Dawn would be a good thing.

CHAPTER THIRTY-SEVEN

It was a little chilly to be hanging out half inside, half outside of Dawn's garage. These Saturday gatherings had become an institution for Jefferson, though, and she always at least stopped by between showings. Today she'd only had one retired couple to squire around, obviously in town for the fall foliage, and they had narrowed their sights to two pieces. She'd gone home after that and put on her jeans and brown leather jacket, which was keeping her warm on this damp day, but was, after half a lifetime of wearing it and working to keep the leather supple, getting snug on her. She needed to lose weight, pronto. When the rain came down they all moved inside the garage, but kept the door open.

Yolanda Whale was working on a six-pack; Rayanne was laying borders around the photos in a scrapbook she was doing of the group and trying to get them to come up with something they could call themselves.

"Jygrs," Dawn said. "There must be way to use our initials. Ryj—"

"The Old Crows," Jefferson suggested at the sight of two crows on a swaying electrical line.

"Sounds like a whiskey," Yolanda commented.

"It would to you," Rayanne shot back.

"Well," Dawn said with a sigh, "the initials I'm coming up with sound like an Icelandic city."

"Maybe Shannon will think of something," Rayanne said. "Where is she?"

Yolanda said, "The Goonies."

"She went to the movies without us?" protested Dawn.

Rayanne said, "That's our name: The Goonies. I loved that film."

"Oh, gross," said Dawn.

"She could be at the movies, though. Or someplace."

"Good thinking, Yo," said Rayanne. "I'd have to agree that she's someplace."

Jefferson remembered the day Shannon helped her work on the boat, how impossible her dilemma was. Iraq was no fit place for a New Hampshire dyke. The service was no fit place for someone who was used to being out or who had a back as sore as Shannon's appeared to be. "Hey, what about loons? They're all over the place now."

Yolanda laughed. "The Loonies! We can be The Loonies."

"You are the loony," said Rayanne.

Jefferson was always amazed that Rayanne was a successful financial wiz, with her lousy people skills, but Dawn said she made money hand over fist for herself and her clients. Drew and Ryan raved about her. Jefferson was surprised to learn that Buck and Serena put what they called their spare change in her hands, whatever they didn't have committed to property. She wondered, if she'd been fifteen years younger, when women were entering fields like finance in greater numbers, if she might have been good at something like that. Real-estate sales seemed to suit her. She used to laugh at the feminists, but they'd really opened up the world for the women who followed them. Still—Rayanne, goonies, financial savvy—it did not compute, as Rayanne herself might say. "Goonies definitely has a fun-loving feel to it," Jefferson said, laughing, "but then, so does the one Shannon came up with last week: The Bean-Supper Gang."

Dawn looked at her watch, then at Jefferson. "This isn't like Shannon. She usually lets one of us know if she isn't going to be here."

"Try her cell," Yolanda suggested.

Dawn said, "I did. And I left her two messages."

"Then her battery must be dead because the day Shannon Wiley doesn't respond to Dawn Northway—"

They all looked at one another. Jefferson was the first to say, "I think Shannon's got a lot on her mind."

The floodgates opened and everyone spoke at once.

Yolanda set her beer down on a sawhorse, hard. "She came to every one of us for help. Who helped her? I know I couldn't."

There was a general shaking of heads.

"And now she's what," Dawn asked, "sitting alone somewhere contemplating—"

"No," said Rayanne. "Not that."

"I didn't mean suicide. Maybe she's just sad."

"Shannon doesn't sit around and think about things, women. She acts. That's how she got into the Guard in the first place," Yolanda told them. "She thought her life was going nowhere so she signed on."

"And now," Jefferson said, "she's stuck again."

"Only this time, the Guard is definitely not the answer," Rayanne told them.

Dawn dialed again, then put the phone down. "I'm driving over to her place."

Jefferson was up and had her keys out. She reached for Dawn and pulled her toward her car. The Avalon's lights blinked as she unlocked the doors while the others grabbed what they needed and followed. Dawn sat in front with her. Rayanne and Yolanda got in back.

She imagined, as she drove, that Shannon was a lesbian, like herself, with ghosts. Would Shannon grow out of her ghosts or would she, Jefferson, someday be as down as Shannon? She could see herself, alone, thrashing in her bed to a nightmare. All the women she'd abandoned would drift through the mist to terrorize her. She'd feel haunted and vulnerable as giant trees dripped loudly around her. Shannon needed to face her ghosts, yell back at their taunts, prod the empty shadows with the sharpened stick of her future, or become another Donna Quixote, a victim of her own too prolific loving—or longing.

Pipsborough was small; the drive over the slick streets was quick except for the mad gray squirrels dashing across streets in search of richer foraging grounds. Shannon's cabin was one of a half dozen that had once been part of a motor court, probably built in the thirties and now in much too bad shape to attract vacationers. A knee-high, once-painted picket fence, snaggle-toothed, sagged backward. She could imagine the old cars parked along the horseshoe driveway, kids in overall shorts and fathers in captain's hats, the mothers wearing wide-legged rayon playsuits. Ginger would like this place. Would have liked.

"Where's her bike?" asked Rayanne.

"Inside?" Yolanda suggested.

Dawn opened the creaky screen door and knocked. "Shannon?" she called. Shannon's cat came streaking out of the cabin and made for the woods in back.

When there was no answer, Jefferson, Rayanne, and Yolanda went to the windows. The cabin consisted of a small combined living room and kitchen and a sleeping loft. The bathroom had a high frosted-glass window. Light flooded inside when Dawn opened the front door. She watched Yolanda enter behind Dawn and knew she'd been watching too many episodes of *Law & Order* when she wondered why their guns weren't drawn.

She felt light-headed and an acrid taste came into her mouth. She slumped against the cabin, nauseous. What was up with her? She'd handled plenty of situations in classes, on playing fields. Was it the thought of another death? She wanted to go lumbering into the woods like a wounded old moose to lie down and die in peace.

"Jefferson!" Dawn called from inside, and she felt the shame that had always come when she realized her clothes were dirty once again from playing in the woods. Emmy's mute disappointment had felt like an elevator at Lord and Taylor's crashing to the ground. That had been a recurrent nightmare in her childhood, the elevator falling with her in it, Emmy many floors above. It plunged; she stood frozen and silent with fear.

Breakfast erupted. They were calling, sounding frantic. She wiped her face with the hem of her shirt. To quell more nausea, she pictured herself at the end of the day, alone in her big soft chair by the fire. Then she wove her way to the car and started it while they put Shannon, limp, on the backseat. Dawn sat with Shannon's head on her lap, Rayanne leapt into the front seat, while Yolanda lifted Shannon's legs and rested them on her own. Even as she started the Avalon, she gagged again at the smell of vomit.

"Shannon's sick?" She searched Dawn's worried face in the rearview mirror.

"She swallowed pills," Dawn was shaking her head, "but she threw up so much, I don't know if they got into her system."

Jefferson reached the street and gunned the car toward the hospital in Laconia. "Let's hope she tossed the pills before they reached her liver."

"What would happen to her?"

Rayanne was dialing on her cell phone, stabbing numbers, cursing, stabbing them again.

"Call nine-one-one," Jefferson advised as she rounded a curve too fast.

"Nothing's happening! Wait—Yeah," Rayanne said into the phone. "We're coming in with a suicide. Me? I'm Rayanne Vishengrad. Is she breathing? I don't know—Dawn?"

"She is, but really slowly. And she's sweating bullets. Jefferson, where—"

"About fifteen minutes out."

"Fifteen minutes." Rayanne pushed the phone toward Dawn. "She's going to walk you through CPR."

"I know CPR," Dawn said. "I'll start again now."

"Geeze, we should have thought of that." Yolanda grabbed the phone.

"I did, on the bathroom floor," Dawn said as she positioned Shannon's jaw. "Tell her we have the bottle. It's ibuprofen."

Yolanda repeated instructions to Dawn. Jefferson focused on the road, passing cars as she never had before, no matter how drunk.

"Jef, the dispatcher is telling the police we're on our way. She said they'd meet us with an ambulance, but it wouldn't save time at this point. The ER is waiting for us."

She pressed the pedal down harder. Ahead a police cruiser, lights rotating, was waving her on, holding her hand up to stop intersection traffic. What a different world, she thought, from the scene in *The Well of Loneliness*, the first gay book she had ever read, where a character, another young lesbian, hanged herself. Not different enough, she thought. All those years she'd spent drinking and chasing women, she thought, she hadn't noticed that she was doing what the straight world wanted her to do. She was killing herself like Shannon, only slower. Killing us—why hadn't she thought enough of her relationship to do right by Ginger? She'd been a mirror for a whole society that thinks gays aren't worth much. Who knew if Ginger's aneurysm wasn't from the whole gay-straight thing eating up her gut? Ginger had never told the Quinn family any more than she had told the Jeffersons. Neither of them was out at work. YOUR SILENCE WILL NOT PROTECT YOU—she'd seen that bumper sticker at the Lake Front Shop. Protect us? It's killing us.

By the time Shannon had been wheeled into the ER, Jefferson had stopped shaking; no one knew she'd gotten sick.

"The Bean-Supper Gang rides again," said Yolanda. "You think they have beer in that soda machine?"

"I think they call it a soda machine for a reason," Rayanne said.

Yolanda had called Shannon's mother and got up to meet her as she came in.

"How is she?"

"We don't know. They might let you in to see her," Yolanda said. "They won't let us. I'll go over to Shannon's later, find her cat and keep him at my place."

"Oh, that girl and her strays," said Shannon's mother. She sighed and looked toward the hallway. "I called Shannon's father. He'll be here in a minute."

Dawn was hugging Mrs. Wiley. She and her husband hadn't helped Shannon either. The poor kid. This wasn't supposed to happen in this new century: Lesbians weren't isolated. They helped each other through these things. Shannon had been out to her family and loved anyway. She was gay in the military, in theory. Jefferson wondered what was really going on with Shannon, with all of them, with the whole group being single. They treated Jefferson like a widow, but she wasn't, really. She was an unattached ex who had taken care of her former lover. A lover who'd left her for a man. Which was like that old well-of-loneliness book.

She was no brain. Probably she'd never figure out what was what, but that was okay. Right now she didn't want to lose someone else in her life. Shannon's community was all gathered, except for Drew and Ryan, and they were on their way. Maybe this was working; maybe they were taking care of one another. "Please let Shannon make it," she prayed to that big old boring god who seemed to be in charge of these things.

"What would Xena do?" she asked aloud, for Shannon's sake.

Mr. Wiley hurried in the door, obviously distraught. "Doesn't she know she's government property?" he asked his former wife. "They can toss her in the brig for doing this." Mrs. Wiley shushed him and they were allowed back to see Shannon.

Jefferson was incredulous. "Government property?"

"My dad told me the same thing," Dawn said.

"He would have told her to go fight," said Rayanne.

Jefferson chuckled to herself. Angela and Tam had been big into Xena too. Café Femmes used to go silent once a week when the show came on.

"In Iraq?" Dawn asked. She was crying. Jefferson, seated next to her, gathered her to her shoulder. Dawn felt fragile in her arms. "Shannon's a kid in her head," Dawn said. "She wanted to go play soldier, but she'd rather patch up an injured enemy soldier than kill him."

"She'd have a better chance of surviving there than she had on whatever she did to herself back in her cabin," said Yolanda.

Jefferson asked, "How many did she take?"

"There was an empty hundred-tablet bottle on the sink," Dawn told her, still resting in Jefferson's arms.

Yolanda added, "And she was lying in a puddle of what came up. Your whole backseat may need to go to the dry cleaners."

"So if Shannon does make it, she could be in bad shape."

"Let's put it this way, Jefferson." Yolanda looked across Rayanne, who sat between them, to meet her eyes. "The Guard isn't going to want her."

"Not true," Rayanne said. "Who would make better cannon fodder than a suicidal dyke?"

CHAPTER THIRTY-EIGHT

That night, a doctor finally told Shannon's parents that her friends had brought Shannon in time and she would be fine except for a very sore throat. He told them everyone might as well go home. Drew and Ryan stayed because they'd just arrived, but Jefferson walked out to her car feeling drained and scared and guilty. Couldn't she have helped Shannon or at least made her feel better about herself?

The hospital was tiny compared to those in New York. She was all too familiar with the place. The ambulance had rushed to Ginger only to declare her dead. She had no desire to stick around tonight, especially since no one but Shannon's parents would be allowed to visit.

She felt so unsettled. In New York, she would have gone to the bar and had a cup of that tranquillity tea Amaretto made up. The act of drinking something she was told would calm her, did calm her.

So when Dawn hugged her extra long and asked her back to her house for tea, an herbal concoction Dawn's grandmother mixed that would practically knock her out, of course she said yes.

"You keep your place shipshape," she told Dawn when they'd settled in her living room, side by side on the couch, mugs and teapot on a low bamboo coffee table before them. From a big boom box on the entertainment center came soft, bouncy electronic music.

"It's easy when the place is too big for me—and I don't have six kittens turning it upside down and shedding everywhere," Dawn said with a gentle smile, then added, "You have your work cut out for you. I should adopt some animals, but I'm away all day." She poured the tea for Jefferson. "Inhaling the steam makes my eyelids heavy."

Jefferson inhaled. It was probably only taking more oxygen in that did it, but she was able to reply, "Yes. Yes," she repeated, breathing again, "it's like taking a Xanax."

"Do you?" Dawn asked, slipping a new-age CD into the player.

"Do I what?"

"Take tranquilizers."

She nodded. "My life's been so full of changes. And now that I don't drink... Well, I started using liquor so early I never learned how to calm myself because I always had my liquid tranq."

Dawn touched her hand. "You've had a tough time."

Something—maybe because of the tea, maybe the aftereffects of her adrenaline spike—had changed radically. No longer was she two streets over from Saturday Lake, in a plain, sparsely furnished ranch house in a little cul de sac cut out of the New Hampshire woods, but she was in a softer world, where hints of a design emerged. A framed picture here and there, of birds, fantastic, long-tailed, crested birds; a piece of woven art, also depicting birds; an unusual orange lampshade and a warm brown carpet; several daffodil yellow pillows, including two very large pillows on the floor—all were knitted into a sheer weightless fabric around her. Dawn was stroking her hand. She was in a safe place with a safe woman whose eyes were tender and whose hands were hot.

At the same time, guilt was tearing her up. How could she be so happy in Dawn's company when Ginger was dead? What was she stealing from Dawn, when they were together, by thinking so much about Ginger? When she added guilt about Shannon, her serenity threatened to flee.

So she reached out to Dawn, to hold her and to be held after the events of the afternoon, but their cheeks touched, Dawn's softer than she might have imagined had she ever tried to imagine it, with little hairs that brushed along the hairs on her own cheek.

A cloud of desire enveloped them, like fog rushing off the lake, exotic as the sea, and they, to Jefferson's pleased surprise, were kissing. Oh, such hungry little kisses Dawn gave her, unusual in their brevity and light quick touches. She couldn't get hold of Dawn, like the woman was a little Yankee sprite in the fog.

Through the fog and her struggle to still Dawn, to get serious, as she thought of it, about what they were doing, appeared a memory of Shannon's face, tight with muteness, trying so hard not to blurt what she felt about Dawn, how she feared Jefferson's handsome looks, how desperate she was for this woman now taking comfort in Jefferson's arms, in arms that right now sought only the warm animal closeness of a desiring woman, Dawn or not.

"I'm sorry to be shaking." Dawn flopped against the back of the couch. "It's been a long time." She straightened Jefferson's collar and smoothed it down.

"For me too," she said, although it felt so natural to move into this space with a woman, with such an appealing woman, as she'd been swimming in Saturday Lake all her life, dipping in, out, stroking, diving, so she felt held up by the buoyancy of her love for all of them, for Dawn, Ginger, Lily Ann—they were one endless lake and she a was a lone long-distance swimmer, immersed in them.

Or was she only skinny-dipping into love with this tomboy femme librarian? Ah, she thought, my first librarian, then erased the thought. She would not be a collector of encounters anymore. She hadn't meant this to happen, never intended to be lovers with quiet Dawn. Her habitual attention to femmes made Dawn seem available and interested whether she was or not, and then she couldn't say no when they thought they were responding to her overtures. She could never say to them that it was very simple: she loved women. She loved the challenge and the acquiescence of them, the touching and the entry to their protected places.

The moment was what she treasured: the moment laughter turned to recognition, the moment a hug got serious, the moment friendship spilled into desire, the moment yearning was released, the moment tenderness flamed to passion. Above all, she admitted to herself, they loved her. For that moment, or for years, they imagined something loveable about her. Weren't lovers all figments of one another's imaginations? Each thought the other had something she wanted. With time, they saw how they had enhanced their simply human lovers and what remained. Ginger had obviously been disappointed, although Ginger, for Jefferson, had always retained her appeal. How did Dawn see her? How long would her interest last? There would be no love-her-and-leave her solution here at the lake. What was she getting herself into?

Dawn said, "It's because of Shannon."

"Do you mean the shock is messing with our emotions?" Jefferson asked.

"Not that." Dawn was playing with the hair that had grown too long down the back of Jefferson's neck.

Jefferson realized it felt good to be touched again.

"Shannon's been so—there—all the time. As soon as I think of being with someone, it's as if I'm being unfaithful to Shannon, as if she's my lover. I want you to know that she is not and never has been. I have brought her home and fed her, found her cottage for her, listened to her troubles endlessly." Dawn turned her eyes up to Jefferson's. "Oh, but I've had my eyes on you since that first church supper. And your hands. Such strong, lesbian hands." Dawn used one finger to stroke with the conscious sensitivity she might use to outline a wild bird's body.

"And you're moving to Concord to escape Shannon?"

"Maybe I was," Dawn said, with a timorous voice. Her tone became animated. "Am I moving? Now?" Dawn gave Jefferson another of her quick kisses.

Jefferson wanted to object that Dawn shouldn't stay around for her, that she wasn't a U-Haul kind of woman, that she might only be running away from her grief, but the kisses were making her nuts so she slid her arms around Dawn's rib cage—so narrow it made her feel protective and Dawn fragile—and pressed herself to her, locking their lips, not hard, but steady, varying the pressure delicately, as she liked to, committing herself and Dawn to what they could give each other.

Dawn pulled away. "I don't do this with just anyone."

A little ashamed, she realized, I do. With just about anyone who wants me. She thought of Dawn's first girlfriend in her unkempt home with her stream of needy married women. She could see the attraction for the women: the forbidden, the other side, the eroticism of the überbutch in her splendid, sordid isolation. Would she become a monied version of her if she didn't get things right this time? The thought was as dismal as the butch's trailer. That was no way to get love. She didn't want to think about how close it was to her way.

"I'm not just looking for some fun." It was clear that Dawn expected from Jefferson a declaration similar to her own. "I don't know what I'm looking for." She touched Dawn's shoulders with the hands she'd been told were competent, confident, persuasive hands, her tools of seduction.

Dawn hadn't struck her as one of those women who needed to process her way into bed. She added, "Except you," and kissed Dawn's neck, just behind the earlobe.

Dawn, hot to the touch, fingers rhythmically kneading Jefferson's upper arms as if to restrain herself, told her, "You're claiming me."

She was taken aback: this little terrier sank her teeth in. Damn. Did she want this? Wasn't she thinking just the other day how much easier life was now that she needn't worry about anyone but herself and the kittens? Why put herself at risk for more pain?

She remembered the hurt. If Ginger had only stayed with her a few more months, the pain would have been simpler, cleaner. Death happened, it was not a choice; but when a woman left a woman for a man—that was 3-D rejection. Whatever the circumstances, she didn't plan to go through it again.

Dawn returned with two bottles of Poland Spring water. "You haven't left," said Dawn, setting down the water.

"No, but let's go the slow route. I need to be sure." Why was she hesitating? It must be some sign of maturity in herself that she could even appreciate and allow a woman like this in her life. Dawn wasn't one of her bad girls, or a woman with love stuck in her craw, choking on it rather than letting it out.

Dawn dug her fingers into her shoulders and massaged so deeply it hurt where she hadn't known she was tense. Dawn kissed her on the forehead and stroked her hair. "I would never leave a woman for a man, Jefferson. You wouldn't have to be scared of that. I'm lesbian to the bone."

She tensed. "I meant that I need to be sure of me."

"These muscles are rock, Jefferson. Let it go."

She did then, letting her shoulders sag, her neck bow forward to Dawn's wise fingers and words.

"Jefferson, I've fallen in love with you. No, I fell for you the first time I saw you. You're what's missing in me. I want to be yours in every way there is. Will you let me?"

She wasn't dreaming, was she? How had she gotten so nuts about this woman?

Dawn began to unbutton her own fancy pearl-like buttons, but Jefferson stilled her hands under one of her own. "Hey, Dawn, let me," she said, "when it's time."

"It's time, Jefferson." Dawn kept unbuttoning under Jefferson's hands.

Jefferson let her and touched Dawn's left nipple through the blouse with the flat of her pinky, sending all the electricity in herself into that light pressure. Dawn slumped against her, but straightened immediately, pushed her hand aside, and pulled up Jefferson's sweatshirt.

Okay, she thought, sighing, the woman wants skin. When their breasts came together, Dawn's were like little birds against her, not the proud crested birds of her prints, but darting wrens she could keep in her hands. Once they were undressed, Dawn did the femme thing, leading her by the hand to her bed, looking coyly but shyly back. Briefly, Jefferson remembered that Bonnie had lived there with Dawn, shared this bed.

Dawn turned some lights off and some on, arranged the bed linens and pillows, smiling and softly chattering. Jefferson, standing naked on a small patterned rug by the bed, worried again; her body was no longer that of a twenty-year-old. Dawn might not like what she saw, or felt, or smelled. She sagged and swelled where she never had before. Jefferson might not be able to keep up with someone years younger. Then she thought of what it would do to Shannon if she knew what was going on right now. Of what it would do to her if she learned about them during her recovery? Would it drive her over the edge again. She considered stopping, but Dawn had mounted the bed and sat, legs tucked modestly to one side, smiling widely. She was so obviously pleased with her catch she wasn't thinking of the incident that had catapulted them into this moment, but only of their pleasure and a future of love.

Who could resist this slight, competent femme? True, she'd been with no one but Brandi since getting sober this time, including Ginger, but what had come of such self-control? First, Ginger had left her; second, left her for a guy; and last, left permanently. No, this was who Jefferson was: a lover of women, a body seeking heat, a heart unable not to love, a woman who felt she had never been loved for who she was, but only for her butchy poses, her intuitive hands, her good looks, for whatever it had been that Ginger thought she'd found in her. Maybe this one, this thirsty Dawn, really wanted to know who she was and could embrace more than her hands and lips, could love her as no other woman had, as her parents never did, as she herself could not. What exactly had Emmy wanted before she could love a daughter? A debutante?

She didn't want to hurt Dawn. That would be like snapping her lovely tender neck, but how long would it be before she learned to stop begging for love on every street corner. It looked like she would find out.

Hope thrummed through her like blood as she caught sight of their clothes commingled on the floor at the foot of the bed. That was a powerful stimulant, that mix of blue-denim legs. Dawn had put a CD of Japanese drumming on the boom box. Jefferson dropped to the bed and enclosed the end of Dawn's breast with her mouth as if suckling for love.

"Hey, Kitten." She brushed her lips along Dawn's incredibly smooth skin. "You're as playful and independent as a kitten."

Dawn laughed and called her a big old tiger, then growled and pretended to pounce on her. As Jefferson wrestled her onto her back and lay atop her to hold her down, she said, "I'm no ravenous tiger, Dawn. I'm a wounded lamb, but I'll try." She would try to be Dawn's tiger.

Dawn reached for her head and pulled it down, then enclosed Jefferson's lips as if to drink her in and pushed her tongue into Jefferson's mouth, her pelvis grinding up into Jefferson. What was there, then, but Dawn? Everything was Dawn: she tasted, smelled, felt the miracle of Dawn. She couldn't get enough of Dawn and heard her quick breathing, saw her closed eyes, a vein throbbing in her neck, her pretty breasts, her thin left leg, her little belly, her fluted labia, slick and puffy.

She was lost in sensation as never before. There was no leading, no following. She reached for Dawn, shaking with a deep desire she'd thought she would never feel again. Dawn reached for her. Dawn kissed the palm of her hand; she licked between Dawn's fingers. Dawn entered her with one slow, gentle finger, and she found Dawn's opening with her forefinger while her thumb stroked her clitoris and she kissed the inside of Dawn's velvety thighs, betraying Ginger again with her mouth. They were seldom still in the next hours, and they moved as one. She felt astonishment at the ease of their lovemaking, how one action flowed to the next and each touch completed a circuit she'd never known was open. Dawn insisted on giving as much as Jefferson gave and knew how. She seemed to genuinely desire Jefferson. The woman was a talented, or perhaps accomplished, lover.

As Jefferson caught her breath, Dawn said, "Finally. Finally I found a woman who fits me."

These were words Jefferson had wanted to hear. Now that they were said, she feared that she needed to feel so powerfully loved and wanted that she believed Dawn, whether she should or not.

Dawn became utterly wanton then, thrashing in Jefferson's arms, twisting on her hand, loudly crying her name. That call, acknowledging Jefferson as the source of her pleasure, as her choice of lover, broke something in Jefferson, broke some raw tendon tie-down that had held a tent of self-protection over her all her life. She trusted this woman, whose boldness inspired her further, and she gave herself over to the force field that enveloped the two of them, to the undeniable power and honesty of their matched desires.

Dawn left her side for more and colder bottled water. Jefferson lay alone on the big bed, naked, uncovered, tired yet energized, and found herself grinning. Dawn reminded her a little of Angela in the innocence of her passion. Dawn's deep sensual responsiveness was healing the lover in her.

"What?" Dawn asked when she returned.

Without thinking, she said, "I'm happy."

They drank, each from her own bottle. Then Dawn lay beside her and gently rubbed her head on Jefferson's breast. "Me too." They lay silent for a while.

Dawn asked, "It's not the sex, is it?"

"No, baby," she answered with a confidence that surprised her. She was not lying. "It's not the sex." She tightened the arm that encircled Dawn's shoulders and wondered how long she could keep her close and if keeping her close would preserve this startling happiness.

Chapter Thirty-nine

The next time Jefferson went out to the farm was like a walking-on-air celebration. She finally knew what walking on air felt like. She thought she'd been in love before, but no, except for Angela and Ginger, she'd had conquests, and Ginger had been a painful, muted kind of love. She'd been won herself and been paraded around like a trophy. She'd used and been used. Now she knew she'd never really loved and never really been loved. She was plain happy when she was with Dawn, when she knew she was going to see Dawn, when they spoke by phone, when she awakened in the morning and remembered that Dawn was in her life.

Dawn pulled on boots and went out to the muddy kitchen garden with one of her sisters, to surprise their mother by getting some Saturday chores out of the way. Mrs. Northway was shopping. She'd be making a Vietnamese meal for their guest that evening. Jefferson accepted the task of reading the newspaper to Mr. Northway, whose leukemia had affected his eyes. When she finished the first section, he asked her to look through business articles for mention of Vietnam.

Dawn joined them and Mr. Northway said, "I would love to go back there with Dawn. Her middle name is Mai: M. A. I., not M.I.A. It means cherry blossom."

She was touched to be allowed into this family, to share this time with the Northways. "Does it bother you," she asked, "what America did to Vietnam? That I was part of that America back then?"

"You weren't a protester during the war?" Dawn asked, looking surprised.

"I barely remember it. Hippies taking over the streets, people setting themselves on fire. I was focused on winning field-hockey games. At one point, before college, I thought about going into the military, but Angela reminded me there was a war happening. After that, I guess I turned my back on the whole thing. I didn't read the paper, I didn't watch the news on TV. Now I can't believe I've lived through all that history."

Dawn gave her quiet laugh. "I love that sense of entitlement. I'm jealous of it. I can't imagine the ease of it. But, if I'd been here during the war? I would have gone to every march. I would have demonstrated outside military recruiting booths. Would have yelled and written letters till my fingers bled."

"Would you have blown up the recruiting stations?'

"Jefferson! How could you ask? Violence will never stop violence."

"No? I guess you're right."

"Oh, Jef. You've been so protected."

"Did I turn my back on the Vietnamese? On our soldiers? On your dad?" she asked, meeting his eyes.

"So many Americans take their easy lives for granted," said Dawn.

"You must have hated us," she said to Mr. Northway while thinking that she would have a hard time fighting for a county that ostracized her for being gay. She remembered the days when she could have been arrested for being herself.

He nodded. "We did. We were stuck in the slime, taking fire, burning, killing, destroying—dying."

"I never thought about whether the kids I grew up with—the boys up the street that I played with—were over there."

Mr. Northway patted her forearm. "Once I got back and got some distance from it all, I didn't hate anyone. I promise you that I don't hate you. It's beyond my understanding why things happen the way they do." He inhaled a cautious breath as if to avoid more coughing. "As long as my kids have love in their lives—that's what matters to me now."

Had that been a blessing of their love? This was new to her. The ghosts of would-be in-laws flickered through her mind, disapproving, disappointed, angry. She caught her breath, stunned with hope. Was she actually getting another chance here, a chance at a lasting, loving, sound union? She watched father and daughter spar affably until they heard Mrs. Northway arrive. Dawn dashed down to the cellar. Mrs. Northway fussed over Dawn's dad and ordered Jefferson out of the room so he could nap. Jefferson washed pans in the kitchen, following crisp orders from the quick, exacting, but frequently laughing woman.

These people were, unlike her parents, adults. Jarvy and Emmy, she remembered again, were a couple of kids, playmates who palled around together. My god, she thought, no wonder I don't know how to be an adult.

She went down to the basement, where Dawn was shelving her aunt's preserves. She pulled Dawn to her and held her close while she told her what she'd realized.

"Do you still want me?" she asked.

Dawn stayed quiet in her arms for too many beats of her heart, then answered, "Yes. I can see where that could cause us some friction, but yes, I do still want you." Dawn gave her that big joyful smile. "I can watch you grow up." She pulled Jefferson up the steps and out to the kitchen garden.

"I think my mom likes you," Dawn told her. "You pitched right in. Nothing impresses her more."

"You learned a lot from her."

"Oh, I did. I always loved to cook, but the bad thing used to be when dad called me Cookie. I hated that name."

"I'll have to remember never to call you that."

"It's what they called the cooks in the war. But, seriously, you name it, I can do it, from the kitchen to the orchard, getting cars out of ditches and helping a goat give birth. My mom and dad both love teaching their skills."

"I can tell. I now know the right way to peel an avocado." She held out the pail of peels and other refuse.

Dawn laughed. "And you'd better do it that way if you ever do it in front of Mom again. She remembers who she taught what. Dump those in here."

Jefferson added her offering and pushed the wheelbarrow filled with weeds through the muck to a compost pile.

"Who cooked when you were with Ginger?"

"Neither of us. We were the kind of people they invented takeout for."

Dawn laughed. "I always wondered who could afford takeout. I shared an apartment with two other women and we took turns cooking a lot of greens and rice. It was all we could afford."

"We spent way too much on restaurants. We could have paid off the loans on Ginger's dance school if we'd cooked. Including the money I put into the school."

"Did you get paid off when she died? From selling the school?"

"A committee from the neighborhood wants to buy it. If they can raise the rest of the money I'll forgive the loan so they'll have operating expenses. As a memorial to Ginger."

She off-loaded the wheelbarrow where Dawn told her to and they headed back.

"Do you mind me asking about you and Ginger?"

"Hey, ask away. Better you learn the worst up front."

"The worst? I'm touched by your memorial, Jef. You really must have loved her."

Jefferson considered what to say. She didn't want to get mired in the mud of her past and risk what might be the best part of her life so far. On the flip side, she wanted to make an honest beginning with the woman. Dawn was so good at showing her devotion, at being sensitive to her desires. She decided she would follow Dawn's lead. Who better to model as a loving partner?

"After Ginger died—and before you—I was, for the first time ever, fine and whole, single, independent, chaste, sober. I've thought a lot about what Ginger and I had, and didn't have. I came to the realization that I had no clue how to be trusting and intimate, not after abusing Ginger's trust over and over. I only knew how to live by lying. I'm afraid of telling the truth, afraid, if I'm honest with you, I'll drive you away."

They reached the barn. Together they hung the wheelbarrow on the wall. Dawn pulled Jefferson down to a bale of hay where they sat, side by side.

"We knew each other so well and so little. It was as if I knew her whole, though the details stymied me."

Dawn squeezed her hand. "Did you have affairs?"

"Affairs? Of course I had affairs," she said, a little too harshly. "Sorry, that anger you're hearing is directed at me, not you."

"And you're angry at yourself because…"

She loved the cool softness of Dawn's hand. Holding it excited and comforted her at the same time.

"I never questioned having affairs. That was part of the old bar ethics. I'm a butch in that society. It was some sort of code of honor to have affairs while the long-suffering femme waited at home and forgave. You know, it was the culture."

Dawn looked at her with a puzzled expression. "What did you get out of it if you loved Ginger?"

"Did I love Ginger? She was my backboard. I couldn't make a basket without her there. She was like a guard that didn't move, didn't speak, blocked me from going too far. I still missed a lot, fell to the boards over and over, but she was only a painted piece of wood and never noticed or, maybe, never cared."

She looked at Dawn to gauge her reaction. Dawn smiled so she went on. "Things were different when I came out. Or maybe they weren't. What I got out of affairs was the thrill of them. They would start with the subtle excitement that came with picking up vibes that a woman was interested. That would build into a big want. It felt good. The desire for the new woman, this stranger, would consume me. It was another way of getting high, I think." She didn't mention that sex was only fulfilling with her clandestine liaisons. That wasn't a problem with Dawn.

"Look," Dawn said. "There's one of those silly blue jays."

The bird was picking up one of the peanuts Dawn had dropped as they walked.

Dawn said, "It's such a delight to see them scoot off with the nuts and to hear their little sounds: dropping the nuts on the ground, their feet scrabbling, the sound their beaks make when they tilt their heads back and try to half-swallow a nut so they can fit another one in their mouths."

They watched the comical blue-gray bird, smiling.

Dawn turned to her, a delighted look on her face. "I love your laughing blue eyes."

She closed them, a sense of Ginger, the waste, the missed life, the new chance she had with Dawn overpowering her.

"Tell me," Dawn encouraged.

She couldn't silence the words that gushed from her. She felt like she was turning inside out, all her feelings and thoughts of the years with Ginger had to be spoken—and to this woman alone. "Hey, I admit I wanted her. I never stopped wanting Ginger, but it was like my feelings had frozen about the time we got together. What I felt about Ginger never changed. It never got deeper or lessened, it never adapted to changes in her or in me. It was like the jump shot the newspaper got of me at an

Academy game. There I am, reaching for the basket, the ball in the air. It never goes in, it never drops, I'm suspended. Ginger is always out of reach, I'm always longing. We were content with that balance." She tried to read Dawn's eyes to see if she should continue and stopped. She was always trying to read eyes. She was always looking for approval before doing anything, then forging ahead whether she got it or not. "I know people can't always help being dishonest, but I can choose not to get involved with my beloved liars, all the other women, anymore. Especially this liar," she concluded, pointing to herself.

"From the outside, I would call what you had with Ginger an imbalance."

"You are so right. With you, Kitten, I have my feet on the ground and my eyes open. You're my friend and it looks like that could grow if I'm honest, kind, if we build history, share family, go deep with each other—" She looked into Dawn's eyes. Dawn was nodding. "And our love of this place, the lakes region. I think we both want to make a home here with the right woman." Dawn had stopped nodding and looked down, as if reluctant to say she was serious about moving. "Dawn, you're not going anywhere. You're staying here because of your family. Because of this piece of land. Because there's no better place to make a home or be a librarian. You can make a life in Concord, but it would be so dreary compared to life at the lakes."

Dawn looked away. Jefferson touched the tear on her cheek with a finger. "Why?" she asked.

Dawn grimaced. "I don't want to watch him die."

Jefferson put an arm around Dawn's shoulder. Nothing in her life had ever felt so real. "I'll be with you, Dawn. I'll do my best to balance out the pain."

"Are you asking me to stay at the lake?"

She froze.

"To stay with you?"

She fought with her warring desires. "I'm not positive. I wouldn't want to treat you like I did Ginger. You've lost so many and so much. You're having trouble with losing and I'm having trouble with gaining."

They sat quietly, holding hands, watching the sun go down. The sky looked like somebody was spreading rose butter and cream across it. Jefferson asked herself, why does Dawn think she loves me? Ginger thought she did because Jefferson solved a problem for her. Ginger didn't have to give her much. Jefferson was able to maintain the illusion of a sort of marriage, a feeling of permanence that satisfied her need for roots. Meanwhile, Ginger could give 98 percent of herself to her real passion, dance. When Jefferson entered Ginger's life, Ginger no longer had to date men and pretend she wanted to get married and have kids. She wasn't out to her family, but they no longer pushed her either. Jefferson stayed pretty much under their radar, but they didn't have to worry about Ginger being alone in the world because her roommate was such a very good friend.

So Jefferson had served a purpose. Maybe that was as good as she could have hoped for, because love was not the word she'd use to describe how Ginger had acted toward her. Of course Ginger said she loved her and of course she'd said she loved Ginger and of course both of them had believed it at the time, but now, with the relationship gone, not so much, she thought.

Dawn, though, what drew Dawn to her? There were the obvious things: Jefferson was new in town, available, not bad-looking. She made it possible for Dawn to stay in Pipsborough, didn't she? The hunt was over. She was from the big city and had a polish and experience the local women lacked. Dawn hadn't mentioned that she'd been with anyone when she lived in New York. Maybe she'd been too shy to find lesbians and was making up for it now.

Or maybe she found something lovable about Jefferson. The thought startled her. Here in New Hampshire she had been trying to be herself. No airs. No more old smoothie, as one girlfriend had called her. Dawn didn't seem to be in lust. She seemed to like being together no matter what they did. And me, she thought, I've had a lot of lovers, but what do I know about love? Can Dawn teach me love?

This was frightening. The happiness she saw in her eyes when Dawn looked at her, the way Dawn wanted to do things for her, little things like make her a sandwich with her favorite mustard, like buying her favorite seeded bread, made her fearful of a trap. Dawn actually wanted to give, as well as take pleasure, whatever the pleasure. It wasn't the loving woman she was scared of this time. She feared that she would reject Dawn, run from the thing she'd most wanted, the thing she'd begged for all her life. The therapist at rehab told her she had a couple of kids for parents. For whatever reason, they had been unable to grow from lovers to parents, unable to include her in the family they had created for each other. They told her they loved her, but she didn't feel it or see it. Even as a kid, she'd been able to see that they wanted to remain the kids in the family. Both sets of grandparents pampered and spoiled their children, got them out of financial scrapes, indulged their expensive tastes. She spent a lot of time sleeping over at her grandparents' homes while Emmy and Jarvy went out to play.

But her grandparents had finished with their child rearing. They had their perfect sons, their perfect daughters. If Cousin Ruth was unavailable to babysit, Jefferson would be delivered and put to bed. Going to Grandmother's or to Grandmother Jefferson's for any length of time had been like going to finishing-school seminars for perfect behavior. By the time she was twelve they gave up on her and she went off on her own on her bicycle with lunch money for whole days of exploring the river and the neighborhoods. Once in a great while, Emmy and Jarvy would hustle her into the city with them.

She was in front of Lord and Taylor's. Emmy had dressed her in a red plaid wool bonnet, matching coat and leggings. She had her hands in a white furry muff to keep them warm. They'd been to see the tree and the ice-skaters at Rockefeller Center.

The scene behind glass was of a family of women, the older ones cooking, the younger doing something at a kitchen table. They wore old-fashioned clothes. They looked happy. She wanted to be one of the little girls in the warm kitchen where her aunts and mother cooked at a walk-in brick hearth.

In the cold night on the street side of the bright window, her mother loomed at her left and her father at her right. Jarvy was smoking. Emmy said how pretty the clothes were and Jefferson felt a chill. She would be dressed like Huckleberry Finn, barefoot at the table, the floor warm under her feet. She'd be fastening a fish hook to a line and tightening it around her bamboo pole. Jarvy was taking her fishing on the Mississippi come spring. They jostled her to the next window. Men in the parlor smoking pipes. She could smell the women's turkey cooking in the kitchen.

She pulled them back toward the warmth of the ladies' window and woke up lying across a rumbling train seat, gritty-eyed, her muff for a pillow, her mother and father silent on the facing seats, wide-awake, Jarvy smoking, the paper folded on his lap, Emmy reading a ladies' magazine. Little Jefferson slept again, woke to a station call, and neither her mother nor her father was there, across from her. That cloud, the dark purple one, hugged her like there was no tomorrow. She cried, cried silently and bitterly, huddled into herself on the train seat, hugging the muff. By the time Emmy and Jarvy returned from the club car she'd gone numb. She hid her face, her fear, her abandonment in the furry muff and slept until the next morning when she woke under pink sheets and blankets in her ivory four-poster bed, despised dolls arrayed around the room, December sun glowing weakly hot through thin, lacy curtains. Her teddy-bear Michael was in her arms.

All her life the Lord and Taylor scenes behind glass were like remembered dreams that had happened to others, and denied to her. She'd always believed that Cousins Ruth and Raymond had come closer to living such homey Christmas fable lives with their stuffy stay-at-home mother and father and each other, but Raymond was dead of lung cancer and Ruth had never stopped drinking. Her husband took the kids and left her. Ruth had moved to Florida where she got so heavy she ended up with diabetes and now had to have a leg amputated.

Dawn felt to her like the Christmas windows. Scared or not, Jefferson wanted to be happy at her side now, while they were both still young and healthy.

They spent that Saturday night in Jefferson's bed, in her cottage by the lake.

"This place is so comfortable," Dawn said.

Jefferson, forgoing electricity, made a fire in the woodstove, lit a lantern, and carried it to her bedroom. "It was built for leisure, for cold nights by the fire, hot days on the porch, and snuggling under a puffy quilt."

Dawn wore a lacy, low-cut bra that shaped her breasts into scoops of lovely pale gold flesh. She pushed Jefferson down and straddled her, letting the bra touch Jefferson's lips. The sight of Dawn engorged her whole being with desire, and she found a nipple through the bra, licking and sucking until the fabric was saturated. Dawn continued to bend forward, supporting herself on her hands. By feel, she rolled Dawn's panties down and reached her with fore and middle fingers, tapping Dawn's hood until Dawn pressed down, squirmed herself open, and rode Jefferson's fingers, eyes closed, hair falling forward until she came with a happy yip and lay on Jefferson's chest.

In a moment Dawn was active again, moving backward to yank down Jefferson's jeans and pull them off.

"Open your legs, Jef." Dawn ran one lace-clad breast along the wet

Lee Lynch

parts between her legs until Jefferson thought she'd come against the breast, but Dawn moved and pressed her mouth where her breast had been, keeping still, forcing Jefferson to rock herself into orgasm.

"You," Dawn said, easing up into her arms, dallying at the highlights, "were built for pleasure."

"Everything has changed, since you," she told Dawn. Her voice was still thick and low with satisfaction. "My mind has changed, my body has changed. My future is rich."

Dawn's eyes shone. The sight of them enhanced Jefferson's feeling of radiance. Dawn whispered, "I'll love you forever, Jef."

"Dawn, Dawn. Don't go making promises. One day at a time, okay?" Those AA slogans held a lot of truth, she thought. "I've learned that promises don't mean anything because I've broken so many myself. After all, forever can be the best aphrodisiac."

"No, Jef. That was then. That was them. This is me, now. I recognized you right away. You may go away, but I won't."

All those years she'd wasted trying to make Ginger happy instead of bouncing her heart around like a basketball, slapping it like a handball, spiking it like a volleyball, kicking it. What a dog she'd been instead of deeply treasuring the woman she'd thought of as her one true love. She'd sunk her fingers into one after another shallow pond, testing the waters of every flirty woman who crossed her path and some she just wanted to tease the flirtyness from.

Despair must have been plain on Jefferson's face because Dawn put her arms around her and said, "There, there, there," and held her, rocked her, made love with her until sleep melded them together with the contentment only warm, sated bodies and hope can know. It was all she'd ever wanted.

She couldn't say it, but Jefferson hoped she could stay too. "There's this empty place in me you're sliding into," she told Dawn. "It's always been there and I've tried every which way to fill it. In the past I thought I knew the way it should be done. I loved hard, partly, I think, to ensure that I would be loved in return. My loving was begging. It did no good, like knocking on the doors of empty apartments on Halloween night, hearing the hollow sound of their vacancy, my pillowcase open, a few stray Mary Janes and sour balls down at the bottom. Now it turns out all this begging for love has been my impatience. When I gave up— abracadabra. Here you are."

Dawn moved closer to her. "Am I a sour ball or a Mary Jane?"

• 304 •

"Neither," said Jefferson, thinking about how generous and gentle Dawn was with her and with her friends and the Northway family. "You're the nice lady who opened her door and gave us little Milky Ways. You're all dressed up as a genie of love."

Dawn nuzzled her neck. Jefferson squeezed her hand.

"Dawn," she said, "I'm so afraid I'm never going to change. I come on so together, then fall apart in the dark. It'll always be Halloween with me—costumes and masks—and I'll always be a beggar of love, on the prowl night and day, taking it from anyone who can give it. What if you give me everything and I'm still not satisfied?"

CHAPTER FORTY

Jefferson was the only one, other than Mr. and Mrs. Wiley, who was free to pick up Shannon from the hospital. Shannon said she couldn't face her parents. Though Jefferson didn't know how she would face Shannon, she sympathized so much with her and was so guilty about being attracted to Dawn, she wanted to drive Shannon home and do whatever would help. The red tape to release her stretched for almost an hour. As they drove north along the lake, Shannon was subdued and sat like a huddled bundle abandoned at the door to a Goodwill shop.

"I've caused everybody a lot of trouble." Shannon was turning herself around. Gone were the limp bleached hair, the chapped lips, the pale, sunken face.

After a while Jefferson was able to put her thoughts into words. "I should have heard your desperation." She grasped Shannon's hand.

The sun was out, but few boats were on the water this late after the season. Wind-driven wavelets made the boats slap the water.

They stopped at a pharmacy for Shannon's antidepressant. Jefferson bought lip balm and gave it to Shannon, then walked the aisles while Shannon's prescription was filled. Shannon was slumped on a red molded plastic chair across from the counter, a long-legged waif with a bewildered fix-my-life look on her face that Jefferson found strangely appealing despite Shannon's butchiness. Several people paced around them as they waited. The pharmacy telephone rang, was answered, rang again.

She plunged out of the vitamin aisle and walked to Shannon. "I can't take you home. You aren't ready to be alone."

"Wings will be there."

"Yolanda has your cat," she reminded Shannon, wondering if the lapses in Shannon's memory were permanent. Shannon's energy was so low this might be the best time to tell her that she was seeing Dawn. The drugs she'd been administered in the hospital might still her reaction.

"I'll be okay. It'll be good to get home."

"Your mom went over yesterday. She said it wouldn't be the first time she cleaned up after you."

Shannon relaxed her face into a small, brief smile.

"She was worried about you being alone in that little cabin, but she knew you wouldn't want to stay with her or your father."

"She got that right."

"I have extra rooms, Shannon. For a couple of days. What do you say?" She'd have to warn Dawn to stay away. If Dawn didn't have a cat of her own, Jefferson sometimes thought Dawn would never go home.

"It would be peaceful on the lake," Shannon said, her voice softer than Jefferson had ever heard it. This was not a butch beside her, this was a woman in pain. No, she wouldn't say anything about Dawn yet.

"You'd have to promise to call me at work—or wherever—if you felt like offing yourself again."

"Not funny, Jefferson."

"I'm dead serious," she answered, straight-faced.

She got a real smile out of Shannon that time, and Shannon got up slowly, with a stiffness she'd only seen before in people many years Shannon's senior.

"Tell me about your back, Shannon," she asked as they walked past the vitamins, into books and magazines, then all the way to the household cleaners. Shannon seemed pretty wobbly, but she wasn't slouching as she had when they first arrived. She experienced the warmth that used to envelop her when one of her students made unexpected and exceptional progress.

"What about it?" Shannon's voice sounded small and rusty.

"Where did you hurt it?" She had her hand on Shannon's back, pressing various points.

"In the Guard."

"How?"

"It was stupid, really. A strap on my gear popped loose. I was supposed to be on this truck, but I stopped to fix the strap. The driver played catch-me. I ran for the open back, tossed my pack up, and missed when I tried to jump on."

"You fell?"

"No, but I heard something pop when I leapt up for my second try. You know how you do? Get all twisted up throwing yourself up and forward at the same time?"

She nodded, remembering a volleyball game that put her on the sidelines for weeks.

"Oh, yeah. That night I felt like the truck ran over me, not away from me."

"You had a base doctor?"

"Sure, but I didn't want to get the driver in trouble. She was my… you know."

"Girl?"

"Not really. She was married to a guy at home, but we fooled around some."

"So you've been living with this messed-up back for how many years and the Guard doesn't know about it?"

"They know. I waited a day and blamed it on something else."

"Wiley," the pharmacy tech called.

She stood back, running her knuckles up and down her cheek, hard, trying to decide how to tell her about herself and Dawn, while Shannon went to the counter. A moment later Shannon exclaimed, "You have got to be kidding."

"What's the matter?' She joined Shannon at the counter.

"They want a hundred eighty dollars for thirty pills!"

"Here. Put it on my credit card." She tugged her slim wallet from her back pocket.

"No." Shannon waved her away with more energy than she had demonstrated yet. "Can't you give me something cheaper?" she asked the clerk.

Eventually, the pharmacist had Shannon call the hospital to see if a generic could be substituted.

"I am steamed," Shannon said, returning to the vitamin aisle after her call and walking swiftly past the seasonal and toy aisles. "What was that doctor thinking? Didn't he know I don't have insurance?"

Jefferson smiled to see Shannon so energized. Whatever works, she thought, stopping herself from taking Shannon's hand as they walked, but not surprised at the impulse. She was so unused to spending time with another butch, except for Gabby, and she didn't find Gabby remotely attractive as anything but a friend. "Won't the VA pay for it?"

"I don't have veteran status so I'm not entitled. The only time I get good medical care is when I'm on active duty." She kicked a mop display and sent it crashing to the floor. "I'm thinking I might as well go back in, Jef. I need to face up to it and take my chances. That way I'd get the benefits, such as they are."

She grabbed Shannon's elbow and faced her. Part of her wanted to encourage Shannon to do that, but she genuinely cared about her. It would make her own life easier, cowardly as she knew that thought to be. She gripped both of Shannon's elbows. "There's no way they'll reinstate you with your disability, is there?"

"Sure, they will. They never acknowledged the accident enough to pay me for it. I wanted out, so I didn't pursue it. Why bother, when you could get shipped to the Mideast waiting for them to make a decision? Better to stay under their radar. They'll check me out enough to maybe keep me out of combat. I can hope for motor pool or a stateside assignment."

"How about recruiting? Then you could stay here."

Shannon laughed, a lively laugh of genuine amusement as they pulled up to Jefferson's cottage. "Dude," she said, "that job is harder than combat right now. Nobody wants to join up."

Two and a half hours after going to get Shannon, Jefferson was back home with Shannon as a guest. Out of habit, she hit the answering-machine play button.

"How're you doing, Tiger?" Dawn's recorded voice asked. "This is your Kitten."

Jefferson's stomach felt like it was plummeting past her ovaries and all her other organs. She turned her head quickly and saw Shannon standing outside, walking toward the dock. Ducks rose from the water to take flight, crying as they lifted. Close call, she thought, and erased the message. After a moment she decided to turn the machine off. She'd go outside and use her cell to call Dawn back later—after she hid the Prozac, ibuprofen, aspirin, and kitchen knives.

As she suicide-proofed the house, though, she realized how wrong it felt to lie about Dawn. Hadn't she learned that hiding the truth only hurt everyone? She would have to tell Shannon eventually, but not tonight, not when she'd offered her shelter in her home. Now it was clear—she couldn't keep the lid on this. Shannon would only feel deceived when she found out Jefferson was protecting her from the truth.

How to say it? She'd never had to face up to such a situation before. The only time her flings got really messy was when they were with someone from their immediate social scene. She simply disappeared from social life while the trouble lasted. Ginger was only marginally interested in the bars so she could always tempt her away with dance recitals or a cozy night at home. It had never occurred to her, back then, that she should come clean to anyone. On the contrary, the quieter things were kept, the less likely it was that someone would get hurt. This thing with Dawn, though, was more than serious. Plus Shannon was so fragile now and their circle of friends was so small. There simply was no place to hide. She hadn't felt this exposed since she was a kid.

She looked toward the water again. It was deep off the dock, but Shannon was in sight. She found a couple of steaks in the freezer and stuck them in the microwave to defrost. She could at least make her a good meal, maybe share her bed with Shannon, to hold her and give her some comfort.

Shannon came back in from the dusk. Jefferson cooked dinner and Shannon, freshly showered, played with the kittens, who had become long, stringy adolescents.

"You get those pills down yet?" she asked.

Shannon was shaking the bottle to catch the kittens' attention. "Can you believe they were sixty-seven ninety-nine? I should put them in my mom's safe-deposit box, not swallow them. He said the other ones wouldn't kill me if I popped all of them. You think these would?"

Jefferson strode from the kitchen to the living room and, pushing Shannon down on the couch with one arm, snatched the bottle from her hand.

"Dude," Shannon protested.

She straddled Shannon, face close enough to kiss her. "You are cut off, girl," she declared. "If I have to drive over to your place to deliver pills daily, I will, as long as you keep talking trash about taking pills—or whatever."

She got up, filled a glass with water, and handed Shannon one tablet.

"Nah," Shannon said, refusing both. "Once you start pills like that you can't stop. I'd be on them all my life. I'm already into you for these. Who has an extra seventy dollars a month? Besides, who needs pills? The bad guys will put me out of my misery soon enough."

Beside Shannon on the couch, she grabbed her arms again, but this time pulled her, roughly, close and kissed her. To her surprise, Shannon didn't struggle. "You really want to give this up? Think of all the women waiting out there for you."

She was startled to see the desire come into Shannon's eyes, kind of a blue cloud that left her looking unfocused.

"The state will help with the costs. Come on, Shannon, we'll find some way to do this by the time these pills run out." She let go and moved back to the kitchen.

"Yeah, like go back in."

"Hey, this is not the best time to be making decisions like that, Shannon. Have a pill before the ones they gave you at the hospital wear off. Start getting well."

Shannon used the arm of the couch to help herself stand.

"I don't think so. I won't need them now that I've made up my mind. It was the indecision that was killing me, no bones about it."

Jefferson moved to her easy chair. "Playing soldier is going to wreck your back. You won't be able to run a B-and-B hurting like that."

"You know I hate this war business, Jefferson, but it's what I signed on for. I tried to find an easy way out. I'd better grit my teeth and go for it." She grinned a sick-looking grin. "You know the slogan: 'There's strong and then there's army strong.' That's me. Sink or swim. I've been sinking and I need to learn how to swim." Shannon had a look of despair. "You'll find a home for Wings if something happens to me over there? Yolanda won't keep her forever. She can be mama cat to your kids. Or maybe I could write a will, leave Wings and everything else to Dawn."

Jefferson's insides constricted. "I've got to talk to you about that, Shannon."

"A will?"

"About Dawn."

Shannon spun toward her, a kitten under each arm. Her eyes looked like broken windows in a ruined house. "No," she said, carefully putting the kittens on the couch, as if afraid of hurting them—as if afraid she was about to be hurt. Jefferson searched her mind for the right words. She knew her face was full of the pain she was about to inflict.

Jefferson was twelve. The boys down the street were at Choate. Jefferson would start at Dutchess Academy in town next September. A new teenager, a nice clean-cut young man, Emmy said, had moved into the Elliots' old place, the brick house with the glass atrium and a heated indoor pool. He kept inviting Jefferson to swim with him. She loved to swim, to dive and pull the water with her arms and kick till her body felt like a speedboat slicing the lake. She swam so fast she would try out for the swim team at the Academy. She bet she could practically tow a skier, swimming fast. That was something else she loved, water-skiing, timing her stand to the second, balancing on the skis, going as fast as the boat, feeling the muscles burn in her legs, kneeling and jumping, lifting one ski, turning on the rope, sinking slowly into the lake when she reached the shore and waiting, eager for her turn again.

She burst out of the water after a breathless swim across the pool and pulled herself up the steps by the silver rail, water streaming from her, a sea monster, smiling at the exhilaration of it—and there he was, the teenager, watching her, his swim trunks on the tiled surround—he was so hairy—examining her body like it was a property he was about to buy.

He said, "There's nothing up here yet," touching his own bare chest with his index fingers.

She looked at her flat front, felt humiliated. No, it was worse, she felt stripped, discarded—weak—then saw her strong thighs and wet feet and knew it was too slippery to safely run.

"Sink or swim," her father had said over and over, teaching her to swim at age three. It was her most vivid preschool memory. Sink or swim. Her dive into the boy's pool gave her the distance she needed from him. When she emerged she had enough time to grab her clothes. He was grasping at her as she opened the door to the garden and didn't care what she trampled as she headed for the hillside into the woods, skirted the backyards between their houses, and pulled on her clothes before entering the screened back patio.

Her mother, listening to opera on the hi-fi, had asked, "Did you have a nice swim?"

She couldn't tell her. There was every reason on earth to say something: so she wouldn't have to go back, so the boy wouldn't do that to other girls, so her mother would comfort her fear away. Emmy wouldn't, though. She'd get upset. She'd ask questions and more questions and cry, as if it had happened to her. She'd tell her father! He'd have to talk to the boy's father. The boy would get back at her.

"Great pool," she cried, and went up the wooden stairs two at a time, frantic to get out of her wet bathing suit. She only realized when she got into her bathroom that she'd run all the way home in her white swim cap. She would go out for field hockey, not the swim team. In an instant, she'd switched from wanting to be a water-ski champ to wanting to pilot the boat that pulled the other kids at the lake. She'd learned all the good ski tricks already anyway. Boating, that would be her thing. You didn't have to wear a bathing suit when you spun that wheel and learned where the rocks lurked.

Facing Shannon, she felt as weak and helpless as she had that day, and once again her head pounded with those words: sink or swim. She had to tell her. What words could she possibly use? She moved to her and pulled her close. Her rush of affection toward Shannon was so strong that she pulled her into a hug.

"I mean it's not time to talk about Dawn and the will," she said, her voice sounding, to her, thin and pleading. Nothing else would come out. "I guess the upside to going back in the service would be a chance to meet the love of your life."

Shannon's breathing seemed quicker. She'd put her arms around Jefferson's back and now kissed her neck. Part of her recoiled and thought, Ew! This felt strange to her, like she was on the wrong side of a volleyball net, trying to spike the ball for her team backward. She had no sexual desire, only a need to repair everything for her friend. She hadn't intended to make love to Shannon, didn't want to, but lovemaking was her language. She didn't know how else to speak these feelings of tenderness and comfort. Dawn would despise her if she found out. Hell, she despised herself. She'd thought herself capable of improving her play on this new course, not acting like a sandbagger.

Moving into automatic seduction mode, she framed Shannon's face with her hands, sliding her fingers into Shannon's yellow hair, still damp from the shower, and explored her lips with all sorts of kisses. This was interesting and repellent, performing passionate acts without feeling passion. It put her in a place where she could watch herself. It was true, the language of seduction was her most articulate and she could not stop the flow of it. She'd warned Dawn, more than once, that she might be a beggar when it came to love, but the minute she noticed someone getting too serious about loving her, she went running to the next bad girl. She explained that she had a certain fascination with a kind of woman, a woman who was adventurous and therefore exciting. Eventually she realized that only made her seem more attractive to Dawn, who had an amazing stash of lingerie in which to entice her when turned on. How lucky was she that Dawn was both a nice person and an adventurous femme?

And then Jefferson had to wonder. Was she some kind of monster incapable of love and fidelity? Had she been hunting for love all these years, or had she been learning to love? She had it in her to hit the line drives, to keep a handball in play, to teach a team to be more than its individuals, but she seemed sadly lacking in the skills she most needed.

She thought of Dawn with the fulfilled feeling that came of sinking a long putt. A hole-in-one was exciting, but putts were the most satisfying. Dawn loved her. That was the simple, magical, undeniable, and incomprehensible truth. Dawn loved her. Yet here she was.

She'd always assumed she was a bad person, first, from her mother's discontent with about everything she did as a kid and from her father's disinterest, and then, because she turned out gay. Gayer than gay, really, with her appetite for women. Was it possible that there was no lack in her? Maybe it was more about bounty. She was so full of—of stuff—happy stuff, loving stuff, how could she keep it all inside? She'd be glad to give it all to one woman, if one woman could accept it all and not run away. Had she overwhelmed poor Ginger, who wasn't used to shows of affection, exuberance, so much focus on her—or to showing love? Ginger must have fled inside herself. She'd quickly thrown up the plywood and the two-by-fours as soon as the hurricane of Jefferson appeared in her life.

She sighed and gave herself over to what she knew best.

Shannon seemed comfortable with the way things were going so she let her hands follow Shannon's tall, thin body. She was surprised by Shannon's responsiveness. Probably it had been a long time for her, the way she had been obsessing about Dawn. This would be good for her, maybe break the pattern, get her thinking about other women. She reached under Shannon's T-shirt and ran her thumbs roughly across her nipples, thinking she should feel guilt or confusion, instead of the hot bubble of excitement in her chest that rose and grew larger. The perfect rapture of making love was not something to be squandered, but neither was it something to be hoarded. She expressed herself more naturally through her hands and limbs than she did with words. This itch of hers for other women might look like betrayal, she thought, but was really a heart on the loose, directing hands that sometimes seemed to heal before they inevitably hurt.

Neither of them would expect to do this again and would not talk about it. Their friendship would be stronger for it. Was she kidding herself? Was she in for some screaming fits with both Dawn and Shannon? She was confident that wouldn't happen, as she was confident that she and Shannon were supposed to be doing this. Here. Today.

She had her thigh against Shannon's closed legs and that way guided her backward to the couch, hands on her hips. She was able to slip Shannon's shirt over her head before Shannon fell back onto the couch and reached to unbutton Jefferson's shirt. Butch, femme, it didn't matter. At the first touch of breasts she always felt an explosion of lust that propelled her onward. Shannon was in sweatpants and was a wriggling naked treat for Jefferson in no time. Jefferson got out of her own pants and they lay, front to front, touching from lips to feet, holding each other on the couch for the longest time, making small, delicately exciting movements with their hips and thighs, breasts and bellies. Their hands stayed out of it.

She was drifting off when Shannon shivered. Jefferson quickly pulled the throw from the back of the couch over them. The light rubbing her movement caused made Shannon gasp. Jefferson scrambled to invert her body. Both expert at this, they parted each other's moist lips simultaneously, and she felt the touch of Shannon's tongue as hers touched Shannon. And then a rush of hot tenderness for the fine troubled woman Shannon was engulfed her. They both adopted a light, slow, rotating rhythm, matching each other. The tension built and she knew she would have no trouble coming, but they went very slowly, teasing each other until their breathing became quick and loud to her ears. When Shannon's thighs tensed, Jefferson moved against her tongue enough to push herself over the edge she'd been avoiding and they breathed audibly together, Shannon bucking, Jefferson arching, coming powerfully, feeling exquisite pleasure for herself, without a worry about taking care of a femme, although that was normally part of her pleasure.

They both sat up then, looking under their eyebrows at each other.

"Are you hungry?" Shannon asked.

"I could do with something tasty. Hey, do you like strawberry ice cream?"

Shannon's grin was like a kid's. No, she thought, it was a kid's.

They sat side by side on the couch, TV tuned to an old *Law and Order*, both acting silly. Now and then Shannon would poke her with an elbow and she would poke back. Neither of them stopped grinning except to suck pink ice cream off their spoons.

Jefferson chuckled as they got into bed together that night. "We're pretty pleased with ourselves, aren't we," she said. As soon as the drugs leave Shannon's system, she thought, Shannon would be gone to start her life over.

Shannon spooned her bottom against Jefferson. "It was really nice," Shannon said before she fell asleep.

She thought for a long time as she lay beside Shannon. Thought about having the freedom to do what she had just done. Shannon had needed this release to her future. She was a bit honored that she could give her that. Yet it would hurt Dawn to know that she had. She needed to marry the two forces of her nature. She couldn't reconcile deceit with honesty; she would have to choose. Was a life with Dawn worth sacrificing the freedom to indulge her impulses? Pick your sport, she told herself. Would it be softball or golf; would she be part of a team or move in the world as a self-styled one-woman wonder?

Wait. Wait. Wait.

In a moment, she was on her porch, pacing in the chill night. What made her think she was the only one who could give all these women what they sought? What did she think she was—some kind of super lover? Who said she could stomp on anyone's heart: Dawn's, Shannon's, or her own, for that matter? All her career, she'd taught her students to play by the rules, and she thought she was exempt?

She sat heavily on the edge of an old wooden Adirondack chair. Good gravy, she thought, do I even want to do this anymore? Give it a rest, Jefferson, she heard Glad say. You've been handed a terrific second chance. Are you going to throw it away for some sleazy fun?

It wasn't sleazy fun, she told Glad, told herself. Bringing women out, making love to lesbians, these were responsibilities and a privilege. So many, many times she'd acted as a bridge for other women. It was, she admitted to herself now, one of her greatest pleasures to hear their struggles and to ease them for a time, sometimes for longer. It made her feel good about herself. Comforting them, making them feel good was her most selfish act. It even, she realized now, turned her on.

Did she have no responsibility to her primary relationship, then?

What had she just done? Stone-cold sober, she'd risked hurting Dawn horribly and losing the chance of a life with her, not because Dawn would ever know about this, not because Dawn wouldn't forgive—she might—but because fooling around like this would prove toxic to the way she herself saw any relationship. The lake, too, she'd almost destroyed the peace of the lake, her Innisfree. She was so tired of this balancing act. So tired of herself.

Except—there was Shannon sleeping inside, full of life once more. And here she was, the lesbian, the butch, who Mother Nature had made this way perhaps with a purpose.

CHAPTER FORTY-ONE

They went down to the city for their four-month anniversary, singing along with old disco songs as they drove. Shannon had gone off to war, apparently cheerful from the relief of having made a decision. So far all the news had been good, including the fact that her truck-driver buddy had divorced her husband, gone up in rank, and was keeping Shannon out of combat, getting her trained in some computer skills that she could use back home in addition to running the bed-and-breakfast. Either that, Shannon had e-mailed, or home would be wherever her buddy was stationed.

Jefferson's heart wasn't exactly simmering with cheer to be back in the city, but she could probably avoid running into most of the people she'd known with Ginger. Not so their ghosts, who inhabited her mind at each sighting of a familiar place. Briefly, she wished for amnesia, but without the life she'd lived how could she have been ready for Dawn or be who Dawn needed? She felt a distinct pull to the West Fourth Street Courts for a handball game. She'd have to teach Dawn some day, though where to find a handball court up at the lakes she did not know.

It was only in the forties that day so they walked into Central Park and back to Jefferson's car for the sheer pleasure of it. This was terrific, she thought, having a chance with Dawn to be seriously new together. She'd considered telling Dawn about Shannon and decided not to. It was the very last time and Shannon was gone, possibly forever. With some struggle, she'd forgiven herself and was determined to prove she could trust herself.

Dawn had wanted to introduce her to some friends. To show her off, was how Dawn put it. The woman was in love. She was glad to see Dawn so happy; it enhanced her own elation. Dawn was smart, funny, appealingly exotic, stable, self-supporting, didn't want to live together yet, imaginative in bed—a wonderful match fueled by more than the physical and, on Jefferson's part, by a trust in someone else, as well as in herself, that she'd never before experienced. Someone had once told her, if you were persistent in love, love would come back with a willing woman. Maybe that was true.

She'd expected Dawn to broach the subject of a civil union, now, shockingly, legal in conservative New Hampshire. Not doing so was very smart on Dawn's part: Dawn had heard the warnings in Jefferson's stories—or confessions—and was appropriately wary.

Dawn was dressed in a spotless white nylon parka too light for fall at home. She had her hair up in a twist and looked sharp on Jefferson's arm. Despite her doubts about this whole jaunt, she started to feel like her much younger self, promenading across from the park, near to skipping with glee at the sight of two striped cats in a window watching pigeons. Her leather jacket would never fit the way it had in her thirties, but she'd sloughed off enough new pounds to be comfortable in it again. When she squeezed Dawn's arm to hers, a memory of walking like this with Ginger ambushed her, like a ghost who quickly left. She breathed in until her lungs would hold no more of this pretty air.

"What is it, Jefferson?" Dawn was watching her face. "That sounded like a sigh of regrets."

She shook her head. "No." She was denying the truth to herself as well as to Dawn. "Or maybe." Her emotions were such a jumble. She clasped Dawn's hand, that soft, always-yielding hand that seemed to exist to be cherished, and said, sadness taking on weight around her, "Not to have found this, not to have found you, until now? Part of me wants to cry because I had to wait so long, the other part wonders how I got so lucky."

They walked past lamp posts and trash baskets and ornate apartment building entrances on their way to their distant parking space. They smiled at each other after they passed a woman in long boots and a gray fur coat walking her long-legged gray dog.

"You wouldn't have wanted me then," Dawn said, pressing her cheek to Jefferson's shoulder.

Without hesitation she replied, "I would always have wanted you!"

"Oh, Jefferson, sometimes you're such a goofy romantic. You never would have gone for a mousy librarian from Pipsborough."

"Hey, Kitten, you're not mousy."

"You wouldn't have noticed me long enough to find that out."

"You would have gotten my attention somehow. Right?"

Dawn slowly shook her head as they waited for a light to change. "No, Jef. When you were drinking I would have run the other way."

"Good girl," she said. "That's one reason I love you. Putting up with my shit is not on your agenda." She put her arms around Dawn and hugged her hard, then let her go and leapt into the street, weaving through the traffic, Dawn's hand in her own.

"Jefferson! You're crazy," Dawn called with a loving laugh.

They reached the sidewalk without any trauma beyond the shout of a cabdriver in a language they didn't understand. She grinned at Dawn. She couldn't wait to introduce her to Angela.

It wasn't only Dawn, was it, she thought. It was laughing at the sight of another dog walker with a brace of four eager poodles heading to the park. It was knowing somebody was crazy about her again. It was the history they'd begun to accumulate, the anticipation of a rich life ahead. It was surviving, still being here though Ginger was gone. Yet Ginger wasn't gone. Ginger, like her old friend Glad, was in the sunshine and the city, the walkers and this sweet lady beside her. Ginger seemed to share her every breath. She wasn't glad Ginger was gone, but she was so happy to have this new life for herself, it seemed to balance the sadness in her. Dawn made her want to swing around lamp posts and serenade her. She'd missed her own exuberance.

Gloom, grief, guilt, she could let all that go. "I love you, little Kitten," she said.

Dawn's always surprising eyes, a shade not unlike the lake in sunshine, flooded with light, the way they always did when she was pleased beyond words. Jefferson relaxed, swung into Dawn's mood, and grabbed her in her arms, singing "Our Lips Are Sealed." They danced and dipped in circles until the end of the block. Dawn, as usual, tripped on her own and Jefferson's feet, managing to smack a shin on a hydrant on their journey.

"I'm such a klutz," Dawn said, laughing as she rubbed her leg. Jefferson went down on one knee, not as easy to do as it once had been, and pushed Dawn's pant leg up to survey the damage. "No blood, but a good scrape."

"My hero," Dawn said.

Jefferson helped herself up using a lamp post, trying to disguise her need for the prop. She loved bopping around the city like this. "You are terrific for my confidence, Dawn." It was true. Being loved was a powerful booster. Not always enough, but powerful.

"Come on, my dancing dyke. We need to get down to Chinatown for Mom's shopping. Wait till you taste what she's going to make us tomorrow night. Oh, let's remember to stop at the notions store for Aunt Tuyat's special thread."

They drove to the library where Dawn once worked and said hello to two friends who were still there, then Jefferson got a tour.

"The staff is almost all straight," Dawn told her. "Can you deal with husbands if my friends visit us up at the lake?" Dawn asked.

Jefferson made a sour face.

"They're such great friends. These women are the ones who gave me the confidence to know I could run a rural library." Dawn chattered on about how she had to do circulation, reference, be the children's librarian, get very creative with grants. No wonder Dawn had such a fiercely loyal Friends of the Library in Pipsborough.

"You're what I call a competent femme."

"And this is a good thing?" asked Dawn.

She stroked Dawn's head and ran her hand down her lovely loose hair. "You're a good thing." The irrepressible pleasure of being with Dawn Northway was a feeling she'd experienced in a few small tastes and moments before, but this continuum of happiness baffled and delighted her. She had to work to simply accept and enjoy it.

"Then why do you look sad? Is it Ginger?"

"No. Yes. A little. It doesn't detract from us, though. Makes you more special, if anything."

"It must be hard. Where do your feelings go when someone you love dies? They don't disappear."

"There was a lot of water under the bridge by the time that happened, Dawn."

They were walking from their distant parking space to the notions store, and Dawn pulled her aunt's list from her purse. Jefferson followed her into the shop at first, then wandered back outside. She hadn't told Dawn her whole story yet. It was too humiliating, but Dawn needed to know that Jefferson's sorrow was more complex than loss itself. Here she was, taking a chance again, risking her heart and risking Dawn's too. Sometimes she felt too damaged, too beat-up by the life she'd lived to deserve the love of this bright-eyed gamin of a woman. Sprite, imp, a woman without artifice, who seemed to sparkle from the inside out—she feared she'd sully Dawn. Instead, when she added confessions to prior confessions, made it clear that she hadn't been only with Ginger all those years, Dawn continued to act pleased and eager to hear more stories of her big-bad-wolf days.

The street was busy with shoppers from the 'burbs and buyers from the garment shops. So much of the industry had moved overseas, but a few diehard specialty stores were apparently keeping their heads above water enough to survive. So many women. So many women to admire. Should she tell Dawn that she couldn't promise fidelity? She didn't want to make Dawn worry.

The women shoppers, always in pairs or threes, were older. She wasn't attracted to the kids. There was something so focused about the twenty- and thirty-somethings. Her peers had never been so hustle-bustle-all-about-making-money. The older women drifting by were laughing, sometimes arm in arm, happy to be out with their girlfriends. Some were real lookers. Their faces told such stories, weathered like her own. She wanted to hear the stories, to make them forget they'd ever been hurt, that they were aging, that they no longer had their whole lives ahead of them. She saw herself in bed with one—that one passing into the store where she stood—listening to her after-lovemaking tales.

The woman held the door while Dawn exited on Jefferson's arm. She saw the woman look at them, at their linked arms, and smile as if in blessing. Jefferson tucked Dawn's hand tighter in her own. God, she thought, spare me from myself. She'd used Dawn's touch to connect with another woman and felt all too pleased about it.

She was getting the second chance she'd heard Glad whisper about, and she knew it. But did she know how to love Dawn? What did it matter when Dawn so obviously loved her? Dawn knew what love was and Jefferson felt like she'd never known. She would give this wholly, unconditionally loved business a chance—no, more than a chance. She wouldn't let herself fight it. What if all the pleasant feelings she had toward Dawn were exactly what comprised love? She smiled at the sight of Dawn; she laughed deeply and genuinely with her. Dawn was a talented and attentive lover who seemed genuinely to revel in making love to her as well as luxuriating, to the nth degree, in Jefferson's touch. Dawn had no hang-ups compared to most women who turned her on, and the more time they spent in bed, the more Dawn, without artifice, turned her on. Jefferson realized that Dawn was right; she'd had her doubts about getting together with a librarian, had harbored an image of a staid, dried-out kind of woman, but that had been a mistake. For all she knew she might have slept with librarians before.

Why shouldn't she end up with a decent, caring, passionate woman who enjoyed pleasing her? Why not fall easy for once, instead of falling hard? Her ebullient self was returning. They planned to stay in the city for the weekend; her parents were on a cruise. She was excited about showing Dawn where she'd lived for so many years. Tomorrow night they'd go dancing. The old Lincoln Center cream-colored vest and tie no longer fit so she'd bought a deep red shirt, a black silk tie, and a charcoal gray wool-front vest for the occasion.

Could she stay with Dawn? Could she stomach a life on the lake where the biggest thrill was throwing a wake of white spume behind the boat into the clean lake air? Could she have a passion for a life without the trauma and drama she'd always created for herself? Could she pledge, to herself, to hold Dawn's hand for the rest of her life, and no one else's, like this?

If she could, was it because she'd stopped drinking, because grief had beaten her down, because her erotic adventures had left her jaded? Was it because, so close to fifty, she was just tired and ready for the shelter of Dawn? She told herself that while all of this might be true, she loved everything about Dawn and would be content with her.

They were passing Lincoln Center on their way back to the car after stopping for a supply of Manhattan Special sarsaparilla. The fountain wasn't operating. She saw her younger self dancing there with Ginger on hot summer nights. There wasn't a reason in the world she couldn't do the same with Dawn come summer, here or at the band shell on the Pipsborough green after wandering the hospital white-elephant sale, with her young bride beside her.

She ushered Dawn off the sidewalk. Despite the chilly weather, steel drummers were beating out a melody nearby. She pulled Dawn into her arms and swung her around, then settled them into the world beat of the drums and danced around the dry fountain, which had once flowed so boisterously it had nearly drowned out the music of her life.

Dawn laughed and this time followed without a misstep. When they had made the circuit, they laughed their way back to the car and drove downtown without hitting one light.

Chinatown was as crowded and hectic as ever. Dawn knew the shops well and steered Jefferson along like a little tugboat with a barge.

They bought a bag of ice and put the groceries in Dawn's cooler, then drove back uptown to the new Greek restaurant Dawn's friends had raved about. She realized she'd been checking everywhere they went to see if Ginger was in sight, an old, old habit left over from when she was out with one of her flings. She'd been careful to the point of hypervigilance.

Three of Dawn's friends were already seated at the restaurant, giggly on late-lunch wine and the rest of the afternoon off. Jefferson felt like a rooster in a henhouse. In front of her, one of them said, "Your friend is utterly charming, Dawn."

"Try these, Jef," Dawn urged. Dawn reached across the table and held a fat, purplish olive on a fork out to Jefferson. The waiter had brought a bowl of them to the table. "Kalamata olives are incredible."

She waved it away with a smile, saying, "I'm not into olives." But Dawn insisted and she worked it off the fork. Willie Nelson's "To All the Girls I've Loved Before" was being performed up-tempo on Greek musak.

Dawn's friend Francesca, who worked at the Brooklyn College library, rushed in late. Francesca, in a floppy green beret, laughed as they were introduced, her eyes holding Jefferson's. As she bent to her seat she displayed enticing cleavage and removed the beret. Down fell a cascade of dark red hair onto her shoulders. Jefferson was caught with her mouth open, about to bite into the still-dripping back olive that she held between her thumb and index fingers. Her hands tingled, grew warm. She popped the salty, oiled olive into her mouth. She laughed now too, feeling the ebullience again, feeling her butch power swell inside her. She'd never tasted olives like these. Were they fresh off some tree in Greece? Would Francesca go with her to some hot Greek isle? Or was there another woman like this one already on that island, waiting to feed her ripe olives? Dawn need never know; it wasn't as if she'd leave her now. For that matter, nothing was stopping her from moving back to the city, a city in which she would now be homeless, jobless, and more loveless than ever, no matter how many Francescas she bedded.

She felt Dawn's eyes on her and looked up. Dawn looked from her to Francesca, then back again. Briefly, Dawn's eyes turned wide and horrified. Then they went calm and she smiled. There was no question in Dawn's eyes and no hesitation as she got up and moved around the table to sit by Jefferson's side. She didn't say a word to Jefferson, but kept up her part of the conversation with the other librarians. Jefferson felt a rush of air beneath her, as if the floor had opened up and she was falling, as she had in her childhood nightmare, falling beyond safety, with no loving arms to catch her. Then Dawn set her drink on the table and laid one hand on Jefferson's forearm, fingers and thumb curved as if to still a live beast. Her message of possession was clear.

Jefferson pulled her chair closer to Dawn. When she put her arm around Dawn's slight shoulders, the feeling of falling stopped.

This sort of claiming was new to her. Ginger never had and, as long as she had been with Ginger, no one else would. Dawn, pleasantly, good-humoredly, was challenging Francesca. Dawn was, incredibly, telling the world that Jefferson belonged to her and no one was to get between them. Jefferson felt a quiver of excitement in her belly and another between her legs. At age forty-nine, she was too big for the restaurant. Her shoulders seemed to have broadened in a moment and her hands, her hands could shape mountains. She sat tall, until she feared the buttons on her shirt would pop off. Dawn's protectiveness had awakened her own and she curled a hand around Dawn's shoulder. When their eyes met, she smiled. This feeling of safety actually aroused her. Dawn might be as much sexual adventure as she needed. Still chatting with her friends, Dawn slipped a hand under the tablecloth and kneaded the inside of Jefferson's thigh, high up. It felt great. She felt great. She and Dawn would go to the apartment as soon as they got out of here and they'd make it theirs.

Lounging back in her chair, she surveyed the friends, but thought of her Dawn. They would add on to the cottage, raise the kittens, cruise the lake on summer nights, ice-skate in winter. Had she learned enough about love from six kittens? She would trust that she would not leave Dawn, that Dawn would not leave her. Dawn had claimed her; Jefferson was no longer a beggar and only had to surrender to the terrific force inside her that was love.

She looked from Dawn to Francesca. God, this was hard. Then she looked back to Dawn.

About the Author

Lee Lynch has been writing about lesbian life and lesbians from the time she came out, almost fifty years ago. She was first published in *The Ladder* in the 1960s. In 1983 Naiad Press published her first books, including *Toothpick House* and *Old Dyke Tales*. Her novel *The Swashbuckler* was presented in New York City as a play scripted by Sarah Schulman. Lynch's play, *Getting Into Life*, caused consternation when performed in Tucson, Arizona, due to its realistic portrayal of lesbians. She is working on her next novel, *Rainbow Gap*. Her recent short stories can be found in *Romantic Interludes 2: Secrets* (Bold Strokes Books) and in *Read These Lips*, at www.readtheselips.com. She has twice been nominated for Lambda Literary Awards and her novel *Sweet Creek* was a Golden Crown Literary Society Award finalist. Her reviews and feature articles appeared in The Lambda Book Report and many other publications.

Lynch's syndicated column, The Amazon Trail, runs in venues such as boldstrokesbooks.com, womenscommunityconnection.com, and camprehoboth.com. She is a recipient of the Alice B. Reader Award for Lesbian Fiction and the GCLS Trailblazer Award, and has been inducted into the Saints and Sinners Literary Hall of Fame.

Her other books are available from Bold Strokes Books. She lives in rural Florida with her sweetheart Elaine Mulligan and their furry ruffians.

Books Available From Bold Strokes Books

The Pleasure Planner by Larkin Rose. Pleasure purveyor Bree Hendricks treats love like a commodity until Logan Delaney makes Bree the client in her own game. (978-1-60282-121-7)

everafter by Nell Stark and Trinity Tam. Valentine Darrow is bitten by a vampire on her way to propose to her lover Alexa Newland, and their lives and love are placed in mortal jeopardy. (978-1-60282-119-4)

Summer Winds by Andrews & Austin. When Maggie Turner hires a ranch hand to help work her thousand acres, she never expects to be attracted to the very young, very female Cash Tate. (978-1-60282-120-0)

Beggar of Love by Lee Lynch. Jefferson is the lover every woman wants to be—or to have. A revealing saga of lesbian sexuality. (978-1-60282-122-4)

The Seduction of Moxie by Colette Moody. When 1930s Broadway actress Violet London meets speakeasy singer Moxie Valette, she is instantly attracted and her Hollywood trip takes an unexpected turn. (978-1-60282-114-9)

Goldenseal by Gill McKnight. When Amy Fortune returns to her childhood home, she discovers something sinister in the air— but is former lover Leone Garoul stalking her or protecting her? (978-1-60282-115-6)

Romantic Interludes 2: Secrets edited by Radclyffe and Stacia Seaman. An anthology of sensual lesbian love stories: passion, surprises, and secret desires. (978-1-60282-116-3)

Femme Noir by Clara Nipper. Nora Delaney meets her match in Max Abbott, a sex-crazed dame who may or may not have the information Nora needs to solve a murder—but can she contain her lust for Max long enough to find out? (978-1-60282-117-0)

The Reluctant Daughter by Lesléa Newman. Heartwarming, heartbreaking, and ultimately triumphant—the story every daughter recognizes of the lifelong struggle for our mothers to really see us. (978-1-60282-118-7)

Erosistible by Gill McKnight. When Win Martin arrives at a luxurious Greek hotel for a much-anticipated week of sun and sex with her new girlfriend, she is stunned to find her ex-girlfriend, Benny, is the proprietor. Aeros Ebook. (978-1-60282-134-7)

Looking Glass Lives by Felice Picano. Cousins Roger and Alistair become lifelong friends and discover their sexuality amidst the backdrop of twentieth-century gay culture. (978-1-60282-089-0)

Breaking the Ice by Kim Baldwin. Nothing is easy about life above the Arctic Circle—except, perhaps, falling in love. At least that's what pilot Bryson Faulkner hopes when she meets Karla Edwards. (978-1-60282-087-6)

It Should Be a Crime by Carsen Taite. Two women fulfill their mutual desire with a night of passion, neither expecting more until law professor Morgan Bradley and student Parker Casey meet again…in the classroom. (978-1-60282-086-9)

Rough Trade edited by Todd Gregory. Top male erotica writers pen their own hot, sexy versions of the term "rough trade," producing some of the hottest, nastiest, and most dangerous fiction ever published. (978-1-60282-092-0)

The High Priest and the Idol by Jane Fletcher. Jemeryl and Tevi's relationship is put to the test when the Guardian sends Jemeryl on a mission that puts her not only in harm's way, but back into the sights of a previous lover. (978-1-60282-085-2)

Point of Ignition by Erin Dutton. Amid a blaze that threatens to consume them both, firefighter Kate Chambers and property owner Alexi Clark redefine love and trust. (978-1-60282-084-5)

Secrets in the Stone by Radclyffe. Reclusive sculptor Rooke Tyler suddenly finds herself the object of two very different women's affections, and choosing between them will change her life forever. (978-1-60282-083-8)

Dark Garden by Jennifer Fulton. Vienna Blake and Mason Cavender are sworn enemies—who can't resist each other. Something has to give. (978-1-60282-036-4)

Late in the Season by Felice Picano. Set on Fire Island, this is the story of an unlikely pair of friends—a gay composer in his late thirties and an eighteen-year-old schoolgirl. (978-1-60282-082-1)

Punishment with Kisses by Diane Anderson-Minshall. Will Megan find the answers she seeks about her sister Ashley's murder or will her growing relationship with one of Ash's exes blind her to the real truth? (978-1-60282-081-4)

September Canvas by Gun Brooke. When Deanna Moore meets TV personality Faythe she is reluctantly attracted to her, but will Faythe side with the people spreading rumors about Deanna? (978-1-60282-080-7)

No Leavin' Love by Larkin Rose. Beautiful, successful Mercedes Miller thinks she can resume her affair with ranch foreman Sydney Campbell, but the rules have changed. (978-1-60282-079-1)

Between the Lines by Bobbi Marolt. When romance writer Gail Prescott meets actress Tannen Albright, she develops feelings that she usually only experiences through her characters. (978-1-60282-078-4)

Blue Skies by Ali Vali. Commander Berkley Levine leads an elite group of pilots on missions ordered by her ex-lover Captain Aidan Sullivan and everything is on the line—including love. (978-1-60282-077-7)

The Lure by Felice Picano. When Noel Cummings is recruited by the police to go undercover to find a killer, his life will never be the same. (978-1-60282-076-0)

Death of a Dying Man by J.M. Redmann. Mickey Knight, Private Eye and partner of Dr. Cordelia James, doesn't need a drop-dead gorgeous assistant—not until nature steps in. (978-1-60282-075-3)

Justice for All by Radclyffe. Dell Mitchell goes undercover to expose a human traffic ring and ends up in the middle of an even deadlier conspiracy. (978-1-60282-074-6)

Sanctuary by I. Beacham. Cate Canton faces one major obstacle to her goal of crushing her business rival, Dita Newton—her uncontrollable attraction to Dita. (978-1-60282-055-5)

The Sublime and Spirited Voyage of Original Sin by Colette Moody. Pirate Gayle Malvern finds the presence of an abducted seamstress, Celia Pierce, a welcome distraction until the captive comes to mean more to her than is wise. (978-1-60282-054-8)

Suspect Passions by VK Powell. Can two women, a city attorney and a beat cop, put aside their differences long enough to see that they're perfect for each other? (978-1-60282-053-1)

Just Business by Julie Cannon. Two women who come together—each for her own selfish needs—discover that love can never be as simple as a business transaction. (978-1-60282-052-4)

Sistine Heresy by Justine Saracen. Adrianna Borgia, survivor of the Borgia court, presents Michelangelo with the greatest temptations of his life while struggling with soul-threatening desires for the painter Raphaela. (978-1-60282-051-7)

Radical Encounters by Radclyffe. An out-of-bounds, outside-the-lines collection of provocative, superheated erotica by award-winning romance and erotica author Radclyffe. (978-1-60282-050-0)

Thief of Always by Kim Baldwin & Xenia Alexiou. Stealing a diamond to save the world should be easy for Elite Operative Mishael Taylor, but she didn't figure on love getting in the way. (978-1-60282-049-4)

X by JD Glass. When X-hacker Charlie Riven is framed for a crime she didn't commit, she accepts help from an unlikely source—sexy Treasury Agent Elaine Harper. (978-1-60282-048-7)

The Middle of Somewhere by Clifford Henderson. Eadie T. Pratt sets out on a road trip in search of a new life and ends up in the middle of somewhere she never expected. (978-1-60282-047-0)

Paybacks by Gabrielle Goldsby. Cameron Howard wants to avoid her old nemesis Mackenzie Brandt but their high school reunion brings up more than just memories. (978-1-60282-046-3)

Uncross My Heart by Andrews & Austin. When a radio talk show diva sets out to interview a female priest, the two women end up at odds and neither heaven nor earth is safe from their feelings. (978-1-60282-045-6)

Fireside by Cate Culpepper. Mac, a therapist, and Abby, a nurse, fall in love against the backdrop of friendship, healing, and defending one's own within the Fireside shelter. (978-1-60282-044-9)

A Pirate's Heart by Catherine Friend. When rare book librarian Emma Boyd searches for a long-lost treasure map, she learns the hard way that pirates still exist in today's world—some modern pirates steal maps, others steal hearts. (978-1-60282-040-1)

Trails Merge by Rachel Spangler. Parker Riley escapes the high-powered world of politics to Campbell Carson's ski resort—and their mutual attraction produces anything but smooth running. (978-1-60282-039-5)

Dreams of Bali by C.J. Harte. Madison Barnes worships work, power, and success, and she's never allowed anyone to interfere—that is, until she runs into Karlie Henderson Stockard. Aeros EBook (978-1-60282-070-8)

The Limits of Justice by John Morgan Wilson. Benjamin Justice and reporter Alexandra Templeton search for a killer in a mysterious compound in the remote California desert. (978-1-60282-060-9)

Designed for Love by Erin Dutton. Jillian Sealy and Wil Johnson don't much like each other, but they do have to work together—and what they desire most is not what either of them had planned. (978-1-60282-038-8)

Calling the Dead by Ali Vali. Six months after Hurricane Katrina, NOLA Detective Sept Savoie is a cop who thinks making a relationship work is harder than catching a serial killer—but her current case may prove her wrong. (978-1-60282-037-1)

Shots Fired by MJ Williamz. Kyla and Echo seem to have the perfect relationship and the perfect life until someone shoots at Kyla—and Echo is the most likely suspect. (978-1-60282-035-7)

truelesbianlove.com by Carsen Taite. Mackenzie Lewis and Dr. Jordan Wagner have very different ideas about love, but they discover that truelesbianlove is closer than a click away. Aeros EBook (978-1-60282-069-2)

Justice at Risk by John Morgan Wilson. Benjamin Justice's blind date leads to a rare opportunity for legitimate work, but a reckless risk changes his life forever. (978-1-60282-059-3)

Run to Me by Lisa Girolami. Burned by the four-letter word called love, the only thing Beth Standish wants to do is run for—or maybe from—her life. (978-1-60282-034-0)

Split the Aces by Jove Belle. In the neon glare of Sin City, two women ride a wave of passion that threatens to consume them in a world of fast money and fast times. (978-1-60282-033-3)

Uncharted Passage by Julie Cannon. Two women on a vacation that turns deadly face down one of nature's most ruthless killers—and find themselves falling in love. (978-1-60282-032-6)

Night Call by Radclyffe. All medevac helicopter pilot Jett McNally wants to do is fly and forget about the horror and heartbreak she left behind in the Middle East, but anesthesiologist Tristan Holmes has other plans. (978-1-60282-031-9)

Lake Effect Snow by C.P. Rowlands. News correspondent Annie T. Booker and FBI Agent Sarah Moore struggle to stay one step ahead of disaster as Annie's life becomes the war zone she once reported on. Aeros EBook (978-1-60282-068-5)

I Dare You by Larkin Rose. Stripper by night, corporate raider by day, Kelsey's only looking for sex and power, until she meets a woman who stirs her heart and her body. (978-1-60282-030-2)

Truth Behind the Mask by Lesley Davis. Erith Baylor is drawn to Sentinel Pagan Osborne's quiet strength, but the secrets between them strain duty and family ties. (978-1-60282-029-6)

Cooper's Deale by KI Thompson. Two would-be lovers and a decidedly inopportune murder spell trouble for Addy Cooper, no matter which way the cards fall. (978-1-60282-028-9)